BB Easton

FOREVER

NEW YORK   BOSTON

Forever
Hachette Book Group
1290 Avenue of the Americas, New York, NY 10104
read-forever.com
twitter.com/readforeverpub

First trade paperback edition: August 2021

Forever is an imprint of Grand Central Publishing. The Forever name and logo are trademarks of Hachette Book Group, Inc.

The publisher is not responsible for websites (or their content) that are not owned by the publisher.

The Hachette Speakers Bureau provides a wide range of authors for speaking events. To find out more, go to www.hachettespeakersbureau.com or call (866) 376-6591.

Library of Congress Cataloging-in-Publication Data
Names: Easton, BB, author.
Title: Star / BB Easton.
Description: First trade paperback edition. | New York : Forever, 2021. | Series: 44 chapters | Summary: "In 1999, I met my Prince Charming. He was the tall, tattooed, wickedly handsome bass player for the up-and-coming rock band, Phantom Limb. But, more importantly, he was mine. I knew it the moment he flashed me that shy, dimpled smile. And he knew it too. Hansel "Hans" Oppenheimer wore his heart on one sleeve and scrawled lyrics about me on the other. Unlike the losers of my past, Hans showered me with tenderness, took me places I'd never been before, and showed me the type of all-consuming love I'd thought only existed in fairy tales. But, like any good fairy tale, my road to happily ever after was paved with challenges, and right when I least expected it...it forked. In 1999, I met my Prince Charming. In 2000, I met my soul mate"—Provided by publisher.
Identifiers: LCCN 2020054038 | ISBN 9781538718445 (trade paperback)
Classification: LCC PS3605.A8555 S73 2021 | DDC 813/.6—dc23
LC record available at https://lccn.loc.gov/2020054038

ISBNs: 978-1- 5387-1844-5 (trade paperback), 978-1-5387-1843-8 (ebook)

Printed in the United States of America

LSC-C

Printing 1, 2021

This book is dedicated to the boy who treated me like such a princess that I never dated another toad again.

Thank you, Hans. Your love broke the spell.

AUTHOR'S NOTE

Star is a work of fiction based on characters and events introduced in my memoir, *Sex/Life: 44 Chapters About 4 Men*. While
many of the situations portrayed in this book are true to life,
many others were added, exaggerated, or altered to enhance the
story. I also changed the names and identifying characteristics
of every character (and most locations) to protect the identities
of everyone involved.

Due to excessive profanity, violence, graphic sexual content,
and themes of juvenile delinquency, this book is not intended
for—and should probably be completely hidden from—anyone
under the age of eighteen.

INTRODUCTION

People love to ask me how much of my stories are true and how much of them are fictionalized. It's a hard question to answer because I base every scene on something that actually happened. The identities of the characters have been altered, and I might have changed the time line or situational details to fit the flow of the story, but the basic plot points are almost always based on actual events.

That being said, some books end up being truer than others. This story, the one I'm about to tell you, is the truest thing I've ever written. I found, as it came pouring out of me, that my relationship with Hans was already so over-the-top romantic, so fantastical, so suspenseful that it simply didn't leave much room for exaggeration. It is a modern-day fairy tale, full of love at first sight and sprawling castles and faraway lands and witches and warlocks. Only in *my* fairy tale, the prince is a tattooed bass player, the princess wears combat boots, and the happily ever after is anything but predictable.

Welcome to my real-life rock-star romance. Enjoy!

PART

I

July 1999

It was the best of times; it was the worst of hangovers.

I awoke, nauseous and confused, in a lilac-colored room plastered with peeling My Little Pony decals. The midday sunlight leaked in through the closed blinds, searing and uninvited. The sheets touching my exposed skin were itchy. Stifling. And my mouth tasted like the inside of a beer bottle that had been used as an ashtray.

Ugh.

I searched my alcohol-logged brain for clues that might help explain why I was waking up inside the magical land of Equestria. Images from the night before began to surface, grainy and out of order. It was like flipping through a stack of Polaroids that I didn't remember taking—scene after scene of teenagers in black lipstick and black vinyl thrashing in the darkness. A house party. Goth Girl, my friend from school, hanging on the arm of the homeowner—a lanky Lord Licorice-looking douche bag named Steven. A keg in the kitchen. A heavy-metal band playing in the living room. I thought their name was Phantom something. Phantom Limb? And there was a guy. A tall guy with messy black hair and a full sleeve of horror-movie tattoos.

The only guy not wearing pleather or lipstick.

The bass player.

My heart skipped a beat as I remembered the way he'd reacted when I'd bumped into him at the keg.

"Hey, Tinker Bell. Going somewhere?"

When that tattooed, spiky-haired giant smiled down at me, it was as if someone had flipped a switch on his whole demeanor. His dark features lit up. His eyes twinkled with some inexplicable recognition, and two adorable dimples broke through his tough exterior. He looked at me as if he'd been looking for *me.*

Before I could even apologize for our collision, the bass player simply chuckled and tucked me up under his arm. Click. *I fit like a puzzle piece. Then, he steered me into the living room and plopped me down onto his lap. As if we were already a couple. As if boundaries didn't apply to us and things like introductions were just a formality.*

"So, what's your name, Tinker Bell?" The dimple-cheeked devil beamed at me, nonchalantly rubbing a slow circle on my thigh with his thumb.

"BB," I croaked. I cleared my throat and tried again, forcing myself to meet his gunmetal-blue gaze. "I'm BB...hi."

"So, Bumblebee, why were you in there getting your own beer?"

I smiled and rolled my eyes. "Well, who else was gonna get it for—"

"Me," he interrupted with a grin. "I think I'm gonna be getting all your drinks from now on."

I scoffed, trying desperately to keep my cool, and said, "I don't even know who you are."

Mr. Tall, Dark, and Tattooed grinned. His white teeth glistened. His dimples deepened. My heart rate skyrocketed. My palms got sweaty.

"I'm Hans," he said sweetly and without a shred of ego. "I'm the bass player."

Hans hadn't taken his hands or eyes off me the entire night—not that I minded. The way he'd touched me, looked at me, spoken to me, it wasn't like a guy who was trying to get into my pants; it was like a guy who'd *already* gotten into my pants... and met my parents.

Locking eyes with Clover, a purple pony with a peeling pink mane, I thought, *This is what Cinderella must have felt like the morning after the ball. Except I don't even have a glass slipper to prove it was real. And also, I'm pretty sure Cinderella wasn't this hungover.*

Clover stared back at me with sad equine eyes. I wished she could peel the rest of the way off the wall and go get me some fucking Advil. My head was pounding.

Groaning, I pulled the pony-covered polyester comforter up under my chin and rolled over.

Onto a body.

I screamed and scrambled backward, realizing a moment too late that, with two people in a twin-size bed, there was no *backward* to scramble to. As soon as I felt myself falling over the edge, I reached out and grabbed the first thing I could get my hands on.

It was an arm. And it was covered with the stuff of nightmares. Hellraiser and Jason and Freddy and Pennywise sneered at me as I clawed at their faces, trying to keep from going overboard.

The arm flexed and jerked away from me, but I held on for dear life. The motion yanked me back onto the bed where I landed face-first with a smack on the bare chest of my unexpected roommate.

Laughter, deep yet boyish, vibrated under my cheek.

"You scared the shit outta me!" the beast chuckled, wrapping his tattooed arm around my shoulders and pulling me in closer. The gesture and the warmth from his body turned my insides to goo.

"You scared the shit outta *me*!" I giggled, smacking him on the chest. I wanted to sit up and look at him, make sure he was real, ask him a million questions about what had happened the night before, but I couldn't. Not yet.

I needed to let him hold me first.

I almost purred as I snuggled into his side and draped my right arm over his bare torso. It had been almost three months since I'd felt the flesh of a boy beneath my fingertips, felt the rise and fall of his chest beneath my cheek. I hadn't gone that long without a boy to cuddle with since... middle school? Elementary school?

As far back as I could remember, I'd had a boyfriend. Boys provided two of my favorite things: attention and affection. At home, I was showered with both, being the only child of two doting hippies. But, when I wasn't at home, I got my fix from boys.

Boys, boys, boys.

Of course, as it was with any drug, the price just kept going up. At first, I'd paid for my cuddles with kisses, glimpses up my skirt. Later, my body had become the preferred currency, but my dealers would also accept blood and tears in a pinch. When times got lean, I'd been known to offer tokens carved out of my own heart, gift-wrapped wisps of my soul. Whatever it took to keep the love and affection flowing.

That May, I'd even paid with three broken ribs and a punctured lung.

I was no quitter.

I inhaled and savored his masculine scent—cigarette smoke and sweat. The smell of rock and roll.

Callused, bass-playing fingertips slid up and down my exposed arm, leaving goose bumps in their wake. The morning scruff of a grown-ass man grazed my forehead. And the steady thump of a heart I felt like I already knew beat beneath my cheek.

Hangover schmangover.

I was high as a kite.

As I smiled against his chest—and let my eyes roam over the hills and valleys of his abs, which were peeking out from under the covers—I couldn't believe this was the same man who'd intimidated me the night before. He might look like seventy-five inches of pierced, tattooed, heavy-metal mayhem, but he was one hundred percent snuggle bunny.

On a sigh, I finally forced myself to sit up. The giant gazed up at me with soft, denim-colored eyes, rimmed in lashes so thick and black they looked like eyeliner, and my heart sputtered. Those eyes and that mouth—narrow and pursed, as if it were on the verge of a smirk or a kiss—betrayed his otherwise severe appearance. Especially in the light of day.

Hans was fucking cute.

Hans.

I'd have to remember to get his last name...and his phone number...and a few of his babies before I left.

Babies. Oh shit. Did we...

I looked down and took a quick mental appraisal.

Clothes?

Still on.

Memories of late-night fuckery?

None.

Vag soreness from what I assume this tall drink of water is packing?

Nope. Nuthin'.

Damn.

"What are you doing in here?" I asked, smiling even wider and trying not to think about the hungover swamp monster I must have resembled.

"I *was* sleeping...until somebody sank her fuckin' talons into my arm." Hans looked down at his bicep. "I'm surprised I'm not bleeding."

I laughed. "You know, for a guy with Freddy Krueger tattooed on his arm, you're kind of a pussy."

"I thought I was being attacked by Freddy Krueger," Hans teased, rolling onto his side and propping his head up on his hand. "He waits until you're asleep, you know." Hans's bottom half was covered by the world's girliest comforter, but his top half...

Drool.

As I tried to drag my eyes back up to his face, something caught my attention.

"What's that?" I asked, reaching for his non-tattooed arm.

Hans offered me his left arm, looking just as curious as I was. Rows and rows of words had been scrawled on the inside of his forearm in blue ink.

We read them together in silence.

I can tell you when they streak the sky,
Where the falling stars go when they leave the night.
I know how they shimmer, infrared.
I know because one fell and landed in my bed.

Hans glanced up at me with a sheepish smile and shrugged. "Guess I wrote it after you passed out last night."

Guess I wrote it after you passed out last night?

Guess I wrote it after you passed out last night!

Does that mean, Guess I wrote it about you after you passed out last night? Did Hans Whatever-His-Last-Name-Is write a fucking song about me? Are we in love? Should we go get matching tattoos now or after the wedding?

Oh shit. He's looking at you. Say something, BB. You're making your future husband uncomfortable!

"So, this is *your* bed?"

Nice. Not awkward at all.

"Well, it is where I crash almost every weekend, so..."

I looked around at the decor and nodded in approval. "I like what you've done with the place."

Hans laughed and sat up with his back against the white-washed wooden headboard. Even when he was sitting up, his legs stretched almost to the end of the twin-size bed. I couldn't begin to figure out how he'd slept curled up next to me on that tiny mattress all night.

Hans folded his art-covered arms across his chest. "Hey, don't judge. Bronies are people too, you know."

I giggled and rolled my eyes. "Okay. If you're such a *bronie*, name *one* My Little Pony character."

Hans looked around the room and then back at me with a smirk. "Flutternuts."

An unexpected laugh burst out of me.

"Sparklesack."

I laughed harder.

"Glitterdick?"

"They don't have nuts"—I cackled—"or dicks. They're girls!"

Hans chuckled as I dried my tears with the hem of my Black Flag crop top. "Okay, fine. You got me," he said. "This isn't my bed."

"Whose is it?" I hiccupped.

"Steven's daughter. She only stays here a few nights a month, but when she's gone, Steven and Victoria throw down."

I vaguely remembered, after Hans had refilled my red plastic cup one too many times, asking Goth Girl where I could sleep. She'd steered my drunk ass down a hall to a place she called "Maddie's room." I guess Maddie was a four-year-old pony enthusiast. Mystery solved.

"So, how long have you been friends with Steven?"

And, more importantly, why? That guy's such a fucking sleaze-ball. I don't know what the fuck Goth Girl sees in him.

"I'm actually friends with Victoria. We went to Central High together until she transferred to East Atlanta last year."

Shit. I didn't even know Goth Girl had other friends. Especially not hot ones. That bitch has been holding out on me.

"Jesus. You went to Central? And you didn't get shivved? That's impressive. You know what they say about that place. You don't graduate—"

"You get paroled." Hans quirked up an eyebrow.

"Yeah." I smiled. "So, when did *you* get paroled?" I immediately regretted the question.

Hans was rocking a five o'clock shadow, a full sleeve of tattoos, and a *very nice* full-grown man body. There was no way he could have been Goth Girl's classmate. She was my age, and this dude had to be in his early to mid-twenties. What if he had some kind of learning problem, and it had taken him, like, seven extra years to—

"In May."

[Insert record-scratch sound effect.]

"Like, *this* May?" I asked, my voice an octave higher than usual.

Hans smiled and eyed me suspiciously. "Yeeeeah…why?"

"Sorry!" I held my hands up defensively. "I just thought you were, like…thirty-five."

Hans laughed. "Yeah, I get that a lot."

"So, how old *are* you?"

"Eighteen." Hans shook his head. "No, wait, nineteen. Sorry, my birthday was last month. I keep forgetting." He smiled and shrugged in a way that made me want to pinch his scruffy, chiseled cheeks.

"I graduated in May and had a birthday in June, too!" I squealed. "Dude, that's crazy! But I'm only seventeen. I graduated early."

"Oh shit!" Hans snapped his fingers in the air and sat straight up. "You must be the girl Victoria was talking about. She said one of her friends at East Atlanta got in a bad wreck right before finals, but she still managed to graduate a year early with honors and shit." Hans's eyes roamed all over my disheveled body. I knew he was scanning for injuries, but the intensity of his gaze still made the butterflies in my stomach do backflips. "You okay now?"

I thought about it. Was I okay? Physically, my ribs had healed. Emotionally, I'd accepted that Harley—my asshole ex-boyfriend who'd been driving—was a cheating piece of shit whom I'd never really loved. And psychologically, I was coming to terms with the fact that Knight, whom I actually did love, was probably better off in the military than here, getting in bar fights and running me and my boyfriend off the road. So...

"Yeah," I said with a smile, "I am."

For once, Hans didn't return my smile. "What about the guy you were with?"

Harley. That motherfucker. I remembered the puppy-dog eyes he'd given me as the cops escorted him out of the hospital, his hands cuffed in front to accommodate the cast on his left arm. Turned out, that asshole had been on parole for grand theft auto, so being found at the scene of the accident with a trunk full of illegal firearms, a vial of LSD, and a female minor who'd been taken at gunpoint didn't exactly sit well with the law.

I snorted and rolled my eyes. "He'll live."

Hans stared at me with an unreadable expression. It only lasted a second or two, but it reminded me why I'd been so intimidated by him the night before. When Hans wasn't smiling, he looked scary as fuck. Heavy, dark eyebrows, one impaled with a silver barbell, shadowed his storm-colored eyes. Wild black hair shot out in all directions. And that hard, stubbled jaw flexed as Hans drew his already-narrow mouth even tighter. Some women have what they call Resting Bitch Face. Hans had Resting Evil Villain Face.

Then, it was gone.

His smile returned, lighting up his features, and he simply replied, "Good."

On that note, Hans threw off the purple pony comforter and got out of bed. His toned physique was on full display as he turned and towered over me, wearing nothing but a pair of black boxer shorts with little yellow bananas all over them.

I ogled him. I couldn't help it. There was just so much to look at. The man's body was a long, lean, chiseled work of art. Literally. One arm was covered in black-and-gray tattoos, the other in handwritten lyrics about falling stars who hijack your bed.

It was all too much. I had to force myself to look away from the banana print and make eye contact.

Thankfully, Hans seemed to be refreshingly unaware of how affected I was by him. He simply jerked his messy bedhead toward the door and said, "You wanna go get some breakfast? I'm fuckin' starving."

I wasn't big on eating—anorexia and all—but for some reason, I found myself with a sudden hankering for banana.

"Sure," I chirped. "Just give me ten minutes."

I tried to re-spike my bottle-blonde pixie cut and reapply my makeup using whatever products I could find in my purse. Nude lipstick, black liquid eyeliner, concealer, and blush—just enough to take me from looking like death to looking like death that was worthy of an open-casket funeral. But I was having a hard time concentrating with Hans's boxer shorts on the floor next to me and the steam from the shower fogging up the mirror.

Somehow, when I'd said, "Just give me ten minutes," Hans had taken that as an invitation to take a ten-minute shower in the same fucking bathroom as me while I got ready.

I tried to act cool and make small talk, but it wasn't easy over the sound of rushing water and my own thoughts screaming, *Hans is naked! Hans is naked! Hans is naked! Holy shit!*

He told me that his last name was Oppenheimer—I at least got that much out of the conversation—and he said that his parents had moved to the US from Germany before he was born. He had two older sisters who had already gotten married and started families, and...

He said some other stuff too, but now that I knew his last

name, I was too busy trying to decide if I would go by *BB Oppenheimer* or *Brooke Oppenheimer* to attend to the rest. Neither option had a great ring to it, but sometimes you have to make sacrifices in the name of love. I gazed into the fogged-up mirror and imagined what my new signature would look like if I were to write it with my finger in the condensation. I finally settled on BB Oppenheimer. If I went by Brooke Oppenheimer, my initials would be B.O.

I giggled to myself and glanced over at the black curtain separating me from a very naked, very wet *Mr. Oppenheimer*. My giggles turned to full-blown belly laughs when I noticed a muscular hand and forearm, still dry, still scrawled with blue ink, sticking out over the top of the shower curtain rod.

Taking a step closer, I reached out and pinched the tip of Hans's long middle finger—the nail bearing the chipped remnants of black nail polish that had long worn off. "What's going on here?" I teased, swinging his hand from side to side. "Are you so tall that your whole body won't fit in the shower at once?"

Hans chuckled. "Nah, I just don't want the lyrics to get washed off before I have a chance to write them down."

Oh my God. Could he be any more adorable? I can't wait to become Mrs. B.O.

Thankful that Hans couldn't see the stupid schoolgirl grin on my face, I chirped, "I'll go write 'em down for you!"

"Cool. Thanks, Tinker Bell. My hand was starting to fall asleep."

Hans laced his fingers through mine and playfully shook my hand back and forth, like I had done to his finger. The contact caused my breath to hitch and a squeal to percolate in my chest. I was holding hands with a very beautiful, very naked man, who might have possibly written part of a song about me on his skin before curling up next to me in a twin-size bed the night before.

"You think you can remember all the words?"

"Yeah, I got 'em," I said, opening the door to a blast of cool, dry air from the hallway.

I got 'em tattooed on my fucking brain.

I dashed out of the bathroom in search of paper and something to write with. I was pretty sure I'd be able to recite those lyrics on my deathbed, but I still didn't want to dawdle and risk losing even a single syllable of what he'd written.

When I rounded the corner from the hall into the kitchen, I found Goth Girl leaning up against the kitchen counter, clutching a mug to her face. She was wearing nothing but an oversize Marilyn Manson T-shirt, and her sleek black hair had been ruffled into something resembling a bad Wicked Witch of the West wig.

"Hey, Victoria!" I blurted, glancing around the room in a tizzy. "Do you know where I can find some paper?"

Goth Girl looked at me over her mug with disinterested doll eyes, then reached to her left with one hand and opened a drawer.

"Awesome! Thanks!" I ran over and rummaged through the junk drawer until I found a pad of paper and a pen. Ignoring Goth Girl, I stood there and jotted down the lyrics to my new favorite song, then tore the page out of the pad and shoved it in my back pocket.

"What...are you doing?" Goth Girl deadpanned as I threw everything back into the drawer and slammed it shut.

I spun around and beamed at her. "I think...I think Hans

wrote *a song* about me last night! Well, part of a song. I mean, I guess it might not be about me *per se*, but it kinda seems like it's about me. And he wanted me to write it down before he washed it off his arm. He's in the shower now. Did I mention that he slept in the same bed with me last night? And he didn't even try anything! I mean, I don't think he—"

"He has a girlfriend, BB."

Blink, blink.

"Her name is Beth. They've been together for four years."

Girlfriend. Beth. Four years.

The bombs just kept falling.

Kaboom! Kapow! Kablooey!

"Then why did he have me sit on his lap last night? Why did he sleep in the same bed as me? He *cuddled* with me, Victoria." I said the word *cuddled* as if I'd just found out he had the bubonic plague rather than a significant other. After being cheated on in spectacular fashion by Harley, the thought of Hans having a girlfriend disgusted me. Disappointed me. Hell, it was down-right depressing.

Goth Girl shrugged. "I dunno. He's a flirty drunk. And he always sleeps in Maddie's bed, so maybe he was just too wasted to figure something else out." Her dark, hungover eyes bored into me as she took another sip from her steaming mug. Her stare felt like a warning.

Holding my hands up in defense, I backpedaled. "I had no idea. I swear. Nothing happened—"

At that moment, Hans came sauntering out of the hallway and into the kitchen, looking like six and a half feet of squeaky-clean sex god. He was wearing black Converse, baggy black pinstripe slacks, a low-slung studded belt, and a black wife-beater. On his non-tattooed wrist, he wore a watch with a thick leather strap, and his shaggy black hair had been towel-dried into a spiky riot that I was just dying to get my fingers into.

I glanced at Goth Girl, silently begging for her blessing, but all I got back was a nasty case of Resting Witch Face.

Hans smiled at me, transforming his sinister appearance into something warm and non-threatening, then turned that dimpled grin on Goth Girl. "Hey, Vic, we're gonna go grab some breakfast. Wanna come?"

She glared at him, as if trying to impart something telepathically, but before she could answer his question, a raspy female voice called out from the hallway on the opposite side of the kitchen. The one leading to the master bedroom.

"There you are," the husky voice crooned. "We were looking for you. Come back to bed."

I turned and watched as the blonde I'd seen doing a keg stand in a Korn T-shirt the night before emerged from the shadows with a sheet wrapped around her body. Her makeup was smeared below her eyes, and her once-perky pigtails had fallen to half-mast. Much like her eyelids when they landed on Goth Girl.

Pigtails shuffled in, completely ignoring the giant hunk standing in the center of the kitchen, and headed straight for Goth Girl. After kissing her with way more tongue than I thought was advisable first thing in the morning, Pigtails took the mug from Goth Girl's hands, set it on the counter, and led her toward the master bedroom without so much as a *Good morning*.

My eyebrows were practically touching the ceiling when I turned back around and looked at Hans.

"The fuck was that?" I asked, gesturing over my shoulder with my thumb.

Hans chuckled as he walked across the kitchen, heading straight toward me. Picking up Goth Girl's mug, he turned and leaned against the counter beside me, mirroring my stance. Our elbows touched, and my entire arm erupted in goose bumps.

Downing the rest of Goth Girl's coffee in one swig, Hans swallowed and shook his head. "Watch. She and Steven are gonna get in a huge fight now. They do this all the time."

"Do what?"

Hans turned around and poured himself another cup of coffee from the pot on the counter. I was sad that his arm wasn't touching me anymore and even sadder that there was some skank out there named Beth who could touch it whenever she wanted.

"They do a bunch of E and find a girl to have a threesome with. Then, Victoria gets all jealous the next morning when she sobers up."

"Shit." I shook my head in disbelief. "How did I not know that?"

I thought about it and realized that, in the three months since Goth Girl and Steven had started dating, I'd basically been grounded—thanks to Harley constantly making me miss my curfew—or recovering from a car accident the entire time. I wondered what else I'd missed.

"She did seem pretty fucking pissy this morning," I admitted.

What I didn't admit was that some of her animosity seemed to be directed at the two of us. I also didn't admit that she'd told me about his girlfriend. I kind of wanted to see how far he was going to take things before I called his ass out. Yeah, that was it.

I'd wait for him to cross the line. Then—*BAM!*—I'd give the signal, and Beth and Goth Girl would pop out from behind a tree and bust his ass red-handed. That was *totally* why I didn't mention the girlfriend. Not because I wanted to pretend like she didn't exist and continue my flirtfest. Nuh-uh. No way. I had serious undercover boyfriend recon work to do.

When Hans and I walked outside, there were only two cars still parked on Steve's quiet, unassuming suburban street—my black '93 Mustang hatchback and a black BMW 3 Series on the opposite side of the road.

"Is that your car?" I asked, trying to hide the shock in my voice as I gestured toward the Beemer. I was a muscle-car enthusiast through and through, but I had to admit, there was something sexy about that little black import.

"Yeah. My parents got a new car, so they gave me their old one. But it's a stick, so I can't drive it for shit." Hans shrugged as we made our way down the steep driveway.

"I can teach you!" I blurted out.

Hans gave me the side-eye.

"For real!" I pointed enthusiastically at the little 'Stang that could. "My car is a stick! I even won some races at a little track not far from here! Oh my God, we could go there to practice. It's the perfect place!"

As soon as the words were out of my mouth, I felt the stinging slap of guilt. After what Harley had done to me, I didn't owe him shit, but for some reason, the idea of taking another man to our special place just felt wrong.

Fuck that, my inner bitch piped up. *Harley only took you there to teach you how to race on* his *track so that you could win* him *money. Not only should y'all go, but you should both take a piss on the finish line before you leave.*

The bitch had a point.

Hans smiled at my passionate outburst and pulled his car keys out of his pocket. "Oh, I know how to drive a stick. I just suck at it. I'm too ADD for that shit." Hitting the unlock button, Hans tossed his keys to me and headed toward the passenger side of his own car.

He's letting me drive?!

"You want me to drive?"

"Only if you wanna live." Hans gave me a lopsided grin. Then, he opened his door and ducked inside.

When I pulled open the driver's-side door, the interior of the car was all shiny black leather and shinier brown walnut, but the floors were all crushed Newport cartons and empty bottles of Mountain Dew. I smiled to myself. I loved how unconcerned Hans was with the bullshit of life. He didn't apologize for his messy car because it didn't matter to him. He wasn't afraid of losing his man card for wearing nail polish or letting a girl drive his car, probably because he was six-foot-fuck tall and had a five o'clock shadow at eleven o'clock in the morning.

And he also doesn't seem to give a shit that he has a girlfriend, my guilt chimed in.

Fuck you, guilt. Nobody asked you.

I, unlike Hans, had all kinds of hang-ups, including an acute fear of asking him where he wanted to go for breakfast. Knight and Harley had each taken me to Waffle House for our first date, and I'd barely survived those two relationships. If Hans said he wanted to go to motherfucking Waffle House, I might have to drive us off the nearest bridge just to save myself the drama.

"Are you cool with IHOP?" I asked as my black pleather-covered ass landed in the black leather driver's seat. My feet couldn't even reach the pedals.

"Fuck yeah, I love that place," Hans said as I fumbled around, looking for the seat-adjustment controls. "When you order coffee, they bring you the whole fucking pot."

"I don't know how you drink that shit," I teased, my fingers finally finding the right button. Before I could press it, I heard a familiar whirring sound coming from Hans's side of the car.

I looked over and snorted. Hans's knees were practically smooshed between his chest and the glove compartment as his seat moved backward in slow motion. I giggled and hit my button, too. My seat moved forward at the same pace that Hans's was moving backward, our smiling eyes locking somewhere in the middle.

I'd never driven a German luxury car before, but as soon as I pulled out of the neighborhood, I wasn't sure how I'd ever go back. Hans watched me with rapt attention from the passenger seat as I gasped at the acceleration and squealed over the handling and gushed about how smooth the ride was. I did miss the deafening roar you get from an American big block, but I'd get over it.

As I pulled onto the main highway that led into town, Hans rolled his window halfway down and lit a cigarette. Gesturing toward me with his open pack, he asked, "Want one?"

"Hell yeah," I said, taking the green-and-white Newport box

from him. I lit up at the next red light. The cool, minty tingle in the back of my throat surprised me. I hadn't had a menthol since I was a kid when my best friend, Juliet, and I used to smoke what was left of the cigarette butts in her mom's ashtrays.

It tasted like sneaky, bad fun.

"Can I open the sunroof?" I asked, my finger poised over the button just above the rearview mirror.

As soon as Hans nodded, I had that bitch open wide, the blazing July sun filling the car and burning my skin in the best way possible. I tilted my head back and inhaled the hot, humid air. After spending almost three months in near isolation, driving a luxury car with a Newport between my fingers, a gorgeous, tattooed cuddle machine in the passenger seat, and the sun on my face felt like absolute heaven.

My reverie was quickly shattered, however, when the light turned green and I stomped on the gas. The wind from the now-open sunroof snatched the ashes clean off the end of my cigarette and sent them swirling around inside the car.

"Shit!" I spat, swatting at the gray flecks in the air—as if that would help, as if I could simply pop them like bubbles.

I waited for Hans to yell at me about his precious imported leather, but he didn't. In fact, he did the *last* thing I'd expected. Hans Oppenheimer rolled his window the rest of the way down, held up the end of his cigarette, and watched as his ashes took flight too, flitting between us in the sunlight like a handful of silver glitter.

"Did you see that?" Hans asked once the ashes had vanished, eyes wide.

"Yeah," I said. The word came out all breathy, as if I'd just witnessed some supernatural phenomenon. "It looked like—"

"A snow globe," Hans and I said in unison.

"Yes!" I cried. "Oh my God! Right? We just created the world's most expensive snow globe!"

Hans chuckled and rolled his window halfway up again. "I'm gonna call the *Guinness Book of World Records* people and report that shit. Maybe we can get on *The Tonight Show*."

"Good plan. Hey, maybe Phantom Limb can be the musical guest!"

Hans gave me an adorable little smile and opened his mouth to reply when a robotic tune interrupted his train of thought. Reaching into his pocket, he pulled out a little black cell phone. I immediately pressed two buttons on my door to roll the windows up as Hans hit the button to close the sunroof.

"What's up, man?" Hans smiled as he greeted the caller. "No shit? Right now? I have BB with me." Hans glanced over at me, his mouth quirked into a tiny smile. "Yeah, the girl from last night. No. Fuck you." Hans looked at me again as his smirk erupted into a full-blown grin. "Right on, man. We'll be there. Thanks!"

Hans hung up and turned his whole body toward me. I could feel the excitement radiating off him.

"Change of plans. We're going downtown."

My black pleather pants, black combat boots, and cropped Black Flag T-shirt felt ridiculously out of place as Hans and I walked out onto what used to be the Falcons football field. Instead of perfect green Astroturf and pristine white stripes, the center of the arena had been buried in shit-tons of dirt and littered with derelict cars. Parked around the edges of the track were about a dozen monolithic monster trucks, and in the center of the track was a group of dirt bikes, their drivers suited up and signing autographs.

Hans looked around the expanse for a second. Then, he cupped his hands around his mouth and shouted, "Lucifer!"

A skinny guy in a STAFF T-shirt who was standing in front of a blocked-off entrance on the other side of the arena yelled back, "Woo!" and pointed at us the way a rock star would point to a crowd.

I looked at Hans in amusement as the little fella jogged over. "Lucifer?"

Hans smiled. "That's our drummer. His name is Louis, but he's batshit crazy, so we call him Lucifer."

I thought back to the night before and remembered thinking the drummer was going to give himself an aneurysm with the way he was thrashing around. It was like watching Animal from The Muppets play drums. Or Travis Barker from Blink-182 but with fewer tattoos.

"He's a crew guy over at The Omni, too, so he gets me into all kinds of shit."

"What's up, LDH?" Louis asked with a grin as he and Hans did that handshake/hug/slap-on-the-back thing that guys do.

LDH?

"Lou, this is BB." Hans gestured toward me. "BB, this is Lucifer."

"Sup?" Louis gave me a chin nod, a ghost of a smile on his amused lips.

I wanted to blurt out, *Stop looking at me like that! Nothing happened, I swear!* but instead, I muttered some shit about it being nice to meet him and how much I enjoyed their show the night before.

Louis walked us around the arena and introduced us to the monster-truck drivers and dirt-bike racers. Everybody was super friendly, not that I knew who any of them were. I was told that Grave Digger, the black-and-green-and-purple SUV/hearse-looking thing, was the star of the show, so I asked its driver to sign my arm.

I would have had him sign my boobs, but alas, I had none.

The trucks were about fifty times bigger up close than they looked on TV. I pulled the little point-and-shoot camera my parents had given me for my birthday out of my purse and asked

Hans to take a picture of me standing inside one of Bigfoot's wheels. The tire alone had to be ten feet tall. After Hans took the picture, he handed the camera to Louis, whispered something in his ear, and then walked over to help me down. At least, that was what I thought he was doing. Instead, he turned around and sat on the edge of the tire with his back to me.

Hans glanced at me and patted his shoulders. "Get on."

My first instinct was to hesitate, to ask why, but one look into those blue-jean-colored eyes had me climbing aboard, no questions asked.

Hans held his hands up for me to hold on to while I straddled his neck. I climbed on, careful not to let my dirty boots touch his clothes. When Hans stood up, the head rush was delicious. I clung to his hands for dear life, dizzy from both the altitude and the sight of Hans's wild black mane between my legs. I felt like I was a mile above the earth, like the atmosphere must surely be thinner, oxygen scarce, but when I glanced behind me, Bigfoot's tire was still a few inches taller.

"Smile, fuckers!" Louis shouted.

I reached up and gripped the edge of the tire above my head just as Hans gripped my spindly thighs with his massive hands. Time froze. I held my fake smile and my breath as I became hyperaware of every aspect of Hans's touch. How firm. How gentle. How high up on my legs.

Pretty fucking high.

But, when the pads of his fingers began massaging slow, tiny circles over the shiny black material separating us, my core clenched, and my mouth fell open in a silent gasp that I was thankful he couldn't see.

Louis saw it though, and he took that opportunity to press the shutter button.

Flash.

That was it. Hans set me down gently and followed Louis to the next truck, assuming I was right on his heels. I wasn't though. I stood there, blinking and mourning the feeling of Hans's hands on me for a solid three to five seconds before I was able to pick my cool back up and carry on.

Once we met every truck driver, dirt-bike racer, and crew guy on the track, Hans and I said goodbye to Louis and made our way to our seats. They were Club Level, which I soon learned meant *where the rich people sit*. Evidently, rich people didn't go to many monster-truck rallies because that section was a ghost town. The rich people restroom didn't even have a line!

I ducked inside to pee and primp, and when I came back out, the sight of Hans Oppenheimer leaning against the opposite wall almost knocked the wind out of me. The man was a walking contradiction. He looked almost unapproachable, standing there with his Resting Evil Villain Face, his scary-as-shit tattoos, and his effortless rocker-chic look, but the boyish smile on his lips and the adorable stuffed Grave Digger doll in his hand had me skipping toward him instead of away.

"Is that for me?" I asked, reaching for the squishy plush monster truck with the chunky little wheels.

"Oh shit," Hans said, not giving it over. "Did you want one too?"

I laughed and snatched it out of his hands, rubbing my cheek on its velvety hood like a cat.

Hans gestured down the hall with his thumb. "They have

Monster Mutt and El Toro Loco too, if you'd rather have one that looks more like an animal."

"Nope. Grave Digger's perfect," I said, holding up my forearm to show off my autograph. "Thank you." I was about to rise up onto my tiptoes to give him a kiss when I suddenly remembered that Hans was not my boyfriend. The realization cascaded over me like a bucket of cold water.

Hans and I had never even kissed.

Hans belonged to someone else.

What the fuck is wrong with me?

It didn't even make sense. Every cell in my body recognized him, reached for him, yet I hadn't even known him a full day. Had we been together in a past life? My hippie parents believed in reincarnation. Maybe they were right. Perhaps we had history, this soul and me. My bones recognized his vibration and hummed along. My heart and his already had a secret handshake. But my brain? My brain told me to stop being a desperate attention whore and go find my own goddamn man.

By the time I shook off my confusion, Hans and I were standing at a swanky-looking restaurant counter in the Club Level lounge. My stomach growled audibly at the smell of roasting garlic and grilling meat. There were tiny versions of famous Atlanta restaurants in every corner. Italian food, barbeque, a steakhouse, a bakery. Hans was salivating over the menu at a place with twelve-dollar hamburgers when the sound of engines revving rattled the stadium.

"It's starting!" I squealed.

Hans handed me one of the passes Louis had given him so that I could run to our seats and watch the beginning of the show. We were in the tenth row, so close that I could smell the exhaust and testosterone. The trucks roared and paraded around the arena, shining, snarling examples of American excess, before splitting up and parking along the two shorter sides of the oval. Next, about two dozen guys on dirt bikes filed in from all directions, taking to the ramps and soaring through the air. After their introductions, they lined up against the two longer sides of the oval.

An announcer bellowed things that I couldn't understand through the loudspeakers, evidently signaling for two dirt-bike racers to take their places at the starting lines on either side of the dirt track.

Starting lines.

They're racing.

This is a racetrack.

I hadn't wanted to take Hans to Harley's track, yet somehow, the track had found me. I didn't want to think about the way Harley had looked in the hospital, in handcuffs and a cast, awkwardly tossing me an engagement ring before being hauled away to prison. I didn't want to think about the phone call I'd gotten from his brother, Dave, the same day, telling me that my worst enemy, Angel Alvarez, had been living with Harley for over a month. And I damn sure didn't want to think about Knight admitting to me in a letter that he was the one who'd run us off the road. That he'd blacked out in a fit of rage when Harley took me from him at gunpoint. That he was beyond help and was going back to Iraq for another tour of duty.

I could feel my heart rate beginning to climb and my hands beginning to shake as I reread the letter in my mind. Even though I'd burned it months ago, I'd committed every angry capital letter to memory. I glanced around the arena, but in the face of every driver, all I could see was Knight sneering at me from behind the wheel of his own jacked-up monster truck, blood smeared across his mouth and a cigarette between his perfect white teeth.

Stop.

I snapped my fingers and pictured a big red Stop sign in my mind. It was a tactic my psychology professor had taught me. The irony was that I'd come to him, looking for strategies to help Knight with his post-traumatic stress disorder. It didn't take long for me to realize that I had a good number of the symptoms as well. *Because* of Knight. Because of what I'd seen him do to other people. Because of what he'd done to me. Thought-stopping helped me stave off the flashbacks and panic attacks that used to hijack my life whenever I saw something Knight-related. I just had to remember to do it.

One of the bike riders did a backflip off one of the ramps, stuck the landing, and sailed across the finish line with both arms raised in victory. The crowd went wild but not as wild as my pulse when Hans showed up with two giant beers, two giant cheeseburgers, and garlic fries.

"How did you get beer?" I squealed, reaching for one of the plastic souvenir cups with grabby hands.

Hans chuckled. "Dude, I haven't been carded since I was, like, sixteen."

"Thank you." I smiled, leaning in to give him a peck on the cheek.

Fuck! Goddamn it, BB! Stop doing that!

I bent over before my lips could meet his face and picked my purse up off the concrete floor. "How much do I owe you?"

Nice save, dumbass.

"Pssh." Hans swatted my purse away. "Your money's no good here." He smirked at me and set a paper-wrapped cheeseburger in my lap.

My stomach growled, and my mouth watered. I felt guilty for what I was about to do. I knew a cheeseburger, fries, and beer would put me well over my self-imposed thousand-calorie-a-day restriction, but fuck it. I hadn't eaten in over twenty-four hours, it smelled *amazing*, and the last thing I wanted to do was reject Hans's gift.

Maybe I'll just cut back tomorrow, I thought as I inhaled half of the burger in three orgasmic bites. *Maybe I'll do some extra cardio tonight*, I told myself as I washed it down with fizzy, ice-cold Budweiser. *Maybe I'll just have one or two fries*, I mused as I shoved a fistful of fried, garlicky goodness into my face.

It's amazing what being drunk on saturated fat and alcohol can do to shut up your inner voices. My guilt curled up and took a nice long catnap for the rest of the rally.

Hans and I spent more time on our feet, shouting and cheering and sloshing our beers around and asking each other, "Did you see that shit?!" than we did in our seats.

The show was phenomenal. Five-ton vehicles careening through the air, landing on top of other cars, rolling over and crashing into one another. But, when Robosaurus came out, breathing fire and chomping junkyard sacrifices in half like some kind of metallic cannibal from hell, Hans and I lost our goddamn minds. And our voices.

We came stumbling out of the Georgia Dome late in the afternoon, drunk, happy, and rambling on about every kick-ass thing we'd just seen. Well, I was drunk. Hans would probably have to drink a few *pitchers* to get a buzz, big as he was.

I sat down on a bench in a shady spot just outside the exit doors and dug a pack of Camel Lights out of my shapeless tiger-print sack of a purse. Hans sat down next to me. Right next to me. Like, so close our thighs were touching. A fiery wave of pleasure radiated outward from that tiny spot, engulfing my entire body in hot, tingly anticipation.

Lighting two cigarettes, I passed one to Hans. He accepted it with a warm smile and leaned back, casually draping his arm over the top of the bench behind me.

Oh my God. He put his arm out! That's like the universal signal for, Come here and let me hold you, *right? He totally wants to cuddle! If I lean back, he'll put his arm around me, and we'll just have a totally friendly, nonsexual afternoon cuddle between friends.*

I took a deep drag, said, *Fuck it,* and leaned back on the exhale.

Hans did *not* put his arm around me.

I rested my head on his shoulder.

Hans did *not* put his arm around me.

I panicked and prayed to the universe for a sudden earthquake to split the earth and swallow me whole.

"Tired?" Hans asked.

I nodded.

If by tired *you mean*, embarrassed as fuck, *then yeah, I'm fucking exhausted.*

"Here." Hans took the plush Grave Digger he'd been carrying for me and set it on the far side of the bench. "You wanna lie down?"

Oh my God, he's trying to get me away from him! He's totally freaked out! I'm totally freaking him out!

Mortified tears stung my eyes, and a prickly heat spread up my neck and stained my cheeks as I lay down on my back with my head on the little stuffed monster truck. I didn't know what to do with my legs, so I bent them at the knees and planted my feet flat on the other side of Hans's thighs, careful not to touch him.

Even in my distress, I had to admit, it did feel pretty damn good to lie down.

It felt even better when Hans rested his right forearm on top of my knees.

What the fuck?

He rocked my spindly legs from side to side slightly, the smoke from the cigarette in his hand creating a zigzag pattern between us. Gazing down at me with soft eyes shining out of that hard face, Hans asked, "What do you want to do now, Bumblebee?"

Run away together. Never look back. Fly to Las Vegas. Become Mrs. Oppenheimer.

"I dunno." I turned my head and exhaled a stream of smoke away from him. "I don't have to work or anything. What about you?"

"My friend's band is playing tonight at the Tabernacle. It's just on the other side of the park"—he gestured with his cigarette toward Centennial Olympic Park—"if you wanna go."

With you? I'd go watch paint dry.

I shrugged in a thinly veiled attempt to pretend like I hadn't already named all of our future children. "Cool. What should we do till then?"

Lie here? Maybe pull you on top of me? I'm pretty sure fully clothed dry-humping isn't cheating. What if I'm the only one who comes? Then it's totally fine, right? Yes. Let's do that.

"We could go to Underground."

Or that. That's totally what I meant. What you said.

5

Fifteen minutes, the beginnings of a sunburn, a liter of sweat, and two cigarettes later, Hans and I walked up to an old train depot on the south end of downtown with a huge sign out front announcing that we'd arrived at Underground Atlanta.

"It doesn't look very underground to me."

Hans chuckled as he led the way around to the side of the building. "You haven't been here before?" He sounded almost dumbfounded.

"I think my parents took me as a kid, but I don't remember it."

"Okay, so all of this"—he gestured around at the streets and storefronts and the plaza out front—"was built in the 1920s about two stories *above* the original roads and train tracks from the 1800s. I think they did it to help with traffic or some shit. All the businesses just moved their shops up two floors, and everybody pretty much forgot about the space below."

"That's fucking crazy," I said, looking around, trying to picture how it must have looked before.

"Well, not everybody forgot. Some of the old storefronts underground turned into speakeasies."

"Dude. Shut up. How fucking cool would that have been?" I pictured myself with a chin-length bob, the fringe on my little black dress lifting and falling in layers as I did the Charleston with some tall, dark, handsome character in a pinstripe suit. I looked down at Hans's pinstripe pants and chain wallet, then up at his evil yet angelic face and smiled. "I always wanted to be a flapper. I mean, look at me." I gestured down the length of my body with the backs of my hands. "Wavy hair, stick-figure body, way too much eyeliner, problem with authority—I would have been fucking perfect."

Hans did look at me, and the heat from his gray-blue gaze made me squirm. He licked his lips subtly before speaking. "Maybe you were."

"Maybe I was a *flapper*? Like, in a past life? Do you really believe in that stuff?" I didn't mean to sound so judgmental. I was really just surprised. I didn't think anybody but my parents believed in reincarnation.

And now me, I guess.

Hans shrugged as we rounded the corner of the train depot. There was an escalator on the side of the building that descended into the ground. "I dunno. It's possible, right?"

Hans and I stepped onto the escalator at the same time. I turned sideways to face him, leaning my ass against the moving handrail. Hans mirrored my stance, facing me. The lights in the tunnel caused the shadows on his face to alternate from left to right as we traveled slowly by.

"I mean, haven't you ever had an experience where, I don't know, like, you knew something you shouldn't have known?

Or you felt like you'd been somewhere that you'd never been before?"

"Or like you knew someone that you'd never met?" I blurted out.

Hans locked eyes with me for what felt like a lifetime—or, in our case, possibly two—then gave me a ghost of a smile. "Yeah," he said. "Ever felt something like that?"

My nose tingled. My hair tingled. My fucking cherry-red toenails tingled as I held Hans's challenging stare. Whatever I was feeling, he felt it too. And he wanted to hear me say it out loud.

"Yeah"—I swallowed—"I have."

When the escalator deposited us at the bottom, I felt like I'd stepped through a wormhole into another time and place. We were at the end of a long brick-paved street, concrete and exposed beams overhead blocking out what had once been bathed in sunlight. Storefronts lined both sides of the lane, their exposed brick facades and hand-carved wooden archways protected from the elements for over eighty years. Antique streetlights illuminated our path, and kiosks made from old horse-drawn wagons dotted the center of the lane.

Within a few steps, the sound of distant jazz music filled the air, and the smell of candied pecans being sold from a wagon cart filled my nostrils.

The urge to hold Hans's hand grew with every step I took deeper into that romantic, forgotten city beneath a city. I needed to smoke. I needed to do something with my hands before my hands did something stupid.

At the first intersection we came to, a man was standing on the corner, playing the saxophone right in front of a restaurant with outdoor seating. Well, as outdoor as you could get under-ground. I didn't know what kind of food they served, but there were ashtrays on the tables, and that was all I needed to know.

A sign told us to seat ourselves, so I chose a table in the back corner of the patio area where the saxophone music wasn't so loud.

A waitress came out and brought us menus and a basket of chips and salsa.

It was a Mexican restaurant.

I lit a cigarette and immediately felt myself relax. Having a table in between our bodies and a Camel Light to busy my way-ward hands calmed my nerves dramatically. I thought of some-thing else that would help me chill out even more.

"Do you think they'd card us here?"

Hans chuckled. "Me? No. You? Fuck yes."

My mouth fell open. "I don't look *that* young."

"Yeah, okay." Hans pursed his lips, trying to suppress a smile.

"How old do I look?"

Hans tilted his head to the side and appraised me, narrowing his eyes so that the blue was overshadowed by a canopy of thick black lashes. He looked sinister when he looked at me like that. "Seventeen."

I huffed out a sigh. "But I'm here with you, and you look twenty-seven, so doesn't that make me look older by association?"

Hans's mouth pulled up on one side. "If you say so. Wanna try it?"

"Really?"

Hans shrugged and pulled a pack of Newports out of his pocket. "What's the worst that could happen?"

Right on cue, the waitress came back and pulled a pad of

paper out of her apron. She looked to be in her early twenties, and she seemed a little apprehensive about approaching us—probably because one of us was a gorgeous raven-haired giant with an evil face and even scarier tattoos. She was also wearing Keds and a scrunchie. If anybody was gonna serve alcohol to a couple of teenagers, it was her.

"My name is Maria. I'll be your server today. What can I get you to drink?"

Hans and I shared a glance. Then he said, in a voice even lower than normal, "We'll have a couple of Coronas, please... Maria."

The swarthy, lopsided grin he gave her had me seeing red and cracking my knuckles under the table. I knew he was just trying to get me a beer, but still, did he have to do it like *that*?

Maria smiled and dropped her eyes, pretending to write down Hans's order. When she recovered from his smolder, she looked at me and asked, "May I see your ID, please?"

Bitch.

I grabbed my purse, pulled a stuffed monster truck out of it, then fished out my wallet.

You want an ID? I'll give you a motherfucking ID.

Pulling a card from one of the slots inside, I handed it to her with plenty of extra salt.

Poor Maria glanced at the card, then at me, then back at the card as uncertainty marred her already-anxious face.

Hans kicked me under the table. I met his look of confusion with one of triumph.

"Um, ma'am, I'm sorry, but this doesn't look like you."

"I know. I cut all my hair off and bleached it blonde."

"No, ma'am. It says here that"—Maria looked at Hans, then

leaned over, and whispered in my ear—"you weigh one hundred and eighty pounds."

Adrenaline surged through my bloodstream. I knew Maria was just doing her job. I knew anyone would question a girl who could eat cereal out of the divots behind her protruding collarbones if she produced an ID saying she weighed almost double, but I didn't fucking care. Maria had questioned my weight and flirted with my soul mate, and for that, she must die.

I snatched the ID out of her hand and spat, "That picture was taken over five years ago. I went on fen-phen after high school, okay? I was sick of being teased about my size, okay? I'm not proud of it, *okay*? You don't have to rub it in my face!"

Maria held her hands up in defeat, then placed one over her heart in an act of genuine remorse. "I am so sorry, ma'am. I didn't—I shouldn't have—I'll go get your drinks right now. I apologize."

And off she went.

I should have felt bad—I'd behaved like a total asshole—but I didn't. I felt like a champion. Nothing made the spoiled only child in me happier than getting my way.

I smiled to myself and went to put my ID back in my wallet when Hans held his hand out and flicked his long fingers at me. "Uh-uh-uh. Let me see that thing."

I smiled in amusement and handed over the plastic card.

Hans burst out laughing. "Who the fuck is this?"

A huge grin split my face. "I have no idea. My best friend, Juliet, found it in a bush outside of Kroger. She would have kept it for herself, but she's Black and Japanese, so it doesn't look anything like her."

"It doesn't look anything like *you*!" He cackled. "I can't fucking believe you just bought beer with this thing!"

Hans handed the driver's license of one Jolene Elizabeth Godfrey back to me, respect and delight shining out of his otherwise dark features. I beamed with pride as I tucked the ID back into my wallet. Then, I pulled my irritated scowl back on when poor, sweet Maria returned with our beers.

Hans tried to feign seriousness as he ordered enough tacos to feed a small army, then burst out laughing again as soon as Maria was out of earshot. Holding up his Corona, he said, "To Jolene."

I smiled and clinked the neck of my bottle against his. "To Jolene."

I took a victory swig and let out a content sigh.

What a difference a fucking day had made. Before Steven and Goth Girl's party the night before, I'd been a shell of my former self. My buzz cut had grown out so much, my head looked like a mushroom. I hadn't worn makeup in weeks. I had been depressed, bored, and nursing not only a few broken ribs, but yet another broken heart. But I'd picked myself up, chopped my hair off, and rejoined the land of the living with gusto. I'd gone from staring at the same four walls every day to waking up in a strange bed with a strange man, driving his BMW downtown with the sunroof open, getting the VIP treatment at a monster-truck rally, and teleporting back to the 1920s. We might not be at a speakeasy, but I did manage to buy alcohol illegally.

That reminded me. "How do you know so much about this place?"

Hans was absentmindedly biting his thumbnail and looking

at something over my shoulder. His eyes snapped to mine when I spoke. "Huh? Sorry, I was listening." Hans gestured toward the saxophone player behind me. "He's really good."

"It's cool. I was just asking how you knew so much about this place."

"Oh, I dunno. I've just always been into history. It was the only class in school that I didn't have to cheat to pass. Besides music."

I laughed. "That's funny. History was the only class that I *did* have to cheat in. I just don't fucking care about what a bunch of angry old white men did hundreds of years ago. Like, I get it. They were dickheads. Let's move on."

Hans snorted into his beer. I loved making him laugh. He had pretty teeth. And pretty lips. His smile wasn't some big, megawatt movie-star smile even though that was how his presence felt. His smiles were small. Shy almost. So fucking cute.

"So, *Jolene*," he teased, "what *do* you care about?"

Your face.

I took a swig of my beer while I tried to come up with a better response. What did I care about? Boys. Cuddling. Sex. Art and music and movies. Psychology, helping people, women's rights. My parents, my dog, my friends. I liked to read and write and draw and paint. I wanted to travel. I loved fashion and photography. I loved drinking and smoking and breaking the rules. So many things floated into my consciousness all at once that I just blurted out, "Everything. I care about fucking everything."

"Everything, except for angry old white men who act like dickheads."

"Correct." I smirked, pointing a finger gun at him. "Except for those. And, also, Chumbawamba."

Hans laughed again, and the sound made me feel like the fizzy beer bubbles in my stomach were dancing throughout my entire body. I noticed that he always looked down when he first started laughing, just for a second, just long enough for his thick inky-black lashes to soften the rest of his hard, brooding face. It was also just long enough for me to sigh without him seeing it.

Hans grabbed his pack of Newports from the table and popped one into his mouth. Just before lighting it, he paused with his cigarette between his teeth. Hans looked at me, all traces of amusement disappearing from his too-serious face and said, "Are you going away for college?"

Now, it was my turn to snort. "Fuck no. I'll be right here." I pointed in the general direction of the Georgia State University campus, which was only a few blocks away. "I got the HOPE Grant, so as long as I stay in-state, my tuition is covered. I've already got some credits from my AP classes, so if I keep busting my ass, I should have a bachelor's degree in psychology before I'm old enough to drink."

Hans smirked and nudged my foot under the table. "You might not want to say that too loud, *Jolene*."

Warmth spread from the tiny spot on the side of my foot where our shoes were touching, up the inside of my pleather pants, and shot straight to the apex of my thighs.

"Oh, right." I blushed, looking around to make sure Maria hadn't been within earshot. "I mean, I'm *totally* already old enough to drink." I raised my voice loud enough for the entire restaurant to hear.

Hans nudged my foot again to quiet me, and I almost came.

"So, are you going to college in the fall?" I asked, trying hard to focus on his answer rather than the fact that his foot was still touching mine.

"Nah." Hans finally lit his cigarette, then held his open pack out in a silent offering.

I took a menthol from him and leaned in so that he could light it for me. The flame warmed my face, and the first drag made my throat tingle.

"I'm just gonna focus on my music for now. My parents want me to go to college and even offered to send me to this fuckin' crazy expensive music school in town, but I don't want to learn somebody else's style. You know? I want to find my own."

I nodded with a new appreciation for the man sitting across from me. Hans wasn't just another wannabe rock star. Hans was an artist. The realization made me a little sad. I knew that affliction. Both of my parents, my uncle on my dad's side, my aunt on my mom's side, a few cousins, and both of my grandmothers were artists. You would think that, in a family full of poets, painters, and piccolo players, I would have been encouraged to let my own artistic tendencies flourish, but no. Being born with the need to create was seen as a burden in my family. It wouldn't pay your bills; it would only break your heart.

My father and his brother, who had grown up playing in rock bands together, were consumed by depression as adults. They couldn't make enough as musicians to meet even their most basic needs, so they worked soul-crushing retail jobs during the day that broke their sensitive spirits. My father used to stay up late into the night, drinking and playing his electric guitar for no one, the amp volume turned down low. His rock-and-roll spirit all but neutered.

"Being smart, now, that's something you can build a future

on—not your talent and damn sure not your looks," my father had preached.

"Smart beats pretty every time," he'd whispered in my ear every night before bed.

"Art will only break your heart," he'd warned.

"In this day and age, you have to have at least a master's degree. Bachelor's degrees are a dime a dozen. Get a job with good benefits, maybe a pension. Then you'll be happy," he'd promised.

Please don't turn out like me, he'd begged with his eyes.

I didn't want to turn out like him either. Being a starving artist held no appeal to me. I knew how poor my family was. How depressed and stressed they all were. I wanted to help people like them, not become one.

Hans certainly seemed to be starving. That motherfucker ate more than anyone I'd ever met. Maria returned with plates of tacos stacked up her arms like porcelain staircases and two more Coronas in her fists—a peace offering.

I took my beer with a genuine smile and decided that I liked Maria after all.

She tried to put a few of the plates in front of me, but I shook my head and directed them all to the other side of the table.

Hans was already polishing off his first taco by the time the last one was set down. "Go ahead." He gestured toward the school of tacos on the table.

"I'm good." I held up my hands, cigarette in one, beer in the other. "Got my dinner right here."

Hans stopped eating and stared at me with his serious face again. The face that reminded me that he might still be a serial killer. "You're not gonna eat?"

"I'm still full from lunch. That burger was huge! Thanks though. Hey, after this, do you wanna go walk around Georgia State on our way to the Tabernacle? I still don't know my way around the campus, but the idea of taking one of those guided tours makes me stabby."

Hans smiled and took another bite. "Sure," he murmured with his mouth full, following my change of subject without a second thought. "I wanna see it too. Hey, maybe I can come down here and meet you for lunch sometime. These tacos are fucking amazing."

"Yeah." I took a swig of my beer to hide the shit-eating grin that was threatening to take over my whole face. "Maybe." I took a drag from my cigarette. "That'd be cool." I exhaled.

Oh my fucking God, I screamed on the inside. *Hans wants to see me again!*

6

Hans paid the check without even looking at it, just handed Maria a credit card. For a starving artist, he sure didn't seem to be hurting for money. I wanted to ask him if he had another job besides being a bass player in a band no one had ever heard of, but I didn't want to get too personal about his financial situation when I hadn't even known the guy a full twenty-four hours yet.

We time-traveled back up the escalator, going from the dark, romantic Atlanta of the 1920s to the blistering hot, noisy-as-shit Atlanta of 1999 in just a few seconds. The contrast was jarring. Not only did we have to raise our voices to hear each other over the cacophony of sirens and car alarms, but we were also approached by at least five panhandlers in as many blocks on our way to Georgia State University.

My dad had always told me never to give homeless people money. He'd said that they would only use it to buy drugs and booze. Evidently, nobody had ever said that to Hans because, by the time we reached GSU, he'd given away all his change and half of his remaining cigarettes.

The Georgia State campus wasn't so much a *campus* as it was just a loose cluster of old, mismatched buildings on the south end of Peachtree Street. Hans and I poked around, trying to get into locked buildings and taking random stairwells just to see where they led. Normally, I might have been a little overwhelmed at the sheer expansiveness of my new school, but I had the perfect two-beer buzz going, so nothing was going to bring me down.

The only common area we could find was a large cement courtyard about two stories above street level. I liked it up there. Hans and I were completely alone yet in the middle of every-thing. The courtyard was flanked by the library, a bunch of buildings that were probably named after angry old white men, and the College of Arts & Sciences.

I elbowed Hans in the ribs, another excuse to touch him, and pointed at the building across from us. "You know, if you're gonna come down here to have lunch with me anyway, you might as well just enroll. Look, our majors would even be in the same building."

Hans squinted at the Arts & Sciences sign, which was being hit directly by the sideways rays of the early evening sun.

"We could carpool!" I chirped. "Wait, where do you live?"

Hans turned away from the building and faced me, shielding his eyes from the sun with his hand. "On Lake Lanier."

"On Lake Lanier? Like, *on* Lake Lanier?"

Hans laughed, turning away from the sun. We kept walking. "Yeah."

"First of all, *damn*. Those houses are super nice," I said. "And second of all, that's like forty-five minutes north of here."

"An hour with traffic," Hans corrected.

"And you're gonna drive down here just to have lunch with me?"

Hans shrugged and stuck his hands in his pockets. "Yeah. Why not?"

I squinted up at him, my heart fluttering faster than hummingbird wings. "You hate to drive."

Hans smiled and looked down at me. Two dimples cratered his stubble-covered cheeks. Midnight-black lashes rimmed his blue-jean-colored eyes. "Yeah, but those were really good tacos."

There was something in his voice, his delivery, that told me he liked more than just the tacos. My legs turned to rubber, and I had to cross my arms over my chest to keep from wrapping them around him and never letting go. I opened my mouth to say something—probably something stupid like, *Hey! I know! You should tell your girlfriend to go fuck herself and get an apartment with me and go to college with me and go everywhere with me and marry me and give me tall, black-haired babies!*—when a fire truck, ambulance, and police car rounded the corner and blasted us directly in the face with their flashing lights and screaming sirens. It was a regular occurrence downtown, but the timing couldn't have been better.

I used the distraction to change the subject, which was never hard to do with Hans. "So, how long till the show starts?"

If it weren't for the illuminated marquee and line of pierced, purple-haired teenagers wrapping around the building, one would assume that the Tabernacle was just another big, old Southern Baptist church. And it had been once. Now, there was enough drinking, dancing, smoking, and toking going on inside to have the original founders rolling over in their graves.

"Oh shit!" I said, reading the name on the marquee as we walked up. "Your friend is opening for Love Like Winter? I just bought their new album! It's fucking amazing!"

"Right? I think I've listened to it eighty times, and every time I hear something different. They're fucking geniuses. And super nice, too. We tried out to be their opener a few weeks ago, but they wanted somebody more alternative. That's the direction I'm trying to take us in, but Trip wants to go more industrial, if that's even possible."

"Who's Trip?" I asked, veering left to go join the back of the line.

"Our lead singer," Hans said, grabbing me by the hand and pulling me to the right, toward the front of the line.

I squealed and stumbled to get back in step with him, acutely aware of the fact that Hans was now holding my hand.

He's holding my hand.

He's holding my hand.

He's still *holding my hand!*

My lungs seized, and the gears in my mind came to a grinding halt as I struggled to decide what to do. I knew I should pull away. I couldn't pull away. I wanted to lace our fingers together and rub his thumb with my thumb—if my thumb was the one that ended up on top, of course—but I couldn't do that either. Instead, my hand remained a limp fish in Hans's grasp, my legs, a couple of wet noodles, as I shuffled along beside him to the front doors of the venue.

One of the guys checking IDs at the door, a little fella with a black bowl cut, saw us approaching and puffed up his chest. "Excuse me, sir," he said, pointing to the other side of the building. "I'm gonna need you to step to the back of the line."

Hans cocked his head to one side. "I'm gonna need you to blow me."

My mouth fell open as the door guy dropped to his knees right there and reached for Hans's belt buckle.

Hans laughed and swatted him away. "Not here, damn it!" He pulled his buddy up off the ground, and they did that same hug/back-slap thing I'd seen him do with his drummer.

Stepping to the side, Hans turned toward me and asked, "BB, did you get to meet Trip last night?"

I knew he looked familiar! I hadn't recognized him without his black lipstick and goth gear on, but that cheekbone-length butt-cut gave him away.

I shook my head and was about to extend my hand when Trip

came over and wrapped his arm around me instead. "Fuck no, she didn't! Your ass went all caveman and claimed her before we even finished breakin' down our equipment." Turning toward me, Trip lowered his voice and asked, "So, BB, have you seen this guy's schlong yet? We don't call him LDH for nothin', you know."

A Cheshire Cat grin overtook Trip's face just before Hans covered it with his massive hand and pulled him away from me. Trip came back swinging, but Hans just held his face at arm's length so none of his punches could connect.

"Trip! Get your ass over here and help us!" a female voice shouted.

Hans released his head, and Trip looked over his shoulder at an angry-looking lady with a red Mohawk checking tickets behind him. He covertly slipped two wristbands into Hans's palm, then sucker-punched him in the stomach before skipping back to his post.

Hans let out a guttural noise and gave Trip a middle-finger salute. Half-laughing, half-coughing, Hans took me by the hand, *again*, and led me into the building.

I felt like someone had replaced my blood with Pop Rocks and Coke. I was a floating cloud of fizzy pheromones. And I was also freaking the fuck out.

I knew it was wrong. I knew I was basically just a hop, skip, and a fuck away from becoming Angel Alvarez—that man-stealing whore—but I rationalized. I told myself that I wouldn't let it go any further. I told myself that siblings slept in the same bed and held hands too. I told myself that it meant nothing. Hans was just flirty, like Goth Girl had said.

But when he slid his thumb over mine, a sense of déjà vu scrambled my senses. I could have sworn I'd felt that particular touch before. Not with my skin, but with my soul.

There you are, it whispered. *I've been looking for you.*

"Sorry about him." Hans chuckled as we reached the top of the stairs. "He's...well, he's Trip."

"He's *a* trip." I laughed, picturing him on his knees in the middle of the sidewalk. "Is that his real name? I like it."

Hans snorted as we joined a long line of people waiting to buy drinks at a cash bar. "Nah. His real name is Cody. We gave him the stage name Triple X because of all the fucked-up porn he watches. Now he just goes by Trip for short."

Hans lifted my hand and adorned it with one of the wristbands, leaning in close to me to keep anyone from seeing what he was doing. It felt intimate, like we were sharing a secret.

When he was done, I took the other wristband out of his hand and returned the favor. With my eyes cast down and my hands busy accessorizing Hans's thick wrist, I asked, "So, what *does* LDH stand for?"

When Hans didn't answer right away, I looked up at him, and I swear to God, I think he was blushing.

"I'll tell you another time," he said.

"No! You have to tell me now!" I cried. "Pleeeeease?"

Hans stuck his thumbnail between his teeth, like he was thinking about it. Then, he smiled and shook his head.

"Are you fucking serious? You're not gonna tell me?"

Hans shook his head again. "It's embarrassing. Well, not really embarrassing, just...awkward."

"Well now I *have to* know." I pouted, stomping one well-worn combat boot on the well-worn hardwood floor. I crossed my arms and turned my head away from Hans in a huff, my eyes landing on the entrance below.

Trip!

I flashed Hans a wicked grin. Then, I bolted back down the staircase and poked my head through one of the six massive, wooden front doors.

"Trip! Hey, Trip!" I yelled.

Trip turned around from where he was checking IDs just a few feet away and spread his arms like he was waiting for me to leap into them. "I knew you'd come running back to me, girl."

I giggled. "Hey, what does LDH stand for? Hans won't tell me."

Trip's face contorted into an evil grin. "So you *haven't* seen it yet."

"Seen what?"

"LDH stands for Long Dong Hans, sweetheart. Your boy in there is packin' some serious sausage."

I burst out laughing, along with everybody else on the front steps of the Tabernacle, except, of course, for Trip's female coworker, who smacked him on the back of the head and pointed at his steadily growing line.

Trip ignored her, focusing on something over my shoulder. "There's the big fella now. Why're you holding out on my girl, bro? BB wants to see the beast!"

I turned and found Hans standing right behind me, a beer in each hand and a one-dimpled smirk on his otherwise hard face.

"Happy now?" he asked, handing me one of the clear plastic cups.

"Mmhmm." I nodded, biting my smile and resisting the urge to look down at the size of his feet.

Hans and Trip yelled some obscenities at each other, then we walked back up the stairs, through a set of double doors on the other side of the lobby, and into the concert hall. It still looked very much like a cathedral on the inside—aside from the black paint and graffiti on every visible surface. The pulpit had been replaced with a raised stage, but the twenty-foot-tall stained-glass windows along the left and right sides of the room remained. The pews had long been removed, but the second- and third-floor balconies were still intact. No one passed collection plates anymore. They let you bring the money to them—at the bar and the merch tables. And, although the statue of Christ on the cross had been taken down years ago, there was no doubt that what went on inside was a form of worship.

Hans selected a spot close to the stage but on the far-right side of the crowd. As the lights went down and the crowd started to rush to the front, he leaned over and whisper-yelled in my ear, "You can go up closer if you want."

I looked up at him with my eyebrows pulled together. "You don't want to come with me?"

Hans shook his head. "I can't. I'll block everybody's view. I just feel bad, making you stand back here with me when there's room up front."

It was so fucking sweet. I wanted to wrap myself around his long, lean body and press my ear to his heart and just listen to the sound of *it* for the rest of the night instead of the music. But I smiled and smacked him on the arm instead. "Don't be stupid."

The opening band was called Miss Murder, and they spotted Hans in the crowd right away. The drummer pointed his sticks in our direction before launching into their set. I could tell they were nervous, their movements stiff and rehearsed, but their sound was pretty cool. Hans had been right; they were heavy, but not Phantom Limb heavy.

As soon as their set was over and the guys started breaking down their equipment, the drummer motioned for us to come over. He and Hans chatted for a minute before Hans hopped onstage to help them clear out.

Evidently, only headliners got roadies.

I had no idea what to do to help, so I did what I always did whenever I felt awkward. I smoked a cigarette and tried to look cool.

It was kind of fun, watching Hans in his element. He looked so comfortable up onstage. He knew exactly what to do and joked with the guys as they worked.

When they were done, Hans came over to the edge of the stage and reached both hands down to me. "C'mon. We're gonna go meet the band."

"The band? Like, *the* band?"

Hans beamed with pride. "Yeah. Like, *the* band. Come on."

I set my almost-empty plastic cup with two cigarette butts floating in it on the edge of the stage and let Hans hoist me up. As he led me across the platform and through a curtain, I became acutely aware that I was wearing the same clothes I'd worn the day before, had re-spiked my hair in a sink that morning, and had been drinking steadily since noon. If I had known I was going to meet Love Like Winter that day, I would have at least showered.

I covertly ducked my head and sniffed my armpit.

Ugh.

While I was busy rummaging through my purse, looking for

breath mints and lipstick, we managed to make our way to a doorway where Hans's drummer friend was standing. He was a sweaty, stocky guy wearing a muscle shirt and a huge smile— the smile of a guy who'd just opened for Love Like Winter.

I don't even really remember what happened; it was so surreal.

There was a room. With famous rock stars inside. Whom I'd seen on MTV. Whose CD was in my car stereo. Who smiled at me and said they liked my pixie cut. Who shook Hans's hand and said they remembered him from the audition. Who laughed about the Grave Digger autograph on my arm because, *How can a truck hold a pen?* And who then put *their* autographs on my arm to add to my collection. Rock stars who said, "Thanks for coming," as they breezed past us and out the door. Who left us alone in a green room, backstage at the Tabernacle.

Hans and I just stood in their wake, blinking at each other.

"Oh my fucking God," I whispered.

Hans's dimples deepened. "You're totally fangirling right now."

"Fuck you! That was Love Like Winter!" I huffed and gestured at the open door. Then I looked down at my arm in amazement, flipping it over to admire both sides. "And they touched me."

Hans chuckled at my dramatics. "They're just people."

I held up a hand. "No, they're not. They're Love Like Winter. Hush your mouth."

Hans raised an eyebrow at me and smirked, effectively hushed.

I looked down at my arm again and smiled. Picking up the Sharpie they'd used, I pulled the cap off and handed it to Hans. "Will you sign it too?"

Hans rolled his eyes. "Put that thing away."

"I'm serious. You're gonna be just as famous as them one day. I can tell. I want to be able to say that I got your very first autograph."

After some stammering and hesitation, Hans finally accepted the marker. I turned my left arm over to expose a blank spot and held my breath as he wrapped his hand around my wrist. I wondered if I would ever get used to the feeling of his skin on my skin. To the violent knocking of memories from a lifetime forgotten on the basement door of my subconscious.

Knock, knock, knock. I heard with my ears.

Knock, knock, knock. I felt in my bones.

When Hans released my arm, I looked down to admire his work. Only, where a signature should have been, a ten-digit number had been written instead.

A phone number.

I lifted my eyes to meet his. Hans's chest rose, and he bit the inside of his lip. He reminded me of a child awaiting a punishment. A sweet, generous, painfully sexy, six-foot-three-inch-tall child with a five-o'clock shadow and a full sleeve of tattoos.

Who had just done something he shouldn't have.

"Honey, I think somebody needs to teach you how autographs work. Gimme that thing," I joked, trying to defuse the situation. I flicked my fingers at the marker in his hand.

Hans handed it over without a word, worrying his lip as I took his wrist and flipped it over.

Five seconds later, Hans burst out laughing when I lifted my hand and let him see my masterpiece. "Are you fucking serious?"

"Oh, wait, hang on," I said, quickly adding the letters *LDH* inside the shaft of the two-inch-tall penis I'd just drawn. "There."

"You think *that's* a better autograph?" Hans asked, gently slipping the marker from my hand.

I grinned and nodded.

"Okay then." He shrugged. "Guess I'd better start practicing." Hans reached out and snatched my arm before I could pull away.

"No!" I yelled, tugging against his grip, but it was too late. I was caught.

When Hans came at me with the Sharpie, I switched tactics and tried to bat it out of his hand.

He chuckled and moved the marker from side to side, taunting me with an, "Uh-uh-uh," before finally holding the damn thing so high over his head that I couldn't reach it, even when I jumped.

I grunted in frustration. Back when Knight used to restrain me or pin me down, albeit under very different circumstances, I'd learned how to wriggle and twist my way to freedom.

I grunted in frustration and spun around backward, trying to twist my arm out of Hans's grasp, like I'd done with Knight years before. But the instant my back collided with his front, my muscles softened and gave up the fight. I sagged backward against Hans's chest, and he pulled me closer, wrapping his Sharpie-holding arm around my middle and resting his chin on the top of my head.

Hans was, once again, holding me.

Dopamine exploded through my bloodstream.

My eyes rolled up into my head.

Ever since that morning, I'd been jonesing for another fix. I'd wanted to feel the weight of Hans's arms around me again even more than I wanted to see that famous *dong* of his. And that was *a lot*.

I closed my eyes and held my breath, thinking maybe I could stop time. Maybe I could live in that space between my breaths forever.

I didn't breathe as Hans loosened his grip on my forearm and gently massaged the freckled flesh beneath his palm. I didn't breathe as I lifted my right arm and gingerly slid the marker from Hans's right hand. And I only opened one eye as I scrawled my phone number down the length of Leatherface's chainsaw, my lungs burning like twin bonfires in my chest.

In fact, I didn't take a breath until the first chords of Love Like Winter's opening song rattled through the walls, proving me a failure.

I hadn't stopped time. All I'd done was deprive myself of oxygen while handing my heart to an unavailable man.

Silly, stupid girl.

With a sigh, I wriggled out of Hans's embrace and placed the black marker back on the green-room coffee table. I took a beat to pull on my most-excited grin. Then, I spun around and asked, "Can we go watch the show now?"

Hans led me back through the narrow hallways until we reached a heavy gray door. I could practically see it rattling from the reverb assaulting it on the other side. With a backward glance and his small, dimpled smile, Hans pushed it open, bathing us in a riot of joyous noise.

We entered the belly of the cathedral to the left of the stage just as Love Like Winter finished their first song. The crowd deafened me with their enthusiasm as I made my way to the bar. If I was going to have to stand next to Hans Oppenheimer in this den of gyrating bodies and sweat and abandon for the next hour, I was gonna need a fucking drink.

A stiff one.

I ordered two Jack and Cokes, holding up my wristband in annoyance, like I wasn't obviously seventeen. Just as I was about to hand over my debit card to pay for them, Hans swooped in and slapped a twenty on the bar. I should have protested a little more or at least offered to pay him back. After all, he'd paid for literally everything that day, but I was flat broke. I hadn't been able to work since *the accident* and was living off of what I'd managed to save from my race winnings.

Thank you, I mouthed as I joined Hans at the edge of the crowd. It was too loud for any real communication.

The old hardwood shook and bounced beneath our feet as hundreds of bodies jumped up and down all around us. Hans smiled and handed over one of the fizzy brown beverages.

You're welcome, he mouthed back.

What? I mouthed, just to fuck with him. *I can't hear you.*

Hans smirked at my silliness and cupped his hands around his mouth. *Yooooou're wellllcooooome*, he pretended to shout, exaggerating every syllable.

I furrowed my brow and shrugged. Then, I waved my hand back and forth between the band and my ear. *It's too loud. Say it one more time.* I took a sip of my drink to hide my stupid schoolgirl grin as I batted my eyelashes at Hans.

But Hans didn't mouth *You're welcome* again. He looked at me and looked at me, and then he said, "You're beautiful," instead.

Out loud.

In his normal voice.

I froze. Clear plastic cup to my lips. Sugary bubbles bursting on my tongue. Sugary bubbles stinging my eyes.

Sugary bubbles tingling between my legs.

I swallowed. I blinked. I blinked again.

Hans swallowed. He blinked. His eyebrows pulled together.

Shit. I made it weird.

With flaming cheeks, I mumbled something that sounded like *thank you.* Then, I turned toward the stage and took a sip from my drink to mask my mortification.

Tell him he's beautiful too!

No way! Guys don't want to be called beautiful!

Tell him he looks like Jared Leto from My So-Called Life*!*

Nobody with a penis watched that show, dummy!

Tell him—

My internal freak-out was interrupted by a callused knuckle against the underside of my chin. Hans gently rotated my face up and to the left, forcing me to look at him. I tried to turn my anxious cringe into a smile as Hans searched my face with soulful eyes. The expression he wore was so sincere, it made my chest ache.

He bent down to my ear, the fingers under my jaw splaying to cup the side of my neck, and said, above the roar of the bodies and speakers and the hormones swirling around us, "You are the *most* beautiful thing I've ever seen."

I blinked back stunned tears as my blushing cheek brushed against his prickly one. I inhaled his scent, caressed his earlobe with my nose, then said, "I'm sorry. I couldn't hear you. Will you say that again?"

Hans laughed and pulled me into his side, where I stood for the next hour, swooning and singing and sloshing my drinks in pure glee.

When the last song had been played and the house lights

came up, Hans and I stumbled out onto the fire escape, arm in arm, and made our way down to the street. The night air was hot and sweaty, just like us. We cut across Centennial Park, which I'd never seen at night, and Hans gave his last Newport to a homeless man asking to bum a smoke.

By the time we found the BMW in the Georgia Dome parking lot, I had already begun to mourn what had quite possibly been the best day of my life. I drove back to Steven's house with the sunroof open and the AC on full blast, going exactly the speed limit and not one mile per hour faster. I wasn't going to let anything ruin my perfect day.

At least, that's what I thought until Hans's phone started ringing.

And ringing.

And ringing.

Every time it went off, he'd silence it immediately and shove it back into his pocket. After the third ring, Hans turned the car stereo on. A haunting, heavy bass line filled the car.

"Do you like the Deftones?"

He was trying to distract me. Well, unlike him, I had a one-track mind. I ate distractions for breakfast.

"Do you need to get that?" I asked, watching him out of the corner of my eye.

Hans opened his glove box and pulled out a new pack of Newports. Tapping the lid of the box on the heel of his palm a few times, he said, "No."

No. That was it. No explanation. No chuckle about Trip drunk-dialing him or annoyance about his mom being a worrywart. Hans, an emotional open book, was hiding something from me.

"What if it's an emergency?" I asked.

"It's not." Hans peeled the plastic wrap off the box and let it flutter to the floorboard, joining the rest of the trash accumulated there.

"But what if it is?"

Hans stuck a cigarette between his teeth and shrugged. "Then they can call somebody else."

They. Gender-neutral. Hans didn't want me to know that it was a girl.

I hadn't asked him about his girlfriend because, honestly, I wanted to pretend like she didn't exist. But there she was anyway, riding shotgun in Hans's pocket.

I felt like the lowest of the fucking low. I'd been that girl, searching for my boyfriend. Waiting by the phone. Crying myself to sleep while he was off drinking and partying and fucking someone else. I glanced down at Hans's phone number on my arm and felt another stab of guilt. Had he pulled that move on her, too? Written his number on her skin? Made her feel special?

I took Hans's fresh pack of Newports from the center console without asking and lit one, savoring one last menthol before I cut him loose. I might have been needy. I might have been recently broken. But I was healing. I didn't need to steal another girl's boyfriend to make myself whole. I wasn't Angel fucking Alvarez.

I was, however, way drunker than I'd realized. The menthol had taken my buzz and cranked it up to eleven. By the time I pulled into Steven's neighborhood, I could barely see straight. My head spun, and my stomach lurched. I clenched my teeth and fought back the bile until I pulled up onto the curb behind my Mustang. Then, I threw the Beemer in park, pushed open the door, and retched all over the sidewalk.

I guess matching a dude who was almost a foot taller than me and twice my body weight drink for drink hadn't been such a good idea after all.

8

One Week Later

"Tell me you are not seriously parking here." Juliet hit the door lock button as I killed the engine and cut off the lights.

"What? It's not that far of a walk. And it's free."

Juliet glared at me. "Great. That just means there's more money in your pocket for the muggers and rapists to take."

I swatted at her, missing on purpose. "Nobody's gonna rape us!" I pointed straight ahead to a figure slumped against an apartment building, silhouetted by a nearby streetlight. "If you give Old Willy there a couple of cigarettes, he'll watch your car for you and make sure you get down the street okay."

Juliet's drawn-on eyebrows rose, and a giggle percolated from her chest. "Please tell me you're fucking kidding."

"What? It's a win-win."

Juliet's laugh turned into a full cackle. "How are you still alive? Like, seriously."

I swatted at her again, connecting with her arm that time. "Whatever. Like your decisions are any better."

I had to bite my tongue to keep from adding the word *Mom* at the end of that sentence. Juliet fucking hated it whenever Goth Girl or I called her that.

Juliet lifted the sleeve of the hoodie she was holding in her lap, pushed the top of a bottle of wine out of the opening, and unscrewed the cap. "Speaking of bad decisions."

"Ugh! Wine? That's all you could find?" I wrinkled up my nose.

"I'm sorry. Maybe, if your twenty-two-year-old boyfriend hadn't gone back to jail, we'd be drinking Perrier right now!"

I laughed. "It's Dom Pérignon. Perrier is water, dumbass."

And I'm pretty sure your twenty-five-year-old baby daddy got locked up first.

Juliet was a bitch, but she was *my* bitch. We'd been best friends for five years even though we were polar opposites. Juliet was snarky and introverted and tough while I was bubbly and extroverted and naive. She had dark skin; I had freckles. She had long black braids; I had a short blonde pixie cut. But we shared a love of eyeliner, cigarettes, booze, and boys. Juliet even more so than me, which was how she'd ended up with a one-year-old at the age of seventeen.

Juliet took a swig from the sweatshirt-wrapped bottle and passed it to me. "I can't believe I let you drag me to a heavy-metal concert. I must really fucking like you."

I drank a few swallows of sour, piss-colored wine and winced, passing the bottle back to Juliet. "Or you just really needed a break from Romeo."

Juliet laughed. "Yeah, that too. God, that little fucker is into everything now that he's walking." She chugged a quarter of the bottle after that statement.

"Oh shit, I almost forgot," I said, turning around and grabbing a T-shirt out of the backseat. "Hans said I was supposed to wear this."

I unfolded the shirt and held it up between us. It was black with a white Phantom Limb logo on the front.

"Uh, that thing is gonna look like a tent on you," Juliet said, curling her lip in disgust. "Give it to me. I'll fix it." She snatched the shirt from me and dug around in her cavernous purse until she found a pair of baby fingernail scissors. "Yes!" As she went to work, hacking away at the hem of the T-shirt with the world's tiniest pair of scissors, she asked, "Isn't it, like, super uncool to wear the shirt of the band playing to their concert?"

I laughed and took another sour gulp of wine. "Right? That's what I thought too. But when Hans and I were saying goodbye last Sunday and he invited me to the show, he dug this shirt out of his trunk and said I had to wear it." I shrugged and kept drinking, trying to calm the gang of violent, mutant, body-building butterflies that took flight every time I thought of Hans. Of his pretty denim-colored eyes that looked like they were rimmed in kohl. Of his little dimples and his little half-smiles. Of his arms around my shoulders and his chin on the top of my head.

"He's fucking claiming you, BB. Like a caveman. He wants everybody to see you in his shirt and know that you're his."

I snorted. "I'm *not* fucking his though. *Beth* is." I rolled my eyes and hiccupped, already beginning to feel a buzz.

"Fuck Beth. Where is she?" Juliet looked around at the crumbling bungalows and burned-out streetlights around us. "I don't see that bitch. And Hans sure as fuck didn't see her last weekend because he was with *you* the whole time. He even took care of you while you were wasted! That's boyfriend shit, B."

I took another sour gulp and felt the embarrassment of that night wash over me. I was suddenly right back there in my mind, staring into my own puke on the sidewalk. Wanting to crawl under Hans's BMW and die. I relived the sequence of events—at least the ones I could remember. Hans picking me up and carrying me against his chest, to Steven's door. Steven letting us in and gesturing toward the hall bathroom in annoyance. Pigtails cutting up lines of coke on Steven's glass-top coffee table. *Where is Goth Girl? Did they get into a fight like Hans had said they would?* Hans rubbing my bony back while I heaved into the toilet, handing me my phone so that I could call my worried parents and tell them I was crashing at Victoria's house again. Hans bringing me a large cup full of water and a small cup full of mouthwash. Hans unlacing my boots and peeling off my tight pleather pants before tucking me into Maddie's twin-size bed. Hans curling up behind me on the mattress, his front to my back, his slow, sleepy breath on my neck.

Hans's erection against my lower back in the morning.

"Then why didn't he make a move on me?" I pouted, about to tip the bottle up and finish it before Juliet snatched it from my pathetic, boy-crazy hand.

Juliet shrugged and polished off the last of the wine. "Let's go find out. If we don't get murdered on the way, that is."

As I laughed at her joke, the wine making it seem extra funny, Juliet tossed my new T-shirt at my face. I pulled off my tank top and slipped my new shirt on over my head, careful not to fuck up the spiky-chic hairdo I'd spent an hour trying to make look effortless. Juliet was right; the shirt had been too big for me, but she'd hacked the bottom half of it off, right below the logo, and widened the neck so that it would hang off one shoulder. I rolled up the sleeves and nodded. It would have to do.

Good Old Willy kept his word, and in exchange for two Camel Lights, Juliet and I made it safely to the box office of the Masquerade.

To anyone but a local, the Masquerade would have appeared to be nothing more than a condemned old factory that had once specialized in manufacturing splinters and sadness. But, to alternative-rock lovers, it was heaven. Well, technically, it was Heaven, Purgatory, and Hell, as the three sections inside the building had been affectionately nicknamed.

Hell was home to the techno crowd, fetish parties, and eighties night. Purgatory was the bar on the second floor, and upstairs, on the third floor where all the live music happened, was Heaven. Fitting, considering that was where I'd get to see Hans again.

Just as my feet hit the top stair, a bass line began to rattle the floor. I didn't recognize the song, but something inside me recognized the source. Juliet and I walked out of the stairwell and into the dark, smoky, sweltering confines of Heaven. The crowd was larger than I'd expected for Locals Only night, filling up most of the warehouse-sized space.

When my eyes swept over the crowd and up to the stage, there was a brief moment where the rest of the world fell away. Hans was all I could see. It wasn't that he commanded attention. He wasn't wearing a fishnet shirt or vinyl pants or leather-studded gloves or any of the other dramatic bullshit his bandmates had on. He wasn't even looking at the crowd. But there was something about him that shone.

Maybe it was all the contrast. Hans's features were dark and hard, but his spirit was soft and light. One arm was completely tattooed in blacks and grays; the other was a blank canvas. His low-slung, baggy slacks were black, but the tight wifebeater clinging to his hard chest was white. Hell, even his Adidas were black and white.

But his bass? His bass was red, red, red.

Hans didn't see me when I walked in, but Trip did. He pointed at us from behind the mic stand just before growling the opening lyrics to one of Phantom Limb's original songs. The crowd turned their heads in our direction briefly, which prompted Hans to look up as well.

And smile.

"Fuck, B. That's him?" Juliet shouted over the music.

"Uh-huh," I said, entranced.

"The bass player?"

"Uh-huh."

"That Jared Leto–looking motherfucker with the tattoos?"

I swallowed and nodded, never breaking eye contact.

"Girl, I don't care if he's fucking *married*. You have *got* to hit that."

Juliet took me by the arm and dragged my leaden feet through the crowd, shamelessly shoehorning us into a gap right at the front of the stage. I was so fucking uncomfortable. Why was I so fucking uncomfortable? I'd spent the entire weekend with this guy. I'd slept in the same bed with him. Twice. He'd seen me barf. Like, thirty times. But for some reason, I felt shy. I wanted to run to the bar and take enough shots to tranquilize the batshit-crazy butterflies in my stomach, but the black Xs on the backs of my hands made that an impossibility.

So I did what I always did when I felt awkward. I smoked. And I smoked. And I smoked.

Every time Hans's eyes landed on me, I smiled like a dumbass. Every time his eyes weren't me, I pouted. It wasn't until their fourth or fifth song that I even realized that people were singing along. Phantom Limb had *fans*. Actual fans.

After the sixth or seventh song, Trip paused to have a little banter with the audience. For a scrawny little thing with an unfortunate haircut, I had to admit, Trip exuded some kind of weird sex appeal up there. He was charismatic, oddly confident, and could command the crowd's attention with a flick of his wrist.

After asking how everyone was feeling, Trip announced that it was his favorite part of the show. "Would all the sexy ladies wearing Phantom Limb shirts in the house please come on up?"

I glanced at Hans in confusion, but he just gave me a one-dimpled smile and beckoned me onstage with a flick of his fingers.

Me?

I looked down and realized that I was wearing a Phantom Limb T-shirt. I had totally forgotten.

Sneaky motherfucker.

Juliet gave me a shove toward the side of the stage, and I ascended the stairs on autopilot along with about ten other girls.

Holding Hans's amused stare, I mouthed, *What the fuck?* as Trip instructed us to line up in front of the drum set.

Sorry, Hans mouthed back, cupping a hand to his ear, *I can't hear you.*

I flipped him off as I took my spot in line just behind him, pursing my lips to hide the girlish grin threatening to blow my cool.

"Now, now, BB. That will have to wait until after the show," Trip admonished me, eliciting a laugh from the crowd. "Okay, folks, you know the drill. The Phantom Girl with the best high kick gets to kiss any member of the band she wants."

The fuck?!

I swear I think I saw Hans blush as the band picked their instruments back up and began playing a hard-rock version of the classic French cancan song. Right on cue, the girls on either side of me threw their arms over my shoulders and lifted their knees high into the air.

Right knee, right kick. Left knee, left kick.

I picked up the rhythm and was about to kick my big-ass combat boot into the air when I remembered that I was wearing a skirt—a little black-and-red plaid skirt with safety pins holding it closed. I never wore girlie shit like that, but I'd wanted to look pretty for Hans. If I did the fucking cancan, everybody in the audience was going to see my panties. If I didn't do the cancan, I would disappoint Hans, who'd asked me to wear that shirt specifically so that I would do the fucking cancan dance onstage.

"What's a matter, BB? You freeballin' tonight?" Trip goaded me. "Come on, show us that pussy." Then he turned to the crowd and started chanting, "Show…us…the pussy! Show… us…the pussy!"

I was going to show them my pussy anyway until Trip

decided to make a thing out of it. Now I couldn't give him the satisfaction. Emboldened by all the attention, fueled by my hatred of being told what to do, propelled by my desire to look badass in front of Hans, and encouraged by Juliet, who was glaring at Trip like she wanted to strangle him with his mic cord, I turned around, lifted my skirt, and showed everybody my bare ass instead.

Okay, so it wasn't completely bare. I'd worn my favorite leopard-print thong that night. You know, just in case Hans decided to ravage me backstage or something. A girl has to be prepared.

I glanced over my shoulder at Hans, and the look of awe on his face made me feel like a motherfucking champion. He stood there, slack-jawed, mechanically playing the cancan song on his bass, while the crowd screamed and whistled and cheered in front of him.

Dropping my skirt, I turned back around and found Trip on his knees before me, doing the We're Not Worthy bow from *Wayne's World*. I laughed and pulled him up off the stage as the other girls stopped dancing in defeat.

"Ladies and gentlemen!" Trip yelled into the mic, pulling me to the front of the stage by my hand. "This is a Phantom Limb first. The winner of the high kick contest didn't kick one fucking time. I hereby crown"—Trip lifted my hand above my head and twirled me around so that I was facing backward—"BB's booty!"

I laughed and turned to look at Hans, who was smiling like *he'd* won the contest. And, in a way, I guess he had.

"Oh shit. Do you guys see what I see? It looks like our winner has already picked her poison. LDH, you ready, man?"

Hans spun his bass around so that it was hanging upside down on his back and spread his arms apart in a silent invitation. He was cool, calm, and collected on the outside, but I saw his throat bob as I began to walk toward him. Saw his tongue dart out to wet his lips. Saw his pulse throbbing in his neck, just as fast and hard as mine.

Hans wanted to kiss me too.

"Uh-uh-uh," Trip said into the mic just as Hans's hands reached for my hips and mine wrapped around the back of his neck. "I didn't say *BB* won. I said *BB's booty* won."

You have got to be fucking kidding me.

The crowd went insane as Hans dropped his forehead to mine. Taking a deep breath, he gave me an apologetic shrug, then used his hands on my hips to rotate me away from him. I was now facing Trip, who was laughing his goddamn ass off, as Hans's hands ghosted down my arms. I shivered despite the steamy, sweaty air. When they got to my wrists, they disappeared, reappearing on my calves, just above my boots. I held my breath and glared at Trip, trying not to let him see how much Hans's touch affected me, as his fingertips danced lightly up the sides of my knees, my thighs. You could have heard a fucking pin drop as Hans's big, rough hands disappeared under my skirt, sliding up my hips, inching the plaid fabric up with them. My panties were soaked. My cheeks were on fucking fire. And my heart shuddered to a stop as soon as I felt the hot, humid air caress my exposed ass. Squeezing my eyes shut in mortification, I held my breath as Hans fucking Oppenheimer pressed his perfect, pouty lips against my right cheek.

And then my left.

As soon as my ass was covered and Hans was back on his feet, the crowd exploded into hysterics, and my face exploded into a supernova of a smile.

Hans wrapped his arms around me from behind and whisper-yelled into my ear, "Sorry about that. I'll beat his ass for you later."

I giggled and was about to tell him I didn't mind having his lips on me *anywhere* when Trip's voice boomed through the speakers. "How does it feel to have your ass kissed by a rock star?"

Hans and I flipped him off in unison as Louis, the drummer I'd met at the monster-truck rally, stomped on his kick drum pedal three times and banged his sticks together in the air. The guys responded immediately, grabbing their instruments and joining the intro of "Closer" by Nine Inch Nails.

I gave Hans one last longing look, then hauled ass to get offstage before Trip decided to torment me further. I got plenty of high fives and unwelcome ass grabs as I made my way back to Juliet. She smiled bigger than I'd ever seen and pulled me out of the clutches of some greasy douche bag with an undercut and a ponytail.

"Holy shit, that was hot!" Juliet screamed in my ear. "I can't believe that just happened! I need to leave the fucking house more!"

I pouted. "I still didn't get to kiss him though!"

Trip's voice rumbled through the floor beneath our feet as he humped the mic stand and snarled about wanting to fuck someone like an animal.

Juliet looked at him and then back at me. "Why the fuck is he so sexy?"

"Right?" I cackled.

Trip must have known we were talking about him because he pointed right at Juliet and hissed that he wanted to feel her from the inside.

She rolled her eyes as I laughed and elbowed her in the side. She was trying to act hard, but I saw the grin threatening to break free from her scowl. For possibly the first time since she'd gotten knocked up, Juliet was having fun.

I glanced over at Hans, ready to engage in some serious eye-fucking, but the look on his face doused my libido in ice water. His jaw was clenched, his eyes were narrowed to slits, and he wasn't even looking at me. He was looking at someone behind me.

Glaring actually.

I turned and saw the source of his sudden anger—the douche bag with the undercut who'd grabbed me. I hadn't even given him a second thought. I'd been to enough concerts and clubs to know what to expect. Guys touched girls whether they wanted it or not. They came up behind you and rubbed their semi-hard dicks on your ass. They grabbed your arm and yelled in your ear with their stank beer breath. They followed you to the restroom and cornered you as soon as you were separated from your friends. That's just how it was.

As soon as the song was over, Hans unplugged his bass and walked offstage while Trip announced that they had one more jam for us. Evidently, it was their big hit because the second he spoke the title, "Apparition," the crowd went nuts. Hans was back just in time to start a deep, ominous bass groove that the rest of the band layered their clanging, industrial sounds on top of. I loved it. I absolutely fucking loved it. It was heavier than what I typically listened to but somehow beautiful and catchy at the same time. I was so into it that I hadn't even noticed that a jacked-up bouncer had grabbed Undercut Guy and hauled him off until I saw him being escorted through the fire-escape exit to the right of the stage.

I snapped my head back to Hans, who was watching me again. A hint of a smile played on his lips. Then, a wink.

A crackling warmth roared to life in my stomach and spread through my extremities like wildfire.

Hans might not have used his fists or his boots or a baseball bat, like Knight would have. And he damn sure hadn't pulled out a gun, like Harley. But he'd protected me. *His way.*

I liked his way better.

After the show, Juliet and I sat on the rusty fire-escape stairs behind the building, smoking and watching the band load their gear into the back of Baker's dad's panel van. Baker—Phantom Limb's stocky guitar player who liked to hide behind his Kurt Cobain-esque shoulder-length blond hair—was the quietest and quite possibly most essential member of the band. He drove the van. He booked the shows. He played some mean guitar. And, most importantly, he was the only one old enough to buy beer.

Once everything was loaded up, Baker pulled a blue-and-white plastic cooler out of the passenger seat and opened the lid.

"High Life?" Trip scoffed, looking inside. "Bitch, you know I don't drink Miller fucking High Life. Where's the Korbel?"

Nobody laughed, except for me.

Trip pointed at me. "BB knows what I'm talking about. We're all sophisticated and shit. Where's my bubbly, bro?"

Baker peeked through the slit in his hair curtain as he plucked a can from the icy water inside. "It's all the way at the bottom, motherfucker," he mumbled. "Go fish."

I decided I liked Baker.

I liked him even more when he handed the can in his hand to Juliet.

Hans reached in next, pulling out two cans for us. As he

walked over to where Juliet and I were sitting, I began to panic. I was at a total fucking loss. I didn't know how to greet him. How to act. What to say. I'd spent an entire weekend cuddling with this guy. I'd let him publicly grope my body and literally kiss my ass. But what were we? Friends? Even if we were more than friends, I wondered if I should pretend like we weren't since he had a girlfriend. Although Trip didn't seem to give two shits about her when he was telling Hans to stick his face under my skirt. Maybe Trip didn't like her. The thought gave me hope.

"Hey," Hans said, giving me his shy one-dimpled smile.

"Haaaay," I said back in a stupid singsongy voice that I regretted immediately. "One of those for me?" I nodded toward the can in his left hand.

Hans's eyes twinkled. "Yep." He tucked the beer I'd been eyeing behind his back. "But you're gonna have to come get it."

Okay. Definitely more than friends.

As I stood, Hans held his right hand out to the side, welcoming me back into his arms. Dopamine flooded my bloodstream immediately, the same way a dog salivates at the sight of food. It had been exactly six days since Hans had fed my need for affection, and I was fucking starving.

Unable to play it cool for another second, I wrapped both arms around Hans's waist and rested my cheek on his chest. I even inhaled the aroma emanating from his warm skin. Hans smelled like rock and roll.

Just as he pulled me in and rested his chin on the top of my head, the unmistakable sound of an entire cooler full of ice being spilled onto concrete crashed behind him.

Hans and I spun around to find Trip delicately plucking a no-longer-submerged bottle of champagne out from inside the no-longer-upright cooler. A sea of ice cubes and chilled water spread in all directions as cans of Miller High Life rolled to freedom across the cracked concrete.

"What the fuck?" Baker said, only slightly louder than his normal mumbled voice.

"That's what you get, asshole." Trip pulled the foil off the top of the bottle and shot the cork at least ten feet into the air with a flick of his thumb. A small volcano of frothy white bubbles followed. "You know the only thing I'd stick my arm elbow-deep into ice water for is Leonardo DiCaprio's cock. And I'm talking *Titanic* Leo. Not some bullshit *What's Eating Gilbert Grape* Leo." Trip shuddered in disgust, then tilted his head to one side. "Now, *What's Eating Gilbert Grape* Johnny Depp? Shiiiiiit. I'd go balls deep in a snowman for a piece of that ass." Trip humped the air a few times for emphasis.

The entire crowd burst into laughter, including Louis and Baker, who usually looked like they were competing for the title of most apathetic. Hans's chuckle was quiet and rumbled in his chest beneath my cheek. I felt the vibration between my legs and was considering wrapping them around his waist for a little more friction when Trip chugged his champagne straight from the bottle and belched loud enough to trigger a car alarm.

Leave it to Triple X to sufficiently ruin the mood.

I turned my face up to look at Hans and mouthed, *Is Trip gay?*

Hans shook his head. "No. That's why it's so fucking funny."

I looked over at Juliet, who was laughing so hard, a black tear rolled down her cheek.

"Everybody fucking knows"—she sniffled—"that *Romeo + Juliet* Leo was the most fuckable Leo."

"That's true," I said, snatching Hans's hidden beer out from behind his back and popping the tab. "That's just fucking science right there."

Trip huffed and stomped his foot. "But I want him to draw me like one of his French girls!"

I spat my first sip of beer onto the ground. Holy shit, I laughed so hard, noises weren't even coming out of my mouth, just convulsions and hiccups. While Juliet and Trip continued to argue about which of Leonardo DiCaprio's characters' cocks was most worth suffering a partial ice-water submersion for, Hans pulled me over to a crumbling three-foot-tall concrete wall on the edge of the loading dock. I was about to hand him my beer, sling my purse behind my back, and try to get a running start so that I could scramble up the side of it, but Hans did the honors for me. One second, his big hands were around my waist; the next, I was sitting on top of the wall with my feet dangling off the ground.

Hans hopped up next to me effortlessly. I don't even think he set his beer down. He was surprisingly graceful for a big dude. And gentle. And funny.

"So," he said, bumping my shoulder with his, "Romeo is the most fuckable Leo, huh?"

My heart skipped a beat at hearing the word *fuckable* come out of Hans's mouth. Then it skipped three more when I realized that he might be a little jealous.

I smirked and rolled my eyes. "Duh. I mean, it's *Romeo*. He would *literally* die for me."

"So that's your type? Guys who would die for you?"

Hans's expression remained playful, but there was a tone of seriousness in his voice that I couldn't quite get a read on. Surely he wasn't insinuating that he would die for me. I mean, we'd just met. Maybe he meant someone else? Like an ex.

Knight would die for you.

What the fuck, subconscious? You're gonna bring him up now? Really?

Sorry. My bad. He would die for you though.

Yeah, and he almost killed me trying to prove it, so... what's your point?

No point. None at all. Shutting up now. Enjoy your night.

Oh shit. Hans is looking at me. Say something, dumbass!

"No." I rolled my eyes. "My type is guys *with tattoos* who would die for me. I have standards, okay?"

"Okay." Hans smirked and took a sip of his beer, but his eyes never left mine. "You're wrong though."

"About what? My type?"

"No, about Romeo being the most fuckable Leo. You're wrong."

He said it again!

I waited for my heart to sputter back to life before taking the bait. "Don't tell me you're on Team Jack too. Listen, I get it. He was adorable in *Titanic*, and yeah, I guess, technically, he did die for Rose, but you and I both know that door was big enough for two people."

Hans's pouty little mouth split into a two-dimple grin.

Damn.

He was all white teeth and black eyelashes and sweat-spiked black hair, and I had to stifle the urge to lick his skin just to find out how salty it was.

Hans held a hand up, laughing. "Dude. Don't get me started on that fucking door. No, not Jack. Jim Carroll, from *The Basketball Diaries*. Hands down, most fuckable Leo."

I threw my head back and squealed, "Oh my God! I totally

forgot about that movie! A drug-addicted future rock star! You *would* say that! How perfect!"

"What?" Hans asked with a shrug. "You don't have a thing for musicians?"

Hans's gaze was too intense. His question too loaded. I broke eye contact and began digging around in my purse, trying to find a cigarette and a better response to his question than, *I do now.*

I popped a Camel between my teeth and looked back up at him with my cool partially restored. "Only musicians with tattoos who would die for me," I joked.

Ooh. Nice save.

Hans smiled as he produced a black lighter from his pocket. When he sparked the flint, a tiny flame appeared between us. I leaned into it, noting the way the flickering light softened Hans's harsh features. He leaned in as well. His eyes were on my mouth. His tongue darted out to wet his lower lip. Adrenaline shot out to my extremities. Hot smoke filled my lungs. Then, he pulled away.

Tucking the lighter back into his pocket, Hans said, almost to himself, "I can work with that."

As I exhaled a shaky stream of smoke and tried to process what the fuck Hans had just said, the face of his wide black leather watch glinted in the streetlight, catching my eye.

"Shit." I grabbed Hans's thick wrist and turned it so that his watch was facing me. "I'm supposed to be home by midnight, and I have to drop Juliet off on my way. I have to go."

Hans's face fell, but he nodded in understanding. Hopping off the wall, he turned and stood between my legs. For the second time in twenty minutes, I had to resist the urge to wrap them around his waist. Hans put his big hands on my bony hips and blinked up at me with long black lashes. My panties were officially ruined.

"You want me to walk you to your car?"

No. I want you to lean forward a few more inches and fucking kiss me. I want you to pull my skirt up again and bend me over this wall. I want you to tell me I'm beautiful again and sleep in the same bed as me again and take me to Las Vegas and fucking marry me already.

"Nah," I said, holding my cigarette above my head so that the smoke wouldn't get in our eyes. "Old Willy on the corner has my back. We'll be fine."

Hans's dark eyebrows shot up. "Please tell me you're fucking kidding."

"Why does everyone keep saying that?"

Hans lifted me easily by my waist and lowered me to the ground. As soon as my feet hit the gravel, a pain sliced through my heart. The night was over.

Hans and I retrieved Juliet, who was already on her third beer and cheering wildly for Trip. He was moonwalking while balancing an empty bottle of champagne on his forehead. That guy was never *not* performing. Before we could drag her away, Baker, Louis, and Trip all came over to hug us goodbye.

Juliet was *not* a hugger.

Juliet was *not* a peopler.

But Juliet was full of surprises. Not only did she hug all the guys, but she also draped an arm around Trip's neck and planted a big, wet kiss right on his cheek. Then she mumbled something incoherent into his ear.

I turned to Hans and whispered through my giggles, "Did she just say, 'Stay gold, Ponyboy'?"

Hans chuckled along with me. "I fucking hope so," he said, tucking me into his side. "He does kinda look like Ralph Macchio."

I looked around at all four guys, overcome with appreciation. They had taken my brash, bitchy BFF and turned her into someone happy. Someone who didn't hate everyone. Someone who quoted lines from *The Outsiders*.

The three of us walked arm in arm around the building and up the street as the lights from the Masquerade slowly faded behind us. The top of the hill was bathed in darkness. And free parking. Juliet swayed and stumbled on my right arm. Hans was solid as a rock on my left.

Juliet looked around me at Hans and slurred, "I liked your show. You guys were really good, but next time, you have to play me a Smashing Pumpkins song, okay? They're my favorite. I'm pretty sure James Iha is my brother."

"Her last name is Iha, and her dad is Japanese," I explained.

"You guys do kind of look alike," Hans said, trying to be supportive of her delusion.

"That's racist," Juliet blurted, sticking her finger in the air. Then she burst out laughing.

"Oh my God." I cackled. "You are so wasted."

"I'm sorry, Hansie." Juliet pouted. "You're not racist. You're pretty and nice, and BB wants to sit on your pretty face."

I groaned and pressed my forehead into Hans's bicep. "Just stop talking. Jesus."

Hans snickered. "Thanks, Jules."

As we crested the top of the hill, Old Willy sprang from his perch on the corner and hobbled over to us, limping worse than usual.

He looked Hans up and down, then spoke to me. "Missy, I done saw somebody snoopin' 'round your car tonight. Big fella, driving a truck with them big ole monster tires. He drove down the highway here"—Willy pointed out to the main street—"and I guess he spotted your car 'cause he done turned around right in the middle of the street and came flying down here." Willy pointed down the side street where my car was parked. "Drove by real slow like, then pulled over down there and cut his lights off like he was gonna wait y'all out."

My blood curdled in my veins.

Hans's arm tightened around mine.

Juliet laughed inappropriately.

"Are you okay, Willy?" I asked through the suffocating lump in my throat. "You didn't try to..."

"I'm fine, missy. I went and stood right next to your car and glared at the sumbitch till he took off. Y'all should be real careful though. That fella had eyes like a gotdamn demon or somethin'. I said ten Hail Marys after he left."

Like a zombie, I thought, picturing the almost-colorless irises and eyelashes of one Ronald McKnight.

"Thanks, man," Hans said, placing a hand on Old Willy's shoulder and sticking a few dollar bills into his hand.

"Thank *you*, sir. Y'all have a blessed night now."

We walked over to my car in a daze. Knight was supposed to be in Iraq. He had written me a letter after the accident, confessing that he was the one who'd caused it, and said that he was signing up for a second tour of duty. Now he was snooping around my car two months later? It didn't make any sense.

"That motherfucker is worse than herpes," Juliet snapped as she headed for the passenger door. "He just will *not* stay away."

"You know this guy?" Hans asked, searching my face as we came to a stop next to my car.

"Yeah." I didn't elaborate. There was no possible explanation that could make the situation sound anything other than worse.

We go way back. He was my first love, but we can't be together because he's mentally unstable and extremely violent. Oh, and thanks to the Marines, he's now a trained killer, too. But don't you worry about him. Just because he beat the shit out of my last boy-friend and ran us both off the road doesn't mean he'll do it again. *He probably got it all out of his system.*

"You gonna be okay?" Hans's eyebrows were pulled together, creating a deep V-shaped wrinkle between them.

I nodded. "Yeah. It's fine."

Hans looked at me like he wasn't convinced but wanted to avoid the topic of Knight about as badly as I wanted to avoid the topic of Beth. "Will you call me when you get home?" he asked instead.

I nodded again.

Hans pulled me in for a hug, but something was off. Something was very, very off. Even though we were touching, it felt like an invisible curtain of sadness had been drawn, separating us from one another.

"Thanks for coming out," Hans said, smoothing a hand down my goose-bumped arm.

Then, he was gone.

9

It felt like high school all over again. Everybody was my friend until they saw Knight coming. Then, *poof*, they disappeared.

Knight had alienated me from every friend I'd ever had, except for Juliet and Goth Girl. He'd chased off every guy I'd hoped to date and beaten the shit out of the ones who didn't take the hint. He'd claimed he didn't want to ruin my future, yet he wouldn't let me have one with anybody else.

I felt suffocated. Suffocated and paranoid and pissed off.

I barely spoke on the drive back to Juliet's house. Of course, she was so drunk, she spoke enough for both of us. Mostly about how dreamy Hans was and how funny Trip was and how psychotic Knight was and how, if she ever saw him again, she was going to kick him in the balls.

After I dropped her off, I drove home in silence. No radio. No CD. No mixtape. My brain was a tangled ball of questions, and every string I pulled, trying to unfurl the mess, only drew the knots tighter.

Why the fuck is Knight still in town?

Where the fuck is Hans's girlfriend?

Why hasn't anyone but Goth Girl mentioned her if they've been together for four years?

Goth Girl wouldn't just make up a fake girlfriend.

Maybe I should just ask him about her.

No. No, no, no. Then he'll tell me it's true, and then I'll have to stop flirting with him, and flirting with him is kind of the highlight of my pathetic fucking life right now.

Maybe they broke up and Goth Girl doesn't know.

If they're broken up, then why the fuck hasn't Hans kissed me yet?

Maybe he's just not that into me.

Or maybe he was going to, but then Knight scared him off.

So, he either has a girlfriend, he isn't that into me, or he's a pussy. Awesome.

Should I even call him when I get home?

He'll probably be driving home by then. Maybe he'll have the music turned up and won't hear his phone ringing. Maybe I can just leave a voicemail…

It turned out that I *could* have left a voicemail because my call went *straight* to fucking voicemail. So, I hung up instead.

Asshole.

10

I'd gone to bed wallowing in despair but woke up squealing in delight when I found not one, but *two* missed calls from Hans *and* a voicemail blinking up at me from the phone on my nightstand. A voicemail that I might or might not have listened to so many times that I made myself late for work. By the time I got to Pier 1 Imports with a blue apron around my waist and a big, dumb grin on my face, I could recite the whole thing from memory.

"Hey, BB. Sorry I missed your call. My fucking phone died, and I was stuck at some club in Buckhead with Trip. He gets so amped during a show that it takes forever to bring him down. This place had a pole in the middle of the dance floor, and Trip wouldn't leave until he figured out how to do some pole-dancing move called a Flying Brass Monkey." Hans chuckled. *"Man, I wish you guys had been there. Juliet would have pissed herself, watching Trip work a pole."*

Hans's voice faltered during the second half of his message. I could almost picture him biting his thumbnail and staring off into the distance as he spoke.

"*Hey, I don't know if you have plans next weekend or if you want to hang out again, but…the guys are trying to convince me to have some people over. My parents just bought an RV and are going on a two-month-long road trip, so…it'll just be me here.*" He paused. "*You could…spend the night…if you want. I mean, most people probably will. There are, like, five empty bedrooms and a shitload of couches, so it's not a problem. Just…let me know. Okay? 'Kay, bye.*"

'Kay, bye.

My body did weird, involuntary things every time I got to his sign-off. My muscles tensed like I was holding in a scream. My feet shuffled. I pressed my lips between my teeth to squelch my smile. Just hearing him say it in my head at work had me diving behind display shelves so that I could have my full-body freak-outs in private.

I didn't know what had taken place between our awkward goodbye and that voicemail, but I didn't fucking care. Whatever Hans's hang-up had been—Beth, Knight, even me—he had clearly gotten over it. And I couldn't wait to be over *him*—in a reverse missionary or maybe a nice side-saddle position—that weekend.

"Girrrrl. You ain't been back on yo feet more than a minute, and you already dancin' around here like you done got yo'self some D." Craig, my favorite coworker and Sisqó impersonator, was leaning against the pillow wall, giving me *the look*. "You don't waste no time, do ya?"

I grabbed a pink satin pillow with beading around the edges and threw it at him. Craig caught it and tucked it under his arm.

"For your information, I haven't even slept with him yet." I raised my chin and eyebrows, trying to look haughty.

"Yet." Craig laughed. "Homegirl, you gon' have that man pussywhipped by the end of the week."

I couldn't contain it. I balled my hands into fists, pressed them against my mouth, and did a little wiggle. I lowered my fists just enough to whisper, "He just invited me to spend the night next weekend."

Craig put a hand in the air and did a little back bend. "The almighty Craig knows all. Can I get an amen?"

"Amen," I whispered over my fists. I didn't even know why I was whispering. I think I was so excited that if I didn't whisper I'd be shouting about my booty call to the entire Sunday afternoon Pier 1 Imports clientele.

"I have to call him, Craig. I still haven't told him that I'm coming."

"Oh, yo gon' be coming all right."

Smack. Another pink pillow, that time right to the face.

I skipped off to take a smoke break and call Hans back when something occurred to me. Turning around, I said, "Hey, Craig? You remember Knight?"

Craig turned to face me, his features hard as stone. "That neo-Nazi-lookin' motherfucker who used to be lurkin' around by your car all the time? The one I had to call the cops on when he and your man was beatin' the shit outta each other in the parking lot? Yeah, I remember." He folded his arms across his chest. "Why?"

"Will you let me know if you see him? I . . . I don't think he went back to Iraq."

One Week Later

I followed Hans's directions to the letter, but I still quadruple-checked the address when I pulled up. It couldn't be the right house. It was a goddamn mansion. Or at least, it was to me. The place was a two-story brick bunker with a recessed stone entry-way. The double front doors looked like they'd been handcrafted out of solid cherry, as did the shutters and matching rock-ing chairs on the front porch. The chandelier above the front doors though—that thing looked like some kind of reclaimed wrought iron from the Byzantine era.

The driveway, which was the width of most major highways, led straight to the front steps, then hooked to the right where a three-car garage jutted off the front of the house, creating an L-shape. Cars had begun to gather in front of the garage, so I parked my little black Mustang among them, relieved that they weren't all Porsches and Ferraris.

I stamped my cigarette out into my ashtray, not wanting to soil Hans's pristine white driveway, as something like dread

began to seep into my blood. I'd only been in a house that grand
one time, and it hadn't ended well. I could still hear the sound
of breaking glass as Knight smashed every cabinet door with a
fireplace poker. I could still see the blood dripping from his forearm as he pulled out a framed photo from his mother and stepfather's wedding. I could still smell the urine running down his
stepfather's leg as Knight choked him with his own necktie. And
I could still see the crazed look in his mother's eyes as I shielded
him from her shaking pistol.

Bad things happen in pretty houses.
Run away while you still can.
Rich people are not to be trusted.
You don't belong here, white trash.

"Stop," I blurted, snapping my fingers.

I looked around and blinked a few times to clear the foggi-
ness that always accompanied a flashback. "It's gonna be fine," I
said to no one. "It's gonna be totally…fucking…fine."

Grabbing my purse—which I'd stuffed with a toothbrush,
some toiletries, and a change of clothes before running out the
door, telling my parents I was spending the night with Goth
Girl—I got out of the car. The sound of music and people
talking and laughter drifted up the hill from the backyard, and I
blew out a sigh of relief. The backyard! I didn't have to go inside
the house at all!

With a spring in my step, I rounded the side of the estate and
bounced down the grassy hill. I could see the lake at the bottom
of the slope, just through the woods, the setting sun splashing
it with pinks and oranges. It looked like something from a postcard. Not real life.

Definitely not *my* life.

The house was three stories tall in the back, thanks to a daylight basement. It had a large screened-in porch off the main floor and an even bigger stone patio underneath. The most notable thing about the patio, besides the built-in stone firepit, was the fact that it was covered in living room furniture. Someone had dragged an expensive-looking brown leather sofa, a love seat, a big screen TV, and a recliner out of the house. Hell, there was even an unplugged lamp on one of the end tables just for looks. These motherfuckers partied *hard*.

I spotted Goth Girl and Goth Guy first. They were sitting on a swinging bench out in the backyard, just beyond the patio, and appeared to be engaged in some kind of heated conversation. When Goth Girl's eyes landed on me, they flared, just for a moment, before she half-smiled and waved me over.

"What are you doing here?" she asked in her signature deadpan.

"Hey, Victoria! Good to see you too. I'm fine. Thanks for asking," I replied in an overly cheerful voice.

"Sorry," she mumbled. "I just…didn't expect to see you here."

"It's cool." I smiled a little too brightly. "Hans invited me. Do you know where he is?"

Goth Girl extended a milk-colored finger in the direction of the patio. "At the bar."

Her face was disapproving, but she at least kept her mouth shut about Beth this time. I'd been bracing myself for another lecture. When it didn't come, I dialed back my attitude.

Turning to Steven, I said, "Hey, thanks for letting me crash at your place when I was so sick that night. That was really nice of you. There was no way I would have made it all the way home."

Steven's face paled at the mention of that night, probably because he'd been having a little sleepover of his own—with Pigtails and a few grams of coke.

Goth Girl's face paled too, if that was even possible. Snapping her head toward Steven, she spat, "BB spent the night again? When were you planning on telling *me*?"

"Jesus Christ," Steven barked. "Calm down! She was there with Hans. I barely even saw her. You act like I fuck every girl who steps foot through my door!" Even while he was defending himself, Steven managed to give my body a once-over with his eyes.

Fucking creep.

"Because you do!" Goth Girl screeched.

"Shit, guys," I interrupted. "I'm sorry. I didn't mean to..."

But they weren't listening to me anymore. They'd picked their lovers' quarrel back up right where they'd left off. I backed away slowly and turned toward the patio; at which point, all the air was sucked from my lungs.

Louis, Baker, and Trip were sitting on an Italian leather sofa with brass grommets, their feet kicked up on the unlit firepit, wearing nothing but swim trunks. But, behind them, leaning against a stone wet bar and talking to a couple I didn't recognize was Hans fucking Oppenheimer. And *he* was wearing nothing but a pair of Adidas athletic shorts.

Black ones.

The sight of him made my mouth water. I'd never thought of Hans as being athletic, but with that much of his body on display, there was no doubt that he could have been a professional athlete of some kind. Maybe a soccer player? He had legs a drag queen would kill for. And those abs...

Slurp.

"Yo, LDH! You got company, bro! And she looks thirrrrrsty."

I turned and glared at Trip, who had obviously seen my little drool session based on the evil grin he was sporting. His bare torso was already impressively sunburned, except for a sloppy white outline around a huge tattoo above his navel that read *ROCK STAR.* The bottle of Korbel in his right hand was almost empty, and the joint in his left hand was snatched away by Louis.

Baker peeked through his curtain of hair at me and said, "Sup, BB?"

Louis gave me a half-smile and a two-finger salute.

I took a deep breath and prepared myself to walk the last few steps over to Hans, but before I could turn around, two thick arms—one tattooed, one not—crisscrossed over my chest from behind.

Stubble grazed my ear as Hans leaned down and murmured, "Hey, Bumblebee," so that only I could hear.

He smelled like all the best things about summer—earthiness and alcohol—and I sank into him like toes into sand.

When I turned around, I kind of wished that I hadn't. Shirtless, sun-kissed, wet-haired Hans was a lot to take in that close.

"Did you find it okay?" He smiled, the whiteness of his teeth making his skin look even more tan.

I nodded. Speaking would have diverted too much energy away from the job at hand: Operation Stop Drooling.

"Do you want a drink? These fuckers have been at it since noon, so you've got some catching up to do. I got you some Jack and Coke, but we have beer too."

Aw! He remembered what I'd ordered at the Tabernacle!

I nodded again and let him steer me over to the bar where a

skinny guy in a short-sleeved button-up shirt and glasses was talking to a girl with short blonde hair. It looked a lot like mine, but she wore hers pushed forward and flipped up in the front. She was wearing no makeup, a vintage-looking Yankees jersey, and khaki cargo shorts.

"BB, these are my neighbors, Kevin and Dani."

"Ugh." Dani scrunched up her nose at Hans. "You make it sound like we live together. Gross."

"Whatever," Kevin said. "I'd make an awesome roommate."

"Yeah, if you were a Yankees fan. No one who cheers for the Braves is allowed under my roof."

Kevin smirked. "Which is exactly why you're still single."

"Oh, really?" Dani snapped back, puffing up her chest, which looked like it was probably being constricted by a sports bra under that baggy jersey. "What's your excuse? Your face?"

"Ooh, burrrrn," Hans said, rolling his eyes as he handed me a red plastic cup full of bubbly brown goodness.

I took a sip and tried not to wince at the sting in my throat.

Note to self: Hans makes strong-ass drinks.

"BB went to school with Victoria," Hans said, flashing me a proud smile. "She just graduated early."

"Congratulations," Kevin said, tapping my plastic cup with his beer bottle. "I couldn't wait to get out of high school. Believe it or not"—he gestured down the length of his nerdy outfit with a small smile—"I was not the most popular guy."

Hans gave Kevin an affectionate shove. "Shut the fuck up, man." He popped the cap on a bottle of Corona and took a swig.

Lucky bottle.

"Kevin goes to Georgia Tech for music production now. He's helping us with our demo."

"No shit? That's awesome," I said. "I can't wait to hear it. When will it be done?"

Kevin opened his mouth to answer me, but Dani cut him off. "Hey, speaking of graduation, is Beth coming tonight? I haven't seen her ass since your graduation party."

I slammed my cup to my mouth to hide my horrified expression and watched Hans like a hawk over the plastic rim. Would he look guilty? Would he tell Dani they broke up? Would he give me one of his one-dimpled smiles and say, *BB's my girlfriend now, bitch*?

No, he wouldn't.

Instead, Hans simply shrugged and said, "Nah, she couldn't make it out. She's moving into her dorm this weekend."

Beth was real.

Beth had been invited to the party.

Beth had better things to do, so I got to be her little substitute for the night.

And Hans didn't even have the decency to act ashamed.

Goth Girl had warned me about him, and I hadn't listened.

Hans is a flirty drunk. Hans has a girlfriend.

I felt so fucking stupid. And angry. And, suddenly, kind of drunk.

My cup was empty, my head was spinning, and my face felt as red as Trip's sunburned chest.

Setting the crumpled plastic cup on the bar, I sputtered, "I just remembered, I, um...need to ask Victoria something. It was nice to meet you guys."

Then, I turned and hightailed it across the patio, through the maze of furniture, and over to where Goth Girl and Steven had been sitting on the bench swing. But when I got there, the swing was empty. I looked around, but they were gone. And I was super dizzy. That cup had to have had two or three shots of whiskey in it, and I hadn't eaten all day. My chest and throat felt tight, like I wanted to cry, and my stomach felt like it was being eaten from the inside out by acid and straight alcohol.

I wanted to leave, just get in my car and go, but it was starting to get dark, and I wasn't confident that I could find my way home sober, let alone tipsy and emotional. I hadn't printed out directions or anything; I was just going to let Hans tell me how to get back in the morning.

I sat on the bench and lit a cigarette.

Digging the toes of my boots into the grass to keep from swinging—swinging made me dizzier—I gave myself a drunken pep talk.

Okay, so you're stuck. An hour away from home. With a bunch of assholes. Well, guess what? Lucky for you, you're Brooke fucking Bradley. You don't pout at parties. You are the party. You don't chase boys—okay, you totally do but not tonight. Tonight, you make that boy chase you. You hold your head high and try not to puke, and you march your ass right back over there and flirt with his best friend.

Ew, not Trip. I wouldn't be able to keep a straight face.

No, the other one. Kevin.

Yes! He's kinda cute—in a nerdy way. Perfect! Kevin, here I come!

I was just about to put my cigarette out on the bottom of my boot and go ask Kevin to tell me more about music production when I spotted Hans walking straight toward me, concern etched all over his face.

Shit.

"Hey, B. You okay?"

No. Fucker.

"Yeah, I just didn't want to smoke on your patio. Everything looks so perfect."

Hans sat down next to me, causing the swing to sway back and forth and my dizziness to come back with a vengeance. I wanted to slap his thigh and tell him to make it stop. I wanted to slap his face for not telling me about his girlfriend. And then I wanted to kiss the shit out of it because, *damn*, he was gorgeous.

"Mind if I bum one?"

I huffed and pulled my Camels and a lighter out of my purse. Shoving them in his direction, I said, "Sure. Knock yourself out."

"Thanks?" Hans said, accepting my bitter offering.

I crossed my arms over my chest and stared straight ahead into the woods between Hans's house and his neighbor's. There was just a hint of twilight left, and the fireflies were having a party of their own just beyond the tree line. The pretty scenery pissed me off even more.

If Hans didn't have a fucking girlfriend, this would be really goddamn romantic.

Hans exhaled to the side while keeping his eyes on me. "Hey, are you sure you're okay? You seem...upset."

"Oh, I'm great," I spat, grabbing my purse and standing up. "I'm gonna go get another drink." As I walked over to the bar, I dropped my cigarette butt into somebody's empty beer bottle on the firepit.

Ooh, I bet that looked badass. I hope he saw that. Asshole.

Dani and Baker were sitting on the love seat, drinking cans of Miller High Life and watching—*surprise, surprise*—a Yankees game. Trip and Louis were on the sofa, unleashing their munch-ies on some chips and salsa. And Kevin was over at the bar, pop-ping the cap off a bottle of Corona.

What a coincidence. That's where I'm headed.

"Hey, Kevin." I smiled, batting my eyelashes. "Would you mind making me a drink? Hans made the last one too strong."

Kevin's face flushed. "Uh, sure. Yeah." He set his beer down and fumbled around, looking for supplies.

While he squirmed and tried to make small talk, I noticed a pizza box sitting on the bar. I remembered the way Knight used to force-feed me before he let me drink with him. It had been so humiliating, but he was right. I never got sick when I ate first.

Sighing in defeat, I opened the box and pulled out a slice of pepperoni. I didn't know who'd ordered the pizza, and I didn't care. I considered it asshole tax.

Kevin handed over my drink with a hopeful look on his face. When I took a sip and bubbles tickled my nose instead of alco-hol scorching my throat, I smiled.

"Oh my God. So much better. Thank you."

He looked down at his hands and smiled.

"This isn't your pizza," I said with my mouth half-full, "is it?"

Kevin nodded. "Yeah, but I got it for everyone."

"Dude. You're my fucking hero right now."

Kevin's smile widened. I wanted to reach over and pinch his nerdy little cheeks.

Just then, Goth Girl and Steven came stumbling out of the basement through a set of ornate French doors, sporting some serious sex hair and nuzzling each other like a couple of honeymooners.

Guess those two made up.

Looking around, Goth Girl suddenly screeched to a stop.

"Oh my fucking God," she slurred. "I thought this was a party. Are you guys seriously watching…baseball?" Her face screwed up in disgust.

Steven swayed on his feet, watching Goth Girl with hearts in his glassy eyes. I knew that look. I knew those grinding teeth too.

No wonder they're getting along so well. They're fucking rolling.

"Ooh! I know!" Goth Girl gasped, turning back toward Steven and pawing at his clothes. "Let's go skinny-dipping!"

Nobody said a word, except for Trip, who jumped up on the sofa cushions and shouted, "Fuck yeah!"

"BB!" Goth Girl yelled even though I was, like, five feet away. "You have to come. Let's go swim in the moonlight."

She took hold of my elbow and dragged me away from the bar. I grabbed my cup and gave Kevin an apologetic look as Goth Girl bumped into and bounced off of every piece of furniture between us and the yard.

I scanned the patio for Hans, but he wasn't there. He wasn't in the recliner, he wasn't on the love seat, and he definitely wasn't on the couch that Trip had just leaped off of.

I didn't spot him until I stepped onto the lawn. He was sitting on the bench swing, right where I'd left him, looking utterly dejected. The light from the patio hit him sideways, splashing all over his tattooed arm and splattering across the convex parts of his body. His pecs. His cheekbones. The lock of black hair that had fallen into his face. And his left hand, which was holding a cigarette up to his scowling mouth.

Gah, all I said was that I was going to get a drink. I didn't tell him he had to wait there until I came back.

I wanted to feel justified in bitchiness as I sauntered by, on my way to do a striptease for everyone on the dock, but I didn't.

Not even a little bit.

I felt like the biggest asshole of them all.

A splash echoed through the trees, followed by Trip's voice yelling, "The water's fine, motherfuckers! Come on!"

Goth Girl, Steven, and I leaned on each other for support as we made our way down the stairs of death to the dock. They weren't so much stairs as they were just flat patches of dirt punctuated by railroad ties going down the hill. I tried not to stumble. Tried not to spill my drink. But most of my effort and concentration was being spent on trying not to look over my shoulder at Hans.

The stairs deposited us right at the water's edge where a narrow dock extended into the lake at least thirty feet before expanding into a deck the size of my parents' living room. Next to the sitting area was a slip where the Oppenheimers parked their speedboat, and above that was a second-story observation deck. Out beyond the end of the dock, floating in the black-ened water, were a half-dozen inflatable rafts, doughnuts, and sea creatures, all tethered to the wooden structure.

Trip had already commandeered the orca.

Grateful that the three people down there were the three I cared the least about seeing me naked, I set my cup on the edge of the dock and began the disrobing process. Of course, by the time I got my big-ass boots, socks, and skintight ripped jeans off, everybody else was down there too.

Louis and Baker dropped trou and dived in right behind Goth Girl and Steven, snatching up two more of the available floaties. Kevin and Dani grabbed a couple of beers out of a fridge over by the boat. Then they climbed aboard and turned on the radio to listen to the rest of the ball game. The last one down the stairs was Hans.

I didn't turn around as he approached, but I could feel him. He was radiating tension, which only amplified mine. I ignored him as he passed by but watched shamelessly as he tore off his athletic shorts and dived into the inky abyss before me. It was too dark to see much more than his perfect ass as it arched gracefully into the air and out of sight, but it was just enough to make me start to forget why I was mad at him in the first place.

Oh, right. Beth.

I didn't know Beth, but I'd *been* Beth. And the fact that Hans was now *naked* in the presence of *three* girls who were not *Beth* made me see fucking red.

So what? So he was just gonna pretend like he doesn't have a girl-friend, invite me over, get me drunk, fuck me in his mansion, and then send me on my way? Maybe call me again the next time Beth isn't available to satisfy his needs? And his bandmates are all completely okay with it? This is exactly why my mom told me to stay away from musicians, I thought as I pulled my Death to the Pixies tank top over my head. Far too angry to feel self-conscious about my flat chest, I unclasped my four-pound liquid-filled prosthetic boobs and dropped my water bra on top of my growing pile of clothes.

As I stepped out of my red cotton thong, hoping that Hans was being gobbled up by an alligator out there, I heard Trip yell, "Holy shit, LDH! Your girl's got titty rings, bro!"

A rabble of laughter, whistles, and mumbles followed, caus-ing my cheeks—already heated by rage—to burn even brighter. I squinted into the darkness and saw five of the six floaties occu-pied. But no Hans.

Hmm. Maybe a gator did get him. I smiled to myself.

I was not about to ruin my hair and makeup by diving in like everybody else, so I grabbed my cup and walked back down the narrow dock to where the lake met the land. Wading in, I was surprised at how warm the water was, how soft the lakebed felt beneath my feet. How loud the crickets were and how many stars were in the sky.

Rich people even have more stars than the rest of us, I thought, taking a gulp from my red plastic cup. Then another.

As I waded in deeper, I spotted a constellation that I'd only read about in school—Cassiopeia. I just looked up, and there it was. I don't know why, but that made me angrier than anything. My whole life, I'd thought I was just incapable of finding constellations. I'd thought there was something wrong with me. It turned out, the only thing wrong with me was my fucking zip code.

The sound of screaming and laughing pulled my attention away from the cosmos to the place where Trip was trying to capsize Baker and Louis, over on the other end of the dock. Everyone was cursing and giggling and splashing Trip as he swam around the floaties, chanting the bass line from the *Jaws* theme song and grabbing their legs. I would have laughed if I hadn't been so fucking pissed.

And if the sight of a six-foot-three-inch raven-haired demigod rising out of the water before me hadn't stolen my breath from my lungs.

Hans's face was villainous as he emerged from the darkness. He ran his hands through his jet-black hair, slicking it back. Water rolled off his hard chest in rivulets, reminding me to cover my own with my free hand.

So there I stood, drink in one hand, breast in the other, waist-deep in shark-infested waters, waiting to see what fresh bullshit Hans was going to pull. I expected him to try to charm me or guilt-trip me or get me to share the last floatie with him.

I did *not* expect him to immediately reach for my boob.

I was about to slap him away and toss what was left of my Jack and Coke in his face when I felt Hans's wet thumb graze my chest-tube scar—an angry-looking gash just beside my right breast. Felt his palm flatten against my recently healed ribs. Felt his soul, my old familiar friend, trying to heal me from the outside in.

Hans lifted his soft gray-blue eyes, which were framed in wet black daggers, and exhaled through perfectly parted lips. "Is that...from your accident?"

"Yeah." I nodded, my voice barely above a whisper. "It's fine though." I swallowed. "I'm fine."

Hans's jaw tightened, and his nostrils flared. "It's not fine."

I squinted at his beautiful, furious face in the dark, searching for a constellation among all the confusion. I couldn't figure him out. I couldn't understand why his touch felt like home when we were practically strangers to one another.

Hans pressed his forehead to mine and growled two clipped words through his gritted teeth. Two words that would change everything.

"Leave him."

Huh?

"What?"

Hans's right hand rose out of the water and clamped around my rib cage on the opposite side. "Leave him, BB. Be with me."

"Leave who?" I asked, pulling away to search his face for answers in the dark.

"Your fucking boyfriend," Hans snapped. "The one who did this to you." Hans's massive hand flexed around my protruding ribs. "The one who was stalking you at the Masquerade. The one who has you too scared to even look at me tonight."

"I don't *have* a boyfriend," I exclaimed. "*You* have a—"

Hans's lips sealed over mine, swallowing my accusation along with my doubts, my questions, my insecurities. It wasn't the kiss of a guy trying to score a piece of ass at a party. It was *the* kiss.

As Hans's mouth moved against mine, coaxing memories forward from a time when that kiss had worn a different pair of lips, I sighed and succumbed. Hans didn't belong to someone else. He never had. He'd been mine since the dawn of time.

"Girlfriend," Hans whispered against my lips, cupping my face with his damp hands. He'd taken the ugly word on the tip of my tongue and turned it into something beautiful. A gift for me to wear.

"Girlfriend," I whispered back, smiling against his mouth.

12

Tossing my almost-empty cup onto the dock a few feet away, I wrapped my arms around Hans's neck and let him pull me down into the lake. He kissed me slowly as we sank to our knees, water sloshing over our shoulders. Hans's hands clutched my face. His lips sucked and pulled against mine. His naked erection pressed against the length of my stomach. Hans wasn't trying to sexualize our experience; his cock simply had nowhere else to go.

LDH. I smirked to myself, threading my fingers into his wet hair.

As Hans's tongue traced lazy circles around mine, I caught myself holding my breath. Trying to stop time again. But I realized that I didn't need to fight time, not anymore because, when that moment passed, there would be another. And Hans would be there, too.

"Holy shit! Are y'all fuckin' under there?"

I broke away from our kiss and looked up, but Trip wasn't chiding *us*. He was on the other end of the dock, shouting at Goth Girl and Steven, who were evidently christening one of the Oppenheimers' inflatables under the cover of a beach towel.

"Come on," Hans whispered, giving me one last peck on the lips before taking me by the hand and leading me back toward the shore.

We tiptoed out of the water and up the stairs as Trip and Louis whistled and cheered at the floating sex show, and Dani cheered about a Yankees home run. I looked over my shoulder and saw Kevin watching us make our escape, the lights from the dashboard of the boat illuminating his crestfallen face.

Up the stairs, through the gauntlet of living room furniture on the patio, into the now-empty basement living area, up another set of stairs, through a sleek, modern kitchen, around to the two-story foyer, up another set of stairs, and around a corner, Hans pulled me, not stopping until his bedroom door was shut behind us. The lights were off, but the blinds were open, letting in just enough light to illuminate a room the size of a studio apartment. There was a couch in the middle of the room, facing an entertainment center on the left. Behind it, on the right side of the room, was a recessed nook lined with windows and filled with musical instruments. On the far side of the room, in another window-lined nook, was a four-poster bed. The ceiling was vaulted. The floor was covered in clothes.

I shivered as Hans locked the door behind me, prompting him to disappear into a doorway next to the one we'd come through. He reemerged a split second later, holding a fluffy white towel.

"Come here," he said with a shadowy smile.

I stepped toward him, expecting him to pull me into his arms, but instead, he dropped to his knees before me.

With care and attention, Hans slid the towel up and around my left leg, placing a small kiss on the front of my thigh as the soft terry cloth grazed my sex. My core tightened, and the piercing between my legs hummed like a tuning fork as Hans moved to my right leg. Starting at my foot and moving at a torturously slow pace, Hans replaced every drop of water on my spindly leg with a thousand brand-new goose bumps. I bit my lip to keep from gasping when I felt his mouth on my other thigh, felt Egyptian cotton slide against a place that was wet for a whole new reason.

Hans's kisses climbed up to my hip as he reached behind me with both hands, spreading the towel across my backside. Hans slid his wide palms up and over my ass, massaging away the moisture, as he planted a perfect closed-mouth kiss on my throbbing slit.

He wasn't fucking me, not yet.

Hans was loving me first.

I watched with my heart in my throat as he made his way up my torso. Everywhere the towel touched, Hans followed with a kiss. A lick. A nip.

He was breathtakingly beautiful. High contrast, as always. Black and white. Soft and hard. Smooth and spiky.

And he was mine.

When the towel passed over my already-hard nipples, they constricted even tighter in anticipation. Hans's generous mouth followed. He didn't say anything about my piercings or give me any salacious looks upon discovering them; he simply worshipped them like any other part of my body. Hans treated my elbows with the same amount of tender love and care as my erogenous zones. No man had ever regarded my belly button before, unless he was lapping tequila from it, but Hans did.

As he swirled his tongue around my pebbled flesh, I had to

resist the urge to press my hands into the back of his head and hold him there. When he captured a steel hoop between his lips and tugged, it took all of my willpower not to slide down onto his straining cock and put an end to the torture. But a second later, when he used that same mouth to place a gentle kiss on my chest-tube scar, it took all of my self-control to keep from crying.

I was not the same person by the time Hans reached my fingertips that I'd been when he started at my feet. My eyes had been opened. My *heart* had been opened. I was no longer the girl whose body had only been regarded as a sex object. The girl whose lovers had pierced, sliced, bitten, restrained, and penetrated her to satisfy their own needs. The girl who'd traded her flesh for affection. Hans was showing me that my very flesh was worthy of affection all by itself.

Even the scars.

"You're beautiful," I breathed into his parted mouth when he finally completed his journey.

Hans smiled against my lips, tossing the towel somewhere behind me. "That's my line."

As he kissed me sweetly, his erection pressed against my belly again. I considered taking three steps backward, plastering myself against the door, hitching my thigh up over his hip, and pulling him into me. Because that was what other boys would have wanted. That was what the old me would have wanted. But this boy was different. Because of him, *I* was different. And together, our bodies were more than a means to an orgasm. They were canvases. Our hearts, impressionists.

Lacing my fingers through his, I walked backward toward the messy, moonlight-drenched bed as our tongues danced, stepping on errant T-shirts, belts, and boxer shorts along the way. I guided Hans to lie on his back, crawling over him on the mattress, unwilling to break our kiss. I had planned on starting at his feet, which hung over the side of his king-size bed, and massaging my way up, but I couldn't bear to be that far away from his mouth. So I changed my plan, straddling his washboard abs instead. Hans's thick, hot length throbbed against my aching flesh, but I ignored it, or tried to, focusing instead on kneading the knots out of his broad shoulders as we kissed.

Hans groaned in appreciation against my mouth, and I felt the vibration all the way between my legs. As badly as I wanted him inside of me, I wanted to make him feel the way I felt even more—adored.

I slid my hands between our torsos, massaging Hans's pecs, sternum, and upper abs as he lavished my lips with attention. I couldn't massage his arms while lying on top of him, so I reluctantly broke our kiss and sat up. Hans watched me under hooded eyelids as I lifted his heavy right arm, draped his hand over my shoulder, and worked the tension from his tattooed muscles. I kneaded my way from his biceps to his wrist. Then, taking his hand in mine, I held it to my chest and massaged his palm with my thumbs, pulling the strain from years of bass-playing out through each callused fingertip.

The sensation caused Hans's heavy eyelids to flutter shut and a deep moan to rumble in his throat. The sound was so sexual, so primitive, his face so euphoric, that I couldn't help myself. I lifted his hand to my mouth, wrapped my lips around the base of his index finger, and sucked the rest of the tension out.

Hans's eyes slammed open, black pupils swallowing the blue, as I smiled and took his middle finger the same way. I could feel my heartbeat pounding in my clit as Hans's left hand gripped my hip. By the time I pulled his ring finger into my mouth, Hans was no longer my passive canvas. His jaw flexed along with his hips, grinding into me from underneath. I was so slippery, and he was so hard, that by the time I took his pinkie finger, I was panting with need.

"Hans," I whispered, releasing his hand, which he wrapped around the back of my neck.

Pulling me back down to him, thrusting his slick girth between my trembling folds, Hans pressed his forehead against mine and rasped, "I want you... just like this. I'm clean, baby. I promise."

I nodded in relief against his face. I wanted him just like that, too. Not with a barrier between us. There *were* no more barriers between us. I thrust my fingers into his messy black hair and stilled, the head of his cock poised at my core.

"Me too," I whispered.

Hans cursed and claimed my mouth, his fingers digging into my hips as he filled me, inch by agonizing inch. My insides clenched around him. My pulse quickened. My fingers curled into fists in his hair. My teeth captured his bottom lip. And when Hans filled me to the hilt, when we were as close as two people could possibly be, when his pelvic bone pressed against my clit, I detonated. Hans held me in his big, strong arms as I whimpered and writhed and tried to survive the most intense orgasm I'd ever experienced. For the first time in my life, I hadn't gotten off from the sex; I'd gotten off from the *connection*.

The connection was better.

Rolling me onto my back, Hans braced himself on his forearms and gazed down at me. He used the pad of his thumb to wipe a tear from under my eye and gave me a one-dimpled smile. "Come here," he said, pulling me into his arms as he sat back on his knees, lifting me off the bed and onto his lap.

I was straddling him again; only this time, we were both on our knees, praying to the gods to let it be real. To let us be that happy forever.

We clung to each other like kite strings in a hurricane as our bodies took over. Pushing, pulling, giving, taking. With every thrust, I rejoiced. With every withdrawal, I mourned. I never wanted to be separated from him again. Not even by an inch. I'd spent my whole life looking for him, and now that we were joined, I was holding on for dear life.

And I knew Hans felt the same way. His arms around my torso squeezed until my breathing became labored, until my newly healed ribs screamed in protest, until stars danced before my eyes and a second wave of life-threatening pleasure gripped my core.

"Hans," I gasped, fighting for air and bracing myself for the orgasm I was sure would drown me. I wrapped my hands around the back of his head and sucked in a breath as Hans's cock stiffened and swelled inside me.

"Fuck, baby," he hissed, pulling my body down onto him as he thrust one final time.

The feeling of wholeness overwhelmed me. I fisted his hair and cried out. Torrents of pleasure crashed over me as Hans buried his guttural groans in my neck. He tested the limits of my body as he came, pouring himself into the deepest parts of me as I struggled to stay conscious.

I must have failed because, the next thing I knew, I was waking up on Hans's chest. He'd flopped onto his back, still inside me, and he was running his fingertips up and down my spine. I shivered under his touch.

"Cold?"

"No. Just ticklish."

"Sorry." Hans chuckled, smoothing his hand down my back to make it better.

I purred and snuggled into the crook of his neck. Spent. Sated. Suspended in the afterglow. "Hans?"

"Mmhmm?" he murmured into my hair.

"Was that . . . *normal* for you?"

Am I special? Do you make everyone feel like a goddess or just me?

Hans got very still. Even his breathing became shallow.

When I didn't get a response, I placed my forearms on his chest and lifted my head. Hans blinked up at me with wide eyes. He was chewing on the corner of his mouth.

"What's wrong?" I asked, my eyebrows pulled together.

Hans's smoky-blue irises dropped to my mouth. "That was . . . not normal," he finally admitted.

I could tell there was more he wanted to say, but I didn't press him. I laid my head back down on his chest and waited, my heart lodged in my throat.

Please let it be nothing. Please let it be nothing.

"BB . . ."

"Mmhmm?"

Fuck. This is it. This is the part where you find out that you read the whole situation wrong. This is the part where Hans tells you he doesn't have a girlfriend; he has a fucking fiancée. This is the part where you get your stupid fucking heart broken all over again.

I felt Hans swallow where my head was nestled against his

throat. Felt his heart thundering beneath my cheek. Felt his cock swell inside me.

"I'm in love with you."

Tears stung my eyes immediately, but it took a moment for the rest of me to shift emotional gears. As the shock wore off, a tentative smile began to spread across my face.

He's in love with me?

I wrapped my arms around Hans's rigid body and squeezed.

He's in love with me!

I kissed his collarbone, his neck. Kissed his jaw, his cheekbone, his eyelids. I kissed his nose and forehead, and then I finally kissed his worried mouth. "Hans," I cooed against it, slowly fucking his now fully hard cock, "I've been in love with you since the night we met."

A relieved laugh tumbled from his lips just before they crashed into mine. It struck me then, as his tense muscles relaxed beneath my palms and his hips finally rose to meet me, how much courage it must have taken for him to say that.

I felt like my heart was going to explode. I buried my face in Hans's neck to keep him from seeing the stupid grin that had consumed it and squeezed him tighter. His body was the only thing keeping me from floating away.

"Waking up next to you was the best surprise I've ever gotten," I confessed on a whisper, my lips brushing against his heated skin.

Then a squeal was torn from me as Hans surprised me again, rolling me onto my back and hitching one of my thighs up over his hip. "You like waking up next to me, huh?" Hans smirked as he picked up the pace.

I tilted my head back and felt his mouth on my exposed neck. "Mmhmm," I moaned.

"Then stay," he rasped against my collarbone between thrusts. "Stay here, with me, until my parents get back from their trip. You could wake up next to me every day."

Twin tears rolled down my face as I nodded and laughed in disbelief. Hans lifted his head and looked down at me, eyes hooded in ecstasy, brows raised in hopefulness.

I gazed into them, through them, at the soul of the man offering me everything I ever wanted, and said, "I'd love to."

To which Hans replied with a two-dimpled smile, "I love *you*."

I put my falling star on a leash,
And I tied her to a post on the mezzanine.
She could easily burn through the rope,
But I think she likes the way it feels around her throat.

I ran my fingers over the words scrawled in blue ink on Hans's forearm as we cuddled in the leather recliner on the patio, smoking our first cigarette of the day. A few tufts of morning fog lingered on the lake. A few popped floaties lay in repose on the dock. And more than a few beer cans and red plastic cups dotted the landscape, glinting like cheerful Easter eggs waiting to be found.

"Are you going to turn this into a song for Phantom Limb?" I asked, resting my cheek on his bare shoulder and pulling my bony knees up inside the black Tool T-shirt I'd found on his floor.

"Maybe. If I can convince Trip to do a ballad."

"It's a ballad?" I smiled.

"Of course it's a ballad." Hans kissed me on the top of my

head. "I've never written one before, but whenever I'm with you, that's just what comes out."

"Not even for Beth?" I wanted to slap my hand over my own mouth.

Oh fuck. I said it. I said the B word.

"Beth?" Hans's voice dropped an octave.

I nodded, trying to seem nonchalant as I took my next drag with trembling fingers.

Hans sighed and absentmindedly began twisting a lock of my super-short hair with his free hand as he gazed over at me. "How do you know about her?"

"Victoria," I admitted, forcing myself to make eye contact. "The morning after the party, while you were in the shower, she told me you had a girlfriend. She said her name was Beth and that you'd been with her for, like, four years." I wanted to pull my head inside of Hans's T-shirt and die from just talking about her.

"Are you serious?"

I nodded, then quickly returned my attention to the lake as my cheeks began to tingle.

"Oh my God." He laughed, pulling me closer. "I'm so sorry, baby. I had no idea you thought that. No, we broke up months ago, before graduation. I guess I just never told Victoria. We kind of lost touch for a while after she transferred schools."

Every muscle in my body relaxed in relief, my fears fleeing on a sigh. The question I'd been so afraid to ask had finally been answered. And it was the best answer I could have possibly hoped for.

But they were together for years, BB. What if you're just a rebound?

Shut up! Why do you always have to piss on my parade?

"It must have been pretty serious if you guys were together for that long," I said, trying to appease my inner pessimist.

Hans shrugged and took a drag from his cigarette, buying himself a few more seconds before he had to admit whatever truth was coming next. I braced myself, thankful that I was already in the fetal position. My heart felt a little more protected behind my knobby knees and beneath the cover of Hans's faded black T-shirt.

He exhaled the smoke on a sigh. "We were friends for a long time, but we only dated for about two years, not four. Honestly, I think we should have just stayed friends, but we were both too damn nice to admit it."

Ugh. It was so hard to hear him talk about someone else even if what he was saying was supposed to make me feel better.

"BB, look at me."

I swallowed and turned my head toward Hans. The sincerity shining out of his black-rimmed blue eyes stole my breath.

"I've never felt anything like this before. *This*"—he gestured between us with the two fingers pinching his cigarette—"is serious. I didn't even know *this* existed."

"Me either." I smiled, the butterflies in my belly doing tiny little backflips. "I feel like I just woke up from a bad dream."

"I feel like I'm still dreaming," Hans said, leaning down to press his smiling lips against mine.

His sweet, lingering kiss made me forget all about What's Her Name. Hell, it made me forget my own name. I wasn't brought back into the present until my fingers started to burn from the approaching ember on the end of my forgotten cigarette.

As I laughed and dropped the butt into an empty beer bottle

on a nearby table, something occurred to me. Something that made my blood run cold. "Hans?" I asked, turning to face him again. "Why did you think I had a boyfriend? Did Victoria tell you that?"

Because that bitch knows I am single.

Hans shrugged. "Sort of. I mean, she told me about you and the accident, and I remembered her saying that your boyfriend was driving. So when I asked you if the guy who'd been driving was okay, I kinda hoped you'd tell me that he, like, died or something"—Hans laughed—"but you didn't. You gave me some kind of short answer, like you didn't want to talk about it. So, I guess I just assumed that you guys were still together."

"Oh my God." My hands flew to my mouth. "Then Knight showed up at the Masquerade the next weekend! You must have thought that was him."

"Dude." Hans leaned forward and dropped his cigarette butt into the beer bottle on the table too. "I felt like the biggest piece of shit ever. Some guy was out there, looking for his girlfriend, and I'd had my hands all over her the whole night." Hans shook his head. "I should have just asked you if you had a boyfriend, but I didn't know what I'd do if you said yes. I had to keep seeing you."

"Oh my God, I felt the same way!"

Hans chuckled. "I think we're kind of the same person."

"Except *you're* athletic." I smirked. "I saw all those soccer trophies on your shelf, *Hansel*."

Hans snorted. "First of all, nobody calls me that but my mom. And second, I *was* athletic. I tore my ACL and MCL in tenth grade, and that was that." He lifted his left leg and gestured to four small incision scars on and around his knee.

"Oh shit. I'm so sorry."

"Don't be. It was the best thing that ever happened to me... until I met you," he added, snuggling his face into my neck and giving me a scruffy kiss on the clavicle. I purred and rubbed my cheek against his soft, wild hair. "While I was stuck in my room, recovering from surgery, I learned how to play all my favorite songs on the guitar. Then I moved on to the bass. Then drums. By the time I started eleventh grade, I could play every song on The Downward Spiral album on three different instruments. I healed up enough that I could have gone back to playing soccer, but the guys needed a bass player, so I joined Phantom Limb instead."

"Phantom Limb!" Trip called out in his rock-star voice, stumbling down the stairs from the first-floor deck.

Hans and I turned our heads and watched his descent. Trip was shirtless, sunburned as fuck, and wearing a green silk kimono.

"Dude, why are you wearing my mom's robe?" Hans laughed.

"First of all"—Trip held a hand up in Hans's face as he breezed behind the armchair and grabbed a piece of cold pizza out of the box on the bar—"that's sexist. Second"—he took a bite and continued with his mouth full—"shit got crazy after y'all left last night."

"Oh shit. You didn't let Victoria and Steven pull you in for a threesome, did you?" Hans asked, only partly joking.

"Let's just say, I found out that I look damn good in pigtails."

I squealed. Hans groaned. And Trip beamed with a mouthful of pizza.

"Pssh. I'm just kiddin'. I wouldn't let Steven touch my ding-a-ling with *Hans's* hand." Trip's deep brown eyes lit up.

"Hey! Speaking of Hans and ding-a-lings, somebody here got the *long dong* last night! Am I right?" Trip pointed at me with his half-eaten pizza. "Girl, I bet you're walkin' with a limp today, huh?"

I laughed as Hans glared at Trip, trying to look mad. "Yeah, it's pretty bad," I said, giving Hans a teasing look before returning my attention to Trip. "Honestly, I don't know if I'm gonna make it. I think he might have ruptured my spleen."

Trip shrugged and took another bite. "The dong'll do that to ya. But you'll be all right; I'm pretty sure you got two spleens. And, hey, if you don't, LDH here'll probably give you his. He's sweet like that."

I glanced back at Hans, who gave me that shy little smile I loved. The one where the corners of his mouth barely turned upward, but his dimples and sparkling eyes gave him away.

"You know," I said just loud enough for him to hear, "I kinda have a thing for guys with tattoos who would die for me."

Hans's shy smile split into a grin as his eyes dropped to my lips. "Well, you found one," he said, leaning in for a kiss. "You already have my heart; why not take my spleen to match?"

As I swooned and kissed my big, tattooed teddy bear, Trip exclaimed, "Dude, that's some good shit!" Drumming on the bar with his pizza crust, he sang, "*You already have my heart, bitch. Why not take my spleen to maaaaaatch?*"

Hans and I cracked up. I loved the sound of his laughter. The feel of his hard, warm body all around my small, cold one. His scruffy five o'clock shadow on my soft cheek. I loved the way he literally wore his heart on his sleeve, scrawling lyrics in ballpoint pen on the tender underbelly of his arm. I loved that Hans was strong enough and brave enough and confident enough to be vulnerable. To show me exactly how he felt without fear of ridicule or rejection. He might not have been as tough or aggressive as Knight and Harley, but to me, Hans was by far more fearless.

But mostly, I loved the way he loved me. The moment Hans appeared in my life, I felt as if a switch had been flipped. I suddenly had access to colors I'd never seen before. Feelings I'd never felt. Memories I'd lost a lifetime ago. And a level of connection I didn't know was possible. I'd found my soul mate.

Now all I had to do was tell my parents.

PART II

14

"Ringo likes him," I said, watching our golden retriever cock his head to the side as Hans scratched him behind the ear.

"So does your dad," my mom replied, handing me another dish to dry. "They have so much in common."

I peeked into the living room again. My father was sitting on the couch, where he spent most of his waking hours, tuning his favorite cherry-red Fender Stratocaster and regaling Hans about his glory days as a long-haired rocker in the late '60s and '70s. Hans was holding the Les Paul my dad had thrust into his arms but was clearly paying more attention to Ringo than my dad's tales of stardom. Not that he would even notice. My dad was in monologue mode. All Hans had to do was nod every once in a while.

I walked back over to the kitchen counter where my mom had piled up a few more serving bowls for me to dry. "God, they *do* have a lot in common, don't they?"

My mom didn't look at me as she scrubbed spaghetti sauce from a pan, the water so hot, it steamed on contact. Her brow was creased, and her long red hair, usually loose and flowing, had been pulled over one tie-dye-covered shoulder in a tight braid.

"What's wrong, Mom? You don't like him?"

She smiled in a way that only touched the bottom half of her freckled face and turned, handing me the squeaky-clean hunk of metal to dry. "Oh no, he's lovely. So handsome. And sweet. And you can tell he's just crazy about you. You deserve to be treated like a princess, especially after ... you know."

You know was the term my mom used to refer to Knight, Harley, the car accident, my hospitalization for anorexia the year before, my birth control prescription—basically anything she didn't want to talk about.

"So, you're okay with me staying at his house for a couple of weeks?"

Or months.

"Honey, I learned a long time ago that telling you no is about as effective as putting a fire out with gasoline." My mom gave me a sad smile. "I'm gonna miss you though. I can't believe you're already starting college and moving out. You're only seventeen. Why do you have to be so damn smart and grown-up already?"

I set the pot and dish towel down and gave my favorite lady a hug. "I'll be back, Mom. It's just a few weeks." I tried to sound nonchalant, but on the inside, my heart was breaking just as much as hers.

I'd never been away from my mom longer than a few days. She was my person. My mother, my sister, my best friend. She was the one who'd helped me pick up the pieces after Knight shattered my heart. After Harley shattered my body. She was the one who'd taken care of me when I was sick, encouraged me when I was well, and comforted me when I was sad. I didn't want to leave her, but our time together had expired while we were busy just trying to get by.

I'd grown up too fast, and now, there was no going back.

"I know." She sniffled. "Just promise me you'll be careful. You know how musicians are."

Our warm embrace turned into an icy prison the second the words left her mouth. I pulled away and looked into earthy green eyes the color of mine, creased in fine lines and wearing far less makeup.

"What's that supposed to mean?" I snapped.

My mom sighed and shook her head.

"What about musicians?"

She frowned. "Honey, you know how your daddy is. Your uncle Chandler. They're very sweet, but they can also be very selfish and...*irresponsible*."

Irresponsible was her nicest way of saying *drunk, full of shit, passed out all day*, and *incapable of keeping steady employment*.

I folded my arms over my chest and glared out the window above the sink, throwing shade at the mildewed birdbath in the backyard.

"He's not like that, Mom. He's...generous. He's levelheaded. He never even gets wasted at parties. If anything, *he* takes care of *me*."

"Good. That's good, honey. I hope it stays that way."

When I didn't look back at her, my mom cleared her throat. "Hey, do you know what you call a musician without a girlfriend?"

"What?" I asked, giving her a sideways glance.

"Homeless."

I snorted out a little laugh. "Where'd you hear that one?"

"From your dad." She laughed too.

"Nobody's perfect, right?" I asked, offering a truce.

"No, I suppose not," she said, accepting it. "Hans seems very nice, honey. If you're happy, I'm happy."

I smiled as the first few bars of "In-A-Gadda-Da-Vida" blared from an amplifier in the living room.

"I am, Mom. I really, really am."

September 1999

"Hey, can you guys turn that down? I'm trying to study!" I shouted from the doorway of the master bedroom.

I'd been holed up in there for hours, burning off calories I hadn't even consumed on the Oppenheimers' top-of-the-line treadmill while simultaneously poring over grainy images of biblical paintings in my European Renaissance Art History textbook.

"What's that?" Trip yelled back from the living room. "You want me to turn it up?" The volume on whatever first-person-shooter video game they were playing got louder, filling all five thousand square feet with the sounds of grunting and gunshots. It was better than the sound of grunting and cum shots, which *usually* filled the air whenever Trip was over and had control of the TV.

I was about to stomp out there and smack the remote out of his hand when I heard Hans do it for me.

"Hey!" Trip exclaimed as the volume finally decreased.

"Thank you, baby!" My voice echoed through the cavernous house.

"You're welcome, baby," he rumbled back.

"Blow me, baby!" Trip chimed in, followed by what sounded like a whack to the back of the head. "Ow! That's not how you do it, fucker. Here, let me show you."

I could hear Baker and Kevin laughing as Hans cursed and knocked over something heavy, trying to fight off Trip's advances. Smiling to myself, I closed the door and turned back around.

The opulence of the room hit me like a solar flare, stopping me dead in my tracks. I wondered if I'd ever get used to it. The space. The splendor. The perfect triangular vacuum tracks left on the plush champagne-colored carpet by the housekeeper. I'd been living in that palace for over a month, and I still had to stop and physically pinch myself sometimes.

Standing in the Oppenheimers' master bedroom with its twelve-foot-tall vaulted ceiling, exposed wooden beams, and billowy custom drapes pulled open to reveal a view of the sunset over Lake Lanier, I was definitely having one of those *please don't let this be a dream* moments.

My feelings of awe and unworthiness only grew when I heard the door open behind me. Turning, I found the handsome prince who'd whisked me away to that castle filling the doorway. He casually reached up and grabbed the top of the doorframe with one hand, causing his black Motörhead T-shirt to ride up a few inches. A sliver of tan skin and rippled muscles peeked out from between the hem of his shirt and the studded belt holding up his low-slung black jeans, just enough to make my breath falter.

Hans and I didn't speak at first. We just stood there, salivating over one another until our pupils finished dilating.

Eventually, Hans held up his cell phone with a smirk and said, "My mom wants to talk to you."

Your mom? I mouthed, my heart rate kicking up a notch. *Am I in trouble?*

"No," Hans whispered, cupping his free hand over the speaker. "But I think I am."

Hans held out the phone again. That time, I took it. Hesitantly.

Holding the little black device up to my ear, I cringed and said, "Hi, Mrs. Oppenheimer," in my cheeriest voice.

"Hi, BB. How are you, my dear?" Her voice was soft and warm, her accent definitely German. I liked her instantly.

"I'm great, thanks. How's your trip so far?"

"Eet's been vonderful. My husband is going a little—how do you say?—stir-crazy. But ve are having a very nice time. Ze Grand Canyon vas my favorite."

"I'd love to see it sometime," I replied, shrugging at Hans.

"BB, I need your help vid somezing. It seems as zough my son forgot to pay ze mortgage and utilities at ze end of ze month. Do you sink you could help him vid zat?"

I stifled a laugh and looked at Hans, who was smiling guiltily. "Sure, Mrs. Oppenheimer. What do I need to do?"

"Oh, please. Call me Helga."

Helga walked me through where to find her checkbook, how to pay the mortgage, electricity, water, gas, cable, and phone bills, informed me about the food allowance, and even put me in charge of watering her plants. She did not tell me I could drive her brand-new BMW Z3 convertible, but she also didn't tell me I *couldn't*.

By the time I got off the phone, I was an honorary estate manager. But, more importantly, I was Helga Oppenheimer's personal hero.

"Dude, your mom fucking loves me," I bragged, pressing the End button and handing the phone back to Hans.

"*I* fucking love you," he said, shoving the device into his pocket. "You done in here yet? I miss you." Hans's bottom lip poked out a little bit in a genuine pout.

"I miss you, too." I wanted to grab his ears and kiss a smile back onto his pitiful face, but I had to stay strong. "I just have so much fucking homework tonight. I'm sorry, baby. I have to know the artist, year, and original location for, like, fifty paintings by tomorrow. And"—I walked over to the Oppenheimers' solid cherry California-king sleigh bed and picked up the VHS tape that had tumbled out of my backpack—"I still have to watch this movie for my film class *and* somehow squeeze in a shower."

I tossed the movie back onto the bed in exasperation as Hans crossed the room and pulled me into his arms.

"Can I help?" he asked, resting his chin on the top of my head.

"Really?" I spoke into his chest as he ran a firm hand down my back. Hans didn't do it lightly anymore. Now, he knew I was ticklish. "I don't even know where to begin."

"What if we do all of it at the same time?"

"What? How?" I grimaced up at his handsome, hopeful face.

Hans tipped his head toward the ostentatious mahogany entertainment console facing the foot of the bed. "What if I hook the TV up in the bathroom? Then we can study, in the tub, *while* we watch the movie."

I beamed at his brilliance. "And I thought boys weren't supposed to be able to multitask."

Hans laughed. "I'm so ADD, all I do is multitask."

"I'm pretty sure that's just called getting distracted in the middle of what you were—"

"Shh." Hans placed a callused fingertip over my lips and whispered, "Multitasking."

Goddamn, he was adorable.

While Hans set up the TV, I went outside to smoke a much-needed study-break cigarette. When I got back, after having my retinas scarred by whatever sick Japanese porno Trip, Baker, and Kevin were watching in the living room, the scene in the bathroom rendered me speechless. This wasn't a *please don't let this be a dream* moment. This was an *I've officially died and gone to heaven* moment. I didn't want to be dead, but if being dead meant I could climb into *that* candlelit garden tub with *that* tattooed, hard-bodied bass player, I would have tap-danced to the executioner's block.

Hans pressed play on *Everyone Says I Love You* and turned toward me, his proud smile falling away as soon as he saw my face. "Hey, what's wrong?"

I pressed my lips together and shook my head, trying to tell him that nothing was wrong, but the tears threatening to spill from my eyes said otherwise.

"Come here, baby." Hans's voice sounded like leather, smooth and warm and strong, as he took a step toward me with his arms spread.

I folded into him on contact, trying to press my very cells into his pores. Much like his house, I wondered if I would ever get used to the beauty that was Hans himself. His thoughtful acts of kindness continually caught me off guard, reopening the poorly healed wounds of my past at every turn.

I hadn't realized that no one had ever bought me flowers until I came home from work and almost tripped over a dozen red roses waiting for me in the foyer. It hadn't occurred to me that no one had ever bothered to take me on a real date until I saw Hans standing outside of a Georgia Dome restroom, holding a stuffed monster truck. And there, staring at a whirlpool tub illuminated by candles and a cozy Woody Allen movie, I realized that I'd never experienced romance at all.

I'd given myself away to assholes, and now Hans was left holding nothing but the wrapper.

"You okay?" he asked, pressing a lingering kiss to the top of my messy, bleach-blonde head.

I nodded into his chest.

"You wanna talk about it?"

I shook my head and sniffled.

Hans ran his hand—firm, not gentle—down my back. "You wanna get in the tub and tell me which one of the Ninja Turtles painted the Sistine Chapel?"

I snorted a little laugh and said, "Michelangelo."

"He's the one who's always eating pizza, right?"

I nodded again.

"He's my favorite."

I squeezed Hans tighter. "Mine too." I sniffled into his T-shirt. "Sorry I'm such a little bitch. I just... I fucking love you so much, it makes me cry, and I'm not even a crier." I laughed in embarrassment, releasing him with one hand to wipe my eyes with the heel of my palm.

"I feel the exact same way." Hans's voice was choked with

emotion. He swallowed, his Adam's apple sliding up and down against the side of my head, and he took a steadying breath. "Last night, after we finished rehearsing in the basement, I came upstairs and found you asleep on my side of the bed. I don't know why, but I...I just sat down and cried."

"Oh my God, baby." I looked up at Hans's hard face, unable to hide all the softness inside. "You should have woken me up."

The corner of his mouth pulled up slightly as he shook his head. "No. You looked so beautiful, so tiny in that huge bed. I couldn't wake you up. I couldn't even process it. You know? That something so perfect had been waiting up for *me*. I felt like the biggest piece of shit and the luckiest bastard on earth, all at the same time."

Beautiful.

Perfect.

Lucky.

Every word he spoke fluttered into my ears, lit up the darkened, self-critical corners of my mind, and attached itself to my heart like a bandage, healing me from the outside in. I pushed up onto my tiptoes to kiss the source of those words but was met with an unexpected obstacle.

When I looked down at the bulge between us, then up into guilty gray-blue eyes, a smile split my face. "Hans!" I giggled, smacking him on the chest.

"What?" He shrugged, both dimples on full display.

"You get emotional boners. Do you know how fucking cute that is?"

If his cheeks hadn't been covered in three days' worth of stubble, I'm sure they would have been bright pink. "Kinda ruins the mood." He chuckled as I unbuckled his belt. Even with me on my tiptoes, Hans had to bend down to meet my expectant kiss.

Unfastening his pants, I took him in my hands and whispered, "I love you," against his parted lips.

"I love you too, baby," he whispered back, his cock swelling in agreement against my palms.

"I love you, too," I cooed at it, bending over to kiss its smiling head.

Hans let out a tiny moan, and I suddenly knew exactly what I could do for him. What I could give him in return for all that he'd done for me.

I didn't stand back up to resume our make-out session. I sank to my knees instead. The tile felt cool under my bare shins—all I was wearing was a thin tank top and a pair of Hans's boxer shorts—but the soft candlelight, the flirty banter between Drew Barrymore and Edward Norton, and the flesh beneath my tongue were velvety and warm. I took my time, knowing with absolute certainty—and for possibly the first time in my life— that I had nowhere better to go and nothing better to do.

I had arrived.

Long, rough fingers wove themselves into my choppy hair as I slowly worshipped Hans's manhood with my tongue. My lips. My hands.

"Fuck," he hissed, gripping my head. Hans's hips began to thrust slightly, and his entire body tensed.

He was holding back; I could tell. He wanted to fuck my mouth, but he was too big, and I was too inexperienced.

Or so he thought.

I gripped his hips with both hands and looked up at him from under my lashes. Hans was watching me. Night had fallen, and the room was now shrouded in darkness, but his eyes burned like blue flames. I'd forgotten how villainous he looked when he wasn't smiling. How intense. There was another side to Hans that I hadn't seen yet; I could feel it.

Goose bumps raced down my arms as I took him all the way to my throat, letting him know that he didn't need to hold back.

He couldn't break me.

He *wouldn't*.

Hans held my tear-streaked stare as he tested my resolve, taking control, guiding my movements. I dug my nails into his hips as he pumped into my mouth, each thrust a little deeper, each withdrawal a little less restrained. I gagged and wrapped my right hand around the base of his dick, holding on for dear life yet encouraging him to continue. Just as I felt his cock stiffen in my fist, Hans pulled away.

"Fuck, baby," he panted, running a hand through his tousled black hair. "You're gonna kill me."

I smiled with swollen lips at my flustered boyfriend, his angry cock jutting out of his open jeans. We stared at each other, eyes wide, chests heaving, then, at the exact same time, we both looked over at the bathtub.

Tearing our clothes off, Hans and I scrambled into the now room-temperature water. With the touch of a button, eight powerful jets roared to life, turning the serene basin into a hurricane of stimulation. Hans sat with his back against the far side of the oval to allow room for his long, muscular legs. I went to straddle him but was stopped by two strong hands around my hips.

"No, baby. Turn around."

My heart crashed in my chest almost as hard as the rapids breaking on the surface of the water as I did what I'd been told, standing back up and turning away from him, slowly. Two massive hands palmed my bare ass, kneading the only ample part of my body. I held my breath as Hans parted my flesh and gasped in surprise when I felt his tongue slide along the seam. It started at the front.

And ended at the back.

My knees almost buckled when he did it again. Releasing my ass with one hand but continuing his sweet torture, Hans slid his palm up my lower back and pressed forward until I bent at the waist for him. I gripped the edge of the bathtub in front of me with both hands and whimpered as he lavished me with his mouth. Nothing was off-limits to Hans. He wanted all of me, and I was more than willing to let him have it.

Sweet, sucking kisses gave way to long, torturous licks.

Kneading hands turned into curious fingers.

Curious fingers filled me, becoming slippery fingers.

Slippery fingers massaged the place no one had ever touched before.

A warm, flicking tongue followed them there.

A trail of desire flowed down the inside of my thigh.

My mouth watered.

Stubble like sandpaper scratched my tender, oversensitive flesh.

An eager tongue filled the place where I was aching.

Hans's thumb, slick with a combination of my lust and his saliva, teased my puckered flesh as he fucked me with his tongue. I arched my back and pushed against it, begging for more with my posture. I'd had no idea anything could feel that good. There were so many sensations all building at once that, when Hans finally gave me what I wanted, when he pressed against my tight little ring and filled me in a completely new way, my core spasmed on contact.

A strangled cry began to climb its way out of my throat, but before it could escape, Hans withdrew, wrapped both hands around my hips, and pulled me into the roiling, chaotic water with him.

With my back against his front, Hans kissed me sideways as he groped me with his hands and filled me with his impossibly hard shaft, allowing me no time to adjust as he pumped into me from underneath.

He swallowed my cries as I came, my insides clenching and clawing at him, struggling to accommodate his size but wanting more all the same. I gripped the sides of the bathtub and bit his lip as the hurricane we were dancing in passed through me and into Hans. Once the fury inside me began to subside, Hans wrapped both arms around my ribs, lifted his hips, and filled me to the hilt with a curse and a kiss.

Water splashed over the edge of the tub and onto my backpack as we fell back down to earth.

Hans kept his arms around me and tucked his stubbled chin into the crook of my neck. I pressed my cheek against his temple and smiled, completely content, perfectly at peace for possibly the first time in my life. People were singing and dancing on the glowing TV, but I didn't pay them any attention. I was floating in my love bubble built for two.

Until it popped.

Until the dark thoughts crept in, like spiders, re-spinning their webs of doubt in the dusty corners of my mind.

No one will ever top this. Do you realize that?

You will never be happier than you are right now. And you're only seventeen.

You're so fucked.

Hans just ruined the rest of your life. All eighty-three years of it. Shot to hell.

You've only been together a month, and you already can't live without him.

What are you going to do if he leaves you like Knight did? If he cheats on you like Harley?

You'll fucking die; that's what.

So you're looking at a life of suckage or death.

Congratulations.

"Hans?"

"Mmhmm?"

"That was…" *Intense. Transcendent. Life-ruining.* "I mean, nobody's ever…" *Loved me like this.* "I…" *Can't lose you.*

"I know, baby," Hans murmured into the tender flesh behind my ear, reading my wayward thoughts. "I know."

Hans and I snuggled deeper into the pulsing lukewarm water. Over the din of the jets and the thrumming of my racing heart, I began to make out the unmistakable sound of bad singing. Looking up at the television glowing on the counter, I saw Tim Roth, aggressively serenading a very posh Drew Barrymore while dressed like some kind of vagabond.

"It's a fucking musical?" I spat.

Hans snorted. "Are you serious? It's almost over."

"It's so bad," I marveled.

"Yeah. It's fucking terrible," Hans agreed.

"We should go put it on in the living room and make Trip watch it as payback for the bukkake porn I walked in on earlier."

"Oh shit!" He burst out laughing. "Trip busted out the bukkake! Are you gonna be okay?"

"No. I'm fucking traumatized. All I see when I close my eyes is—"

Hans lifted his hand and pressed a wet finger to my lips. "Shh. You're safe now."

I giggled and kissed the callused pad, feeling the weight of that statement settle into my bones.

"You're safe now."

For a moment, I almost believed him.

16

"We need vegetables in our lives, baby. Like, literally. To stay alive."

Hans wrinkled his nose as he scanned the produce section. "But they're just so . . . *vegetabley*."

We'd been living on pizza and Hot Pockets for weeks. Well, Hans had. I'd been living on Diet Coke, whiskey, and ciga-rettes, per my usual.

"Just pick one vegetable. And a fruit, too."

"*A fruit, too?*" Hans pouted, absentmindedly slipping his left hand into my back pocket as he considered his options.

We were never *not* touching. If we were in the same zip code as one another, we were touching.

It was disgusting.

Hans and I wandered through the colorful, foreign wonder-land of fresh food until he finally settled on a bag of baby carrots and a large container of pre-cut fruit salad.

"Not *that*," I said, intercepting the container and putting it back on the shelf.

Hans's eyebrows pulled together in confusion until I pointed at the price tag.

"Twenty bucks!?"

"Right? I always wanted the pre-cut shit, too, but my mom would never buy it for me because it's such a rip-off. I'll just make you a fruit salad if that's what you want."

"You're gonna make me fruit salad?" Hans beamed, leaning in to give me a peck on the lips. "You do love me."

"Maybe. Or maybe I just want to save enough money to buy a carton of cigarettes while we're here."

Hans gave me the side-eye and smirked. "I thought you were trying to keep me alive."

I smirked back. "It's called balance, Hans. You have to eat your fruit to get your cigarettes."

After I went around collecting everything I needed to keep my boyfriend from dying of malnutrition or scurvy, I pulled my pen and grocery list out of the shopping cart and crossed off *HEALTHY SHIT*.

Hans looked over my shoulder as I studied the list and rested his hand on the shopping cart handle. I glanced over at his forearm and looked straight into the eyes of Count Dracula himself. I didn't appreciate his creepy, bug-eyed stare, so I reached over and drew a blue mustache on Hans's black-and-gray tattoo.

"Hey, what did Bela ever do to you?" Hans chuckled as he inspected my work.

"Who?"

"Bela Lugosi, the actor who played Dracula."

"Oh, I'm sorry. You must be mistaken. There is only one true Count Dracula, and that is Gary Oldman. And Gary Oldman's version has a mustache. Actually, gimme your arm. I need to add his goatee, too."

I lunged for his forearm with my pen, but Hans clapped his opposite hand over it, shielding poor Bela from further desecration.

"I love *Bram Stoker's Dracula* too, but that movie wasn't out when I was a kid," Hans said, defending his choice in body art.

"So? It was out by the time you got that tattoo."

"Yeah, but that's not the point," Hans said, dropping his guard when I finally put the pen away and began pushing the cart toward the deli section. "I'd been planning this sleeve since I was, like, ten."

I stopped in front of a case of deli meat and shivered violently from the cold. "Um, not to sound judgy, but where were your parents while you were busy watching"—I looked his arm up and down—"*Hellraiser* and *The Texas Chain Saw Massacre?*"

I grabbed a package of Oscar Mayer sliced turkey. I had a coupon for it. Fifty cents off. That was like two-and-a-half cigarettes' worth of savings.

"Fighting."

I dropped the processed meat into the cart and looked up at Hans.

"I went upstairs and watched movies whenever they were fighting," he clarified.

I studied his face, searching for clues, but Hans's dark features were neutral.

Glancing at his arm again, face after horrifying, deranged face staring back at me, I said, "They must have been fighting *a lot*, huh?"

When I lifted my eyes to his, it was like looking through

the portholes of a ship during a hurricane. A tiny glimpse at an ocean of turmoil.

"Yeah," Hans said, holding my stare.

I felt my adrenaline surge, my fight-or-flight instinct kicking in. The only other boy who'd ever talked to me about his traumatic past was Knight, and handling him in an emotionally activated state had been like learning how to charm a snake through trial and error. One wrong move, one wrong response, one wrong fucking look, and he'd strike.

But these eyes weren't serpentine; they were sentient. They didn't warn me off; they welcomed me in. This was Hans, *my* Hans, the man who wore his heart on his tattooed sleeve. I didn't need to be afraid anymore. I just needed my brain to realize that.

"So, when your parents were fighting, you would go watch horror movies?" I asked, trying to implement what little I'd learned in my Interpersonal Relationships class so far.

Summarize. Validate. Lean in and nod.

"Yeah," Hans said, furrowing his brow and chewing on his thumbnail. "That's weird, huh? I don't know why I didn't just watch cartoons. I guess, maybe, because I was scared? You know, like, maybe it tricked my brain into thinking I was scared because of the movie and not because my dad was downstairs, putting his fist through the wall."

My heart ached as I imagined a terrified, wide-eyed, wild-haired little boy hiding in his room, replacing one nightmare with another. It wasn't fair. Hans was the kindest, most loving person I knew. He deserved to be tucked in and read to every night. He deserved to be cuddled and reassured, like I was, that monsters weren't real. Instead, he'd turned to them for comfort.

My sympathy bubbled over into rage. My thoughts began to race. I pictured myself destroying all the precious bullshit in their house. The framed art. The porcelain vases. The fine china on the formal dining room table that no one ever used. I imagined myself yanking Hans's phone out of his pocket and calling them up, telling them they were pieces of shit who didn't deserve him.

Stop it, BB. Nod your fucking head and validate that man's feelings.

"That's not weird," I said, choking on my anger as I placed a gentle hand over Bela Lugosi's new blue mustache. "I think it makes perfect sense."

One of Hans's dimples deepened, but he didn't quite smile. "It worked. After watching the scariest shit I could get my hands on for years, I realized one day that I wasn't afraid anymore. I was only twelve, but I was already almost as tall as my dad. So, instead of hiding in my room when they started fighting, I decided that I was finally gonna go downstairs and break it up."

Hans swallowed and looked off into the distance. "When I got down there, I saw my dad slap my mom across the face. I'd never seen him hit her before, and..." He looked back at me. "She's so tiny, BB. Wait until you meet her. She's, like, barely five feet tall. And my dad is this fucking angry giant German. I don't know. I just...snapped. I jumped on him, and we basically wrestled on the ground and beat the shit out of each other until the cops came and broke it up."

"Oh my God, b-b-baby. I'm so s-s-sorry." I was vaguely aware that my teeth were starting to chatter.

Hans wrapped his arm around me and pushed the cart with his free hand away from the meat cooler.

"Don't be. That was the final straw for my mom. She let him spend the night in jail and told him that he couldn't come home unless he stopped drinking. He's still a fucking asshole, and he and my mom still argue a lot, but it's definitely better than it was."

"So that's why you got the tattoos?"

"Yeah," Hans said, stopping to grab a few dozen boxes of Cinnamon Toast Crunch from the cereal aisle. "I used to have a lot of anxiety. At school I was always fucking up and forgetting shit because of my ADD, and then I'd be worried about how my dad was going to react when he saw my grades. I couldn't even take Ritalin because it just made my anxiety worse. The only thing that ever helped me get over my fears was watching those movies when I was a kid, so the day I turned eighteen, I went to Terminus City Tattoo and started working on this piece." He smiled and looked down at his arm. "Having these guys with me wherever I go . . . it sounds crazy, but it, like, cured me. I haven't had a panic attack in over a year."

I wanted to lean in and nod, summarize and validate, but I couldn't. I couldn't fucking breathe. I was the one who was about to have a panic attack, and it was all because of three little words.

Terminus. City. Tattoo.

A flood of memories overwhelmed me at once. All involving Knight. All involving pain. His tattoo chair where he'd fucked me, pierced me, inked me, got drunk with me, slept with me. The way it looked, lying on its side, stuffing flying everywhere as Knight ripped it to shreds with his butterfly knife in a fit of PTSD-induced psychosis. The fire-escape stairs where Knight had told me he loved me—the same ones he'd shoved me down a few months later. The wallpaper in the restroom, covered in busty naked she-devils that always made me feel inadequate and self-conscious while I peed or puked after drinking too much on an empty stomach.

"Stop." I snapped my fingers and blinked my eyes.

Hans stood on the other side of the cart, staring at me with a box of Pop-Tarts suspended in his outstretched hand. "You okay, baby?"

I just stared back, breathing hard and listening to the ringing of my pounding pulse in my ears. I wanted to tell him that I knew exactly how he'd felt. That I knew what it was like to love someone who was sick and violent. Someone who could never truly be what you wanted him to be, even on his best day. Someone whose worst days were so bad that they might haunt me forever. But I couldn't find the words.

Hans dropped the box into the cart and bent down to look me in the eyes. A deep V creased between his brows, and his blue-jean-colored irises flicked back and forth between mine. "Baby, talk to me."

I wanted to. I wanted to share my trauma with someone as freely as Hans had just shared his with me. There were so many hurts I'd never said out loud before because I'd been worried about protecting Knight. Worried that people wouldn't understand, that they'd think he was just another abusive boyfriend.

Was he?

As I opened my mouth to say something, anything, the sound of a different girl filled my ears. A happier girl. A girl who knew my boyfriend's stupid fucking nickname.

"Oh my God! LDH? Is that you?"

We turned to find a buxom brunette in a red crop top and

baggy jeans bounding toward us with a shopping basket in the crook of her arm. She reminded me of Little Red Riding Hood skipping through the forest.

Only way skankier.

Hans's face flipped from concerned to delighted in an instant. "Hey! What's up?"

"Oh my God, it *is* you! I knew it!" Little Red Riding Ho wrapped her arms around Hans's neck and smooshed her ample tits against his chest. He chuckled at her enthusiasm and patted her back awkwardly. Releasing him, *finally*, she squealed, "I love your music! I go to Locals Only at the Masquerade every month just to see you guys!"

"Oh shit!" Hans said, genuine recognition alight in his eyes. "You came onstage for the kiss contest last month."

"Every month! Trip hasn't picked me yet though." She pouted. Just then, her eyes flicked over to me. "Oh my God, I remember you! You're the girl who mooned everybody!"

If I have to hear the words oh my God *one more time…*

I smiled through my gritted teeth. "Yep. That's me."

"Girl, that was awesome!" Little Red Riding Ho lifted her palm into the air.

Oh, for fuck's sake. Now I have to high-five this idiot?

I tried not to roll my eyes as my hand came up to meet hers rather unenthusiastically.

Turning her attention back to my boyfriend, Little Red said, "What are you doing here? You don't live around here, do you? Oh my God, are we neighbors?"

Hans opened his mouth, but I interjected before he had the chance to tell this rando fangirl his fucking home address. "He's up here recording an album. His producer lives here."

"Oh my God, really? That's so exciting! I can't wait to hear it!"

"Thanks," Hans said, giving me a quizzical sideways glance. "It's coming along."

"Oh my God, can I get your autograph?" Little Red asked, digging in her purse for a pen and a piece of paper.

Hans ended up signing the back of a gas station receipt, a Taco Bell napkin, and a gum wrapper for Little Red Riding Ho before she finally let him go, but not until she gave him another disgustingly tight, smooshy hug.

As soon as she walked away, with a little extra sway in her curvy hips, Hans pulled me into his arms and spun me around. My combat-boot-covered feet came off the ground and damn near cleared a shelf of Pop-Tarts.

Hans was so genuinely happy I couldn't even be annoyed anymore. He had just been recognized for the first time out in public. That was a big deal. If he wanted to make a living as a musician, he was going to need fans. Lots of them.

Even cute ones with hourglass figures and limited vocabularies.

When he set me back down on my feet, I smiled up at him, basking in his elation. Hans's happiness was infectious, and I found myself perusing the aisles with him, fantasizing about things like agents and signing bonuses and recording studios and tours. The intensity of our earlier conversation had completely evaporated. My awkward flashback, long forgotten.

By Hans at least.

Love bubble?

Love cocoon?

Love shroud. Ooh, I like it. That sounds kinda morbid, like a Phantom Limb song.

I opened my mouth to tell Hans what it was that we were floating in and then giggled because I'd already forgotten.

"What's so funny?" he whispered into my ear, barely audible over the roar of the bonfire and other fucked-up party guests.

"I don't even know!" I giggled back, nuzzling my face into the soft crook of his hoodie-covered neck. "I'm just so happy right now."

"Me too," Hans whispered, turning his face to mine. His low voice rumbled through me, and when his lips found mine, the invisible layer of fuzzy, tingly electrical pulses surrounding us intensified tenfold.

It felt like every hair on my head was standing on end as Hans's tongue slid along the seam of my lips and swept into my mouth. I couldn't hold on to a thought long enough to think. I could only feel, and everything felt important. Amazing. Symbiotic.

We couldn't have gotten out of that lawn chair if we'd tried. Hans and I had merged into a single eight-limbed monstrosity. A freak of nature. We'd become joined from our necks to our knees, and we didn't give a single solitary fuck who saw us like that.

All of a sudden, the rickety metal and nylon chair shook beneath us as if we were in an earthquake. I clung to Hans's hoodie as the sound of laughter erupted behind us. I looked up to find Trip staring down at us, pupils the size of saucers, gripping the back of our chair and grinning like the Cheshire Cat.

"Time to play, lover boy. We gotta be done by dark so the cops don't get called again. Tuck your boner in and get your ass in gear." Trip ruffled Hans's hair and headed toward Steven's patio where Baker and Louis were already setting up.

I stuck out my bottom lip and looked back at Hans. "You can't go. We're stuck together forever."

Hans smiled, warmth shining out of his dilated denim-colored eyes. "Forever," he whispered against my lips.

"Forever." I beamed against his.

"Hansel Gretel Oppenheimer! Get your sexy ass over here!"

"I gotta go, baby."

"Wait. Can you even play on ecstasy?" I glanced around him at the spot where I knew he would stand, just to the right of Trip's microphone.

"Fuck yeah. It's amazing. I don't even have to think about it. I just play."

"Okay. I guess you can go." I pouted. "I'll miss you."

"I'll miss you more."

"Don't make me come over there, motherfucker!"

Hans stood up and set me down in the empty seat we'd been sharing by the bonfire. Steven had attempted to make a half-pipe in his backyard over the summer, but it hadn't gone well. Evidently, it takes more than just a shit-ton of plywood and some nails to successfully build a skateboard ramp. So after he'd busted his ass on it a few times, Steven had gotten pissed off, torn it down, and set it on fire.

Not super mature, but it was a great excuse for a party.

Goth Girl scooted her lawn chair over next to mine. "You two are so fucking cute," she deadpanned.

"You're so fucking cute," I said, tugging on one of her long Wednesday Addams braids.

Goth Girl rolled her eyes, but I could tell she wanted to smile.

"He's always that sweet, isn't he?" she asked, watching the guys setting up.

"Mmhmm," I hummed dreamily. "Always."

"Oh my God, is this the first time you guys have rolled together?"

"Mmhmm," I hummed again, smiling at my lover from across the lawn.

"You're so fucking lucky," Goth Girl lamented, resting her head on my shoulder. I could feel her teeth grinding against my bony joint. "Steven's such an asshole. Sometimes ecstasy is the only thing that keeps me from cutting his dick off and throwing it out the car window."

I laughed, a little too hard, and rested my head on top of hers. It felt good to talk to her again. I think that was already the longest conversation we'd had since she started dating Steven.

"Where is he?" I asked. "You guys are usually all over each other."

"He's inside, making Maddie dinner."

"Maddie's here?" I sat up and looked at her.

"Yeah. Her whore mother dropped her off an hour ago with no warning."

"I've been out here for an hour?"

Goth Girl sat up and laughed—or came as close to it as her dry, apathetic personality would allow. "You've been out here for, like, two hours."

"Really? No wonder I have to pee so bad." I giggled.

"Go pee. And bring me a beer on your way back."

I nodded and planted a little kiss on her pale cheek. Then I stood up on two rubbery legs and stumbled toward the house. The band was tuning their instruments, so I mouthed to Hans that I was going to pee, hoping to be back before they started playing.

He cupped a hand to his ear and mouthed back, *What? I can't hear you.*

Then we grinned at each other like loons.

When I stepped into the kitchen through the back door, it was like falling from heaven into the pits of hell in an instant. Someone was crying. Someone was yelling. And something crashed against the wall next to my head.

A little girl with bright red curls was standing next to the kitchen table. Her arms were folded across her chest, and her sleeves and pant legs stopped a few inches higher than they were supposed to. "I wanna go home!"

"You *are* home!" Steven shouted back at her, slamming an empty beer bottle down on the kitchen counter. He swayed a little on his feet after the motion.

"I don't want you! I want Mommy!"

"Well, that's funny because your mommy didn't want—"

"Hey, Maddie!" I interrupted before I even knew what I was saying. "It's so nice to meet you! I love your room! Will you show it to me?"

Maddie and Steven both turned toward me, the hurt they'd inflicted on each other still fresh on their faces.

I walked slowly toward Maddie, as if she were a wild beast. "Will you show me which My Little Pony is your favorite?"

Maddie huffed and glared at her dad. "I don't even wike My Wittle Pony anymoh."

"Really?" I said, coming to stand between her and Steven. Crouching down so that I was on her level, I asked, "What are you into now?"

Maddie's golden-brown eyes shifted to mine. "SpumBob StwarePants," she said with every ounce of sass she possessed.

"Oh, I haven't seen that show yet. It's new, right?"

The back door opened behind me, letting in the first few bars of Phantom Limb's fast-paced thrash-metal opening song, "Death Rattle." Maddie watched her father leave, then returned her gaze to mine once the door slammed shut. Her eyes softened fractionally, and her shoulders seemed to relax a little.

"Yeah, it's new. It's so funny. SpumBob wivs in a pineapple undoh de sea."

"Really? That's awesome!" I put my hand on the floor to steady myself as the room began to tilt. My stomach lurched, and my mouth filled with saliva.

No, no, no. I can't puke. Not now. I need to eat. Eating will help.

"Maddie, sweetie, what did your daddy make you for dinner?"

"Leftovoh pasketti. I hate pasketti."

Yeah. I can tell from the way it's dripping down the wall.

I crawled over to the fridge and pulled it open. Condiments, Chinese food containers, expired milk, and at least seven cases of Miller Lite.

Awesome.

"I wike toast."

I turned and looked at Maddie, who was sucking on the end of her sleeve.

"Wif cheese on it."

"Girl, you have excellent taste."

After Maddie and I finished our gourmet cheese toast, Maddie stole all the paper out of Steven's printer so that we could draw pictures of "SpumBob StwarePants" for her room.

She sat on my lap so that she could reach the table better, and that whole love bubble/cocoon/shroud thing I'd been in with Hans sucked Maddie right up. I loved her. I loved her take-no-shit attitude and her adorable gap-toothed smile and her squishy little hands, still plump with baby fat. I wanted to ask Hans if we could take her home. No one would even know she wasn't mine, except for the fact that it was biologically impossible for me to have a six-year-old.

Details schmetails.

Just as I was putting the finishing touches on my pineapple sketch, I heard the front door open and close. A guy I'd never met before walked into the kitchen through the living room and squatted down next to Maddie.

"What's up, homegirl?" he asked, holding up his fist.

"Uncle Jason!" Maddie squealed and smashed her tiny, little balled-up hand against his.

The dude had an interesting vibe. I was so high, I could practically see people's auras, and his read *relaxed, smart, cool, outsider.* He had a nice smile, and if it weren't for that frat-boy haircut and wardrobe, I totally would have thought he was cute.

I can only imagine what I looked like to him. I'm sure my aura was blinking yellow like a caution sign, screaming, *Ninety-eight-pound crackhead who is clearly fucked up and should not be supervising a goldfish, let alone a six-year-old child.*

Mr. Crew Cut extended his right hand to me with a smile. "Hey. I'm Jason."

He even shakes hands? Who shakes hands?

"So I heard." I smiled back, accepting his hand with my much clammier one. "I'm BB."

He was polite enough not to recoil like most people did when they felt how cold my hands were. He also didn't make a big deal about my pupils being the size of quarters.

I decided I liked him.

"Are you Steven's brother?" I asked, narrowing my eyes but still not seeing the resemblance.

"No." Jason glanced between us at Maddie. She was humming the *SpongeBob SquarePants* theme song to herself while furiously coloring in my pineapple sketch. Lowering his voice, he said, "I'm his dealer," with a wink.

I burst out laughing. "And she calls you Uncle Jason? No offense, but that's fucked up." I immediately clapped my hands over my mouth and looked down at Maddie to make sure she hadn't been listening. "Messed up."

Jason laughed. "I'm here a lot. Maddie and I usually bro out for a few minutes whenever I stop by, don't we, Mads?"

Maddie nodded as she concentrated on staying in the lines, her little pink tongue poking out the side of her mouth.

"Are you sure you're a dealer? You look more like"—I tilted my head to the side in contemplation, then pointed my marker at him—"a stockbroker."

Jason laughed, showing off those pretty teeth again. "Ouch." He held both hands over his heart.

"Not in a bad way!" I backpedaled, holding my hands up in apology.

Jason stood up and walked over to the fridge to help himself to a beer. "It's cool. I do corporate web design and IT support during the day. I want to start my own company in the next few years, so I'm just doing this to help raise enough capital for all the start-up costs."

"Kind of like how I'm gonna be a stripper in a few years when I have to pay for grad school."

Jason snorted as he took his first sip of Miller Light. "You're cool." Tipping the neck of his bottle at me, he asked, "So, how's that roll treating you?"

Shit. He can tell that I'm rolling. Am I that obvious?

"Ugh...great."

"Good. That's one of mine. Evidently, they were pretty popular tonight because Steven called me to come replenish his inventory." Jason pulled a ziplock baggie out of his khaki pants pocket and shook the little white tablets inside.

"Do you make those?"

"Nah, I just sell 'em," he said, tucking the bag back into his pocket, "but I want to make sure they're good, you know. I like to keep my customers happy."

"Well, I feel pretty damn—I mean, *darn* happy." I turned

to look at Maddie but found her sound asleep with her head on the table. The sun was almost down outside, which meant that it was probably around nine o'clock. I turned back to Jason and laughed. "I think we bored her to death."

"You need some help with that?" he asked, gesturing toward the unconscious child on my lap.

"Nah, I got her." I wrapped my arms under Maddie's armpits and scooted my chair out, but that only caused her head to fall forward once we cleared the table.

Jason chuckled and came over. Setting his beer down, he picked Maddie up like she weighed nothing and carried her into her room.

I turned on the small lamp next to her bed and began unlacing her too-tight shoes.

"Why don't you ever come to any of Steven's parties?" I asked, wriggling off one beat-up, old sneaker.

"Oh, that's 'cause I ran out of black lipstick and nail polish. And, also, because I don't want to."

I laughed as I pulled her other stinky shoe off. "Yeah, it's not exactly my scene either, but Goth Gir—Victoria . . . is my friend, and my boyfriend's in the band, so . . . here I am."

I unzipped Maddie's stained pink hoodie and managed to get it off of her without dislocating one of her shoulders. *I hoped*. Tossing her My Little Pony comforter over her, I smiled, remembering waking up under that same comforter with Hans. It was crazy to think that that was only two months ago. I felt like I'd known him my whole life. And maybe a few other lifetimes before this one. I couldn't wait to get back outside, climb back onto his lap, and cuddle and kiss and whisper sweet nothings until our bodies disintegrated, and we got new ones all over again.

With my aura now a rosy shade of pink, I turned off Maddie's lamp and stumbled directly into the footboard of her bed.

"Fuuuck!" I shouted, grabbing my knee in the dark.

Jason stood in the doorway, laughing at me, as I hopped around, rubbing the fresh bruise.

"Fuck you," I spat through my clenched teeth, limping past him and into the hallway. "Your evil drugs did this to me."

"I'll report your complaint to the customer service department." He chuckled, grabbing me by the arm to help stabilize me.

I'd never had a brother—or a sister, for that matter—but in that moment, I kind of felt like I had both. All I'd wanted to do was to come inside and pee, but somehow, I'd ended up bonding with two complete strangers in the most amazing way.

Just before we went outside, Jason pulled an elegant-looking card out of his wallet and handed it to me. "Hey, I have people over every Sunday to watch football and *The Sopranos*. It's usually an all-day thing. You and your boyfriend should come."

I took the business card and studied it. *Jason Priest, Information Technology Specialist, 770-555-8730.* Slate gray with embossed white font. Very nice.

Looking up at him with my other hand poised on the door handle, I said, "One question: do we have to wear khakis to this shindig?"

Jason smiled. "No. Chinos are also acceptable."

Stepping from the house to the yard was like going from heaven to hell all over again; only this time, hell was outside, in the form of fire. The band had finished playing, the sun had completely set, and everyone was engaged in some kind of fire play. The bonfire was now at least ten feet tall, licking at the dried leaves on the early-autumn trees. A few people were twirling flaming sticks like batons, and Steven was standing—barefoot—at one end of an eight-foot-long bed of hot coals.

"Fuck yeah!"

"You got this, man!"

"Do that shit!"

"Go! Go! Go! Go!"

Steven had a cheering section that consisted of most of the Phantom Limb guys, at least a dozen black-lipstick-wearing regulars whose names I'd never bothered to learn, and Goth Girl, who was also barefoot and raring to go.

Before I could go get the garden hose, Steven howled at the moon like a werewolf and took off. I grabbed Jason's arm and watched in horror as Steven's feet lifted and sank, one after the other, into the glowing orange coals. I readied myself to run back into the house and call 911 as soon as it was over, but much to my surprise, Steven seemed okay. He kind of danced around and rubbed his feet in the grass, but he still had feet, and he wasn't screaming, so that was good.

Everyone else was screaming though. Holy shit. Walking over hot coals was a real crowd pleaser.

Especially when the entire crowd was high on ecstasy.

I let go of Jason's arm and clasped my hands over my mouth. "Did you just see that shit?"

Jason looked at me with wide eyes. "I'm doing it."

"No! What?"

Jason chugged the rest of his beer, kicked off his loafers and socks right there on the patio, and sprinted over to get in line.

Fucking men. Always trying to prove how big their balls are.

Speaking of men, there was one in the crowd who I knew

for a fact didn't have shit to prove to anybody. When you're the tallest, most beautiful male at the party and your nickname literally refers to the size of your massive cock, you get to take an automatic pass in the pissing contests.

I scanned the crowd gathering around the hot coals, looking for a handsome dark head sticking up above the rest, but I didn't see him. I glanced over at the two flaming baton twirlers. Nope. No Hans.

Then, I found him. He was sitting in a lawn chair, our lawn chair, but he wasn't alone. A girl with frizzy brown hair was standing in front of him, excitedly moving her arms in an attempt to regain his attention. But Hans was nothing if not distractible, and at that moment, his entire focus was on me.

Warmth radiated from my chest throughout my extremities as I drank in the sight of him. Hans was almost a shadow with his faded black jeans, black Converse, black Phantom Limb hoodie—which I couldn't wait to steal—and wild black hair, but his aura was red, red, red.

Like his bass, I thought as I crossed the yard. *Like the roses he's always surprising me with. Red like his heart.*

Once I got closer, I realized that Hans's aura wasn't red for romance at all.

It was red for rage.

It radiated off of him with every heave of his chest, mirroring the flames rising from the wreckage behind him. As I approached, my pace slowed. My senses went on high alert. What had I missed? What was wrong? I hated that my brain wasn't operating at full capacity. I wished Jason had a pill in his pocket that would make me sober again so that I could assess the situation better.

"Hey, baby. You okay?" I asked, my eyes flicking back and forth between Hans and the girl with the unfortunate hair.

Was she upsetting him? She looked as confused as I was, her black lips pulled down into a frown, so I didn't think so.

Hans was backlit by the bonfire, but there was enough ambient light coming from the house for me to see the outline of his jaw flexing as he ground his back teeth together.

"You missed it," he spat.

"Missed what?"

Hans stood up abruptly, causing the collapsible aluminum chair he'd been sitting in to fall over backward, and jerked a hand in the direction of the patio. "The whole fucking show."

My heart seized in my chest as the weight of Hans's words sank in.

He was mad *because of me.*

The frizzy-haired girl graciously tiptoed away as I struggled to breathe. It had never even occurred to me that Hans was waiting for me. The thought of him spending his entire performance searching the audience for me made me nauseous.

"Hans..."

"You didn't come outside for one fucking song." The hurt broke through the anger, causing his voice to shudder at the end.

"I'm *so* sorry. I was taking care of Maddie. When I went inside—"

"Maddie? *That's* who you were inside with? Because I saw who you *came out* with, and it definitely wasn't a six-year-old girl."

My head was spinning. There were so many thoughts flying around in my scattered brain, but I couldn't reach out and grab just one. I'd grab like four and drop them all before one could

even make it out of my mouth. "Hans, please...it's not like...
Maddie was...I wasn't..."

"Who is he?" Hans asked, glaring at me in the dark.

"Who?"

"Whoever the fuck you were hanging all over when you came
outside." Hans gestured toward the patio again.

I closed my eyes to block out the look on Hans's face. I never
wanted to see it again. The accusation. The anger. Hans and I
were joined, had been since before we met, and the drugs only
intensified that bond. If he was happy, I was euphoric. If he was
in pain, I was in agony.

I couldn't think out there with the blazing inferno and fire
walkers and fire twirlers and two dozen screaming goth kids
all vying for my attention in the background. I put my hands
over my ears, kept my eyes shut tight, and shook my head in
frustration. I focused on the words swirling around in my head
and spat them out before something had the chance to distract
me again. "I'm sorry! I'm fucked up, okay? I was taking care of
Maddie, and I didn't think you would miss me with all these
people here. Jason is just a friend. He invited us to watch *The
Sopranos*. He said we have to wear khakis or chinos. I don't even
know what chinos are! And now you're mad at me and people
are walking on hot coals and I don't know what the fuck happened, but I just want us to be happy again."

I could hear Hans talking, but I couldn't make out what he
was saying with my ears covered and the extreme noise in the
background. I felt his fingers, rough yet gentle, wrap around my
wrists and slowly pull my hands away from my head. I opened
my eyes, reluctantly, as the screaming and cheering and music

and laughter and snap, crackle, pop of the fire came flooding back in. Hans was crouched down in front of me, pupils like inky-black oceans, awash in regret.

"Stop it. I'm sorry, okay? I just…freaked out. As soon as you left…this horrible feeling came over me. Like dread. I felt like everyone was laughing at me while I was playing. And I couldn't find you. And then I worried that something had happened to you, but I couldn't get to you because I was stuck out there, playing music for people I don't even fucking like. People who were laughing at me. And I got so fucking pissed off, I wanted to bash all their faces in with my bass."

I wrapped my arms around Hans's neck and burst out laughing.

"What?" he snapped.

"You wanted to bash their faces in?"

"God, yes. I just got so fucking paranoid and pissed off."

"Your brain is on backward!" I giggled. "You drink coffee to calm down, you focus *better* when you're high, and you're the only person I know who hates everyone after taking ecstasy!"

Hans grinned and pressed his forehead against mine. "I don't hate *you*."

Something shifted in the atmosphere around us. Molecules quickened. Particles merged.

"You don't?" I cooed.

Hans shook his head slowly from side to side, causing mine to turn with it. "I worship you."

My body melted and slid to the ground, leaving Hans with nothing but my soul to hold on to.

My soul and my lips.

I kissed away the darkness. The doubts and the fears. I kissed Hans until I couldn't tell where he ended and I began. I kissed him until I felt the corners of his mouth curl up in joy. And once I knew I had him back, I took him by the hand and led him to bed.

18

"Shit," I whispered, closing the door to Maddie's room as quietly as I could in my fucked-up condition. "We don't have anywhere to sleep."

Hans pulled me back into his arms. "We have a whole house on the lake we can sleep in."

"Can you drive?" I knew I couldn't. I could barely find my next thought, let alone my way home in the dark.

"I think so."

Good enough for me.

Hans and I left without saying goodbye and drove away with our hands clasped over the stick shift. It felt so nice in the car. Calm. Cozy. It smelled like leather and menthol cigarettes. The heater warmed my bones. The dashboard lights were a soothing blue. Not bright and flashing like the ones on the police cruiser, fire truck, and ambulance that flew past us as we neared the entrance of Steven's neighborhood.

I vaguely wondered if they were going to Steven's house, but the thought drifted away as the first notes of Jimmy Eat World came swirling from Hans's speakers. The BMW's engine

was so quiet, the ride so smooth, that I felt like we were floating over the road. Hans seemed to drive better fucked up than
sober, just one more way that his brain worked in reverse, and
I smiled, thinking about what a unique, magical snowflake he
was. Even his packaging was reversed—dark and hard, manly,
intimidating—the complete opposite of the soul housed inside.

When I looked out my window and saw acres of water instead
of the usual wall of hundred-foot-tall pine trees, I knew we were
almost home. To get to the Oppenheimers' estate, you had to
drive across the lake, over the top of a hydroelectric dam. That
stretch of road always made me nervous because the only thing
separating the cars from the lake was a few feet of grass, a simple
guardrail, and a sheer drop-off to certain death. So naturally,
Hans chose that exact spot to stop and admire the view.

When he slowed down and pulled onto the grassy shoulder, I
panicked, thinking we must have gotten a flat tire or something,
but Hans didn't seem worried or upset. Instead of calling a tow
truck or busting out a tire iron, he rolled down all four windows
and cranked the stereo up.

"C'mere." He grinned, squeezing my thigh before hopping
out of the car.

I followed him without question, drawn to the pulsing glow
surrounding his body. Hans's energy field wasn't red, red, red
anymore. It was pink, pink, pink. I wanted to touch it. To swirl
my fingers through it to see if it would dissipate like steam or
flicker like a hologram.

Hans stepped over the metal guardrail, causing my breath to
hitch, then turned and held his hands out to help me over. I forgot my fear when I reached out to grasp his glowing hands and
perceived a faint pink light surrounding my own.

We matched.

"Listen," Hans said as I sat beside him on the guardrail. He wrapped his arm around my shoulders and planted a kiss on my disheveled blonde head as the next song on his Jimmy Eat World CD began to play.

Hans had told me to listen, but I was too busy admiring the view to hear anything. The surface of the lake looked as if someone had taken the night sky and spread it out like a picnic blanket before us. A million crystalline points of light billowed and swayed below us while a million more floated overhead, just out of reach.

"Did you hear that?" he asked. "The first star you see might not be." I blinked at him in confusion, then realized he was quoting a line from the song. "What do you think it means?"

I loved Hans's random deep questions. There was an intimacy to them.

What's in your brain? Can I see it? Will you show me yours if I show you mine?

"I don't know," I said, lacing our fingers together and watching the pink glow intensify everywhere that our skin touched. "But he's right. Usually, the first star I see is actually a satellite or a planet or an airplane. Tonight, I didn't really notice the stars until I saw them reflected on the water, so I guess those stars aren't really stars either." I gazed at the glittery black expanse before us and breathed it in. "It looks like two skies, doesn't it?"

Hans nodded, rubbing his thumb over mine. I smiled, remembering how, just a few short months ago, that simple gesture had made my heart skip and my knees go weak.

"I know what it means," Hans said, looking down at me with eyes as black as the lake below. "*You're* the first star I see. Before anything in the sky, I see you."

I could barely make out the features of his face, but I kissed the first one that came into view. I think it was his chin. Then another. His nose? "I'm pretty sure you're the star in this relationship, *LDH*," I teased, finally kissing his lips.

"You're wrong," he murmured against my mouth, sliding his tongue along the top edge of my bottom lip. "You're so fucking wrong."

The insides of my eyelids glowed hot pink as I accepted Hans's kiss. Felt it light me up from the inside out, making my bones hum like neon tubes.

I stood up, ignoring the precipice behind me, the black mirror below that would swallow me whole with one wrong step, and climbed onto the lap of my beautiful, backward boy.

I trusted him to hold on to me, and he trusted me not to let go.

I kissed Hans slowly, deeply, like I had nowhere to be and forever to get there. But he wasn't as patient. Hans kept one arm locked around my waist but let his other hand roam. He unzipped my hoodie—covered in the patches of punk rock bands that I no longer listened to—and slid the threadbare cotton off my shoulders. I slipped my arms out of the sleeves, one at a time, and gasped as a gust of wind caught it like a boat sail and carried it away. Poof. My old life, my high school identity, my facade…into the abyss.

I didn't mourn it for a moment.

I shivered as the cool night air whipped across my freckled skin, but Hans's breath was soon there to chase the chill away. As he marked each brown imperfection with a kiss, his hand continued to travel. He slipped his fingers underneath the straps of my bra and tank top and pulled them down, first over my left shoulder, then over my right. I tilted my head back as he kissed his way across my collarbone. My eyes naturally landed on the brightest speck in the sky, and I smiled when I realized it was moving.

"The first star you see might not be."

My bra slid down to my waist under its own weight, and my nipples hardened instantly against my thin white tank top. Hans's one roaming hand took advantage, palming me over the fabric, as my hips gave up the fight and began to grind against him in slow circles.

"Listen," he said again, returning his free hand to my back.

He used both arms to support my weight as he leaned me backward and kissed his way down my breastbone. I tensed, squeezing my eyes shut and fisting his hoodie, but when I felt Hans's warm, wet mouth close around my cotton-covered nipple, my body surrendered. I opened my eyes, stared at a satellite, and listened as Jim Adkins sang about taking a night drive and making love in the moonlight.

It felt as if the entire universe had conspired to make that moment happen. The sky had shooed away the clouds and thrown a little extra sparkle on the stars to lure Hans off the road. Jimmy Eat World had whispered in our ears to go for it. And the gods had stopped all traffic on the dam just long enough for Hans and me to follow orders.

I stood and locked eyes with my twin soul as we reached for each other's belt buckles at the same time. Our movements were in perfect concert with one another, as if the music were the puppet master and the stars on the water below were our audience. I leaned forward and kissed him, our tongues possessed by slippery synchronicity as we unzipped each other's jeans.

I shimmied mine down below my ass just as Hans reached into his and freed himself. Without breaking our kiss, I turned my body toward the mirrored sky and gasped as Hans spread my cheeks with both hands and guided me to sit all the way down on his lap, filling me inch by euphoric inch.

Once Hans and I were finally joined in the one remaining way we knew how, he wrapped his strong, warm, sweatshirt-covered arms around my waist, rested his chin on my shoulder, and sighed. The breeze cooled the damp spots on my tank top where his mouth had been, causing my nipples to strain against the thin fabric. I rolled my hips, moaning in response to the friction inside. The roar of the wind and the water caught my cries and whisked them away.

No need to be quiet out here, they said.

I rolled my hips more, feeling bolder, and slid my hands down to grip Hans's knees.

"Mmm," I hummed, feeling the vibration everywhere.

"Fuck," Hans growled as his hips began to thrust.

"Mmmmmm," I hummed louder, turning my head to capture his beautiful face in another kiss.

Hans sucked my tongue as he thrust into me harder.

I whimpered, as loud as I wanted, and ground against him between every advance.

"God, I fucking love you," Hans groaned, sliding one hand down my stomach to cup my sex.

"I love you too," I cooed, sliding my left hand up to cup the back of his head. "So much."

With those words, I felt Hans swell and stiffen inside of me. My eyes slammed shut, and my heart soared as he tightened his grip around my waist, plunged himself into me from underneath, and pressed his firm fingertips against my clit. We came together and apart and together again in a hot-pink explosion so bright, it probably could have been seen from space. Our molecules mixed in the air, and when they fell back down to earth, Hans and I were forever changed.

Changed but not for the better.

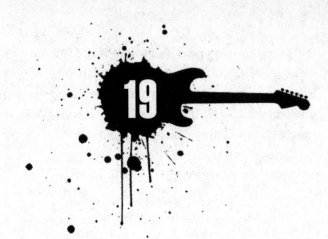

When grown-ups told you to stay away from drugs, when they lectured you on all the ways that they'd ruin your life, they were right, of course. But what they didn't tell you was *how* they'd ruin your life. You assumed they meant that you'd lose your job and borrow money from loan sharks and contract hepatitis and maybe do a little jail time for prostitution or possession. But the reality was that they'd ruin your life in much, much subtler ways. They'd steal your joy. Because, once you'd experienced reckless, vulnerable, soul-baring teenage love amplified to the *nth* degree by ecstasy, the rest of your life would pale in the shadow of that experience. Your happiest moments would never be as euphoric, and your darkest days would feel even darker when compared to that artificial high.

The day after our night of bliss on Buford Dam, Hans was quiet. Lethargic. Preoccupied. I asked him what was wrong, but he just said he had "the blue Mondays."

When I asked what that meant, he explained in a clipped, annoyed tone, "It's when you feel like shit the day after doing ecstasy because you blew out all your serotonin the night before, and there's nothing left."

Okay. That made sense. Coming down from an experience like that had to take its toll. I felt pretty tired and *blah* myself.

But Hans's mood didn't improve.

He was still asleep when I left for school on Monday. Still quiet when I came home from work that night. And he barely touched the spaghetti I made for dinner on Tuesday. As I preserved his plate with plastic wrap and stuck it in the fridge next to the one from the night before, I began to worry that the drugs had done permanent damage. I felt better, so why didn't he?

I got my answer when I began sorting through the mail Hans had left on the counter. I pulled out all the utility bills and set them aside, making a mental note to pay them ASAP since it was almost the end of the month.

Almost the end of the month.

As Hans sat on the back deck, smoking and solemnly staring at the lake, I rushed over to the pantry and threw open the door. There, on the other side, written elegantly on Mrs. Oppenheimer's cat calendar, were the words *HOME FROM TRIP* on Friday, October 1.

We only had two days left.

And Hans knew it.

20

October 1, 1999

When I awoke in Mr. and Mrs. Oppenheimer's plush California-king for the last time, I smacked the alarm clock and rolled over to find Hans's side of the bed already empty. I opened my eyes, expecting the space to be dark, like it usually was at six thirty in the morning, but noticed that a small reading lamp had been turned on in the corner of the room. It illuminated the over-stuffed armchair next to it where a tall, troubled, tattooed man was chewing the fingernails on his left hand down to the quick while scribbling frantically in a small notebook with his right.

"Baby?"

Hans kept writing for a few more seconds, then lifted his head.

His eyes were bloodshot. Puffy. Miserable.

"Have you been up all night?"

Hans nodded once, then looked away. He wore his pain like a beautiful brass birdcage—on the outside for all to see but for no one to enter.

Not even me.

He closed his notebook and set it on the small table next to him, beside the lamp. The sun hadn't come up yet, but Hans stared out the window anyway.

"Hey. Come here," I pleaded, scooting over to his side of the bed and lifting the covers.

For a moment, I thought he wasn't going to budge, but with a heavy sigh, Hans eventually got up and came back to bed.

As he approached with the grace of an athlete, I noticed that Hans was wearing nothing but a pair of plain black boxer shorts. Not leopard print. Not banana print. Not four-leaf clovers. Just black. Like his mood.

And mine.

Hans slipped under the covers and pulled me against his chest. My thigh slid between his legs, my arms wrapped around his torso, and my cheek rested on Freddy Krueger's sneer. Hans stroked my upper arm with his left hand, giving me a glimpse of the new blue ink etched across the inside of his forearm.

Gripping his thick wrist, I gently pulled his arm away so that I could read the words he'd spilled while I was sleeping.

I was wrong. She cannot be contained.
She tricked me with her laugh and her falling ways.
I didn't know until it was over.
She's not a falling star. She's a supernova.

The last line blurred as my eyes welled with the reality of our situation. I'd found my Prince Charming, and he was even better than anything I could have imagined. He loved me with every cell in his body, with every ounce of his soul, and he didn't give a shit who knew it. But while we'd been busy dancing and admiring the stars, I'd lost track of time. The clock had struck midnight. My carriage had turned into a pumpkin, and my gown had reverted to rags.

I wasn't Hans's princess. Not anymore. I was just a poor girl from the wrong side of town, and my night of pretend play was over.

I pulled his forearm to my lips and kissed the words written there, careful not to blink an errant tear onto them while I tried to come up with something comforting to say.

"It's not over," was the best I could do.

Hans took a deep, shuddering breath and held me tighter.

"Hey"—I craned my neck back, trying to get a glimpse of his face—"I'm not going anywhere."

I watched his Adam's apple bob as he swallowed.

"You're going home." It was the first thing he'd said to me all morning.

"You're my home." The words came immediately, and I was shocked to discover that they were true. My parents' house no longer felt like home. My old room was as foreign to me as a motel suite. The things I'd left behind, relics from another life. Right there, in Hans's arms—that was where I belonged.

"As soon as I turn eighteen, we can get an apartment together. That's only . . . eight months from now. Then we can wake up next to each other every day for the rest of our lives. It's not that long."

"I don't want to wait," Hans grumbled into my hair. "I don't want to fucking miss you. I don't want to go back to living separate lives. This is the life I want. This one, right here, with you. Nothing has ever been more perfect, and I feel like I'm losing it. All of it. I feel like I'm losing you."

"Hans…"

"I'm gonna see you, what, like, two hours a day? After work and on the weekends?"

"Not if you come to school with me." The solution fell out of my mouth before I'd even given it conscious thought.

"What?" Hans pulled away so that he could make eye contact with me.

"It's perfect!" I beamed, gripping his shoulder. "Come to GSU with me. We could see each other before school and between classes, and we could even go to Underground Atlanta every day for lunch."

Hans blinked.

"Please?" I begged. "I'll fill out your admission paperwork and everything."

"I don't know, baby." Hans's dark eyebrows bunched in the middle as he shook his head. "I hated school. And with my ADD—"

"You don't have attention problems when you play music, right?"

"Riiight…"

"So, go to school for music. I can help you with the other classes."

Hans narrowed his tired eyes at me and chewed on the inside of his lip. "Do they have a music production program? I do kind of want to learn more about recording."

"I know they do," I lied. I had no fucking idea.

"Okay."

"Okay?"

Hans smiled. It was a worried, unsure, tiny little smile, but there was hope behind his sleepless eyes. Just a glimmer. "Okay."

I squealed and squeezed the shit out of his shoulder. "I love you!"

Hans pulled me against his chest and rolled back and forth with his arms wrapped around me. "I *must* fucking love you to be considering going back to school."

"Hey, do you want to come with me today?" I asked, holding on for dear life. "You could probably sit in my classes with me, and nobody would care."

"No, you need to focus," Hans said, ironically choosing that exact moment to get distracted by my lack of panties. He gripped my bare ass under the oversize Phantom Limb T-shirt I'd slept in and positioned me so that I was straddling the rapidly swelling bulge in his boxer shorts.

"What are you gonna do today?" I asked in a breathy voice as he lifted his hips slightly and captured my earlobe between his teeth.

Releasing it, he murmured, "I'm gonna call the guys and see if we can get together and work on this song."

"Your ballad?" I whimpered as his hips rolled against me again.

Hans nodded, and I felt him smile against my cheek. "I think it's done."

21

"I thought most places had, like, a green room or a dress-ing room or a fucking couch for the bands to hang out on." I cracked open my bottle of Coke and poured half of it onto the gravel loading area behind the Masquerade.

"Well, this isn't most places, princess." Trip winked and tipped his bottle of Korbel in my direction.

Baker snorted in agreement and handed me the fifth of whis-key I'd asked him to buy. I smiled at the round face peeking out from behind that curtain of dirty-blond hair, but my smile fell as soon as I realized that he'd gotten me Southern Comfort.

SoCo.

Knight's fucking brand.

I could almost hear the sound of his latex gloves snapping into place as he readied his piercing needle. I could practically smell the antiseptic and taste the sweetly astringent shot of "*SoCo*" he'd given me to dull the pain. Over and over, I'd bared myself to him, and each and every time, I'd come away scarred.

Some were just deeper than others.

I quietly snapped the fingers on my free hand, shook the

unwelcome memories from my consciousness, and filled my Coke bottle the rest of the way up with whiskey. So. Much. Whiskey. I squealed when it began to bubble over and immediately wrapped my mouth around the entire opening of the bottle to keep from losing any of the precious alcohol-caffeine mixture.

"Yeah, girl. Take it all," Trip teased, humping the air.

Hans slid the bottle out of my hand and tipped it back, swallowing the caramel-colored liquid like it was sugar water as Trip congratulated him on his girlfriend's deep-throating skills. Hans managed to both smirk and flip him off mid-chug.

I pulled the Coke bottle out of my mouth with a slurp-cough combo that was anything but dignified, then laughed in embarrassment.

"Dude. I heard a scout from Violent Violet Records might be coming out tonight," Louis said, sitting on the hood of the van, twirling a drum stick in one hand and pinching a freshly lit joint in the other.

"No fucking way." Trip belched from the champagne. "That's Love Like Winter's label."

"He probably won't come. They say that shit all the time." Hans tucked a finger into the waistband of my pleather pants and pulled me into his side.

It had only been a week since I moved back into my parents' house, and the distance hadn't been easy on either of us. I'd seen Hans every night that week, called him on my lunch break at school and again on my smoke break at work, but I still missed the shit out of him.

I couldn't wait for him to start coming to school with me. I did my best to make Hansel David Oppenheimer sound like a goddamn musical savant on his GSU application, but even if he got in, he wouldn't start taking classes until January. Until then, all we could do was try to comfort each other and wait it out.

And drink. We could fucking drink.

By the time the guys got the green light to start setting up, our bottles were empty, our laughter was loud, and our auras were a fizzy caramel brown.

"Break a leg." I hiccupped into Hans's ear with a kiss as I left him backstage and wandered out into the sea of rock fans beyond. I wriggled my way to the front of the stage, grateful for the crush of people who were helping me stay upright.

Triple X sauntered out first, grabbed the microphone like a lover, and screamed, "What's up, Atlantaaaaa?" into it.

The crowd replied with a shit-ton of noise while the rest of the band quietly took their places.

Trip was fired up, even more so than usual, but my eyes were glued to Hans. Other than a few stolen glances and tiny smirks cast my way, he hardly looked up at all. He really had no idea how beautiful he was. Hans didn't see every girl in the audience—and probably some of the guys—staring at him the way I did. He was completely absorbed in the music. Just like he had been the first time I laid eyes on him—eyes closed, head down, playing in Steven's living room for no one but himself.

They started off with a bang, playing their heaviest shit first, which got the mosh pit going, then they brought it down a notch to give people a rest before playing their more danceable, alternative stuff right before the kiss contest. It was their best show yet. Absolutely perfect. So perfect that my drunk ass bounced up and down until my stomach felt like an acidic, carbonated volcano of SoCo and bile.

The lights were suddenly too bright. The air, too thick. The room, too spinny. My mouth pooled with saliva, and the edges of my vision got fuzzy. I didn't want to miss the kiss contest—I'd worn my cut-off Phantom Limb T-shirt in preparation—but I'd felt that way enough times to know that I had about sixty seconds to sit the fuck down and get some fresh air before I either puked or passed out.

I pushed my way out of the crowd and made a mad dash for the fire escape. As soon as the cool October air hit my face and the screaming fans were quieted behind the heavy steel door, the nausea and tunnel vision began to subside. Thankful that I hadn't just barfed in front of my boyfriend and about five hundred other people, I sat on the steps high above the loading dock and dug a cigarette out of my purse.

I noticed all of our empty bottles stacked in a cute little row on the half-wall below—champagne, Coca-Cola, Southern Comfort, Miller High Life, and Jägermeister. Poor Baker. We had all asked for something different. I smiled, picturing him pushing a little shopping cart through the aisles of the liquor store, cursing our names as he fulfilled our wishes.

But he hadn't fulfilled my wish. Not really. I'd asked for Jack and Coke. So, why was there a bottle of Southern Comfort staring at me?

It wasn't like Knight had personally switched the bottles in Baker's cart, but the simple coincidence still gave me the creeps. I never saw him, never heard from him, but I *felt* him. I felt his zombie eyes watching when I walked to my car after work. I smelled his cinnamony cologne on the breeze during my smoke breaks. And whenever I saw a number on my caller ID that I didn't recognize, I always let it go to voicemail on the off chance that it might be him.

I didn't feel like I was being stalked. I felt like I was being haunted.

My deep, drunk thoughts evaporated the moment I registered the unmistakable beat of the cancan song vibrating through the wall.

Fuck!

I stood up and yanked on the door handle, but it didn't budge. In a panic, I rattled the handle and banged on the metal surface, but nobody was going to hear me. Shifting to plan B, I scurried down the fire-escape stairs, ran around the side of the building, and flew through the main entrance, flashing my orange paper wristband at every security guy along the way. I ascended the industrial metal staircase in the center of the converted old factory as fast as my spindly legs would carry me and up through Purgatory to the top floor where I was prepared to leap onto that stage and secure my title as the ass-flashing, high-kick champion of the world.

But, instead, I stood frozen in Heaven's doorway as my whole world came crashing down around me.

The cancan song was over.

The contest had been decided.

And all I could see was red, red, red.

Hans's red bass hanging upside down on his back.

Glossy red fingernails gripping his shoulders.

And glossy red lipstick smeared on the side of his mouth when Little Red Riding Ho finally pulled away.

I stumbled backward, as if I'd just taken a sucker punch to

the gut. I couldn't breathe. My eyes stung. My knees buckled. And the vomit I'd just successfully tamed shot back up into my throat with a vengeance.

I wanted to scream. I wanted to cry. I wanted to take one of my steel-toed combat boots off and bludgeon her pretty little face in with it, but my limbs were moving of their own accord. My right hand clamped over my mouth while my legs turned and sprinted back down the stairs.

Back down into Hell.

Where I fucking belonged.

As soon as the soles of my boots hit the cement floor below, I bolted past all the Day-Glo-painted ravers and welcomed the slap of the cold night air across my face.

But I didn't stop there. My feet kept pounding the pavement, carrying me away from there, up the poorly lit sidewalk to the street where my car was parked. Evidently, my body had decided it was time to go. My brain, on the other hand, was spinning out of control.

He kissed her! I can't believe he fucking kissed her!

Technically, she kissed him.

He kissed her back!

You don't know that.

He's a fucking guy, BB! He's drunk, he's onstage, she's super hot, AND his girlfriend had just left in the middle of his show. Of course he fucking kissed her back.

Oh my God. He totally kissed her back.

And even if he didn't *kiss her back, this is just gonna keep happening. Every show. Every kiss contest. You're fucked.*

The sound of my own voice was replaced with Goth Girl's as

her warning replayed over and over in my mind. *"He has a girl-friend. He's a flirty drunk."*

Great. Now I'm *the girlfriend. How did I get to be this fucking stupid?*

I breezed right past Old Willy as I rounded the corner, lost in my own spiraling thoughts. He jumped up and hobbled after me, but I hardly even noticed.

"Missy! Miss Missy! Don't go down there! That truck I's tel-lin' you about, it's ba—"

Old Willy's voice disappeared the moment I looked up and saw it. There, at the end of the block, parked on the curb with its lights off, was the Battle Ram Chariot itself. Satan's steed. The bearer of all things evil.

Knight's rusty white monster truck.

Adrenaline flooded my alcohol-stream. The sound of my own heartbeat pounded like Louis's kick drum in my ears. I knew I should run. My car was right fucking there. I could make it before he caught up to me. But on that particular night, my desire to scream at someone was even more powerful than my desire to stay alive.

So I stomped straight...fucking...over there.

Honestly, I had no idea what I thought was going to happen, but marching up to Knight's truck to find it completely empty was not it. I circled the entire vehicle with my senses on high alert, just waiting for the big, bad wolf to jump out and try to eat me.

I knew he was watching me. I could feel it. The idea of him snickering as I stood on my tiptoes to peek into the window of his truck made me even more livid.

I tipped my head back and yelled into the overgrown tree limbs stretching out over the dimly lit street. "Where the fuck are you? I know you're here!"

Standing behind his truck, where I'd started, I swung my head from left to right, peering into the shadows surrounding every dilapidated bungalow and crumbling Craftsman on the block, until a tiny orange ember caught my eye. A faint stream of smoke trailed up and away from it, carrying with it my courage the moment my gaze landed on the pair of ice-blue eyes glowing behind it.

Zombie eyes.

Knight was standing on the tilted porch of the tiny house his truck was parked in front of. The lights were off and looked like they had been for years. The windows were boarded up. The roof was sagging. And there was a tattered white piece of paper affixed to the splintered front door.

"Your boyfriend let you walk back here by yourself?"

Knight's voice sounded exactly the way I remembered it. Clear. Deep. Simmering with rage. Begging for an excuse to boil over into madness.

I could relate.

"That's none of your fucking business!" I yelled.

"You will always be my fucking business, Punk." Knight pointed the lit end of his cigarette in my direction. "Always!"

"No! You lost the right to give a shit about me the moment you told me you were going back to Iraq. Which, as we can clearly see, was complete bull—"

Before I could finish my accusation, Knight leaped off the porch. He stomped toward me in his military-issued combat boots and camouflage pants, fallen autumn leaves crunching violently under every footfall. I held my breath and froze like a fawn as Knight stepped out of the shadows and into the street.

Wrapping a thick, hard hand around my mouth and jaw, Knight pointed the end of his lit cigarette at my face and hissed, "You don't get to fucking tell me who I can and can't give a shit about." Knight sucked in a deep breath through his nose, causing his nostrils to flare. "You are *mine*. I don't know what it's gonna take to get that through your thick fucking skull, but you are the only person on this entire shithole of a planet that I care about. *That* makes you mine. You will never be my girlfriend again, but you will always be my fucking girl."

I narrowed my eyes at him and mumbled something into his palm. Knight removed his hand from my mouth and flicked his cigarette butt into the street.

Working my jaw for a second, I said, "If you care about me so goddamn much, why did you lie to me about going back to Iraq?"

"I never fucking lied to you." Knight gritted his teeth. His undead, ghost-colored eyes mere inches away from my mine. "I signed up for another tour of duty the second that ambulance took you away. I ship out next week. October through May, just like last time."

I stared back at him, steam billowing from my nostrils. "So, you've just been hanging out, shooting the shit, I dunno, *stalking me* for months while I was worried sick, thinking you were off in a war zone this whole time?"

Knight's stare softened. "You were worried?"

"Fuck you."

"Fuck me? *Fuck me?* Do you have any idea how hard it's been for me to stay away from you, Punk? Fuck, I can't!" Knight began pacing back and forth in front of me, rubbing his hands over his buzzed blond head. "I watch you leaving work. I watch you at the train station before school. I watch you walk to your car after your pussy-ass boyfriend's shows." He thrust a hand in the direction of my little black Mustang. "I watched them cut your lifeless body out of a car that *I* ran off the fucking road!"

"A car that I only climbed into because *Harley* put a gun to my head! You were trying to save me, dumbass!"

"And I'm trying to save you now—by staying the fuck away."

"You know what?" I took a step toward him and stood up a little straighter. The alcohol and anger and adrenaline weren't done with me yet. "You're right. You should stay the fuck away. Because I'm happier now than I ever was with you. I've found somebody who treats me like a fucking princess. He tells me I'm beautiful every day. He buys me flowers and writes me songs and doesn't put his fucking hands on me when I say something he doesn't like!" My volume grew. "Somebody who can touch me without making me bleed! Somebody who's not *fucked up* like you!"

The second those two words left my mouth, I clamped my hands over it, wishing to God that I could shove them back in. My protective bubble of anger popped, leaving me completely exposed. My eyes widened in horror while Knight's narrowed like a laser scope. My breathing ceased altogether while his nostrils flared and his muscular chest heaved under his tight black USMC T-shirt.

I shook my head as tears pricked my eyes. Not because I was afraid of him, although I was. I was petrified. But because I knew nothing was more hurtful to Ronald McKnight than those two little words. It wasn't his fault that he was fucked up.

I knew that. I knew every dark secret and unspeakable trauma that ate at his once-innocent soul. I knew that, in an alternate universe, Knight could have easily grown up to be just like Hans. A sensitive artist who poured himself into his craft and loved with every ounce of his soul.

But, unlike Hans, nobody had ever loved Knight back.

Not until me.

And now, I was calling him fucked up too.

I opened my hands enough to speak. "Knight…I…I'm so sorry. I didn't mean that. You know I—"

"Flowers?" he snapped, cutting me off. "You want fucking flowers, princess?"

Knight's wild eyes landed on something next to me, and he stomped back into the leaf-littered yard in front of the abandoned house. I watched in suspended terror as Knight stopped in front of an azalea bush by the front porch. It was dotted with dark-pink blossoms and looked as though it hadn't been trimmed in ages. Bending down and grasping the center of the shrub with both hands, Knight came unglued. He grunted and yanked and twisted and pulled the bush in bursts of superhuman power until the earth conceded the fight and released the damn thing, roots and all, into the clutches of a madman.

Turning, Knight's crazed gaze landed on me. Veins bulged in his neck and forehead and powerful arms, which were weeping blood from a dozen or so raised, red branch scratches. I thought about running as he stalked toward me. Pictured myself turning and sprinting toward my car. I begged my feet to cooperate, but it was no use.

All I could do was wince and wait for Knight to uproot me too.

Stepping back into the street, Knight threw the bush on the ground between us and spat on it. "There's your fucking flowers, *princess*. Happy now?"

Hot tears spilled from the corners of my eyes in unison. I was so scared and so sad. Sad that I'd hurt Knight. Sad that he was too fucked up to be fixed. Sad that every romantic gesture he attempted ended in bloodshed.

Sad that Hans had kissed somebody else.

Knight cocked his head to one side and studied my face. That predatory stare sent shivers down my spine. Only one of two things happened whenever Knight looked at someone sideways like that, and both were a form of attack.

"What's the matter, Punk?" Knight took a step toward me, kicking the bush to the side with his boot. "You don't look very *happy*."

I took a step backward and flinched when my lower back collided with his bumper.

"That *is* what you said, isn't it? That you're so much *happier* now?" Knight took another step in my direction, stopping right in front of me. Reaching out, he wrapped his hand around my mouth again, this time pushing the corners of it up into a forced grin. "Smile, Punk. Show me how *fucking* happy he makes you. I wanna see it."

More hot tears slid down my mortified face as I tried to slap Knight's hand away. "Fuck you!" I mumbled through my misshapen mouth, shoving his hard chest with both hands.

Knight shook his head from side to side. "*Tsk-tsk.* That's not very ladylike, *princess*."

"Stop calling me that!" I yelled, kicking him in the shin.

The asshole didn't even flinch.

"But you like being a little princess. You said it made you *happy*." Knight's grip on my mouth tightened, pushing the corners of my mouth up even higher.

I closed my eyes, causing more tears to spill down my cheeks, and whispered through my clenched teeth, "I hate you."

Knight leaned in and pressed his forehead against mine. He smelled like Southern Comfort and Camel Lights.

Just like me.

"Good," Knight whispered.

Without releasing my distorted smile, he slammed his mouth against the upturned seam of my lips.

I waited for the spark. The zap of electricity that coursed from my head to my feet like a lightning bolt seeking the earth whenever Knight's lips touched mine.

But it never came.

Instead, all I felt was humiliated. Violated. Weak.

No! I thought in my small voice inside my small head. *Let go of me! Stop!*

But Knight didn't stop. Instead, he loosened his grip on my phony smile just enough to deepen his kiss. His assault on my mouth. I wanted to bite his tongue off, but that was something a big girl would do.

And I wasn't big. Not anymore.

Knight had made me small.

I realized that he was right. I did belong to him. I was his favorite little doll. He could play with me, burn my hair, tear off my dress, and leave me out in the rain, but as soon as he wanted to play again, there I'd be, waiting in the same puddle of sorrow that he'd left me in.

I let him slide his hands up inside the shirt Hans had given me. I let him shove my bra up under my armpits and palm the nipples he'd impaled himself with steel barbells two years before. I let him do whatever he wanted with my body because I wasn't there anymore. In my mind, I was standing a safe distance away, imagining more satisfying scenarios than the one playing out on Mable Drive.

I pictured myself shoving Knight off of me. Kneeing him in the balls. Screaming at him for touching me when I wasn't his to touch. I fantasized about Hans showing up and rescuing me from my tormentor like the fairy-tale prince I imagined him to be. Maybe he would sneak up from behind and bash Knight in the head with a fallen tree branch. Or his bass! That would be so poetic. Or maybe he would just pull up in his BMW, I'd jump in, and we'd speed away, hand in hand.

I was so wrapped up in my inner world that I hardly noticed when Knight unzipped my pleather pants and shoved them down around my ankles. When his hands grabbed my ass and lifted me onto his back bumper. When he freed himself from his camo pants and rubbed the head of his cock against my slippery flesh. My traitorous body was wet for him, ready as always, but my mind was far, far away, my heart was in hiding, and my pride was in pieces on the ground.

When Knight pushed his way into me, I stared over his shoulder at my car. How different the night would have turned out if I had just left when I had the chance. I daydreamed about driving down the desolate back roads to my parents' house. How peaceful they were at this time of night. Nothing but twists and turns and tall, tall trees. I wondered what I would have listened to on my way home. The Cure maybe? Hole? No.

Jimmy Eat World.

Knight clutched me tighter and buried his face in my neck as the pace of his thrusts quickened. My legs dangled on either side of his, bound at the ankles. My hands gripped the edge of the rusty chrome bumper I was perched on, and black tears leaked in steady streams from my dead eyes. Knight could have my rag-doll body, but that was all he was going to get.

My heart belonged to someone else.

With a frustrated growl, Knight pulled out of me and shoved his brutal erection back into his pants. "Fuck!" He stomped away from me, rubbing his head and muttering before unleashing his rage on the azalea bush in the middle of the street. "Fuuuck!"

I watched Knight rip the shrub limb from limb as I slid off the bumper and pulled my pants and panties back up, unsure of what had just happened. What was happening.

A dark pink blossom landed at my feet as I shimmied my bra back into place. I stared at the beautiful, dying thing, and it stirred something in me. Reignited my anger. I wasn't capable of feeling anything for myself at that moment, but I felt rage for that flower. The injustice of it all. The unfairness. That flower was just a baby. It hadn't even had a chance to reach its full potential before Knight isolated it from its friends, intimidated it into submission, hurt it, scarred it, then cast it aside in the street when he was done with it.

Well, fuck that. This flower's not gonna die on my watch. This flower's about to get a whole new life, a better life, in a sunnier yard, with more room to grow. This bitch is gonna thrive because of what happened tonight. Aren't you, Mable? Come on, let's get you the fuck out of here.

I leaned over and scooped up the azalea blossom and my purse, which had fallen off my shoulder at some point during the altercation, and tucked the tiny, traumatized bud inside. Then, I did what I'd been wanting to do since the moment I saw those zombie eyes again. I turned and power-walked the fuck away.

"Punk," Knight called after me, dropping what was left of the mangled bush and falling in step beside me.

I didn't look at him. I didn't respond. I kept my eyes on the prize and marched straight toward my car.

"I'm sorry. Fuck! I didn't...you didn't say anything. Why the fuck did you just let me do that? Why didn't you tell me to stop?" His voice wavered and cracked, remorse leaking from the fissures.

"Would it have mattered?"

"Yes, it would have fucking mattered!" Knight screamed. "I'm not a fucking rapist!"

I nodded slightly, still staring straight ahead. "Okay."

One foot in front of the other, girl. You're almost there.

"BB, stop."

I kept going.

"BB, fucking look at me." His voice broke, and with it, so did my resolve.

Stopping beside my car, I turned to face him.

Tears shone like diamonds in the corners of his crystalline-blue eyes, but his jaw was clenched in anger. "I would never—"

"What?" I snapped, surprising myself. "You would never do anything to hurt me? Well, guess what? That's *all* you do, Knight. That's literally all you fucking do."

Knight nodded once. "I know." His deep voice was barely above a whisper. His features were sharp. Severe. "That's what I've been *fucking* telling you. That's why I've been trying to stay away from you. That's why I didn't fucking tell you when I'd be shipping out." Knight's volume rose steadily as he spat his words at me through bared teeth. But for once, his eyes didn't hold the same venom.

They held tears.

"And that's why I'm giving up my freedom, my whole *fucking* life, to go back to the desert. To go back to sleeping on cots and eating fucking dog food and getting shot at and watching my buddies get blown up because that is *still* better than the hell I go through every time I make you cry."

Knight's jaw flexed and his chin buckled as he reached out to wipe the mascara from under my eye. Without thinking, I flinched and pulled away. Such a small gesture—the twist of my neck, the fractional lean backward—but so significant. The heartbreak on his face made *my* heart break as well but for myself. Because I'd spent two of my seventeen years on this planet in a relationship with someone I was afraid of.

"Punk, please look at me. I love you."

Since meeting Hans, I had learned a lot about love. What it was. What it wasn't. What it felt like. How it healed and delighted and made me glow. For years, I'd thought Knight loved me because he'd told me he did. He'd screamed it at me. He'd scrawled it in his psychotic all-caps handwriting in his notes at school and his letters from Iraq. But now I knew better. I knew that Knight didn't truly love me, because true love didn't hurt. It didn't humiliate. It didn't take everything you had to give, suck you dry, and then discard your lifeless body when the guilt made it too hard to look at your corpse.

I wanted to tell Knight that he was wrong. That he wasn't capable of loving anyone, but I couldn't. Whatever he felt for me, it was the closest thing to love he'd ever known. So I let him keep it.

Without it, he'd have nothing but his hate.

Staring at my hand where it rested on my door handle, I took a deep breath, looked back over my shoulder at Knight's tortured face, and I lied.

"I know you do, Knight. I know."

Then I opened the door, climbed inside, and pulled it shut.

As I drove away, I glanced one last time at the man in my rearview mirror. I will never forget the way he looked, standing in the street, illuminated by my taillights. Knight was red, red, red.

Inside and out.

22

I wanted to go home, but when I pulled up to the corner, my car didn't turn right, toward the modest gray house in the suburbs where I kept my things. It turned left, toward the Masquerade. Hans was my home now, and I had to find him. I had to tell him that I didn't care. That it didn't matter if someone else had touched his body. My body. One day, our bodies would burn, just like all the others before them, and our souls would hold hands and dance around the fire.

When the Masquerade came into view at the bottom of the hill, my heart leaped into my throat. Baker's white panel van was still parked in the loading dock. My foot flattened the clutch as I prepared to pull in, and my sweaty palm slid off the gearshift when I yanked it down into second. I turned left onto the access road that ran beside the old factory and then left again into the gravel loading area behind the building.

My headlights illuminated everything from the fire escape to the half-wall, but the guys were nowhere to be seen. I cut the engine and got out of the car, but I didn't hear them either. All I heard was the repetitive electronic pulses coming from the bottom floor of the building.

Hell.

I left my car parked there and ran around to the front entrance. Flashing my wristband yet again at the door guy, I blew past and dashed up the stairs to Heaven. The crowd had dissipated. The bars were vacated. And the stage contained nothing but some speakers, a few mic stands, and a blow-up sex doll, probably tossed onstage by an enthusiastic fan. Dashing up the stairs to the elevated platform, I peeked into the curtained backstage area and found a couple of guys wearing *CREW* T-shirts, smoking a joint.

"Hey," I panted, "do you guys know where Phantom Limb went? Are they still here?"

The curly-haired one took a big hit and held the smoke in his lungs as he squeaked out, "Yeah...I saw Trip down in Hell not too long ago." He exhaled and coughed.

His long-haired friend added, "Dude, I want whatever that motherfucker's on."

"I know, right?" Curly passed the joint with another small cough. "Little dude's on fire tonight."

"Thanks!" I chirped, hauling ass back down the rickety metal staircase.

I passed through the layer of smoke that clung to Purgatory, the world's saddest blues bar, and turned left at the bottom of the stairs, into a huge warehouse-style rave. The black lights and strobe lights and disco balls were in full effect. Everyone was wearing fluorescent clothing and Day-Glo body paint. You could practically smell the ecstasy being sweated out by the writhing, grinding, glow-stick-waving, pacifier-sucking ravers on the dance floor. The concrete vibrated under my feet to the *unce-unce-unce* of the DJ's house beat. And standing on the bar, spraying a bottle of champagne on the crowd below, was Triple X.

I pushed my way over to the bar, sidling up next to Baker and Louis, who were being loved on by a couple of girls in sexy Rainbow Brite costumes, but I didn't see Hans anywhere.

Not wanting to interrupt Louis's and Baker's little flirt session, I tugged furiously on Trip's too-baggy vinyl pants. "Trip! Trip!"

He glanced down at me with foggy, smiling eyes and slurred, "Hey, errrybody! Look who d'cided to grace us with her presence!"

"Where's Hans?"

Trip wobbled on his feet, then sat on the bar, dangling his legs over the edge. The bartenders kept serving drinks to the fluorescent ravers on either side of him, as if he wasn't even there.

"You missed it, baby cakes!" he shouted in my ear. "That scout came, the one from Violent Violent. Violet Violent. Vi— you know what I mean. That muhrfucker came. And he said he wants *us*...to play a show...in Times Square...on New Year's Eve."

"Oh my God, Trip! That's amazing!"

"Yeah." He nodded enthusiastically. "Go tell that to your boy."

"Where is he?"

"Prolly cryin' in his beer like a lil' bitch with all the other sad bastards."

Purgatory.

"Thanks, Trip! Congratulations!" I hugged Trip around the neck and got the fuck out of there.

Purgatory was worse than I'd expected. I'd never been in there before, and I could see why. Purgatory had nothing to offer but jukebox blues, overflowing ashtrays, and plenty of dark corners to wallow in.

I spotted Hans immediately. He was sitting at the bar in the center of the room, staring into the heavy glass beer stein cupped between his palms. His black hair flopped over one eye. His broad shoulders were hunched. And every frightening face on his right arm stared at me in disapproval. He didn't look like a guy who'd just been asked to play a concert in Times Square by a record-label scout.

He looked like a guy whose girlfriend had run off in the middle of his show.

I walked up behind him, unnoticed, and wrapped my arms around his torso. His black wifebeater was still damp with sweat, but I pressed my cheek against it anyway, relieved to have him back in my arms.

Hans flinched in surprise, then relaxed and hugged my arms where they crisscrossed over his taut stomach.

"Hey," I said, kissing the tan skin on his shoulder blade.

"Hey," he echoed, tipping his head back to rest it on top of mine.

I don't think either of us knew where to begin. Or maybe we didn't want to begin at all. Maybe we just wanted to let our feelings and our body language have the conversation for us.

Eventually, Hans broke the silence. "Why'd you leave?" The hurt in his voice drove a spike of guilt into my heart.

If I had just stayed, none of this would have happened.

"I felt like I was gonna throw up, so I went outside to get some fresh air. But when I came back in, I saw you kissing that girl from the grocery store, and I...I freaked out. I'm sorry. I shouldn't have left."

Hans pulled my arms around him tighter. "No, baby. I'm sorry. I didn't kiss her back, I swear. She just...attacked me."

Somebody attacked me tonight, too.

"It's okay."

"It's not okay if it hurts you."

Hans let go of my arms and turned around on his barstool to face me. Pulling me to stand between his legs, Hans glanced up at my face, and I watched as all the color drained out of his.

"Oh my God!" Hans lifted both hands and swiped his thumbs across my cheeks. I didn't flinch when *he* did it. I closed my eyes and relished his touch. "That's it. I'm telling Trip we can't do the kiss contest anymore."

"No." I shook my head. "Seriously. It's fine. The crowd loves it."

"Fuck the crowd! Look at you!"

I opened my eyes and tried to imagine what Hans must have seen. Black makeup streaked down my face. Wild hair. Puffy eyes. I hadn't planned on telling him about Knight, but I couldn't let him think he'd done all that to me. That guilt didn't belong to him.

"Knight was waiting for me at my car," I blurted, dropping my eyes to the floor. My heart pounded against my ribs as I debated on how much more to say, waited for the questions that would inevitably come. I could feel Hans's entire body tense and heat up. I could sense his eyes scanning me from head to toe.

"What did he do?"

I couldn't say it. I wouldn't. I wasn't even sure I knew what had happened myself. Something bad. Something that I didn't want. Something that could change everything. Right then, I just needed Hans's love. Not his sympathy, not his judgment, not his anger or his hurt. I needed him to hold me and tell me it would all be okay.

"Baby?"

His sweet voice was almost enough to break me, but I kept my eyes on the ground. "I don't wanna talk about it, okay?"

"Hey...what happened? You can tell me."

I shook my head.

"Did he touch you?"

"Hans..."

"Did he hurt you?"

"Please..."

"He put his fucking hands on you, didn't he?" The anger in his voice had me squeezing my eyes to keep the tears from falling out.

I didn't need more male aggression. I needed somebody to fucking hold me.

"Where is he? Tell me where the fuck he is!"

"I don't know. It doesn't matter. He's gone."

Hans slumped back against the bar and stared at me, shell-shocked. "This is my fault. If it wasn't for that kiss, you wouldn't have gone up there alone."

It was the exact reaction I'd hoped to avoid. He wasn't comforting me. He was looking at me the way you would look at your favorite lamp after a careless elbow had sent it crashing to the ground. Like I was broken. Like I was a situation that required cleaning up.

"Stop looking at me like that!" I cried far louder than I'd intended. "Just tell me it doesn't matter! Please?" I could hear my voice cracking, feel my chin trembling, but I was too far gone to care. "Tell me you don't care what happened. Tell me we're gonna be okay. Just . . . tell me you still love me!"

Hans sat up and pulled me into his arms right as the dam burst. Running one hand down my back—firm, not gentle—he shushed my sobs and kissed my head. "Of course I still love you. Why would you even say that? You're my fucking soul mate. I've loved you since the moment I met you. Not loving you isn't even an option. Don't you understand that? Don't you understand what this is?"

I nodded against his chest and wrapped my arms tighter around his waist.

"What is it then?"

I sniffled. "What?"

"This. *Us.* What is it to you? Because I *know* what it is for me, and if you think I can just fall out of love with you because of something you had no control over, then maybe you don't feel what I feel."

This was it. The moment of truth. The very thing I'd come back for.

I looked up at Hans's gorgeous, angry, determined face and answered him quietly, "True love?"

With those words, the light was flipped back on. The one that illuminated Hans's villainous features from within, making them appear warmer somehow.

Hans grinned down at me. Then he gave me a dramatic, confused look and mouthed, *What? I couldn't hear you.*

An unexpected laugh burst from my lungs.

I replied silently, a ridiculous smile splitting my face, and exaggerated every syllable, *I said, true love.*

Blue glove? Hans smirked, holding up one hand to model where a glove would go.

Standing up so that we were eye-to-eye, I cupped my hands around my mouth, took a deep breath, then silently shouted, *TRUUUUE LOOOO—*

Before I could finish my pantomimic declaration, Hans leaned in and kissed my open mouth.

His touch was so different from Knight's. He didn't take from me; he gave. He gave, and he gave until I was so full of love that it leaked out of my eyes. I think that's why I cried so much whenever he was around. Because I was overflowing.

Wrapping my arms around Hans's neck, I kissed him back. Relief and gratitude flooded every cell in my body, making them all tingle at once.

How was this man actually mine? How had I gotten so lucky?

I didn't deserve him. The events of that night proved it, but I was going to keep him anyway.

"True love, huh?" Hans whispered against my lips.

"Mmhmm," I whispered back. "Something like that."

New Year's Eve 1999

"F-f-f-fuuuuck. Th-th-th-thissssssss." My teeth weren't chat-tering. They were crashing together at a rate of forty-two col-lisions per second. My bony fingers had turned into worthless flesh-cicles. And the steel shells of my combat boots had frozen through, encapsulating my toes in two matching ice prisons.

For some reason, I'd always assumed that freezing to death wouldn't be that bad. I'd imagined that your body would just go numb, and then you'd fall asleep and wake up in heaven or haunting your old apartment or whatever. It turns out that hypothermia *actually* feels like having all twenty of your fingers and toes smashed by ball-peen hammers simultaneously while seizure-like convulsions rack your body.

I don't recommend it.

Twenty-three degrees, one of the thousands of digital signs in Times Square announced.

Twenty-three degrees.

For an anorexic Southern girl whose entire winter wardrobe

consisted of a few long-sleeved shirts to wear under her regular T-shirts, a flight jacket, and the Phantom Limb hoodie she'd stolen from her boyfriend, standing outside for hours on end in below-freezing temperatures was a fate worse than death. Even hell would have been an improvement over New fucking York on New Year's Eve.

At least hell was warm.

"Steven, BB's cold. You should go snuggle with her," Goth Girl suggested, tonguing his ear.

I kind of wished that it would stick, like the kid who licked the flagpole in *A Christmas Story.*

"I'm f-f-f-fine," I lied.

Goth Girl and Steven had tossed back a handful of ecstasy each before we got on the plane, so they were definitely feeling no pain. Juliet and her new boyfriend, Mike, had flown up with us too. But they'd wandered off in search of food and restrooms, leaving me to babysit Tweedledee and Tweedledum by myself.

The band had to drive up the day before because of all their equipment, so I hadn't really gotten to see Hans except for a few seconds before and after their show. Even though they were on a stage a few blocks away from Times Square and performed six hours before the ball dropped, people were already shoulder-to-shoulder that far back and then some. They'd estimated that over a million people would fill those streets by midnight, and Phantom Limb rocked the faces off of at least a few thousand of them.

I'd never been prouder of anyone or anything. It had been so surreal, watching my man, *my person,* fulfilling a dream right before my very eyes. All the guys had looked nervous as shit when they first came onstage—except for Trip, of course—but by the end of their second song, Hans was smiling. Not a huge smile. Not a cocky smile. But a two-dimpled smile, nonetheless.

His joy had felt like my joy. I'd gotten high off of it. Lost track of time on it. Danced my ass off on it. And the fact that they couldn't do the kiss contest because of the barricades only made me that much happier.

After the show, Hans had given me a quick kiss over the barricade and told me that he and the guys had to haul their equipment back to the hotel and load it into Baker's van but that they'd come right back.

No one had heard from them since.

It had been five hours.

Five more bands had played.

My high was long gone.

My cell phone sat silent.

And I was at risk of losing my lips, nose, and eyelids to frostbite.

The night, my mood, and my life expectancy had taken a vicious turn for the worse.

I stared at the digital clock just below the disco ball on a stick that was supposed to drop at midnight.

11:41. Where the fuck is he?

Goth Girl came over and wrapped herself around me like a mink shawl as I pulled my phone out of my jacket pocket and checked it again. Still nothing.

"I'm just so happy right now. Aren't you just sooo happy?" Goth Girl droned in my ear.

I nodded, my teeth chattering too hard to even bother trying to talk.

Yeah. I'm fucking ecstatic.

"We are in Times Square for Y2K. This is, like, the center of the universe right now. A new millennium is about to begin—right here, right now—and we're gonna watch it happen together."

"It's gonna be fuckin' crazy," Steven chimed in, pulling his girlfriend back over to him. "They think the whole power grid's gonna go out because their old-ass computers are gonna think the year two thousand is just zero-zero. All of this"—he motioned at the digital jungle of animated billboards flashing all around us—"is gonna be pitch-black in a few minutes. Just watch."

"It feels like the world is gonna end," Goth Girl mused, kissing her man in a fit of madness.

"If the world ends, then at least I'll melt with you."

I rolled my eyes as hard as I wanted to, completely confident that neither one of them would notice.

"I saw that, bitch," Juliet said with a smirk as she and Mike ducked under the metal barricade keeping the crowd on the street from spilling over onto the sidewalk. Her hands were full of woolly goodness. "Here. Can't have your bony ass dyin' on us."

I accepted the bundle from her and began sorting through it. It was a beanie, gloves, and a scarf, all embroidered with the NYPD logo.

"Wh-wh-where did you g-g-g-get these?" I asked with hearts in my eyes.

"The police department has a table set up back there. They're selling all kinds of shit for donations."

"Oh my G-G-God, you're my f-f-fucking hero." I pulled on the cold weather accessories as quickly as I could.

"You have no idea. Look what else we brought."

Mike appeared next to her, holding a cardboard pizza box.

"Never m-m-mind," I said, eyeing the Sbarro logo on the side. "M-M-Mike is my h-h-h-hero."

Mike smiled and puffed up his chest. He was a nice guy—kinda nerdy with his short, curly brown hair and glasses—and he was smart, funny, and worshipped the ground Juliet and Romeo walked on.

I was so happy for Juliet. Hell, I was even happy for Goth Girl—at least when she and Steven were rolling and in love. But, as I watched the clock approaching midnight on the most significant New Year's Eve of this or any lifetime, I wasn't happy for myself.

I was alone.

And slowly dying from exposure.

I checked my phone again. "What do you th-th-think is taking the guys so l-l-long?" I asked no one in particular.

Mike gave me a sympathetic half-smile and a shrug.

Juliet folded her arms over her chest and shivered. "I'm sure they just got held up. I mean, look at this place. You can't get fucking anywhere. And the cell towers are probably all jammed."

I opened my mouth to ask a few more irrationally rhetorical questions, like, *Why the fuck did I agree to come here?* and *Will I still be able to walk after they have to amputate all of my toes?* but before I could get the words out, somebody shoved a pair of two-foot-long inflated tubes into my chest and handed me a pair of sparkly plastic glasses that looked like the number two thousand. I looked around to find the source of the gifts and realized that the entire crowd was now wearing sparkly *2000* glasses and clapping those phallic inflatables together like some kind of maniacal flash mob.

We were several blocks down from Times Square, but I could still make out Dick Clark's face when it appeared on the massive monitors in the heart of the madness. The clock below the glowing orb read *11:53*.

No, no, no. I wanted to stop time. I wanted to shoot a flare gun into the air to help Hans find his way back to me. I wanted to punch somebody in the face out of frustration. But I didn't have to.

Because, just then, I heard the cops outside the barricade yelling.

"Section's full."

"Ya can't stand here. We gotta keep the sidewalks clear."

"Keep it movin', guys."

I looked to my right to see the source of the scuffle, and there, standing six inches taller than the police officers blocking his path, was my favorite person in the whole fucking world. I finally got my wish; when our eyes locked, time really did stand still.

Hans's name tore from my bluish-purple lips as I pushed my way through the crowd. There were three uniformed men standing between him and the barricade.

"He's with m-m-m-me!" I shouted, tapping one of them on the shoulder.

The officer tossed me an annoyed glance, but then his face softened. "Aye, I like ya hat."

I smiled and held up my mittens and scarf, showing off the gold NYPD logos on those as well.

The officer glanced up at the clock, then back at me and smiled. "All right, guys. You can come in but only because ya girl here has such good taste in clothes."

The officer opened the barricade by a few feet to let the guys in, and I hugged his arm over the metal fence.

"Th-th-thank you!" I stuttered.

He smiled at me, a gold tooth glinting in the lights from Times Square, just before I was lifted off my feet and carried back into the crowd.

I wrapped my arms around Hans's black-beanie-covered head as we made our way over to our friends. "Wh-wh-what took you so l-l-l-long?" I yelled over the deafening noise from the crowd.

Hans looked up at me and smiled bigger than I'd ever seen him smile before. "They offered us a contract!"

"Who?"

"Violent Violet! They took us out to dinner and offered us a recording contract! We're getting signed by Love Like Winter's label, baby!" He squeezed me tighter and bounced me up and down just as Trip announced the news to the group.

"Violent Violin Records, muthafuckas!" he slurred.

I threw my head back and laughed into the frosty night. Delighted. Excited. In love and alive.

Before Hans could set my frozen boots back on the ground, Dick Clark began the countdown. I was above it all, looking down 7th Avenue at the hundreds of thousands of my fellow humans who'd gathered in peace and love and harmony to celebrate the new millennium.

A million voices rose above the skyscrapers in unison. "Five…four…three…two…"

Hans slid me down his warm body and pressed his warm lips against purple ones as the last second of the twentieth century ticked away. I kissed him with reverence and gratitude and awe at the difference his presence made in my life. Before he'd shown up that night, I'd thought I might die. Now that I was in his arms, I felt as though I could fly.

A blizzard of confetti poured from the sky. Everyone cheered and hugged and clapped their inflatable baguette-shaped noise-makers together. The lights were still very much on. And it felt like the entire world was celebrating with Phantom Limb that night.

Except for Steven, who was clearly disappointed that the power grid had not gone out.

24

January 2000

I squeezed Hans's hand and bounced on my toes as we rode the escalator back in time, back to my favorite city beneath a city. *Our* city.

That December, I'd decided that going to school downtown was the worst fucking idea I'd ever had. Not only was the city hotter in the summer because of all the asphalt, but it also turned out to be colder in the winter because the tall buildings blocked out the sun and turned all the sidewalks into wind tunnels. And speaking of wind tunnels, the outdoor subway platforms were even worse. The train only ran every fifteen minutes, and I'm pretty sure its only heat source was the anger radiating off its passengers. Between waiting for the damn train, riding the damn train, walking from the goddamn train station to campus, walking from building to building between classes, and then doing it all over again in reverse, I was spending *waaay* more time freezing my ass off than I'd ever thought possible.

But that was December.

This was January. And in January, Hans started coming to school with me. We could have been in Alaska, for all I cared. I had my big, hard-bodied teddy bear to keep me warm.

Hans smiled down at me as the smell of candied pecans hit my nose. With our fingers laced together, we stepped from the modern moving staircase onto the vintage brick-paved street of Underground Atlanta. All four of our backpack-burdened shoulders relaxed as we strolled past the ornate light posts and shop fronts toward the sound of saxophone music.

When Hans ran his thumb over mine, the moment came full circle. I lifted our joined hands to my lips and kissed his thumb, which *always* landed on top of mine.

"The last time we were here, the only thing I could think about was how bad I wanted to hold your hand," I admitted with a wistful smile. "I can't believe that was only six months ago."

Hans's dimples deepened, and his cheeks flushed under his five o'clock shadow. "You want to know what I was thinking about?" he asked.

"What?"

"Don't laugh."

I pressed my lips between my teeth to secure them and gave him my most serious face.

"I was wondering if anyone had ever gotten married here before, or . . . if maybe . . . we would be the first ones."

My eyes began to water, and my tightly drawn mouth fell open in a silent gasp.

Hans stopped walking and turned to face me. "I know you're still too young, and I don't want to freak you out or put any pressure on you, but—"

"It's perfect," I whispered, gazing up at him through blurry, waterlogged eyes. "It's so fucking perfect. I wanna do it right now."

Hans smiled in relief. Then, he leaned forward and kissed my goofy grin. "You're not even old enough to buy cigarettes."

"Pssh. This is the South. I can get married with a forged note from my parents."

Hans laughed. I watched his eyes shift to something over my shoulder. Then his face lit up. "A forged note and a ring. C'mere."

Taking my hand, Hans led me to an old-timey cart in the middle of the street that had been converted into a jewelry store kiosk. An older man with a bushy gray mustache was sitting on a stool on the opposite side, reading the newspaper.

"Pick whatever you want. It's just for now. I'll get you something better later."

The man glanced up from his paper and scoffed at Hans's comment.

We snickered under our breath as I perused the cases of rings. They were fancy. Signs boasting *14k Gold* and *Real Diamonds* surrounded the merchandise. I didn't really wear jewelry, other than my piercings, so I was at a total loss.

"Will you pick one for me?" I asked, hopeful. "I can't decide."

Hans smiled and tapped on the Plexiglas above a small white gold band with a channel of inlaid black diamonds going across the front. "I like this one," he said. "The black diamonds are kind of badass, don't you think? And, after I get you an engagement ring, you could keep it and wear it as your wedding band."

My beautiful, backward boy.

Only Hans would give a girl a wedding band as an engagement ring and an engagement ring as a wedding band.

And it was black and white, just like him.

"I love it." I beamed up at him.

Hans leaned over and gave me a chaste kiss. "I love *you*," he whispered.

The irritated man measured my finger and pulled a size five version of the ring Hans had chosen out from a drawer on the back of the cart. As I slipped it on and admired the way it looked on my left hand, Hans handed the man his debit card and signed the receipt.

Arm in arm, we continued on toward our favorite Mexican restaurant. I pointed out good places to take wedding photos along the way, making sure to point with my left hand, and Hans occasionally leaned over and kissed me, mid-sentence. At the restaurant, we tossed our backpacks and coats onto one side of the booth and sat on the opposite side together, drunk on love and dreams and saxophone music.

Hans ordered every taco on the menu while I drank in the sight of my ring for lunch. We went over his schedule, strategized the best places to meet up for a cigarette between periods, and laughed about the Women's Studies class I'd signed him up for as an elective.

Life was good underground.

Too good.

When I finally tore my eyes away from my ring and looked at the clock on my cell phone, I realized we were going to be late to our one o'clock classes.

Hans waved over our waitress and handed her his card. Before we even finished pulling our coats and backpacks back on, she returned with an unhappy look on her face.

"Your card was declined."

Hans furrowed his eyebrows. "Really? Will you try it again?"

"I tried three times, sir. It won't go through."

I laughed and took the card from the woman's hand. Reaching into my purse, I pulled out my wallet and handed her my own debit card, tucking Hans's worthless piece of plastic into the slot next to it. "That's it. I'm keeping this," I said to Hans with a teasing smile. "You cannot be trusted with it."

The woman disappeared.

"Damn it. I meant to deposit that money my mom gave me for books yesterday. Shit. I'll pay you back."

"Don't worry about it," I said, accepting the receipt and a pen from our waitress. "But, from now on, *I'm* keeping up with your checking account. You've overdrawn that thing three times in the last month."

Twenty-five bucks plus tax just for tacos? Ouch.

I signed the slip of paper and handed it back to her with a smile.

"C'mon. Women's Studies waits for no man," I teased, grabbing Hans's hand. I laced our fingers together as we speed-walked toward the escalator that would lead us back to modern-day Atlanta.

I became aware of the ring on my fourth finger as it slid between his knuckles.

I also became aware that my thumb had landed on top of his.

It never landed on top.

Something new and exciting and something nagging and uncomfortable were both competing for my attention in that moment.

Guess which one I chose to ignore.

25

February 2000

It'll be fun, I'd thought.

I've always wanted to go to Mardi Gras!

Riding in a van with four dudes for ten hours won't be that bad.

First of all, the van ride was absolutely *that* bad. Trip insisted that we listen to his heavy-ass Death, Murder, Mayhem playlist on repeat. I got stuck riding bitch in the middle of the backseat the whole way, which made me super carsick, and by the time we pulled into New Orleans, I could identify each guy's farts by the smell alone.

Second, I discovered pretty quickly that during Mardi Gras, Bourbon Street should be renamed Bourbon River—only because the more appropriate name, Barf-Body-Fluids-Beer-and-Beads River, is too long to fit on a street sign. I trudged through the four-inch-deep muck for what felt like miles, trying to find the best place to watch Phantom Limb's float go by. I was thankful that I'd worn my boots but also sad because it would probably take a priest to get them clean again.

And third, nothing about watching teenage girls and grown-ass women waiting to flash their breasts at your boyfriend is *fun*. Nothing. Especially when all you have to offer under your shirt is a four-pound water bra and a couple of bee stings fitted with a pair of stainless steel door knockers.

At least New Orleans in February was warmer than Atlanta. I'd give it that. And the architecture was pretty cool too. And the music. And all the lights. And the palm trees. If you just removed the street slime, the breasts, and the ten hours of open asshole I'd had to smell to get there, I guess it was pretty cool.

I gave up on finding the perfect spot somewhere around mid-Bourbon Street and sat my tired, hungry, pouty ass down on some random steps. They appeared to lead up to a novelty shop or a corner store or a fucking voodoo doll vendor—hell if I knew. To me, it was simply the place where I would watch my man look at other women's tits.

Woohoo.

A tall, extremely thin guy wearing overalls came bursting out of the store and leaned against the handrail next to where I was sitting on the top step. "Oh my *God*. Dat last lady was pregnant! Now my back hurts, my feets hurt, an' I'm cravin' pickles!" His accent was Cajun, his cowboy boots were snakeskin, and his head was shaved completely bald. Lighting a cigarette, he inhaled and exhaled dramatically. "Be happy you ain't knocked up, *mon cher*. Dis shit is da worst."

I looked up at him, then everywhere else, unsure if he was actually talking to me. Furrowing my brow, I tried to figure out how to respond to such an odd statement. I finally settled on, "Uh...congratulations?"

The thin man laughed and looked down at me. His face was

all high cheekbones and pale skin. His head was shiny bald. And his eyes were alight with madness.

He lifted a hand and clutched some kind of amulet hanging from a cord around his neck, then stroked the underside of his chin with it. His eyes rolled up in the back of his head for a moment before they settled on me again.

The man nodded slowly, humming in approval. "You ain't pregnant, and you feisty as hell. I like you." He grinned. "I'm John."

"BB," I said, extending my hand up toward him.

John jumped back and held his hand up as if I'd tried to hand him a live rattlesnake. "No, no, no, no, no. You gots to pay fo' dat."

"I have to pay to shake your hand?" My question came out a lot sassier than I'd intended. I was still super fucking annoyed at being left alone all day so that Hans could literally float down the Boobie Bayou, and my people skills were suffering.

"Ooh!" John shook his head and let out a long whistle. "You got dat fiah in you, girl."

"Sorry." I swallowed and tried to compose myself. "I'm just... in a bad mood. It's nice to meet you."

John smiled and pointed at me. "You in a bad mood 'cause all dese people heah"—he extended his bony, cigarette-pinching fingers out across the landscape—"and none o' dem payin' you *no* attention." He coughed out a chuckle and took another drag.

"You're right." I shrugged. "You're totally right."

"I know! I'm always right! Dat's why dey pay me."

"Who pays you?"

"Dese people." He looked out over the crowd. "Dey come to me. I tell dem de troof. Dey pay me."

"Are you a psychic?" I asked, cocking my head to the side.

"Yes! I know tings." He tapped his temple with his middle finger.

"That's really cool. How does that work? You have to touch people?"

I was suddenly the one giving John all the attention. I'd never met a psychic before. I was skeptical about a lot of things, but for some reason, psychics weren't one of them.

Neither were ghosts or aliens, in case you were wondering.

"I touch yo hand, I know yo life. I look at yo hand, I know yo fucha."

"Really? Can I pay you to look at my hand?"

John smiled and closed his eyes like he was listening to something.

All I heard was a bunch of drunk *woohoo*s from the titty patrol on the street and some loud bass coming from one of the clubs farther down Bourbon Street, but John was on a whole other wavelength.

"No," he finally said with a smile.

"No?"

John took another drag from his cigarette and shook his head. "No. You so bright, I see yo fucha from heah."

"Really?" I sat up a little straighter and turned toward him fully. "What do you see?"

John looked me in the eye. "I cannot tell you. You tink you grown up, but you just a baby. You gonna have to learn some tings de hard way. I cannot take dat away from you."

"So you're not gonna tell me what you see? Oh my God, is it that bad?" I turned and stared blankly into the sea of people as a sense of dread gripped my body. It had never occurred to me that I might get bad news. My stomach flip-flopped as if I'd just gone over the first hill on a roller coaster.

John smiled and closed his eyes. Rubbing his amulet under his chin, he said, "Oh…no, no, no, no. Not bad. You gonna live a long a life, child. You gonna *enjoy* yo life. You gonna have two kids, you know—a boy and a girl. And de man, he not even gonna drive you dat crazy. You gonna be wit' him fo-evah. But de rest…" He shook his head slowly. "You got to find dat out fo yo'self. You got suhprises comin', *mon cher*. And when dey come, you gonna find out what you made of."

I stored everything he'd said away, every single syllable, but at that moment, the only words my insecure teenage brain could process were, "*You gonna be wit' him fo-evah.*"

A grin split my grumpy face. "Thank you, John. I feel so much better. You have no idea. Wow. Can I…give you a hug?"

John walked over and stubbed his cigarette out in a potted plant by the shop door. "Why not?" He shrugged. "I already got yo big energy all ovah me."

I hopped off my step and bounced over to where John was standing by the door. I wrapped my bony arms around his bony midsection and squeezed. But, instead of hugging me back, John's tall, lanky body went rigid in my embrace. I let go and took a step back, afraid that I'd hurt him or crossed some kind of line.

But John wasn't even there. His eyes had rolled up into his head as if he were about to have a seizure, but he didn't convulse. He simply stood there, still as a white-eyed statue.

Then he whispered the number *eleven*. Twice.

Eleven eleven? The fuck does that mean?

"John?" I was about to shake him but decided it might be best if I didn't touch him again.

John's eyes slowly rolled back into their normal positions, and he shook his head as if waking from a dream.

"Okay den." John smiled, pulling open the shop door. "*Laissez les bon temps rouler!*"

Then he disappeared inside.

The fuck?

I sat back down on my step, ready to ponder and overanalyze every word John had just uttered, when I heard the booming of a marching band thundering in the distance. Every thump of the bass drum sounded louder than the one before it.

The parade had begun.

The energy on the street was joyous. Alive. Kinetic. Infectious. I let it lift my spirits. I let it remind me that I was Brooke fucking Bradley. Lover of life. Wearer of combat boots. Thrower of caution to the wind. I wasn't a pouter. I mean, I was a pouter, but not when there was a good time to be had.

So I did what Brooke Bradley always did at parties. I pulled a soda bottle full of premixed Jack and Coke out of my purse, poured it into my empty stomach, and set my sights on a boy.

There were fire-breathing dragon floats, scale-model riverboat floats, and dozens of alligator floats, but the only one I cared about was the one with the fifteen-foot-tall harlequin jester on the front that I knew would be delivering my guy. I peered into the darkness as far down Bourbon Street as I could see, ignoring the plastic beaded necklaces I was being pelted with, until it came into view.

The jester float belonged to a local bar called Jokers Wild that was known for its live rock music. Phantom Limb's new manager, courtesy of Violent Violet, had an in with the owner and booked the gig. It was great exposure. There were thousands of people in the French Quarter that night, and I'm pretty sure every damn one of them heard Trip's screaming vocals at some point.

The jester on the front of their float was at least fifteen feet tall and looked like he'd just snorted a bushel of blow. His eyes were crazed. His smile, maniacal. Kind of like how Trip looked once he came into view. He wailed and gesticulated and made love to the mic stand as the band played a surprisingly good Love Like Winter cover, which I suspected was at the request of their record label.

The crowd went fucking nuts. Other than a few marching bands, there hadn't been any floats with live music, and this was clearly a rock-'n'-roll audience. Tits were flashed. Beads were tossed, quite happily, by Trip, who was starring in his own personal *Girls Gone Wild* fantasy. And there was Hans, standing at the back of the float, playing his bass with his head down.

I shouted his name, but between the amplifiers and crowd noise, he couldn't hear me. I shouted louder even though I knew it was no use. In a panic, I grabbed one of the decorative metal poles holding up the second-story balcony and pulled myself up onto the handrail by the stairs.

"Hans!" I screamed, waving my one free arm. "Hans!"

He never even lifted his head, but luckily, my flailing caught Trip's attention. Taking two steps to the right, he smacked Hans on the arm and pointed at me with a grin. I held my breath as my guy looked in the direction of Trip's outstretched finger. Tingles spread from the top of my head to the tips of my toes as his gaze swept across the crowd.

Look at me, baby. Over here…

I waved my free arm like a lunatic, nearly losing my balance, but just before my favorite steely stare found me, a burly dude standing on the sidewalk in front of me lifted a very drunk, very blonde girl up on his shoulders.

Mardi Gras Barbie immediately yanked her shirt up with both hands, gave a little shimmy, and shouted, "LDH!"

My blood ran cold as Hans's eyes landed on *her* instead of me. When his pursed lips pulled up in a flirty smile for *her*, not me. When he blushed and shook his head at the sight of her bouncing titties, which I'm sure were full and jiggly and didn't look at all like they belonged to a starving orphan boy like *mine*.

"Hans!" I screamed again, leaning around the competition and swaying like a newborn giraffe on the railing, but it was too late.

His eyes had already fluttered back down to his bass, a ghost of a smile still evident on his handsome face. It was that tiny smirk that made the ice water in my veins begin to boil. Heat rushed to my face and my fingers as I gripped the pole so hard, I'm surprised it didn't collapse in my fist like an aluminum can.

Evidently, John had been right. I must have wanted some attention pretty damn bad because, before I knew it, my drunk ass had hopped off the railing, scooped a fistful of beads up off the ground, and chucked them directly at Hans as he passed. The second those purple, green, and gold pearls left my hand, I regretted the action, deeply, but it was too late. All I could do was cringe and hold my breath as the tiny projectiles flew over the crowd, toward my lover.

Luckily, plastic beaded necklace wads are not terribly aerodynamic. They nosedived somewhere between Mardi Gras Barbie and the float, missing both of my preferred targets by at least a yard.

Ugh! I threw my hands up and stomped down the four stubby little stairs that separated John's shop from the street as the giant jester carried my guy away.

"Fuck Mardi Gras," I muttered as I elbowed and shoved my way against the current of bodies lining Bourbon Street.

It was no different than any other Phantom Limb show. Random guys grabbed my arms and hands and hoodie as I passed, trying to pull me toward them, but I was so engrossed in my own inner dialogue that I just kept trudging through the Bourbon Street sludge, full speed ahead.

Fuck Hans. Fuck Mardi Gras. Fuck waiting.

Goddamn, I'm pissed. Why am I so pissed? Hans didn't ask to see those boobs.

No, but he sure liked what he saw.

So what? He's a dude.

Exactly. Two girls were competing for his attention, one that he loves and one with her tits out, and guess which one he saw? Typical fucking guy.

I yanked my elbow out of the clutches of some other typical fucking guy and kept right on walking.

That's kind of understandable though. I mean, what if two guys were competing for your *attention and one of them had his package hanging out?*

Nuh-uh. Hans would still win. Hands down. Have you seen him? He's fucking gorgeous. Especially compared to some rando's scrotum.

Touché.

Another hand grabbed my wrist. I twisted it free without a second glance.

I shouldn't have come with them. This was a stupid idea.

Yeah, let's maybe not go to any more out-of-town shows for a while.

For real. You threw beads at Hans's head tonight! What the fuck is wrong with you? What if they'd hit him?

They didn't.

But what if they had?

Listen, nobody saw me do it, so it never happened.

I sidestepped some dickhead trying to talk to me and hustled across an intersection blocked off for the parade.

Did that guy really just ask me if I wanna party? Like I'm out here trying to pick up a prostitute?

I flipped the hood on my Phantom Limb sweatshirt up to try to look less approachable.

Maybe he just thought you might want some coke?

Well, I do, but not if it means I have to wake up in a bathtub full of ice, missing my spleen the next morning.

I crossed the street at another intersection and found myself staring up at a huge three-story building that seemed to take up the entire block. The second-story balcony railing was draped in rainbow-print fabric, bass-heavy techno music pulsed from every seam, and there were so many people dancing outside and on the balcony the place resembled a psychedelic human anthill.

Just as I began to consider busting out the old Jolene Godfrey driver's license so that I could see the inside of this Technicolor playground, my view was suddenly obstructed by a man-shaped silhouette. His uninvited lips smashed against mine then retreated, like a drive-by kissing.

My mouth fell open in shock as I watched a person who looked like he'd been carved out of marble—hard, hairless, perfectly sculpted marble—scamper off in a skimpy, sexy angel costume. And by *costume*, I mean a white thong, a pair of huge feathery wings, and a light-up halo. He stopped next to an equally drool-worthy specimen wearing the Satanic version of his ensemble, and the two beefcakes watched me, giggling like schoolgirls.

I flipped my hood back and glared at them, trying to act offended. The truth was that I appreciated their strange, unsolicited attention, but I couldn't let *them* know that.

As soon as my face was exposed, both guys stopped laughing. The devil gasped and placed a hand over his mouth, then they cracked up even worse than before.

"Oh my God, honey! I'm so sorry!" Beelzebub squealed, his flashing red horns lighting up his frosted blond tips. "We thought you were—"

"Somebody else," the archangel of abs interrupted with a smirk and an elbow to his buddy's ribs.

I crossed my arms over my chest and raised an eyebrow at them, genuinely offended that time. "You thought I looked like a boy, didn't you?"

"What?" Satan screeched, moving his hand from his mouth to his heart. "No!"

"Whatever. It's fine. It's not the first time I've been kissed by a gay guy."

"What makes you think we're—" The chiseled cherub couldn't even get through his question before he snorted and doubled over laughing, his wings and glowing halo bouncing with every chuckle.

The devil gestured toward his friend. "Sorry about her," he said with a full-lipped smirk. "This one's had a little bit too much pixie dust."

The angel stood back up and put his hands on his narrow hips. Sucking in a few steadying breaths, he flashed me the most mischievous grin ever worn by somebody in a halo headband and asked, "You want some?"

I'd always suspected that the devil and angel on my shoulders were thong-wearing, coked-up gay men. I just never thought I'd get to meet them in real life. Within minutes, I was jumping up and down on the dance floor of what had to be the largest gay nightclub in the southeastern US with a head full of "pixie dust" that came from a vial hanging around an actual seraph's neck.

"I love Mardi Gras!" I announced, spinning under the disco ball to a jungle remix of "Just a Girl" by No Doubt.

When the DJ started dipping into the boy-band volume of his catalog—and my celestial friends began making out with each other—I decided it was time for me to make like NSYNC and go "Bye Bye Bye" too.

Or at least go outside for a smoke break until some better music came on.

Everything felt like it was in fast-forward as I made my way out the door—my thoughts, my movements, time. I dance-jogged in place as I dug around in my purse for my cigarettes, but I found my cell phone instead.

Oh, yeah. This thing. I should probably use it. I wonder if the guys made it back to the van yet. I wonder if Hans even remembers that I'm here. I wonder if he's off judging a wet T-shirt contest somewhere.

When I hit the button to illuminate the screen, a hysterical cackle bubbled out of my throat.

Not because I had eight missed calls and five voicemails.

But because the clock read *11:11.*

Eleven eleven.

Make a wish, a voice inside me said.

So I closed my eyes and wished for Hans. No, I had Hans. I wished for LDH. I wished for him to see me the way Hansel Oppenheimer did. I wished for him to look up from his music once in a while and acknowledge that I was there. I wished for him to play *for me* instead of playing *near me* for himself.

When I opened my eyes, I moved my thumb to the green Talk button to begin playing my voicemails, but the sound of my name off in the distance stopped me. Even over the thumping Backstreet Boys remix behind me and the sea of drunk people in the street, I swore I'd heard it. My ears perked up, and I listened.

Just when I was about to chalk it up to mixing coke with my Jack and Coke, I heard it again. It sounded like it was being shouted through a bullhorn very far away.

I stood up on my tiptoes and looked in every direction, not seeing anyone I recognized. Then, I heard it again. Louder.

"If anyone"—*unintelligible*—"drunk girl"—*unintelligible*—"Brooke Bradley"—*couldn't understand this part either*—"this float for a reward."

Float? Reward?

I jumped up as high as I could to see over the crowd, and there it was, about four blocks away—the head of a giant jester, parting the sea of drunks on Bourbon Street like Moses parting the Red Sea.

I took off in a sprint, leap-frogging over puking party girls and spin-dodging handsy assholes with ease.

"If you guys see a tiny drunk girl with short blonde hair named Brooke Bradley, bring her to this float for a reward, okay?"

It was Trip's voice, and he wasn't shouting through a bull-horn; he was shouting through his microphone!

"I'm here! Over here!" I waved one hand as I ran, clutching the shoulder strap of my purse with the other.

I saw the wheels turning in a few people's heads as I passed, like, *Oh, that's the girl. I should return her and get a*—

But by the time their sluggish, inebriated brains formed the thought, I'd already blown past them.

"What's up, New Orleans? Would y'all do us a favor and go find a little blonde chick named Brooke Bradley? If you do, Baker here will give you a BJ."

"Hans! Hans!" I pushed my way through the wake of people gathering around the float and held up my hands. "Down here! Hans!"

Everything had been in fast-forward until the moment Hans peered over the side of the float. Then, it all shifted into slow motion. Shaggy black hair, slightly spiky from sweat, flopped over one gray-blue eye. Jet-black lashes blinked in relief. Narrow, pursed lips split into a two-dimpled smile. And long, strong, hoodie-covered arms reached for me.

My wish had come true. LDH, of Phantom Limb, had seen me.

I beamed up at him, tears of joy and disbelief stinging my eyes, and accepted his outstretched hands. Hans helped me scramble up the side of the float, which appeared to be crafted out of a flat-bed truck with side panels, and pulled me into his arms.

Grabbing my face with both hands, Hans looked at me as if he were trying to convince himself that I was real. Then he kissed me hard on my closed mouth.

Pulling away, he glared at me with a deep V-shaped crease

between his glistening eyes, all traces of his earlier relief gone. "You have got to stop disappearing like that! Fuck, BB! We couldn't find you anywhere!"

I felt like Hans had just kissed me and punched me in the gut, all at the same time. It had never even occurred to me that he might be wondering where I was. Or that he'd thought of me at all. Did I really think that little of him? Did I really think that little of myself?

"Oh my God, baby. I'm so sorry. I had no idea—"

Two hands clapped me on the back mid-apology, one heavy and one light.

I looked over my shoulder and found Trip and Baker, both looking at me in annoyance.

"You scared the shit outta my boy, blondie. Glad you're okay," Trip said.

"Glad you're okay," Baker mumbled.

Returning to his spot behind the microphone, Trip announced, "We got her, folks! And since you guys didn't even murder her, like Lucifer here said you would, you *all* get a reward!"

I craned my neck to see Louis, who winked at me from behind his drum kit just before smacking his sticks together three times. Right on cue, Louis, Baker, and Trip launched into America's favorite sing-along song of all time—"Don't Stop Believin'" by Journey. Trip didn't even get out the first syllable before the entire French Quarter chimed in, including me.

I smiled up at Hans and sang the lyrics, making exaggerated facial expressions to go along with them.

Hans smiled back, my silliness chipping away at some of his anger, and cupped a hand behind one ear. *What?* he mouthed. *I can't hear you.*

I rolled my eyes and smacked him on the chest. Standing up on my tiptoes, I pulled Hans's face down to my mouth and said, "I'm so fucking sorry, baby. I had no idea you guys were looking for me," directly into his ear.

Hans kept his cheek pressed against mine and shouted back, "I called you five times. I thought you'd been fucking abducted."

Only five? I had eight missed calls.

"I was at Oz. I guess it was too loud for me to hear my phone ringing."

Hans's volume dropped. "Did you even watch us perform?"

I pulled away and leveled him with a shocked stare. "Of course I did! I was standing right"—I looked around until I saw John's shop behind us—"over there. I waited for hours, and you didn't even look at me when you passed by."

I felt my face begin to flush at the memory of his eyes on Mardi Gras Barbie's body.

"Damn. Sorry, baby."

I could barely hear him over the crowd. They were going nuts over Trip hilariously butchering the super-crazy high note in the middle of the song. I had to read Hans's lips to comprehend the next words he said to me.

"I knew I shouldn't have brought you here. It was selfish. I just...didn't want to miss you. I didn't even think about you being all alone...*out here.*" Hans surveyed the madness below with his eyes.

My sweet, backward boy, apologizing when he'd done nothing wrong.

I pushed up onto my tiptoes and kissed his frown, trying to turn it right side up.

"Hey," I shouted as something occurred to me, "how did you

guys get this thing back onto Bourbon Street? Didn't the cops try to stop you?"

Hans grinned.

There it is. A smile. Mission accomplished.

"The guy driving it has a brother on the police force. They let him right through the barricade when he told him we were looking for a lost little girl."

"A lost little girl, huh?" I giggled. "That was pretty badass. Thank you."

Hans's eyes softened. "I love you." He shrugged. "You sure nobody fucked with you?"

I shook my head. "Nah. Nothing worse than any other concert. I did meet a psychic though! His name was John, and he said that we're gonna be together forever!"

Hans shrugged, unimpressed. "I already knew that."

"Well, maybe you're psychic too. Quick, what number am I thinking of?"

Eleven eleven.

"Four."

"Yep. Totally psychic."

Hans smirked and gave me one last lingering, toe-curling kiss before grabbing his bass and joining his bandmates in a hard-rock rendition of "Baby One More Time" by Britney Spears.

I laughed as Trip twirled an imaginary pigtail and serenaded all the drunk girls on the sidewalk, who were too busy singing their hearts out to Britney to expose their breasts.

Feeling awkward just standing there next to the band, I sat cross-legged on the floor of the flatbed with my back against one of the side panels and lit a much-needed cigarette. As I exhaled, I felt my body relax—the coke all worn off, the alcohol all danced out—and smiled up at my very own wish come true. I was onstage with LDH, and *nobody* had their tits out.

But, even through my bliss, something tugged at the back of my mind. A nagging little pull that whispered, *Check your phone.*

Sliding it back out of my purse, I peeked at the call history to see who all the missed calls had been from. Sure enough, there were five from Hans, but the other three? Those had come from a number I didn't recognize.

An international number.

March 2000

"No."

"*No?* What do you mean, *no?*"

"I mean *hell to the nah* is what I mean. You can't just up and leave me here." Craig crossed his arms and leaned against the dumpster behind Pier 1 Imports, glaring at me as if I'd just left him for another man.

And in a way, I guess I had.

"Craig, you've been working here longer than me. You'll be fine." I lit a cigarette and took a few steps away from the back door that we'd propped open, to keep the smoke from wafting in.

"No, I won't. Who am I gonna throw pillows at now? Who's gonna dance to the 'Thong Song' with me after we lock up every night? Did you know that you were the only person here who knew that my hair was Sisqó platinum? Everybody else thought I was tryin' a be a black Eminem or some shit."

I smiled and shrugged. "Who's Sisqó?"

Craig pointed directly at my nose. "Woman, I'ma smack that grin right off yo face."

"You'll be okay, babe. I still have two weeks left. And after that, I can give you my employee discount at Macy's. They're putting me in the streetwear section. All the Phat Farm and FUBU you want, twenty percent off."

That made Craig's lips curl up, just a smidge. "They got Sean John?"

"Pssh. Sean John, Ecco, Rocawear—"

Craig held up one hand and adjusted his waistband with another. "Stop it, girl! You're gettin' me hard over here."

"Never thought I'd hear you say *that*."

We both burst out laughing, but Craig's smile faded fast. "Macy's is so far away though," he whined.

"I know, but it's right by Hans's house. Now I'll be able to see him after work instead of just at school and on the weekends."

"Damn, girl. You really got it that bad?"

"Yeah, I do," I said with a wistful smile.

Craig pushed off the dumpster and took a step toward me, motioning toward the cigarette in my hand. I handed it over.

"You sure this don't have nothin' to do with a certain skinhead-lookin' motherfucker who keeps callin' your phone?" Craig took a long drag from my Camel Light before handing it back.

"Knight? Why would I get a new job because of him? He's in Iraq."

"For now. But he's gon' be back, and when he get here, where do you think he's gon' show up first?"

Craig and I both turned our heads toward the employee parking lot.

There was a time when finding Knight's rusty white monster truck parked out there when I got off work had been an exciting thing. Then, it'd become a scary thing. Then, it'd become a reason to lock the door and call the cops.

"He doesn't even call me that much." I shrugged. "And it's not like I answer or anything."

Craig gave me the side-eye and plucked the cigarette out of my hand. "You might *think* you runnin' toward somethin', but I know you, girl. You runnin' away."

"Whatever," I huffed, trying to act unaffected by his statement. "The only thing I'm running away from is this guy I work with who refuses to buy his own damn cigarettes." I snatched what was left of my Camel Light back with a smirk, took one last drag, and flicked it toward the dumpster.

"Ah, man. Why you gotta be like that, B? I thought you was my suga' mama."

Now *that* was laughable. Thank God Macy's was going to pay me an extra two fifty an hour. Cigarettes were about all I could afford on minimum wage.

"I'm *not* your sugar mama, but I will hold the door for you, Your Majesty."

I opened the heavy back door and smiled as Craig breezed past me, straightening his invisible crown.

I really was going to miss him.

Before letting the door close, I turned my head and glanced at the back corner of the parking lot one more time. I knew it was a mistake as soon as I did it. My heart slammed against my ribs as image after image began flashing behind my eyes. Knight's truck lurched up on the curb. That one streetlight illuminating his pallid, murderous face. My manager driving off and leaving me there with him. Him screaming at me, dragging me into his truck, hog-tying me with the seat belts. Him telling me he was leaving for the Marines.

Him actually doing it.

"Stop. Stop. Stop!" I snapped my fingers three times, and like Dorothy clicking the heels of her ruby slippers together, I was back, and it was all just a bad dream.

"What?" Craig asked over his shoulder, already halfway across the warehouse. He must have seen the frightened look on my face when he turned around because he immediately began patting himself down. "Shit. Is it a spider? It's a spider, ain't it? Don't just stare at it! Help me out, B!"

Craig spun in circles, trying to look at his own backside, as my cackle echoed through the warehouse.

"Relax. It wasn't a spider," I said, sauntering past him toward the break room. "It was a cockroach."

27

April 2000

"So, how do you know this guy again?" Juliet asked as I backed out of her mom's steep driveway.

She had her hair in skinnier braids than usual. I wondered if she'd gotten it done just for the party. She looked amazing. She'd even caked on her signature smoky eyeliner, which had been sadly absent ever since Romeo was born.

"He's Steven's drug dealer." I smiled, trying to soften the blow.

"Awesome. And does Hansy-Poo know you're hanging out with drug dealers while he's away?"

"Hansy-Poo hasn't called me all weekend, so Hansy-Poo doesn't get a say in whom I do or don't hang out with."

Juliet's mouth fell open. "He what?"

I gave Juliet a disgruntled look and turned left onto Highway 78, heading toward Atlanta.

"Let me get this straight. Your man is in Panama City Beach, during spring break, with a bunch of single dudes, and he hasn't called you *once*? It's Sunday! He's been gone since—"

"Friday. Yeah. I'm aware."

"Have you tried calling him?"

"No." I tightened my grip on the steering wheel. Saying it out loud made me feel so stupid.

Juliet snorted. "Why not?"

"Because."

"So, you're testing him."

"Yeah. And he fucking failed." There was so much sass in my voice I wanted to slap *myself.*

"So now you're going to a party at a drug dealer's house to, what? Punish him?"

"No. I'm going to have fun. Remember fun? I sure as fuck don't. Ever since Hans got signed, all I do is go to school and go to work and wait by the phone for him to call me and tell me when he's back in town."

"Why don't you just go with him? You used to."

I could feel my cheeks begin to heat.

Because I always fuck things up. Because I'm too jealous. Because I get wasted and disappear and get into trouble by myself, and then we both get upset with each other.

"I have to work on the weekends."

"Pssh. You could get off work."

"I have to study, too."

Juliet snorted again. "Yeah, okay." Mercifully changing the subject, Juliet asked, "So, this is a party... to watch a TV show?"

"Not just *a TV show. The Sopranos.* And it's the season finale. There is no way I'm watching this shit at home by myself."

"So, you just called this guy up and invited yourself over?"

"Yep."

"Are Victoria and Steven coming?"

Shit. I didn't even think about the possibility of them coming. God, I hope they're not there. Victoria would totally tell Hans.

"I don't know. Maybe."

I turned left onto a side street, then pulled up to the gated entrance of the Midtown Village apartment complex.

I looked at the code scribbled underneath my handwritten directions and typed it into the keypad. The sleek wrought iron barricade swung open without so much as a squeak. The complex inside consisted of about six geometric, ultra-modern gray buildings, and the parking lot was filled with cars that probably cost as much per month as the rent of the apartments they were parked in front of.

I mentally renamed the place Bachelor Village.

We parked in front of the three hundred building, adjusted our lipstick and bra straps, and then made the hike up four flights of concrete stairs to the top floor.

Taking a moment to catch our breath, Juliet and I squared our shoulders, and with a nod, I knocked as loud as I could.

The door swung open almost immediately, revealing a very posh, very sloshed Jason.

"BB! What's up, girl?" He was sporting a drunk, sleepy-eyed smile, a rumpled white dress shirt with blue pinstripes, and a crisp pair of flat-front khakis.

Upon seeing his pants, I gasped and covered my mouth with my hand.

"Oh no!" I squealed. "I forgot to wear my khakis!"

Jason laughed so hard he doubled over, propping himself up on the doorknob. When the door began to swing open, I thought he was gonna go down for sure.

"Whoa, man." I caught him by the elbow. "Somebody's

excited about the season finale, huh?" I cast a nervous look back at Juliet, who shrugged in response. "Thanks for having us. Do you mind if we come in?"

Jason stood up and looped an arm over my shoulders. The gesture seemed friendly, but I think he really just needed me for stability. "Of course! Come in! Come in!"

The apartment was gorgeous. Super-high ceilings, thanks to being on the top floor, stainless steel hardware, sleek lines, gray everything. Except the couches. Those were black leather.

The entryway had hallways jutting off both sides, leading to two separate bedrooms and bathrooms, and the main living area was just through the foyer. Jason walked me into the living room where about six dudes were lounging on various pieces of furniture, drinking and yelling at a baseball game on Jason's big screen.

"Errrybody!" Jason slurred. "This is BB and..." Jason looked down at us with glassy eyes.

"Juliet," I finished for him.

"Buttercup and Juliet!"

The guys all cast us a quick glance, then did a double take when they realized that we had vaginas. Two dudes, dressed as preppily as Jason, leaped to their feet and motioned to their now-vacant seats on the couch.

"You guys can sit here. We were just going to play pool."

"Thanks," I said, leading the way to the couch.

Juliet followed behind. I could feel her bristle with defensiveness. She kind of hated people, but she loved to drink and desperately needed a break from Romeo, so...she'd get over it.

"What kind of whiskey are you guys drinking?" I asked, noticing a few highball glasses on the coffee table. I took the middle seat on the couch so that Juliet wouldn't have to sit next to a stranger.

"It's not whiskey! It's scotch!" Jason announced, stumbling through the living room into the stainless steel kitchen.

"Scotch *is* whiskey," a voice next to me mumbled.

I turned my head and found a guy with an extra-disinterested expression on his face and light-brown hair flipped up in the front, staring at the TV. He had a nice profile—button nose, square jaw—but instead of a beer, he was clutching a bottle of purple Gatorade.

And instead of khakis, he was wearing *pajamas*.

Okay, maybe not pajamas, but, like, workout clothes. To a party. Weird.

"Is it good?" I yelled back at Jason. "I've never had it."

Jason reappeared holding two highball glasses, spilling over with amber liquid. "It's fuckin' delicious." He smiled. Then, he took a sip from each of them and plopped into a vacant leather recliner, spilling half of his precious beverages on his oxford cloth shirt.

Pajama Guy chuckled. I turned to look at him again, and that time, he met my gaze. His eyes were almost turquoise, framed by long sable-colored lashes.

"Is he always like this?" I asked.

"Only every time he drinks." It sounded like a joke, but Pajama Guy didn't smile when he said it, so I couldn't be sure. "I'll get you guys something," he offered. "What do you want?"

"I guess I'll try the scotch, if there's any left. Hey, Jules, you want some scotch?" I asked my BFF, smacking her on the thigh.

Juliet wrinkled her nose at Jason, who looked like he was on the verge of passing out. "Uh, no. A beer is fine. Thanks."

Pajama Guy nodded once, set his sports drink down on the coffee table, and stood up. I thought he was going to go get us some drinks, but he stood in front of the big screen instead.

Every dude in the apartment stopped what they were doing and stood up with him. Juliet and I shared a confused glance.

Then, Pajama Guy shouted, "Fuck yeah! Run, motherfucker! Run!"

The announcers on TV said that somebody on the Braves had just hit a home run. The two guys on the love seat did karate chops and high kicks in celebration. The two guys over at the pool table—which, in Jason's bachelor pad, had taken the place of a dining room table—high-fived. And Jason slept through the whole thing.

When Pajama Guy returned with our drinks, Juliet looked happy to have a distraction from the two guys sitting on the love seat next to her. They looked like brothers and had been putting the moves on her pretty hard while he was gone.

"So, how do you know Jason?" she asked, desperate for a new conversation.

"We went to high school together." Pajama Guy gestured toward the guys on the love seat. "So did the Alexander brothers over there—Ethan and Devon." He pointed at each one as he said their names. "And Allen—he's out on the balcony."

"Who are those guys playing pool?" I asked.

"That's Bryan and Scott. They work with Jason. Hopefully, not too closely." Pajama Guy raised an eyebrow and looked over my shoulder at Jason.

Dude had the driest sense of humor. I couldn't tell if he was being funny or being an asshole.

"That's cool that you guys have all been friends since high

school," Juliet replied, desperate to keep the conversation going. "BB and I went to high school together, too. Until this bitch had to go and graduate early." Juliet shot affectionate daggers at me with her eyes. "What high school did you go to?"

"Peach State."

"No shit? So did we!" I blurted out.

"I know." Pajama Guy looked directly at me.

There was something in his stare that told me there was more to that comment, but before I could probe him further, somebody switched the channel and *The Sopranos* opening credits began.

Jason leaped out of his chair, as if being woken from the dead, and thrust what was left of both of his beverages into the air. "Fuck yeah, muthafuckas!"

Allen, the guy on the back porch, came flying in, shoving his flip phone into his pocket just in time. He was a stocky dude whose kind eyes were magnified by thick glasses.

"Is Amy gonna let you have your balls back tonight?" Ethan called from the love seat.

"Fuck you, bro. I'm not whipped," Allen snapped back. "Amy just had a bad day."

"Whhh-pssh," the two brothers said in unison, pantomiming a whip being cracked in the air.

I giggled. I couldn't help it.

Allen looked at me and furrowed his brow. "Hey," he shouted in recognition, "did you go to Peach State?"

Oh God, here it comes.

"Yeah! You had a shaved head, and you dated that Knight guy!"

There it is.

I forced a smile. "Yep. That's me. I'm BB. This is Juliet."

"What's up?" Allen smiled at us, then shifted his attention to Pajama Guy. "Ken, you remember Knight, right? That skinhead—"

"Yeah, I remember," Pajama Guy interrupted in a clipped tone.

So, Pajama Guy's name is Ken, and evidently, he's not too keen on Knight either. Interesting.

"Would all you bitches shut the fuck up?" Jason shouted, swaying on his feet. "It's the fuckin' S'pranos." He threw both hands in the direction of the big screen, sloshing scotch all over the carpet.

A hush fell over the apartment as we watched Tony Soprano get food poisoning, have a sex dream about his therapist, murder a guy on a yacht for being an informer, and throw a party for his daughter's high school graduation, all in the span of fifty minutes.

When it was over, the guys all grumbled as Allen pulled a piece of poster board out from behind the TV stand. Studying whatever was written on it, he said, "Damn. *Nobody* picked Pussy?"

"Excuse me?" Juliet snapped.

Allen looked up from the poster. "Ha! Sorry. Pussy was the name of the guy Tony killed tonight. Every week we take bets on which character is gonna die."

He turned the poster around so that we could see. Along the left side were the names *Jason, Allen, Ethan, Devon, Bryan,* and *Scott.* Along the top were the dates of every episode that season, and in each box on the grid was the name of a different character. Judging by all the ones circled in red, Jason was surprisingly good at plot prediction for a guy who could barely keep his eyes open through an entire episode.

I turned to Ken. "I don't see your name up there. You didn't want to play?"

"I'm not giving these assholes my money," he said with an arched brow.

"So, you don't bet"—I glanced at the now-empty Gatorade bottle on the coffee table—"and you don't drink..." The puzzle pieces were starting to come together. "Are you, like, a Mormon or something?"

Ken laughed. Hard. Like eyes-closed, head-back laughed.

He had really nice teeth.

"Hell no," he said once he finally recovered. "I just hate spending money." And with that, Ken stood, shoved his empty plastic bottle into the pocket of his Nike running pants, grabbed his car keys and cell phone off the coffee table, and said, "Nice to meet you, Brooke. Juliet."

Brooke. Ugh. Nobody calls me that.

Ken had given the group an obligatory wave and taken two steps toward the door when Allen tackle-hugged him from behind, followed by Ethan, Devon, and finally Jason, who hit the manwich like a wrecking ball and took them all down.

A chorus of "But Ken, I love you," and "Don't leave me, bro," and "Shh...just go with it," blended together until Ken fought his way out of the dog pile and bolted out the door.

The room exploded in laughter the second he was gone, guys rolling around on the floor holding their stomachs.

"He fucking hates us so hard right now," Ethan or Devon cried.

The other Alexander brother snickered. "I'm gonna get that motherfucker to tell me he loves me if it's the last thing I do!"

Jason was laughing too hard to speak.

"I just want a hug," Allen lamented. "Dude's been my best friend for six years. Is a little hug/back-slap action too much to ask?"

"So, Ken hates drinking, gambling, *and* warm hugs?" Juliet giggled.

"Basically," Allen said, pulling himself up and crawling toward the coffee table where he'd left his beer. His hair was all disheveled, and his glasses were on crooked. "Fucker's the enemy of fun, but I love him."

"*. . . the enemy of fun, but I love him.*"

Something in those words struck a chord deep within me.

I had loved somebody like that once.

An enemy of fun.

A buzzkill with zombie eyes.

But I didn't love him anymore.

Nope. Not even one little bit.

May 2000

"We've been sitting out here for, like, an hour, and they just keep coming!" Juliet shouted, flicking her cigarette butt into the street where it was immediately smashed under the tire of a snarling, slow-moving Harley-Davidson. And then another. And then another.

"I know. It's crazy!" I yelled back, watching the never-ending parade of black leather and shiny chrome roll down Ocean Boulevard.

"You know what's even crazier?" she asked, looking at me. "They're all white. All of 'em. I haven't seen a Black person since we left Atlanta."

"Oh my God." My hand flew to my mouth as I scanned our surroundings. Mentally retracing our steps all the way from Atlanta to Myrtle Beach, I was horrified to realize that she was right. "How is that even possible? Black people ride motorcycles too! Remember when we used to go to the track with Harley? None of those moto guys were white. What the fuck? It's Bike Week, not White Week!"

I was pissed. Pissed but most of all ashamed. How had I brought Juliet here and not even realized how uncomfortable she must have been? Or even what it was?

I hopped down off the cement block that supported the sign for our one-star motel and approached a man walking by who looked like a biker version of Santa Claus.

"Excuse me? Sir? Can you tell me where all the, um ... people of color are?"

Santa gave Juliet a quick glance and seemed to catch my drift. "Oh, y'all are lookin' for Black Bike Week. That ain't till Memorial Day."

"Excuse me?" Juliet snapped, standing up to join me.

Santa held up his hands. "Sorry, miss. Didn't mean no disrespect. That's just what they call it. This here is the Harley-Davidson Bike Week. Then, next week, the, uh ... *minorities* do their Bike Week up on the north side of the strip. They ride them fancy crotch rockets and such. Lotta young folks, like yourself. It gets real wild though. Not laid-back like this. Coupla folks got shot last year, so y'all be real careful if you go."

"Uh ... we will. Thanks."

Santa gave us a friendly smile and went along his merry way while Juliet and I stood there, like we'd just been sucker-punched in the guts.

"Oh my fucking God," I said, blinking at my best friend. The girl I would move heaven and hell for. The girl who'd been there for me through every breakup, every trauma. The girl whose baby I'd helped deliver and name.

She was acting angry, but I knew what she was feeling went much deeper than that.

Juliet pursed her lips and raised one of her expertly drawn-on eyebrows. "Did we fucking travel back in time? I'm gonna ask the next person we see what fucking year it is. This is bullshit."

"I'm so sorry I brought you here, Jules."

"Sorry? Why are you sorry? All Hans said was that we were going to Bike Week. Well, here we are." Juliet spun around in a full circle with her arms out.

I grabbed my purse off the cement block and tossed it over my shoulder. "I'm gonna make it right, boo. C'mon."

"Where are we going?" Juliet huffed.

"North. We're goin' fucking north."

Juliet and I turned our backs on the Happy Holiday Motel, tossed our empty Jack and Coke bottles in a nearby trash can, and headed north along Ocean Boulevard.

We walked about a mile, which felt more like three with all the bobbing and weaving we had to do around the Harleys and choppers parked along the sidewalk. The sun was beginning to set before we finally heard it—deep, thumping bass.

We had struck hip-hop.

Juliet and I looked at each other at the same time and grinned.

We followed the sound to an unassuming building on the beach side of the street. The sign out front said, *Dougan's Bar and Grill*, and underneath it, written in black letters on the marquee, were two words that delighted me like no others.

Karaoke Night.

I squealed and sprinted arm in arm with Juliet across the street. Inside the place was dark, dingy, wood-paneled, and packed full of people.

People who *did not* look like me for a change.

The main open area of the restaurant was filled with round high-top tables, all facing a decent-sized stage, and each one had about two people too many shoved around it on narrow barstools.

By some miracle, Juliet and I scored a table in the back corner. Just as the hostess walked away, an announcer called out a name over the loudspeakers. Juliet and I watched as a heavyset man in a three-piece suit walked up to the mic. Poor guy was already sweating profusely and looked like he might throw up.

When the music came on it sounded familiar, but it wasn't until he opened his mouth and sang the words, "If I," in a soft, high-pitched voice that I realized what the fuck was about to go down.

"Oh shit!" I slammed my hand on the table and stared at Juliet with eyes like saucers. "No! No fucking way!"

Juliet's mouth fell open as she stared at the stage.

Fishing my phone out of my purse, I dialed Hans's number prepared to leave him a voicemail. I knew he was at some radio interview and probably wouldn't answer, but I had to share this shit with somebody.

"Hey, baby!" He picked up on the second ring.

"Hans! Oh my God, I didn't think you'd answer. Can you hear me?"

"Barely. What's up? You guys having fun?"

"Yes! Dude, we're at this place on the strip called Dougan's and it's karaoke night and—oh shit, he's about to sing the chorus. Listen!" I held the phone up just before my new hero hit the highest high note in "I Will Always Love You" by Whitney Houston.

The crowd lost their damn minds—jumping up and down, throwing their hands in the air, screaming and whistling. The energy was glorious. I got high just being near it.

"Did you hear that?" I screamed.

"Yeah, that was amazing. Did you say that was a guy?"

The crowd was still deafening, so I ran outside to finish my conversation.

"Yes! And he looks like Cedric the Entertainer!" I cackled. "You guys have to come here when you're done! We have a table in the back."

"Okay. We've been done for, like, half an hour, but Trip won't stop flirting with the DJ. He thinks he can sweet-talk her into giving us air time, but he's probably just gonna get us banned."

I laughed. "Good luck with that."

"I'll be there as soon as I can, okay? I miss you. I'm glad you have somebody to hang out with this time though."

"Yeah, me too." I smiled into the phone. "Oh shit! I hear Tupac. Gotta go! Love you. Bye!"

Hans chuckled. "Love you too, baby. Bye."

As I walked back into the restaurant, I patted myself on the back for my maturity. *Look at me. Came to an out-of-town show and didn't even get jealous or pouty or wasted or lost or anything. I'm basically a full-grown, mature adult at this point. Somebody, get me a drink and a mortgage and register my ass to vote. I have arrived.*

When I got back to my seat, I was pleasantly surprised to see that the drink part of my adult wish list had already been fulfilled. A tall glass filled with smoky-gray liquid sat untouched in front of me on the table. Juliet was sipping on an identical one across from me.

"Who are these from?" I asked, eyeing the murky beverage suspiciously.

"Those guys." Juliet cast her eyes sideways to a high-top about ten feet away with a group of six dudes sitting at it.

Two of them were watching us.

"Ah, man. Great. Now they're gonna expect us to suck their dicks."

"Pssh. Whatever. I got us free drinks, didn't I?" Juliet rolled her eyes and took another long pull from her big, haunted-looking drink.

"What the hell is this?" I stirred the gray matter with my straw, praying I wasn't going to find a finger or a toe floating in it.

"It's called Fuck Me in the Graveyard."

"How romantic." I took a sip and was pleasantly surprised. It was strong as hell but had a fruity aftertaste. Like maybe pineapple? Or grapefruit? Or cranberry? Or all of the above? Whatever it was, it hit my empty stomach and bounced right back up into my brain, telling me things like, *You should get up there and sing. No, you're a terrible singer. You should get up there and rap.*

"I think I'm gonna go put my name in," I slurred ten minutes later over my almost-empty drink.

"What? Here? What are you gonna sing?"

I shook my head. "Not sing. Rap."

"Oh, Jesus Christ. What are you gonna rap?" Juliet started laughing before she even got the word *rap* all the way out.

"The 'Thong Song,' of course. I know all the words. Craig and I have a whole choreographed dance to it." I gasped. "Oh no, Craig's not here. Do you know how to twerk?"

Juliet snorted so hard, Fuck Me in the Graveyard came out of her nose. "I am a *mother*. I do *not* twerk."

"Okay, bitch. Have it your way. More glory for me."

I got up and stumbled over to the DJ booth where there was a huge binder filled with songs. After mustering all the concentration left in my inebriated frontal lobes, I found the "Thong Song" and scrawled the number next to it down on a tiny piece of paper, using one of the equally tiny golf pencils provided.

As I walked behind the table of guys who'd paid for the drink that got me drunk enough to consider doing karaoke, one of them turned in his barstool and clotheslined me with a thick arm around my waist. He was a skinny white dude with a shaved head, who was wearing a wifebeater and about three gold chains. When he smiled, he had a gold tooth to match.

"Where you goin' so fast, Smalls?"

"Uh, I'm just goin' to sit with my friend."

"Y'all like them drinks?" His lips were thin, and they disappeared when he smiled.

"Yeah. Thanks. That was, uh, really nice." I stuck my thumbnail between my teeth, absentmindedly adopting Hans's nervous habit, and looked over at Juliet with pleading eyes.

"Is that a weddin' ring?" Slim Shady asked.

I looked at the black diamonds circling my ring finger and beamed in relief. "Yep!" I chirped. Donning a thicker version of my subtle Southern accent, I added, "My boyfriend done knocked me up, so my daddy said we had to git married, 'fore I started showin'. Just did it at the courthouse last week."

That did the trick. Slim's face fell, as did his arm from around my waist. "Uh, congratulations?"

"Thanks!" I grinned, turning to scamper off.

I'd only gotten about three feet away before Slim called after me, "Hey, if you're pregnant, how come you're drinkin'?"

Shit. Uh . . .

I spun around, fake smile back in place, and swatted at him

playfully. "Oh hush, you. It was only one! My mama said she drank while she was pregnant with me, and I turned out just fine!"

When I turned around and headed back toward our table, I let my mask slide off, revealing the death stare Juliet deserved.

"Well, he seemed friendly," she said, biting her bottom lip to keep from laughing.

"I hate you."

"You didn't hate that free drink."

"I hate that I smell like Michael Jordan cologne now."

"Brooke Bradley to the stage. Brooke Bradley to the stage."

"Fuck, that was fast!" I downed the rest of my drink and the rest of Juliet's too, shook out my arms, and said, "Wish me luck!"

I bounced up to the stage on my toes like a boxer who'd just been called into the ring, already feeling that last injection of alcohol. Luckily, I was born with about eighty-seven percent fewer inhibitions than most humans, but the science beaker of alcohols I'd just poured into my body got me all the way to one hundred.

The folks in the crowd were clearly confused about what a ninety-five-pound white girl with a punk haircut wearing a David Bowie tank top was doing on their stage, but I didn't worry about them. As soon as that cheesy violin intro started, they all disappeared. I was operating on blissful, beautiful muscle memory as I stepped to the right on the first line, slid to the left on the second line, turned around and shook my ass—the only place that jiggled on my whole body—on the third line, and looked over my shoulder to rap the fourth line with a wink.

The crowd died laughing, and the girls stood up and shook their asses with me during the chorus. I pointed at a few pro twerkers in the audience and motioned for them to come up onstage. By the second chorus, I had a whole army of booty-shaking fly girls behind me, and by the third chorus, I managed to get the big guy who'd sung the Whitney Houston song onstage. His face turned bright red as we freak-danced all over him. One girl even took his suit jacket off and threw it out into the crowd.

My heart was racing and I was panting and laughing and forgetting the lyrics by the last verse, but nobody cared. It was the most fun I'd ever had in my life.

As I climbed back off the stage, my knees shaky from the adrenaline and my mouth numb from all the smiling and rapping, I looked to our table, ready to make an *Oh my God!* face at Juliet, but she wasn't even watching me. She had her back to the stage and was yelling at two of the guys from the douche-bag table who must have come over to hit on her again while I was gone.

I was about halfway to the table when I saw Juliet shove one of them in the chest.

Oh fuck.

I broke into a sprint and was almost to the table when Prince Charming picked up a very full, very gray drink off the table—I assume a gift for Juliet—and dumped the entire thing over her head.

What happened next is still a blur. All I know is that I heard two hits—and felt one.

When I came to, I was outside Dougan's, sitting on the sidewalk with my back against the brick building. I had a splitting fucking headache, and all I wanted to do was slump over on the concrete and go back to sleep.

"BB! Wake up! Wake up, damn it! We gotta go!"

I opened my heavy lids just enough to make out Juliet's blurry face. Something wet was dripping on my hands. I opened my eyes a little more and saw that it was liquid falling from the ends of Juliet's braids. She was drenched.

"Get up, damn it. The manager probably called the cops, and we're underage. Get up!"

"What happened? Where'd those assholes go?"

"I'll tell you on the way back to the hotel. C'mon."

Juliet grabbed me by my forearms and hoisted my bony ass off the ground. It felt like somebody was squeezing my skull with both hands, and their thumbs were right between my eyes. When I touched the spot, it exploded in pain.

"Fuck!"

Juliet swatted my hand away as she dragged me down the sidewalk. "Don't touch it. We'll get you some ice at the motel."

"What the fuck happened?"

"Those guys showed up with another round of drinks, but I was trying to watch you rap, so I asked them to move. The one with the Wayans brothers high-top fade called me a bitch, so I turned around and told him to fuck off, and then that piece of shit poured a drink on my head!" Juliet's grip on my arm tightened, but I could feel her hand shaking still. "So I punched him right in the fucking face! Who does that? Who fucking pours a drink on a girl just because she's not interested?" Her voice faltered like she was on the verge of tears, but I knew she'd suck that shit up. Juliet never cried.

"His buddy grabbed him to pull him away, but then the two of them started scrapping, and his buddy's elbow flew back and caught you right between the eyes."

I went to touch the tender spot, but Juliet swatted my hand down again.

"Knocked your little ass out cold. And that asshole manager—"

Honk! Honnnnnnk! A car horn blared behind us.

"What's up, ladies? Y'all wanna party?"

We turned around and glared at Trip, who was hanging out the passenger window of Baker's van. As soon as Trip and Baker saw our seriously pissed-off, wet, swollen faces, their smiles disappeared.

"Damn. What happened to y'all? Wet T-shirt contest gone bad?"

"Fuck you, Trip," Juliet spat. Grabbing my arm, she spun us back around and kept marching toward the motel.

Motorcycle engines revved and cars honked as they swerved to go around Baker's van, which was crawling down Ocean Boulevard next to us.

I heard the side door of the van slide open and knew that Hans must be hopping out. As much as I wanted to turn and run into his arms, Juliet's anger was contagious. I wanted someone to yell at too, someone to blame, and who better than the man who never seemed to be there when I needed him?

"Baby, are you okay? What happened?"

I huffed and ignored him.

He's gonna grab my arm in three, two—

Hans's long, rough fingertips hooked around my tiny bicep, but he didn't grab. He didn't pull. His touch was so gentle, it hurt me to shrug it off.

But I did it anyway.

"Hey...talk to me." Hans jogged ahead of us and turned around, blocking our path. When his eyes landed on mine, he looked as if he were the one who'd been elbowed in the face. "Oh my God! Is that a black eye?"

Is it?

I turned and searched Juliet's face for confirmation. She just kind of shrugged and nodded.

Awesome. I have a black eye.

Hans rushed to me and took my face in his hands. He placed three gentle kisses just above my left eyebrow, causing tears to blur my vision even worse than the alcohol and swelling already had.

I closed my eyes and turned my head away.

"What the fuck is going on? Why won't you talk to me?"

Juliet grunted and dropped my arm, stomping off without us.

"We'll meet you back at the hotel, okay?" Hans called to the guys in the van.

They pulled ahead but continued to crawl along the sidewalk next to Juliet, who was power-walking with her arms folded across her chest. Trip was hanging out the passenger window, talking to her. I couldn't hear what he was saying, but I knew he was probably trying to make her laugh.

Good luck with that.

"Come here," Hans said, taking my hand. At the next gap in traffic, he led me across the street and through a parking lot on the other side.

"What are you doing?"

"What I should have done the second we got here. I'm taking you to the beach."

The parking lot had a trail through the sand dunes that led out to the water. Juliet and I had played in the ocean a little bit that morning, but it was completely different at night. The

ocean breeze chilled my damp skin instead of heating it. The
roar of the waves seemed louder, drowning out the sound of the
motorcycles cruising up and down Ocean Boulevard. The sun-
bathers had been replaced by drunks passed out in the sand.
And the clouds had been dressed in their finest evening wear—
midnight-blue velvet with sparkling white diamonds.

My combat boots sank deep into the powdery sand with
every step as Hans led me toward a lifeguard stand. Without
even looking to see if anyone was watching, Hans climbed to
the top of the wooden structure and held out his hand to help
me up. I climbed up behind him.

But I didn't take his hand.

I wasn't a child.

Okay, legally, I was still a child, but fuck him. I could climb a
goddamn lifeguard stand. Black eye or no black eye.

There was only one seat at the top, so Hans claimed it and
pulled me into his lap, my back to his front.

Between Hans's rhythmic heartbeat against my back, his
scruffy jaw against my shoulder, his warm arms around my
waist, and the steady ebb and flow of the sea spread out before
me, my body gave up the fight and allowed itself to be soothed.

"I don't know what happened, and you don't have to tell me,
but I'm sorry I wasn't there to stop it."

That sweet, simple sentence took away any hope I'd had of an
argument. I'd wanted to shout those words at him.

You weren't there! I'd have yelled, making myself feel better
by making him feel like shit.

But he'd taken the words right out of my mouth and handed
them to me on a silver platter.

"Me too," I sighed.

"Are you okay?"

I nodded. "Juliet got into a fight with some guys while I was onstage at that karaoke bar."

"*You* were onstage? Like, doing karaoke onstage?"

And just like that, my anger roared back to life with a vengeance.

"Uh, yeah. I fucking love karaoke."

"Sorry. I just didn't know you could sing."

Ooh, you think you're so goddamn special just because you have a talent. Like you're the only asshole who knows how to work a stage. I have talents too, motherfucker. I have talents you don't even know about. Like twerking. And making an ass out of myself. People love that shit.

"I can't sing," I snapped. "That's why I rap. Anyway"—I let out an exasperated huff—"I ran over to break up the fight and got elbowed in the fucking face." I winced just thinking about it.

Hans took my chin in his hand and turned my face toward his. His eyes were hard instead of soft. His jaw clenched and unclenched. Then he kissed me right between the eyes. Right on the place where it hurt the most.

Hans didn't say a word. He didn't have to. He was trying to appear concerned, but the anger radiating off of him and the disappointment in his eyes said it all.

I'd fucked up again.

He'd probably had fun that day while I wasn't around. He might have even achieved his dream of being on the radio, for all I knew.

But I wasn't there for the good parts.

I was only there to bring him down.

I opened my mouth to ask about his day when Hans pulled a Hans and changed the subject completely.

"Did you know that the stars are so far away that it takes *years* for their light to reach Earth?" he asked in a serious tone, gazing past me at the sky. "I think the closest star is four light-years away." Hans's eyes seemed to cloud over as if he were lost in thought, his mouth set in a straight line. "All of those stars could be burned out right now, and we'd never know. We'd just go about our lives, looking at the ghosts of dead stars every night, never knowing that we were already in the dark."

A lump formed in my throat. "That was…beautiful." I tried to swallow the uncomfortable bulge, but it didn't budge. "You should write that down, baby. Here…"

As I dug in my purse for a pen, grateful for an excuse to hide my emotional face, I hoped and prayed that Hans hadn't been talking about us. Lately, it felt like his light was always too far away, took too long to reach me. And now that it had arrived, I was beginning to wonder how long it would take for me to realize if it ever burned away for good.

June 2000

Party, Party, Party, Party. That's what we were calling it. It was my eighteenth birthday. It was almost Hans's twentieth birthday. And Juliet and Goth Girl had both just graduated from high school.

Two Birthdays + Two Graduations = Party, Party, Party, Party.

I wanted to call it Party to the Fourth Degree, but that was kind of a mouthful, so I kept that idea to myself.

Party, Party, Party, Party took place at Steven's house because the rest of us still lived with our parents. I had hoped that Hans's parents would take another road trip that summer, but they were too busy being separated for all that.

Hans's dad had been living in their RV on a different part of the lake for weeks while his mom still lived in that big-ass house with Hans. Nobody talked about it, and nobody seemed terribly upset about it either. It simply was what it was.

Wait, I take that back. *I* was upset about it.

All year, I'd been counting the days until Hans and I could finally return to our fairy-tale life, living rent-free in the Oppenheimers' estate, swimming and laughing and watching the sun set over the lake with a couple of beers. Making love all night and waking up in each other's arms at noon. Driving around in Helga's brand-new Z3 and coming home to find sparkling countertops and perfect triangles vacuumed into the carpet. So, when Hans had broken the news to me, I was devastated.

But that loss only made me more determined to save up enough money to cover my half of an apartment. Hans and I were going to live happily ever after, goddamn it, with or without the fairy-tale castle.

I peeked inside my purse for the hundredth time that night to make sure the red envelope with Hans's name calligraphed on the front was still there.

"What you got in there?" Hans asked, stroking my left thigh, which was draped over his right one.

We were sitting in the exact same spot on Steven's couch where we'd gotten to know each other the first night we met. That night, I'd felt as though we were floating on our own little leather island built for two; the black lights and strobe lights and goth kids and industrial music swirling around us had seemed as far away as distant continents. Hans's eyes on my face and his fingertips on my skin had been all I could register. The rhythm. The heat. The tiny jolts of electricity I'd felt with every touch, every dimpled smile.

Eleven months later, and the visceral response Hans elicited from me had only intensified. Sitting that close to him lit me up. My body tingled in anticipation of his touch. My heart leaned in, waiting to soak up every sweet nothing he uttered. And my mouth twisted up into a poorly contained smile, unable to hide the joy I felt whenever his distractible mind was distracted by me.

"Nothing." I grinned and smooshed my purse shut, shoving it against the armrest next to me.

"Nothing, huh?" Hans gave me a devilish side-eye just before reaching across my body with his long, tattooed arm and snatching my bag.

"No!" I yelled, grabbing my once-fuzzy, now very matted and sad-looking tiger-striped purse. "Let go!"

Hans laughed and poked me in the ribs with his free hand, causing my torso to contort in response.

"Fuck you! Don't tickle me!" I squealed.

"Whatcha got in there, baby?" *Poke, poke.*

"Dicks!" I screamed, causing every head in the dark, pulsating room to turn. "Big ole dicks! You want one?"

Hans chuckled and pulled me effortlessly into his lap. Releasing my purse, he wrapped both arms around my waist and grazed my cheek with his stubbled smile.

"No, but I think I got one for your collection." Hans pressed his growing erection against my pleather-covered ass and nuzzled his face into the crook of my neck.

I let go of my purse with one hand—still keeping a death grip on it with the other—and wove my fingers into Hans's unruly black hair. He hadn't performed that night, so instead of smelling like sweat and cigarette smoke, it smelled like floral shampoo and cigarette smoke. I giggled, picturing the bottle of Herbal Essences I'd seen in his shower.

Hans's lips found a tender spot just below my ear as his hands found their way just under the hem of the Birthday Bitch crop top Juliet had given me. I moaned unexpectedly and felt his cock jerk beneath me in response. I regretted nothing more in that moment than my decision to wear pants instead of a skirt that night. If I could have simply pulled my thong to one side and let him fill me right there on the couch, I would have.

My heavy-lidded eyes swept across the darkened living room. Everyone was paired off. Everyone had their hands on each other. And from the looks of things, if we didn't claim Maddie's bedroom right then, we might have to take a number just to reserve it for an hour.

Standing up, I grabbed my purse and adjusted my clothes. Hans followed suit and led me by the hand into the kitchen and straight toward our little pink-and-purple Pony-covered home away from home.

The kitchen was much brighter than the living room, and the party guests in there were much less bumpy and grindy. I squinted and tried to avoid making eye contact with anyone as we passed through.

"Hans!" a voice called from somewhere near the sink.

Goddamn it.

I sighed audibly as we both turned toward Goth Girl, who was waving us over. She and Trip were standing next to the counter, facing one another. Their arms were folded across their chests, and it appeared as though a battle of wills had begun.

"Will you tell this asshole that he has to clean that shit up?" Goth Girl barked, shoving a black fingernail toward the floor where a small yellow puddle of either pilsner or piss was fizzing on the linoleum.

Hans laughed and veered off course, leaving me bereft in the middle of the kitchen. "Yeah. With his tongue."

I walked over to the keg and poured myself another beer. That shit was going to take a while; I could tell. Goth Girl was wasted. Trip was having way too much fun fucking with her, and Hans, successfully distracted, was laughing at them both as he lit a cigarette.

"Hey, Birthday Bitch," Juliet said, sidling up next to me by the keg.

"Hey, Regular Bitch." I smirked and leaned into her arm.

"Excuse me. That's *High School Graduate* Bitch, thank you very much." Juliet raised her drawn-on eyebrows and snapped her fingers in an arc in front of my face.

I smiled and pulled her in for a hug. "I'm so fucking proud of you," I cooed into her hair as she stood, rigidly tolerating my affection. "I can't believe you have a two-year-old at home and you still managed to graduate on time. You're fucking amazing."

"Yeah, well, he watches a lot of *SpongeBob*, so"—Juliet wriggled out of my embrace—"don't be too impressed."

"Shut up," I said, nudging her arm with my elbow. I could tell my lovefest was making her uncomfortable, so I changed the subject. "It's too bad that Mike had to work tonight."

"Huh." Juliet was staring at something over my shoulder. Flicking her black-brown eyes back to mine, she said, "Oh, yeah. His job sucks ass."

I turned and looked behind me. Smiling in recognition, I teased, "Uh-oh...did I just catch you checking out Triiiiiip?" in a singsongy voice.

Juliet's face fell as she pinned me with a look that most teenage girls reserve solely for their annoying younger siblings. "Uh, *no*. Look again."

I turned and gave the clique another once-over, but I didn't see anything out of the ordinary.

"What?"

"Is she always that flirty with your man?"

"Who? Victoria? She hardly even talks to him." I turned around and peeked again.

Goth Girl, who was usually about as perky as Daria on chloroform, was...*smiling*. At Hans. I didn't even know the girl had teeth.

"Whatever. She's just wasted." I rolled my eyes and turned to face Juliet, who gave me an unconvinced half-shrug.

"Call it what you want." Looking over my shoulder again, she said, "Speaking of wasted, guess who just showed up?"

I glanced in the direction of the living room entryway and saw a cute guy with an unfortunately preppy crew cut stroll in...wearing khakis.

"Shit!" I grabbed Juliet and practically dived into the hallway leading to Maddie's bedroom. It turned left after the bathroom, giving us a place to hide.

"What the hell, B?"

"Shh! Hans doesn't know we've been hanging out!" I whisper-shouted.

Juliet snorted. "Still?"

"No! I didn't tell him 'cause I didn't think he'd find out and because it's totally not a thing, but he'd make it a thing 'cause he got all jealous the first time he saw us talking and I don't want to deal with it when it's not even a thing."

Juliet's eyes lifted over my head. "Well, you're gonna have to deal with it now."

"What's up, BB?"

I spun on my heels, smiling from ear to ear in the darkened hallway. "Hey, Jason! What's up? You droppin' off some party favors?" I waggled my eyebrows, indicating that *party favors* was code for drugs, like a total dork. "I haven't seen Steven in a while." I looked around as if he were going to magically appear. "Do you need me to find him for you?"

Jason raised one eyebrow. "Noooo. I'm here 'cause it's your birthday."

"Oh! Wow. Really? That's so sweet! Thanks for coming!"

The only thing I was actually thankful for in that moment was the low level of light in the hallway, preventing Jason from seeing my crimson fucking cheeks.

"You haven't come over in a while," he said, rubbing the back of his neck.

It was weird to see him sober. I hadn't seen him not wasted since the first time we met. Of course, he'd just arrived. By the time Hans and I'd left that night, Jason had been shit-faced and walking on hot coals.

I liked sober Jason better.

"Yeah, well, now that *The Sopranos* is over I figured you guys would be taking a break."

"Nah. We just switched to *Survivor*. You should come watch with us."

"Yeah, okay. Sounds like fun. Hey, I'll, uh... be right back. I gotta pee," I stammered before turning and bolting into the hall bathroom.

I locked the door behind me and set my red plastic cup and purse on the counter. Looking up at my reflection in the mirror,

I stared at the waifish eighteen-year-old glancing back at me, wearing more black eyeliner and glittery eyeshadow than a go-go dancer at Studio 54, and tried to figure out why I felt so . . . weird.

Was it because I was hiding my friendship with Jason from Hans?

Possibly.

Was it because of what Juliet had said about Goth Girl flirting with him?

Maybe.

Was it because my birthday was almost over and nobody had sung me "Happy Birthday" or bought me a cake that said *Happy Birthday* on it or given me a present wrapped in Happy Birthday paper yet?

More than likely.

I wriggled my skintight leopard-print velour pants down below my knees and sat on the toilet in a state of quiet, drunken self-reflection.

So this is adulthood, I thought as I pissed out at least three Solo cups' worth of beer so cheap that it looked the same coming out as it had going in.

No more candles.

No more cake.

Just a keg full of Pabst Blue Ribbon and a house full of people I don't even know. Woo-fucking-hoo.

I tore off three squares of Steven's cheap single-ply toilet paper, and of course, as soon as my hand was between my legs, I heard my phone ring.

Shit!

I hustled to wipe, flush, and fish my Nokia out of my

bottomless pit of a bag, but by the time I pulled it out, I was too late. I'd missed the call.

I hit a button to illuminate the screen and saw three words appear that drove a frozen stake into my heart.

Terminus City Tattoo, my caller ID said.

It was June.

Knight was home.

I swallowed and forced myself to keep breathing, staring at the words until the screen went dark.

It's fine. You're safe. If he's calling from Terminus City, that's at least fifteen, maybe twenty miles from here. He doesn't know where you are. It's fine. You're fine.

Then my phone lit up again, all by itself.

Ding!

A voicemail.

Knight had only called me a few times from Iraq, but every time I'd deleted his messages without a single listen. I knew my limits. I knew I was weak when it came to him. I knew the sound of his voice was bad for me.

But it was my birthday, goddamn it. And if you can't do things that are bad for you on your birthday, then when?

I held the hunk of glittery plastic up to my head with a shaky hand and held my breath with burning lungs. Then my thumb found the rubber Talk button and mashed it flat.

"Hey, Punk. I knew you wouldn't answer. You never do... anymore. It's cool. I get it. I just wanted to tell you happy birthday. You're finally old enough to buy your own fucking cigarettes. If I ever see you again, maybe you can bum me one for a change. Hope you had a good day. I...love you."

Click.

I immediately regretted my decision.

Knight's words had been light, but his tone had sounded darker than ever. The waver in his voice when he'd said, "It's cool," the pause and swallow before, "love you," it made me want to run to him. To soothe him. To ask him what had happened while he was away. To help him work through it, no matter how horrific.

But Knight was beyond help. I had known it the moment I saw him rip that bush out of the ground with his bare hands. I had seen it in his zombie eyes as he grabbed my face and twisted my frown into a fraudulent smile. And I'd felt it as he forced his way into my body without my consent. Perhaps I'd always known it; I just hadn't wanted to accept it.

I still didn't.

Bang! Bang! Bang!

"Everybody! Stop fuckin' and get out here! We have an announcement to make!" Trip's voice drifted away from the door, and I heard his fist pound on Maddie's door just down the hall. "Bust a nut and wrap it up, motherfuckers! Major announcement in five!"

Dropping my phone back into my bag, I wiped the smudged mascara from under my eyes, washed my hands, re-spiked the ends of my choppy blonde pixie cut with my wet fingertips, pulled my shoulders back, and threw open the door. Just as I stepped into the hallway, Steven emerged from Maddie's room, looking like a vampiric version of the scarecrow from *The Wizard of Oz*. His straw-like black hair was disheveled. His black vinyl wardrobe hung from his too-skinny frame. And, like the scarecrow, he appeared to be a little wobbly in the knees.

Following him was an equally cracked-out-looking chick with mussed scarlet hair and smudged black lipstick. Considering that Steven's face was lipstick-free, my guess was that the rest of her makeup was smeared on his dick.

No wonder Goth Girl was feeling so needy.

Piece of shit.

We all filed into the living room where Trip, Baker, Louis, and Hans were standing in front of the entertainment center. Trip had opened the glass cabinet door and turned off the music in preparation for his "major announcement."

I had no idea what it might be, which made me feel a little nervous, and Hans's concerned face when I walked in made me feel even worse.

Glancing at the digital clock on the VCR, which said *11:58*, Trip yelled, "Ladies and gentlefucks! I know it's not a party without a performance from your favorite band of all time, Phantom Limb"—Trip spread his arms wide, gesturing toward his bashful bandmates as the partygoers cheered—"but this isn't just any party. This is Party, Party, Party, Party. And Party, Party, Party, Party deserves a special, next-level kind of performance."

Reaching into the cabinet behind him, Trip turned the large silver volume dial on Steven's stereo receiver all the way up. The speakers crackled in protest as the voice of a radio DJ vibrated through the living room.

"Heeeeey, everybody! This is Rick Dixon, and you are listening to WATL, Atlanta Rocks Radio! It's midnight, which means it's officially Saturday. And what do we do on Saturdays? Weeeeee rrrrock!"

My eyes opened wide as they lurched from the stereo to Hans's face. He rocked back on his heels with his hands in his pockets and gave me a mischievous one-dimpled smile. Baker blushed and stared at his feet. Louis stood there, looking bored. Meanwhile,

Trip was holding an invisible microphone and opening and clos-ing his mouth with every word the overly enthusiastic DJ spoke.

"On tonight's show, we've got new singles by Creed, Papa Roach, Incubus, Limp Bizkit, and of course, Metallica! But to kick things off, we want to spotlight a local band who's been burnin' up the Southeast this year with their high-energy, high-octane shows. If you guys ever get the chance to go see Phantom Limb perform live, you are in for a treat. And ladies, if you wear your Phantom Limb T-shirt to a show, they'll even pull you onstage for a kiss contest."

With those words, my fluttering heart dropped into my bowels like a stone. I pictured a line of girls in Phantom Limb T-shirts waiting outside the Masquerade to buy tickets as the DJ made a loud, exaggerated kiss noise, just to drive the point home.

"This is their debut single, 'Falling Star.' Enjoy!"

I held my breath and stared at Hans as a melody I'd never heard before lilted through the speakers. It wasn't heavy. It wasn't one of their usual songs. It was... a ballad.

When Trip's usually screamy voice began to sing the words that had been scrawled on Hans's forearm, tears filled my eyes. When he growled about putting his celestial pet on a leash, I swooned. And when he keened with velvety sincerity about his delicate fallen star being an explosive supernova in disguise, I knew exactly what he meant because my heart felt like it was about to explode and kill us all.

When the song was over, all two dozen partygoers screamed and jumped up and down and bum-rushed the guys in the band, but I got there first.

Leaping into Hans's waiting arms, I wrapped my legs around

his waist. I kissed his cheeks. I kissed his nose. I kissed his fore-head, eyelids, and chin. Eventually, I kissed his mouth but not before saying, "Oh my God," and, "I'm so proud of you," and, "That was amazing," at least a hundred times.

Hans smiled against my lips when they finally collided with his. "Happy birthday," he cooed, just loud enough for me to hear.

"Happy birthday back," I squealed. "Your song was on the radio!"

"*Your* song was on the radio." He bumped my nose with his nose.

"But how? You've never even played it for me before."

"I wanted it to be a surprise."

I tightened my grip around Hans's waist with my thighs and dropped my forehead to his.

"Did you like it?" he asked.

I nodded, causing his face to move up and down in sync with mine. "I loved it. I love *you*."

"I love you too, baby."

My heart swelled, as did Hans's emotional boner, which thickened between us. He clutched my ass tighter, pulled my wet center closer, and kissed me like we were the only ones in the room.

The chorus to the best gift I'd ever been given played in my head as Hans carried me to Maddie's room and kicked her door shut behind us.

I know it's wrong to keep her.
She belongs light-years away.
I know it's wrong to keep her,

So every day I pray.
Don't let my falling star fade away.
Please let this falling star…
Fall for me.

And fall I did—onto Maddie's pony-covered bedspread.

I might not have gotten a cake for my birthday or had any presents to unwrap. Nobody sang me "Happy Birthday" or presented me with eighteen tiny candles to blow out. But, as Hans crawled on top of me in the place where it'd all begun, none of that mattered. I'd already received the best gift I could have ever asked for.

And he'd written me a song.

30

July 2000

The second "Falling Star" started getting radio play, the band's tour schedule ramped up dramatically. Not only were they being asked to join the summer rock festival circuit, but places they'd already played as an opening act were asking them to come back to headline. I was incredibly happy for Hans, but with me taking a full summer semester course load and still working part-time while he traveled, it seemed like the only time I got to see him was before and after his local gigs.

And his local gigs had seriously changed. Headlining brought with it a whole new experience. We weren't drinking Jack Daniel's in the loading dock, shooting the shit anymore. We were drinking Jack Daniel's in green rooms while people came and went, asking for interviews and sound checks and photo shoots. So basically, I was drinking Jack Daniel's by myself while Hans worked.

Headlining also brought with it a whole new caliber of fangirl—the *groupie*. Fangirls I could deal with. Fangirls were intense, but once they got their kiss, their hug, their autograph, they usually just giggled and ran away. Groupies, on the other hand, they didn't just want to kiss my man; they wanted to fuck him, marry him, have his babies, divorce him, collect alimony for the next eighteen years, and then release a secret sex tape when the money ran out.

Standing in the pit waiting for Phantom Limb to come out always made me feel a little nauseous, but standing in the pit surrounded by grown-ass women whose Phantom Limb T-shirts looked like they had been shrink-wrapped onto their curvy bodies, made me feel more than sick.

It made me feel invisible.

At least I'd worn a dress that night. It might have been black with little white Jolly Rogers all over it, and I might have accessorized with combat boots, but it was the girliest I'd looked since the fifth grade.

When the house lights went down and the crowd rushed the stage, I found myself pushed at least four rows back before the guys had even made it to their places.

Shit. That was mosh-pit territory. I knew better than to stay put.

The front four rows were packed way too tightly for me to squeeze through, so I wriggled over to the edge of the crowd instead. I was on Hans's side, only about ten feet back, close enough to see the panic on his face when he glanced at the front row and didn't see me there. I screamed his name and waved my arms just in time to catch his attention before Trip began his opening banter with the crowd.

When Hans's eyes found me, I swear to God, my knees went weak. His manager had convinced him to start wearing eyeliner to their shows, and the result was fucking panty-melting. I wanted to run up onstage and wipe it off.

He smiled at me with one dimple as those black-rimmed blue eyes twinkled in the spotlight. His tattooed arm draped over the body of his glossy red bass guitar flexed in preparation. A wide studded belt holding up baggy slacks glinted in a flash of movement. And then our connection was gone. Hans cast his gaze down as he began to play and kept it there for the remainder of the show.

Until the kiss contest, I assume.

I didn't stick around for that shit anymore. That cancan music was my cue to get the fuck out of there. I'd go pee, smoke, flash my fraudulent ID at a bartender to get a drink, balance my checkbook, anything to avoid seeing somebody else's lips on my soul mate's. That usually meant I'd get a good groping on my way in and out of the pit, but whatever. I didn't have anything for them to grab anyway.

After finishing their second encore with a killer cover of "Terrible Lie" by Nine Inch Nails, the guys exited stage right to the deafening sound of screaming and declarations of love from the crowd, which no longer included me. I was already clawing my way out of the pit, making every effort to get my scrawny ass backstage and into Hans's pinstripe pants before my competition.

I ran toward security with my backstage pass thrust out before me like an FBI agent waving a badge. Sprinting through the dark corridors backstage, I got lost repeatedly before finally catching a glimpse of Trip through the half-open green room door. He was hovering over a table covered in snacks and cold cuts, eating a rolled-up slice of turkey while some grade-A groupie was on bended knee before him, massaging his balls with both hands through his leather pants.

My stomach lurched. Not because of what I saw, but because of what it meant. If there was a woman desperate enough to worship over Trip's weaselly, measly little pecker, then...

Hans must already be taken.

With a balled fist at the ready and my pounding heart in my throat, I took a deep breath and pushed the green room door the rest of the way open.

Sure enough, there he was, lounging on the couch across the room. Hans's left arm was draped casually over the back of the sofa, and his sweet smile was trained on the bimbo with the bad Jennifer Aniston haircut sitting next to him. She was wearing a tank top so low-cut, he could use her cleavage as a beer koozie. Hans looked totally at home, his posture open and inviting, his attention fixed on the floozy who'd gotten there first.

I watched in suspended strike mode as Jennifer Skankiston handed Hans a Sharpie, then hooked an index finger into the top of her tank top. With a giggle, she tugged the stretchy fabric down, and just before her entire right breast sprang free, just as I reared back to launch myself at her, Hans caught a glimpse of me out of the corner of his eye.

"Hey, baby!"

The smile that illuminated his chiseled face temporarily disarmed me as Hans leaped from his seat and rushed toward me. He'd gotten up so quickly that J. Skankiston had to hold on to the cum-encrusted upholstery with both hands to keep from falling on her stupid fucking face.

Hans snatched me up in a lung-crushing hug that I made

absolutely no effort to reciprocate. Setting me back on my feet, he looked me over with a furrowed brow.

"What's wrong?" Hans's jovial mood turned sour at the sight of my scowl. His voice dropped an octave too. "What is it, baby? Did something happen?"

"Ugh!" I huffed and shook him off, stomping out of the green room and back into the labyrinth. The halls were lit at random intervals by red party bulbs, ominous shadowy darkness filling the stretches in between. It looked underworldly.

Fitting, I thought, seeing as how I was already in hell. I'd finally found the perfect man, and I was doomed to watch other women try to fuck him for the rest of eternity.

Following the exit signs, I eventually found an external door to thrust myself out of. Only instead of being revived by a crisp, invigorating blast of cool night air, like I'd hoped for, I barreled headlong into the thick, hot simmering gravy that passes for air around here in the summertime.

I leaned over and placed my hands on my knees, trying to catch my breath and stave off the angry tears threatening to spill, but the motion caused half the contents of my purse to spill out instead. Makeup, cigarettes, Jolene Godfrey's driver's license, and birth control pills rolled like dice across the finely ground bed of broken bottles and cigarette butts at my feet.

Awesome.

Just as I knelt down and began to collect my belongings, a dark figure knelt beside me. Five long, masculine fingers reached out in front of me and picked up the last item—a fat red envelope.

"Hey, you okay?" Hans's voice was quiet as he ran his free hand down my back. Firm, not gentle.

I stood up straight and tall, rage boiling inside of me hotter and thicker than the July air, and snatched the envelope out of his hand. "No, I'm not fucking okay! That girl was about to pull her tit out, Hans!" I shoved the card into my purse and closed the flap, thankful he hadn't seen his name scrawled on the other side. "I'm not fucking blind! Or did you just think that I was gonna look the other way, like I do with everything else?"

Hans didn't stand up with me. He simply raised his hands in a pleading gesture. "Baby..."

"What if I hadn't shown up tonight? What else of hers would you have *signed*?"

I felt like I couldn't catch my breath. My chest constricted as the mountain of things I'd been ignoring suddenly became too heavy for me to carry any longer. It wasn't just about the girl. It was the question of whether or not his lips had been the kiss contest prize that night. It was the question of how many other girls had kissed him that I didn't even know about. How many other girls had gotten backstage at how many other shows that summer and what had happened when I *wasn't* there to break it up. It was the countless gray-area transgressions that just came with the territory. And they all crashed down on me at once in an avalanche of insecurity.

I took a step back, beginning to hyperventilate. "I...I can't do this anymore." I was shocked to hear myself say the words, but they were true. I couldn't do it anymore. It was eating away at me. At my self-respect. At my sanity. I felt like I was going crazy.

Hans's mouth fell open in stunned silence.

"I love you, Hans. I love you so fucking much that seeing this shit, knowing it's happening, knowing nobody fucking thinks it's a big deal but me, it's too much. I can't pretend like it's not killing me anymore. I can't pretend like I don't lie awake at night, wondering how many other girls have kissed you since we've been together. How many other skanks have snuck into your green room. How much of you they get to touch when I'm not around to run them off." My chin began to wobble as I shoved an angry finger in the direction of the venue. "I can't do this shit anymore, Hans. I'm sorry. I'm just... too fucking jealous to be your girlfriend!"

I spun around, ready to march back to my car, crank up the AC, lock the doors, and cry myself to death when two massive hands clamped around my midsection.

Hans spun me back around to face him. He was kneeling in front of me now, holding my waist and looking up at me with glistening, kohl-lined eyes. "I'm sorry, baby. I'm so fuckin' sorry." Sincerity squeezed his usually soft voice until it sounded like it might break. "That girl had a media pass and said she was with WATL. I was just gonna sit down and answer a few interview questions until you got there, but I guess she was just a fangirl who wanted an autograph."

"Oh, I think she wanted more than just an autograph," I snapped.

"I didn't know, baby, I swear." Hans shook his head back and forth in earnest. "I just thought she was gonna interview us."

I threw my hands up and tried to step away again, but Hans's death grip wouldn't allow it. "Ugh! This is exactly what I'm talking about. You're so fucking naive! You don't realize girls are hitting on you until they're practically riding your cock! I can't be around twenty-four/seven to fight them off, and you're *obviously* not up to the job." I was seething. I hissed my words at him with a venomous tongue even though, deep down, I knew he couldn't help it.

Hans was simply too sweet to see the bad in anyone. That was part of why I'd fallen in love with him.

According to my Interpersonal Relationships class, there was a term for what Hans and I had—*fatal attraction*. It's when the very qualities that attract you to someone eventually lead to the death of the relationship. I adored how kind and gentle and romantic Hans was. Whenever he wrapped those bulging tattooed arms around me, I felt as though I'd just shrugged on a fur coat made from live puppies that could sing "Lovesong" by The Cure a cappella. The only problem was, Hans made everybody feel that way.

And this Cruella de Vil was not down with sharing her puppy trench.

"Let me go, Hans. Your fans await."

As angry as I was, the look of despair on his face after that statement made me want to take back everything I'd just said. Hansel Oppenheimer was a unicorn. A myth. A fairy-tale prince. And what was I doing? Guilt-tripping him while he knelt in a bed of rusty screws and lightbulb shards at my feet?

He should be the one leaving me.

I opened my mouth to retract my words, but the only sound that came out was a surprised gasp as Hans wrapped his arms all the way around my waist and buried his face in my belly.

He turned his head sideways, just enough to speak, but kept a death grip around my midsection. "Please don't leave, baby. Please. You can't. I know you see the fans and the groupies, but I don't. I swear. All I see are people who aren't you, and you. That's it. Everyone else is just a walking, talking hunk of flesh that I need to get around to get to you."

Hans's grip tightened as his voice grew louder. More frantic. "You want to know why I don't look at you anymore when I'm onstage? It's because I fucking can't. Because every time I do, I see some dickhead trying to buy you a drink at the bar or knock you down in the pit or press his dick into your ass when you're in the front row. You think *you're* the jealous one?"

Hans lifted his head and pinned me with a crazed, angry gaze I'd never seen before. "The entire time I'm up there, all I want to do is leap into the crowd and smash some motherfucker's teeth down his throat." His voice was gravelly as he twisted my black cotton dress in his free hand. "It throws me off my game so bad, I can't even look up anymore. It takes everything I have to just focus on the music and ignore it. All I want to do is protect you, and I'm fucking helpless up there."

Tears and mascara and relief poured out of me as the implications of Hans's words sank in. I grabbed his face with both hands and pulled him up to meet my salty, wet mouth. I kissed him with everything I had and realized in that moment that the real problem was never Hans. Clearly, he was even more perfect than I'd feared. The real problem was that I'd never truly felt worthy of him.

Hans kissed me back like I was the last canteen in the Sahara, and I decided that my self-doubt and jealousy had to stop. He obviously loved me if he was willing to kneel in a bed of what looked like human teeth and used syringes just to keep me from leaving him. It was time for me to accept that love and get the fuck over myself.

Hans broke away from our kiss and pressed his forehead to mine. "I want you to move in with me."

"What?"

Hans pulled away a few inches, just enough to look directly into my stunned, blinking eyes. "You said you can't do this anymore. That you're too jealous. Well, so am I. I want you all to myself." The lump in Hans's throat bobbed up and down. "Ever since you moved back home, I've been losing my fucking mind. I want to fall asleep with you in my arms again. I want to wake up next to you every morning. I can't wait any longer. I need you back."

Every square inch of my body tingled violently as the giddiness I was trying to contain leaked out through my pores. Even my eyeballs tingled as fresh tears sprang forth, blurring my vision. Without a word, I reached into my purse and handed Hans the red envelope he'd retrieved for me earlier, my bottom lip clamped between my teeth.

"What's this?" Hans asked, admiring his own name calligraphed on the front. When I didn't answer, he tore open the flap and slid a homemade card out that said *Happy Birthday* on the front in matching calligraphy. "My birthday was a month ago," Hans said, the V reappearing between his stormy eyes. "Why didn't you—" His voice trailed off as he opened the card.

I watched his face go through a myriad of emotions as he flipped through the contents—a brochure for the Midtown Village apartment complex, enough hundred-dollar bills to cover the deposit on a one-bedroom unit, and finally, the stupid fucking poem I'd written, back before Phantom Limb took over the airwaves. Back before I'd convinced myself that a rock star wouldn't want a live-in girlfriend. Back before I'd taken a step back.

I miss you when you're gone,
But I know you have to go.

I miss you when you're here,
And I'm sleeping all alone.
I miss you when we're together,
If you're too many feet away.
I missed you for seventeen long years,
Before I found you, my soul mate.

I want to be there in the morning
When you rub your sleepy eyes.
I don't ever want to miss another
Mundane Tuesday night.
When I first woke up beside you,
I knew that's right where I should be.
So, now that I'm finally old enough,
Will you move in with me?

As his eyes traveled down the page, Hans's pierced eyebrow lifted, his mouth curved upward, and his scruffy cheeks dimpled adorably.

"What's all this?" he asked softly, his black-lined blue eyes lifting to meet mine.

"It's a yes."

31

Hans held my hand, his thumb tracing lazy circles on top of mine, as he walked me to my car. I'd parked about half a mile away, in a nearby neighborhood, but I wished it were farther. I wanted that walk to last forever.

The humid air hugged us like a warm, thick blanket. My cells sang along with the crickets. My molecules buzzed to the hum of the streetlights. And my heart fluttered with every blink of Hans's long black eyelashes whenever I caught him smiling down at me.

Or should I say, *LDH*'s long black lashes. I couldn't believe that my sweet Hans was the same tall, toned, tattooed badass that I'd just seen perform in front of a few thousand people at Variety Playhouse. He could have left with any girl he wanted that night, but he'd chased me down and knelt in broken glass just to get me to stay.

As the taillights of my trusty black Mustang came into view, just as I began to mourn the end of our evening stroll, I felt myself being tugged away from the street and onto someone's lawn.

"Look," Hans whispered as he led me deeper onto the property of a beautifully renovated antebellum home.

I was about to try to steer my distractible boyfriend back on course when I caught my first glimpse of the ethereal wonderland he was dragging me toward. The backyard of the estate had been wrapped, swathed, and wallpapered in thousands upon thousands of tiny white Christmas lights—in the middle of July.

They must have hosted a party or a wedding there earlier, some grand celebration, but by the time we found it, there was no evidence of life anywhere. The backyard sloped downhill to a swimming pool, which was as still as a pane of glass, reflecting the twinkling lights coiled tightly around every tall pine tree surrounding it. The back of the plantation-style house, all three stories of it, was dark. In fact, the only movement at all came from the ceiling fans quietly spinning on the patio under the main deck.

I couldn't even process all the beauty at once. The way my attention was flitting from one shiny object to the next must have been what Hans's brain felt like all the time. As my head swiveled and my eyes darted around that sparkly, glowing jewelry box of a backyard, I failed to notice that Hans was pulling me farther and farther onto this obviously very private property.

It wasn't until my body fell onto Hans's lap that I realized he had escorted me all the way down to the patio, and we were sitting on one of the cushy lounge chairs under the deck. I froze, highly aware that these people had a stupid amount of money and probably owned a state-of-the-art security system with invisible lasers and paralysis-inducing mist. Not that it mattered. Between Hans's strong arms around my waist, the secluded coziness of the covered patio, and the majesty of a hundred thousand tiny lights dancing in the trees and on the water before me, I was already paralyzed.

Hans and I sat in silence, enjoying the view. The fiery tree branches flickered in sync with the sounds of crickets and cicadas and air conditioners in the distance, creating a concert of white light and white noise that was playing just for us. As we watched the show, tucked into and around each other, Hans and I had an entire conversation telepathically, one that was full of promises and shiny rings and *I do*s and baby names.

When Hans began trailing featherlight kisses from my shoulder up to my neck, I tilted my head and bit my lip to keep from humming out loud.

When he repeated his delicate assault on the other side, he surprised me by biting down on the haphazard bow holding my halter dress up and yanking it loose. Within seconds, the black fabric covering my chest was replaced by warm, damp air.

My first instinct was to snatch my dress back up and scurry off before the owners had a chance to loose the hounds, but when Hans took both of my pierced nipples between his fingertips and tugged gently, I was a goner.

My head rolled back onto his shoulder, my back arched involuntarily, and I surrendered to his impulsive will.

"You are so beautiful," Hans whispered, his teeth grazing my shoulder.

I squeezed my eyes shut and tried not to whimper, his words giving me as much pleasure as his expert hands. Then, he stood up and came around to the foot of the lounge chair and knelt before me. It was reminiscent of our postures from just minutes ago in the parking lot. Only now, everything had changed. Hans's shy, one-dimpled smile had returned to its rightful place, and I was ready to book a flight to Las Vegas instead of booking it to my car to cry.

After gazing at me for a moment, his eyes soft and loving yet dark and daring, Hans grabbed the hem of my dress with both hands and slipped it off. Before I had time to process the fact that I was almost completely naked on the patio of a complete stranger, Hans bent down and captured my left nipple ring between his lips. He swirled his tongue around and around the sensitive pink flesh as he laid me flat on the overstuffed chaise lounge cushions.

Hans then turned his attention to my other breast, fondling and sucking, while I desperately tore at his sweat-soaked tank top. As I peeled the cotton off his torso, Hans made his way down mine, planting a trail of torturously unhurried kisses along the way. I stared at the ceiling fan overhead, its breeze causing all the wet places Hans had left behind to tingle, as his mouth hit the apex of my *very* wet panties. The feel of his tongue probing me through that thin piece of fabric was glorious, electric agony.

My hips began to thrust involuntarily, begging him to end the torture, when I felt a thick finger hook the sopping wet fabric between my legs and pull it to one side.

As soon as Hans's mouth made contact with my aching flesh, I felt my entire body contract. It was too much. I was spread-eagled, practically naked on a stranger's chaise lounge, with my breasts exposed to the steamy night air. Fingers that had just skillfully shredded a bass guitar in front of thousands of people were stroking my G-spot, and the playfully wicked black-rimmed eyes of a rock star were gazing up at me from between my thighs where his expert tongue was flicking and teasing the barbell piercing my clit.

Just as a tidal wave of an orgasm began to build, I heard the sound of Hans undoing his belt and fly.

Oh, thank God!

Hans shimmied out of his baggy pants and Adidas with ease and scooped me up into his arms. I wrapped my legs around his waist and my arms around his neck, hoping he would take me against the wall of the house so that we wouldn't have to worry about any unexpected squeaks from the patio furniture.

As Hans carried me, the feel of his callused hands gripping my ass and his thick, firm cock grazing the inside of my thigh had me writhing in need. I thrust my hands into his sweaty hair and sucked at his swollen, tart lips. My senses were so overwhelmed with desire that I didn't even notice how far we'd traveled until I felt lukewarm water sloshing into my boots.

My eyes shot open as the water continued to rise up my legs.

Hans had carried me into... the motherfucking... *pool!*

Before I could yelp or thrash in protest, Hans thrust his tongue into my mouth and his monolithic cock into my needy body, both silencing and sating me at the same time.

My awareness dived below the surface of the water to where our bodies were now joined. Hans was all I could feel. There was simply no room in my consciousness to process anxiety, fear, wet, dry, hot, cold, past, future. Every sensation was flooded with him.

Once we were completely submerged, Hans pressed my back against the cool tiled wall of the pool and filled me completely.

With his lust, with his loyalty, with his love, with himself. Every achingly slow withdrawal felt as though it was peeling away another layer of separation between us until we were no longer two people in a pool. We were the pool.

We were the unending, undulating sea.

Hans broke our kiss just long enough to whisper into my neck, "I love you."

Tears stung my eyes. Hans had said those three words to me a thousand times before, but that was the first time I'd truly allowed myself to *hear* them. To believe them. To hope against hope that the fairy tale might actually come true.

I grasped his beautiful face with both hands and urged him to look at me. When he finally complied, tiny white lights from the trees around us danced across the shiny surface of his eyes, giving me the sense that, through those black holes of eyeliner and dark lashes, I could see directly into the heavens.

I smoothed the worried V between his brows with one thumb and whispered back, never breaking eye contact, "I love you too, baby."

Hans tightened his grip on my ass and buried himself into me as far as he could go, pressing his forehead into mine. "I love *you*."

Hans's words were forceful. Resolute. They echoed through me, bouncing into and out of all the hollow places they'd never managed to reach before, leaving a satisfying vibration in their wake.

After a moment of reverie, Hans slowly withdrew and then plunged into me harder than before. I moaned unintentionally. His next thrust was harder still.

I grabbed a handful of his messy black hair and hissed into his mouth, "I love you."

My sentiment was immediately rewarded with a pounding so forceful that water sloshed over the edge of the pool.

Kissing me just below my ear, Hans growled as he ground his hips into mine, "I love *you*."

Abruptly, Hans tightened the grip he had on my ass and stood upright, exposing both of our naked torsos to the warm night air. I reached behind me and propped myself up with my arms on the ledge of the pool, baring my breasts to the rock star before me and my soul to the sensitive artist within. Hans responded to my submission by taking my left nipple ring between his teeth and thrusting fully into me just as he bit down.

Fire.

I might have been submerged in water, but my loins and heart and lungs were ablaze with pleasure. My eyes rolled back, and my body erupted in a volcano of curse words and whimpers and *I love you*s and tears as Hans withdrew and attacked, harder and faster. The once-mirrorlike body of water around us had become an uncontainable riptide of waves and lust spilling over the edges of the pool and crisscrossing through the cracks between the surrounding terra-cotta tiles.

Hans slid two wet fingertips into my mouth to silence me and growled with every advance, "God...I...fucking...love you," before he stilled, pouring the last ounce of himself into me.

We stood there in the water, eye makeup running down both of our faces, slumped over one another, panting in a tangle of hot, wet bliss until our brains were able to process outside information again.

How long? Who knows? Time doesn't exist in heaven. But I do know that, when I finally looked up at the house, something was different.

"Um, Hans? Was that light on before?"

"What light?" Hans's head snapped around, and the look that flashed across his face as soon as he caught sight of that illuminated second-story window was all the answer I needed.

But the sirens in the distance confirmed it.

32

Hans was a fucking ninja. In the time it took me to slosh my way toward the stairs with those water-filled, steel-toed cement blocks strapped to my feet, he had already leaped out, run to the patio, shimmied into his pants and shoes, and returned, clutching the rest of our clothes and my purse in the crook of his arm like a football. Although his face was playful, Hans wasted no time in pulling me out of the water and whisking me away from that magical, twinkling fairyland.

Hand in hand, we tore through the neighbors' backyards in the direction of my car. The sound of our shoes slapping the earth ricocheted through the darkness and silence surrounding us. I just prayed that the owners of the million-dollar yards we were destroying were adrift on a creamy burgundy sea of red wine and sleeping pills and couldn't hear us giggling and shushing each other outside as we tromped through their perfectly manicured flower beds.

With every panicked yet elated breath I sucked in, the approaching sirens grew louder. Finally, between two houses, my little black Mustang hatchback came into view. Hans and I tiptoed around the far side of the castle it was parked in front of and peered around to see if the coast was clear.

Slinging my purse over my shoulder, I looked at Hans and held up one fist in what I hoped was the universal TV cop show signal for *hold*. He waited next to the house as I scampered across the front yard, remembering on the way that I hadn't put my dress back on and was wearing nothing but a red thong, which had happily shifted back into place during that five-hundred-yard dash.

It's fine, I told myself as I stood naked in the middle of the street, digging in my purse for my car keys. *You're so not naked. You're basically wearing a whole bikini, just without the top part. No big deal. There are beaches in Jamaica where you'd be considered overdressed right now.*

When I finally found my keys, I hit the unlock button and dived inside. I watched through the passenger window as Hans's athletic, half-naked, six-foot-three-inch-tall silhouette sprinted across the yard toward me.

Slurping the drool back into my face, I jammed the key into the ignition just as Hans climbed in and slammed his door shut. I was just about to crank the engine and get the fuck out of there when flashing blue lights illuminated my rearview mirror.

Shit!

I spun around and saw the cop car pull up right in front of the McMansion we'd just defiled. Although I was parked at least a block away in the shadow of a huge magnolia tree, I still didn't want to draw any attention to the suspicious '93 Ford lurched on the curb in what was obviously an import-driving kind of neighborhood, so Hans and I decided to slide down in our seats and wait them out.

Even though we were both topless and hiding from the police, Hans flashed me a confident rock-star smile and reached over to brush my cheek with his thumb. "That was amazing."

Looking into that dreamy face was like mainlining Xanax.

What was I so worried about again?

The sound of a car door slamming shut reminded me.

Oh, yeah. The fucking cops.

Snapping out of my love-drunk trance, I fished my dress out of the pile of clothes in Hans's lap and shimmied it on over my head. I couldn't quite tie the halter top from my fetal position under the steering wheel, but at least my bottom half was covered.

Hans was still slumped down in his seat too, but his eyes were glued to his side mirror. Curious to see what had him looking so serious, I climbed out of my hidey-hole and leaned across the center console. Resting my cheek on his warm, damp chest, I peered into the mirror he was studying.

The cruiser still had its headlights on, and one police officer was at the ready behind the wheel. The cop who'd been riding shotgun was now standing in the doorway of the McMansion, talking to a middle-aged man wearing a bathrobe. I couldn't make out much from that distance, but I distinctly saw the homeowner raise an angry-looking finger and point it directly at my car.

"Go!" Hans yelled, prompting me to stomp on the clutch, crank the engine, and hit the gas at once.

I peeled out of there with my headlights still off and cringed as the cruiser's sirens screamed to life behind me.

Shit, shit, shit!

Luckily, I'd driven through that neighborhood looking for

free parking enough times to know a back way out, but I didn't know if I could make it without getting caught.

My body operated on muscle memory alone as my consciousness completely abandoned ship and spiraled in a million different terrible directions.

Let's see. Where to begin? Underage drinking, being in possession of false identification, trespassing, indecent exposure, disturbing the peace, speeding, evading the police... I'm going to jail. I'm going to jail wearing nothing but a halter dress and a thong. Fantastic.

I turned right onto the first street I came to, stomping on the accelerator halfway through the turn just like Harley had taught me at the track. I hadn't raced in over a year, but evidently, I could still tail-brake a corner without spinning out.

Just pretend like you're back at the track, B. You used to do this all the time. It was fun. You're having fun.

Redlining in second gear, I braked hard just before the next turn to transfer some weight to my front end before cutting the wheel. As soon as I was halfway through the turn and my RPMs were just right, I punched the gas and hit the straights, shifting into third within seconds.

See? It's just like riding a bike. You got this.

"Damn, baby! Where the fuck did that come from?"

It was the first thing Hans had uttered since we peeled out. I glanced over and found my rock-star boyfriend gripping the roof handle with one hand and the center console with the other, a look of shock and awe on his face. It was all the encouragement I needed. After spending a year feeling inadequate around this man, I'd finally found a way to set myself apart from the hordes of ho-bags beating down Hans's door.

I could drive this fucking Mustang, and I could do it topless.

I redlined her again and muscled through the last turn in the neighborhood. I could still hear the sirens right behind me and see the occasional reflection of a blue light off a house or a street sign, but I'd managed to keep enough distance and turns between us that I didn't think the police had been able to get a decent visual on me.

The next turn would make or break us though.

If I could pull out of the neighborhood and onto the highway without having to stop, we'd be home free. I could have us tucked away into the club parking lot within ten seconds. But, if I had to stop and wait for traffic... that was it.

Game over.

I downshifted to second and held my breath as we approached the intersection.

Please be clear, please be clear, please be clear...

"It's clear! It's clear! Go, go, go!" Hans was on the edge of his seat, looking left and right and left again, making sure I wasn't about to kill us both.

I crushed the accelerator with all forty pounds of wet steel and leather strapped to my right foot and was rewarded with a satisfying yelp from my tires and an even more satisfying glimpse of Hans's head being slammed backward into the headrest by the torque.

I flicked on my headlights as I raced toward the entrance of the club's parking lot, just a little over a block away. A few hundred yards, and we'd be in the clear.

Two hundred...

One hundred...

Hans was now turned around completely backward in his seat with both fists gripping the headrest and wide, excited eyes scanning the expanse behind us for any sign of the police cruiser. I bit my lip and held my breath as I made the final turn into the parking lot. The instant all four tires were off the highway, I killed the headlights and careened into the first available parking spot I could see.

Hans erupted into a fit of hysterics, pounding the headrest with his fists and yelling "Wooooooo!!!" as if he were Triple X greeting a sold-out stadium.

I'd never seen anybody so amped in my life.

The moment I killed the engine and turned to face him, Hans had his giant hands around my shoulders and was practically shaking me like a rag doll.

"Holy shit, baby! You lost 'em! You fucking lost 'em!" A manic grin split his face. "Where the fuck did you learn to drive like that?"

Ever distractible, I watched Hans's eyes flick down to my still-exposed breasts mid-thought. His hand impulsively reached out to stroke one of my nipple rings. Hearing my gasp, Hans glanced back up at me and swallowed.

"That was the sexiest fucking thing I've ever seen."

Before I could formulate a response, I found myself plastered against the driver's-side door as seventy-five inches of tall, dark, and tattooed ravaged my still-swollen lips and half-naked body with everything he had. Hans was ravenous. I thrust my fingers into his wild hair and held on for dear life, not knowing where he was going to take me next. I might have been in the driver's seat, but with Hans, I was the one along for the ride.

And what a ride it had been. In our year together, Hans had taken me places I'd never been. Given me experiences I'd only dreamed of. He'd made me pull over and look at the stars when

I would have just sped on by. And that night, in that car, Hans showed me that he'd rather have a boyish, smart-ass trouble-maker than all the curvaceous, red-lipped groupies in the world.

He showed me my worth.

And I would never be able to unsee it again.

August 2000

"Oh my God! Hans! Look! How fucking cool is this?"

Hans walked up behind me, carrying a stack of heavy-looking boxes. With his chin holding the top one steady, he smiled. "It's stairs."

"I know! You open the door like you're gonna walk into an apartment, but all it is is stairs!"

I giggled maniacally and bounced on my toes as I held the door open for Hans to walk through. As soon as he crossed over the threshold, I breezed past him, ran up the carpeted staircase, and gasped as it opened up into the most adorable little apartment six hundred dollars a month could buy. The stairs led into the living room, which was open to the kitchen and a little dining area. The back wall had a brick fireplace and two sliding glass doors that led out onto a balcony. To the left of the stairs was a little hallway that housed the bedroom, laundry room, and bathroom.

It was just like Jason's apartment, only half the size and with zero upgrades.

It was perfect.

I zoomed through the nine-hundred-square-foot paradise like a flea on crack, throwing open all the doors, squealing at the size of the walk-in closet, oohing and aahing over the builder-grade appliances in the tiny kitchen, and finally turning to find Hans, who was standing in the middle of the empty living room, watching me with a sweet smile on his gorgeous face.

I bounded over to him and leaped into his arms. Peppering his face with kisses, I cried, "We did it! We fucking did it! Look at this place! I can't believe I live here! I can't believe *we* live here! Hans, we live here!"

Hans chuckled and buried his face in my neck. "Fuck yeah, we do."

Hans set me down, and I ran over and threw open the sliding glass door. "Look at this view!"

We were only on the second floor, but our balcony faced the woods behind the apartment complex instead of the parking lot and another building, like Jason's.

I knew it was probably wrong to get an apartment in the same unit as my secret friend, but it made me feel better to know somebody close by. I mean, what if something happened while Hans was gone? What if I needed something, like entertainment or attention or alcohol? I was a young woman now. I had to look out for myself.

Hans followed me onto the balcony and wrapped his arms around my waist from behind. "I love it."

"I love you," I cooed back.

"I wonder how long we're gonna live here," Hans said, resting his chin on the top of my head. "Do you ever think about that? All the places you'll live before you die. What they'll look like. Where they'll be."

"Not really. I just assumed I'd live in Atlanta forever. I like it here."

"No way," Hans said, releasing me to pull his pack of Newports out of his pocket. "We're gonna live all over."

I turned to face him, and he handed me a cigarette with an impish gleam in his eye.

"We might even move to New York if Violent Violet gets us the producers we want for our next album."

"What? Really?"

"Maybe." Hans grinned as he lit the cigarette dangling from my surprised mouth.

I took a drag and tried to formulate a response that would come across better than simply screaming, *There is no fucking way I'm moving to New York!* like I wanted to.

"That's really exciting, baby, but"—I took another drag— "I'm applying to graduate programs right now. You know I'm trying to finish my bachelor's degree early, and all the master's programs I'm applying to are in Georgia."

Hans flicked his ash over the edge of the balcony. "You can transfer. They have great schools in New York. Plus your grades are, like, perfect. They'll have to let you in."

"But . . . it's cold there."

"We'll get you a big-ass coat."

"But . . . what about your degree?"

Hans shrugged and exhaled a stream of smoke away from my face. "I'll take a year off or whatever. It's cool."

What about my parents? I don't want to move away from them.

There are no trees in Manhattan. I love trees.

What if we have kids? I'll need help, and you're never home.

But... but we just got here.

"Hey"—Hans tilted my chin up and gave me that two-dimpled smile I loved so much—"it's gonna be great."

"Promise?"

"It doesn't matter where we live. I could share a cardboard box under the Brooklyn Bridge with you and be the happiest man alive."

I melted into a puddle of swoon juice right there on the balcony. Hans was right. He was my home now. It didn't matter where he had to go. If he had a dream, then I was going to support him. Even if that meant moving to the cold concrete jungle of New York.

"You're right," I sighed. "I already lived with you and had to give it up once. I don't think I can do it again."

Hans beamed. "I *know* I can't. That shit was horrible."

"Right?" I laughed, stubbing my cigarette out on the metal railing and flicking it overboard. "I'm so glad—" I squealed in surprise as Hans picked me up and cradled me against his chest.

"What are you doing?"

"What I should have done downstairs. I'm carrying you over the threshold."

I giggled as Hans slid the glass door open and waltzed through.

"Welcome home, baby," he said, gently setting me down on the kitchen counter.

"Welcome home," I replied, wrapping my legs around his waist. "You know," I said, sliding my hands under his tank top, "we've never had sex in a kitchen before."

Hans smirked, grabbing my hips and pressing his already-thickening cock against the seam of my little cutoff jean shorts. "Or on top of a washing machine."

"Or in front of a fireplace," I said, pushing the black fabric up over his defined abs.

"Or on the stairs," Hans added, reaching between his shoulder blades to pull his shirt the rest of the way off.

"Or in a walk-in-closet." I giggled, lifting my arms so that he could relieve me of my tank top as well.

"Think we should hit 'em all right now?" Hans beamed, raising that one pierced eyebrow.

I unhooked my bra and tossed it onto the growing pile of clothes on the linoleum floor. "But what will we do when we run out of places?"

Hans unbuckled his belt, and I actually salivated in anticipation. "We'll just have to move."

Aaaaand . . . my saliva dried right back up.

34

October 2000

"So, we're cheering for the guys in black. Got it." I discreetly slid my phone out of my pocket for the third time that hour and illuminated the screen. Still no word from Hans.

"And what's their name?"

I tucked my phone away and rolled my eyes at Ken. "The Falcons."

"And who's their quarterback?"

I pointed at the big-screen TV in front of us. "The one in the tight pants with his head up that other guy's ass."

Ken tilted his head and raised his eyebrows. "His name."

"Uh ... Chris?"

"Chris what?"

I looked around, hoping to find a clue hidden somewhere in Jason's sparsely decorated man cave. Just as I was about to give up, Allen walked by wearing a black Falcons jersey with the answer to Ken's question in bold red letters across his back.

"Chandler!" I shouted. "Chris Chandler. Number twelve.

Boom." I tapped my temple with my index finger and gave Ken a smug smile. "Got it all right here."

Ken glanced over his shoulder at Allen and laughed. "Really?"

"Man"—I stretched and pretended to crack my knuckles—"all that learnin' wiped me out. I'm gonna take a smoke break. Wanna come?"

I didn't actually expect the Gatorade-drinking dude in the workout clothes to join me on the balcony so that I could blow secondhand smoke in his face, so I was pretty surprised when he stood up and said, "Sure."

Not that I minded. Ken was actually really easy to talk to and smart, and he didn't hit on me or make me feel weird like some of the other guys at Jason's house. The Alexander brothers had practically dry-humped me against a wall the week before.

At the same time.

Ken opened the back door for me, and the crisp night air stung my cheeks. I flipped the hood on my Phantom Limb sweatshirt up over my head and pulled the drawstrings tight. It was almost coat weather.

I loathed coat weather.

Ken took a deep breath and exhaled. "I fucking love fall. It smells like football season."

I inhaled the scent of burning leaves and smiled. Every October, when the forest Atlanta is carved out of sheds its crinkly, rust-colored fruit, people have to either bag it or burn it to keep from being buried alive under it. And since Southerners love to burn shit, the whole region smells amazing for a while.

"*You* love something?" I teased. I set my beer down on the railing and held my cigarette over the edge to keep the smoke away.

"I love stuff," Ken retorted, taking a seat in one of Jason's patio chairs. He rested an ankle on his knee and draped his plastic bottle–holding hand over the armrest, casually waiting for me to reply.

I'd never seen somebody so comfortable just *sitting*. I always had to be doing something. Smoking, drinking, talking, gesticulating with my hands, playing with my hair, but not Ken. He just *sat still*. And looked at me when I spoke. And listened. And then, when it was his turn to talk, he would say some smart-ass shit that made me question whether or not he was an asshole.

I'd never met anyone like him.

"Oh, really?" I said, taking the bait. "What do you love?"

"Football."

"Okay." I rolled my eyes.

"And baseball," he added.

"And let me guess...basketball."

Ken grimaced. "Nah. Fuck basketball. They score too often. It gets boring."

"Did you play sports in high school? You look...athletic."

And also, you wear running pants like they're regular pants.

"Yeah. I played pretty much everything, but football was my favorite. I played until my senior year. Then I quit."

I coughed in surprise. "You quit? You just...quit? During your senior year? You could have gotten a scholarship and shit."

Ken shrugged. "I didn't want to do it anymore. I was sick of getting up at five in the morning and staying late after school every day and having coaches scream in my face. So one day I just...quit going."

"Wow. Were your parents pissed?"

"Fuck yeah. Everybody was pissed," Ken said with a smile. A

wicked, middle-finger-up kind of smile that made me see him in a whole new light.

Pajama Guy had a defiant streak.

"So, what I hear you saying is that you *don't* actually love football. See? You love nothing. I told you so."

Ken laughed in defeat. He had a nice smile. I felt weird, noticing his nice smile, so I busied myself by pulling my phone out of my pocket to check the time.

"Oh shit!" I cried. "It's eleven eleven!" I held the illuminated screen out for him to see. "That's my lucky number! Make a wish!"

Ken lifted an eyebrow and glared at me as if I'd just asked him whether or not Santa Claus was real.

"Don't tell me you don't make wishes either." I held up my left hand and dramatically counted off Ken's *don'ts* on my fingers. "You don't drink. You don't smoke. You don't gamble. You don't make wishes. What about when you blow out your birthday candles? You have to make a wish then."

"I don't celebrate my birthday. Or holidays."

"What? Why?" I gasped and covered my mouth. "Oh shit. Are you a Jehovah's Witness?"

Ken laughed again. More pretty white teeth.

"Fuck no." He chuckled. "I'm an atheist."

"Then why do you hate all things good and wonderful?"

Ken stood up and crossed the balcony, leaning on the railing next to me. He was wearing a plain gray hoodie and smelled like he had just pulled his entire comfy wardrobe out of the dryer. "I don't believe in blindly buying things just because of a number on a calendar. Like Valentine's Day. Who says we all have to uniformly buy heart-shaped bullshit just because it's February 14? Hallmark made that shit up. It's corporate brainwashing."

I laughed as I exhaled, causing my stream of smoke to come out more like a dotted line. "How does your girlfriend feel about that?"

Ken stared out into the parking lot and lifted an impassive shoulder. "Never had one."

I held up a hand. "So, let me get this straight. You don't drink, you don't smoke, you don't gamble, *and* you don't believe in holidays, religion, or evidently, commitment. Next, you're gonna tell me you don't eat chocolate."

"Actually..." Ken peeked at me out of the corner of his eye.

"Oh my God!" I squealed. "No way! You really are the enemy of fun! What about caffeine?"

"Nope."

"Sex?"

My eyes went wide as soon as I heard my own question.

Shut up, BB! What the fuck?

I was just about to apologize when Ken turned to face me, wearing a smirk that said he was anything but offended.

"I'm a fan."

"Oh, you're a fan." I smirked back, arching a brow.

Lifting my almost-empty beer bottle in a toast, I said, "Well then, to sex and cursing, the only two things we have in common."

Ken smiled and lifted his Gatorade bottle. "Cheers." The plastic container met my glass bottle with an unsatisfying thud.

As we drank the last swallows of our beverages—mine piss-colored, his purple—I watched Ken's mouth and wondered who he was having sex with.

Not that it mattered.

Nope. Not at all. I was totally *not* into Pajama Guy. And

besides, I had a boyfriend. Who lived with me, most of the time. And he was going to be home from Nashville any minute.

"Well, I gotta go. I have school in the morning."

Ken polished off his sports drink and screwed the cap back on. Sticking it in his pocket, he said, "I should go too. I'll walk you out."

He opened the door for me and slid my empty beer bottle out of my hand as I passed. When I looked over my shoulder at him in confusion, Ken explained, "Jason doesn't recycle."

I snorted as I grabbed my purse off the couch and waved goodbye to the Alexanders and Allen, whose eyes were glued to a buxom blonde giving a blow job on Jason's big screen.

Ugh! Do all guys fucking watch porn together?

Jason was standing—or I should say, *swaying*—in front of the television, transfixed.

"I gotta go, man. Thanks for having me," I said, giving him an awkward side hug.

Jason brought his arm down around my shoulders and slurred, "Look it. This is the most expensive porno ever made. Jenna Jameson in *space*. Fuckin' final frontier, man."

"Please tell me it's called *Fucking in the Final Frontier.* Because if not, that was a missed opportunity." I giggled, struggling to get out from under Jason's arm, but he had pretty much shifted all of his weight onto my shoulders, turning me into a human crutch.

"C'mon, man," Ken said, pulling him off me. "Here we go." He helped Jason into his armchair where he passed out pretty much on contact.

"It must get pretty fucking old, hanging out with drunk people all the time when you don't drink," I said as we descended the four flights of stairs to the parking lot.

Ken shrugged. "It's cheap entertainment."

"Technically, it's free entertainment."

"Even better." Ken snapped his fingers and pointed at me in one fluid motion.

I chuckled as we reached the parking lot and followed Ken to a burgundy Mitsubishi Eclipse convertible parked in front of Jason's building.

"Is this your car?"

"Yep." Ken pushed a button on his keychain, causing the headlights to blink.

"Looks awfully *fun* for somebody who hates everything."

"Don't worry," he said, turning to face me. "I drive it really, really slow."

I cracked up. Ken didn't laugh with me, but he smiled as I doubled over at his expense.

"I guess you'd better leave now if you wanna get home by sunrise, old man," I teased, standing up and sucking in a breath.

Ken didn't reply. He just stood there, watching me.

"What?" I asked, my hysterics dying down.

"Nothing. I'm just gonna wait to leave until you get home safe."

"Oh, I just live over there," I said, pointing to the shittier two-story building across the parking lot.

"I know."

"Oh. Okay. Well... maybe I'll see you next week?"

"Maybe." The corner of Ken's mouth pulled up slightly as he folded his arms across his chest.

With that awkward salutation, I took a few hesitant steps away from Ken and his shiny little convertible, then turned and headed for the home that didn't feel like home yet.

Pajama Guy didn't even hug me goodbye. All my friends hug me goodbye. Are we not friends? I wondered, my feet carrying me closer and closer to my empty new apartment. I knew without even scanning the cars parked out front that Hans wasn't there. Hans was never there. But I was trying real hard not to think about that.

Just before I reached my front door, I remembered the way Ken had fought his buddies off like an unaffectionate ninja the first night we met.

Ha! I totally forgot! I snickered as I shoved my key in the lock. *Ken hates hugs, too! That motherfucker really does hate everything!*

I turned and waved across the parking lot at my non-hugging new friend.

Ken replied by nodding once.

I snorted as I stepped into my pitch-black apartment. *He even hates waving! What an asshole!*

35

"Hans?" I called out even though it was obvious he wasn't home yet.

His car wasn't even in the parking lot. I flipped on the lights at the bottom of the stairs and headed up, pulling my phone out of my pocket. No missed calls.

I dialed his number, and he picked up on the last ring.

"Hey, baby!" Hans yelled into the phone. Wherever he was, it was definitely *not* Baker's van.

"Hey!" I yelled back, hoping he would hear me over the riot of joyous noise in the background. I dropped my purse on the table next to the couch and switched on the lamp next to it. "Where are you?"

Hans laughed. "I don't even know. Hey, where are we?" His voice sounded muffled for a minute, then came back full-volume. "We're at the Hard Rock."

"In Atlanta?"

"No, in Nashville."

My heart sank. Another night by myself.

Hans's voice got muffled again as he shushed somebody and told them he was on the phone. "Baby? You still there?"

"Yeah, I'm here." I walked into the kitchen, flipping on every light in my path. Opening the cabinet next to the stove, I pulled out what was left of the last bottle of Jack Daniel's Baker had bought for me. "I thought you guys were coming home tonight. You know we have class in the morning."

I took a long pull straight from the bottle, then carried it with me back through the living room, around the corner, and into the bathroom.

"What?" Hans yelled in my ear.

"Nothing," I sighed, reaching into the shower and pulling the lever all the way to H.

"Sorry. It's so fucking loud in here!"

"I can tell," I muttered, taking another swig. It burned like hell. I put the phone down long enough to take off my hoodie, shirt, and bra.

When I picked it back up all I heard was, "And he said that we got it! Can you fucking believe it?"

I held the phone between my shoulder and ear as I shimmied out of my boots and jeans and underwear. "I'm sorry. I didn't hear you. You got what?"

"We got *it*! We're opening for Love Like Winter's spring tour! Can you fucking believe it? He said we might even get to do the European leg if it goes well!"

Something crashed to the floor in the background, and the already-raucous crowd exploded in cheers.

Meanwhile, I stood paralyzed, naked and alone, staring at the gaunt girl trapped in my mirror.

Somebody should help her, I thought. *She looks lost.*

"Baby?"

"That's amazing," I said, watching the lost girl's mouth move at the same time as mine. "I'm so happy for you. That's incredible."

More words came out, but I didn't hear them. All I heard was Hans telling me that he had to go. That he loved me. That he'd see me tomorrow. I don't even know if I pressed the End button on my phone before I set it down on the counter, picked up the bottle of whiskey, carried it into the shower, and cried in a ball on the floor until the water ran cold.

November 2000

"You okay?"

"Huh?" Ken's words pulled me out of whatever death spiral of negative thoughts I'd been traveling down and back into the present. I blinked at Jason's big screen, watching the game come back into focus, then turned and faced Pajama Guy.

"Sorry. I'm fine. I just...I'm stressing out over this test I have tomorrow. I should really be home studying right now, but instead I'm here"—I swept my hand in the direction of the TV like Vanna White revealing a new prize on *Wheel of Fortune*—"pretending to watch football."

"So why'd you come?" Ken draped his elbow casually over the back of the couch and turned to face me. Waiting. Listening.

"Because Jason's bossy ass literally came and pulled me out of my apartment. He says I'm the Falcons' good-luck charm, and I'm not allowed to miss a game until they win the Super Bowl."

Ken chuckled. "Well, I have good news for you. There's no way they're even gonna make it to the playoffs."

I gave him a half-assed smile, then turned my fake attention back toward the big screen.

"Hey, I have an idea. Why don't you get your stuff and study over here?" Ken asked the back of my head.

I turned and blinked at him for what felt like five minutes.

Why didn't I think of that?

Who the fuck is this guy?

Why is he so . . . smart?

And observant?

And cold?

"You're a goddamn genius," I finally said.

Ken didn't acknowledge my compliment. "What's your test over?"

"Ancient Egyptian art history. It's horrible. It's a master's level class. All these assholes have been to Giza and can read hieroglyphs and shit. I have no idea what I'm even doing in there."

Ken's face lit up as if I'd just told him that the Falcons *were* going to the playoffs, and they wanted *him* to be their backup tight end. "I fucking love ancient Egyptian art history."

"Liar," I said with a smirk. "You love nothing."

It turned out, Ken really did love the shit out of ancient Egyptian art history. *And* early eastern renaissance art history. And traveling. While he quizzed me, using the ten-pound stack of homemade flash cards I'd retrieved from my apartment, Ken regaled me with stories about the museums he'd visited while touring Europe after high school. The Sistine Chapel, the *Mona Lisa*, *Winged Victory*, the crown jewels, he'd seen them all.

Egypt was next on his list, he said.

I told him to take me with him.

He said I'd need three grand and a passport.

I told him to send me a postcard.

That made him smile his big smile again. The one that had me questioning my stance on jocks. And guys without visible tattoos. And guys who don't drink or smoke or hug or gamble or eat chocolate or celebrate holidays or birthdays.

"So, are you an art major?" he asked.

"No." I pouted, stacking my cards up after finally getting all four hundred eighty-seven of them correct during Ken's relentless quizzing. "I probably would have been if my parents were rich and I didn't have to worry about things like rent and utilities. But they're not, so I'm a psychology major instead. I just take art and film classes as my electives."

"Film classes, huh?"

"Mmhmm," I mumbled, tapping the cards on Jason's kitchen island until the corners lined up just right.

"You know I manage a movie theater, right?"

I stared at him with my mouth hanging open. "No way. Really?"

Ken rolled his eyes. "Go ahead. You can ask."

"Ask what?"

"What everybody asks when they find out I run a movie theater."

I blushed at his insinuation, then decided to go for it. "Can you get me in for free—"

"Nope," Ken cut me off with a smirk.

I laughed and threw a handful of flash cards at him. "Asshole."

"Now I'm really not letting you in."

"I take it back! I'm sorry!"

"Nope. It's too late now. You blew it." Ken gave me a wicked look. Then he stood up and grabbed his keys and empty

Gatorade bottle off the island. "Look. It's your lucky number." Ken pointed to the blue *11:11* on Jason's sleek digital microwave clock.

"You gonna make a wish?" I asked, standing with him. "Come on. You know you want to."

Ken's aqua irises softened. He didn't smirk. He didn't give me some smart-ass quip. Instead, he pushed my barstool back under the island, handed me my flash cards, and said, "You can have mine."

"You can have mine."

That statement lingered in my ears as we said our goodbyes, as I walked through the door that Ken held open for me, as our footfalls echoed in the stairwell on the way down to the parking lot.

How could somebody be kind of an asshole *and* a total gentleman at the same time? Pajama Guy made no damn sense.

"Thanks for helping me study tonight," I said as Ken headed toward his little burgundy Eclipse. "I feel so much better. You have no idea."

Ken stopped next to his driver's-side door and hit the unlock button on his key fob. "And the Falcons won, so I guess Jason was right." He turned to face me. "It's a good thing you stayed."

"Oh, so you don't believe in religion or holidays or commitment, but you believe in good-luck charms?" I teased.

Ken spread his arms. "Hey, whatever helps the Falcons win."

I don't know what came over me. Maybe it was the beer. Maybe it was the isolation. Maybe it was sheer gratitude. But, for whatever reason, as soon as Ken spread his arms, I took two steps forward and wrapped mine around his waist.

I expected him to freeze or do that awkward get-the-fuck-off-me back-pat thing that people who aren't huggers do when they feel uncomfortable, but the moment my cheek touched Ken's chest, his arms immediately pulled me in closer. He was hard and warm underneath all that soft, dryer-scented cotton, and he held me the way a five-year-old holds on to a balloon string. Like I was precious. Like my very existence made him happy. Like the thought of watching me float away would break his ornery, apathetic little heart.

I wanted to stay there, feasting on Ken's unexpected affection for as long as he would let me, but I couldn't. I had to let him go. I had to take a step back, and smile, and tell him good night. Not because it was the right thing to do, but because the man who'd been starving me was watching us from across the parking lot.

37

I could feel Ken's eyes on my back and Hans's on my front as I crossed the expanse from one man to the other. I was usually overjoyed to see Hans, but something in his posture, in his hollow cheeks and sunken eyes, something in the flex of his jaw and the straight line of his mouth told me that this would not be a happy homecoming.

"Hey, baby," I said, full of false cheer as I approached.

Once I got close enough, I could see that he was still wearing his eyeliner and stage clothes from the night before. Hans hadn't come home; LDH had, and he'd clearly been partying like a rock star.

"Who the fuck is that?" Hans snapped, his bloodshot eyes flaring as they looked past me toward Jason's building.

"Just a friend." I smiled and held up my flash cards. "I needed a study buddy for this test—"

"Oh, you got all kinds of new friends, huh?" Hans's words were acidic.

He cocked his head to one side and narrowed his eyes at me, daring me to take the bait. Motherfucker was looking for a fight, but he wasn't going to get it out there in the parking lot.

I grabbed Hans's arm, which was completely bare despite the November chill in the air, and hauled his ass inside the apartment. I didn't look back at Ken as I closed the door behind us and locked the dead bolt.

I didn't want him to see my fear.

"It's nice to see you too," I quipped, trying to sound more annoyed than anxious.

I flipped on the light above the stairs and watched Hans recoil like a vampire in the sun. I hated this version of him. Still in LDH mode, coming down off the high of performing and the high of whatever he'd taken that kept him up all night after performing.

I headed up the stairs, trying to get some distance from him.

"I know about Jason." His words were sharp. They stuck in my back like porcupine quills as I continued up the stairs.

"What about Jason?" I asked flippantly, crossing the living room to turn on the lamp.

"Don't give me that bullshit! Victoria told me you've been hanging out with him behind my back, and I just saw you leaving his fucking apartment!"

I continued making my way through the tiny living area without giving Hans a second glance. "It's not like that," I said, flipping on the dining room light with a shaking hand. "He's our neighbor." I walked into the kitchen and turned on the harsh fluorescent bulbs. "He's the only person I know in this complex, and he has people over every Sunday. If you were ever home, you could come with me."

I realized my mistake a moment too late. By walking into the kitchen, I'd painted myself into a corner. Hans was now standing in the doorway behind me, blocking my exit.

I knew he would never hurt me. At least, my brain did, but my nerves and heart and muscles and lungs remembered other fights, terrifying fights, with a very different boyfriend. They told me I wasn't safe. They told me to run.

"Are you fucking him?" My gorgeous, high-contrast boy was now more black-and-white than ever. His skin was pale from weeks spent sleeping during the day and partying all night. His black beard scruff shadowed the hollows of his cheeks. His black eyebrows were pulled down into a V. And his black pupils were still swollen from whatever the fuck he'd been pumping into his bloodstream all weekend.

"No!" I yelled, taking a step farther back into the kitchen. "Why the fuck would you even ask me that?"

"Oh, I don't know. Maybe because you've been spending every weekend with him while I'm out working my ass off and *fucking lying to me* about it!"

"No, I spend *Sunday afternoons* with a *group of people* that just happens to *include Jason*, and I didn't tell you about it because I knew you'd act like a jealous...fucking...asshole!" My words were aggressive, but my posture was anything but.

I backed up again, bumping into the wall at the end of our skinny kitchen. My heart was pounding in my chest as the tunnel vision of a panic attack began to cloud the edges of my awareness. I could feel myself beginning to hyperventilate. My eyes darted left and right as Hans approached, looking for a way out. Looking for a weapon.

I considered jumping over the counter into the living room, but Hans would catch me pretty easily. I considered trying to dart through the opening next to him, but those long arms would snatch me in an instant. So, instead, I pulled the biggest kitchen knife we owned out of the wooden block on the counter to my left and held it in front of me like a sword.

"Stay back!" I screamed, unable to catch my breath.

There would be no snapping of fingers. No invisible Stop sign in my mind to save me. I was too far down the rabbit hole. In my history, fights like those ended in bruises and bloodshed and humiliation. I had to protect myself. No one would save me.

No one ever saved me.

Hans froze where he stood in the center of the kitchen and held his hands up. "Jesus, BB! What the fuck?"

Between gasps of air, I pleaded, "Just...stay back. Please."

"Baby, I'm not gonna hurt you." Hans took one hesitant step closer, holding his hand out as if he were trying to earn the trust of a frightened animal.

"Stay the fuck back!" I pointed the knife at him, now violently shaking in my puny grasp.

I hadn't touched him, but Hans looked wounded nonetheless. His mouth fell open as if I'd just stabbed him in the gut. His hands hung lifeless at his sides. And his eyebrows lifted in an expression of pain and remorse.

"I didn't mean to scare you." His voice was quiet and sincere.

I didn't answer, just watched his every move with stinging, tear-filled eyes as my chest heaved and my body jerked.

Hans spread his arms, leaving himself open and vulnerable. "I'm so sorry, baby. I'm so sorry. I just...I can't lose you."

I lowered the knife and concentrated on trying to slow down my breathing. My heart rate. My racing thoughts.

"I love you so fucking much," Hans continued, taking another hesitant step toward me. "It kills me to be away from you. I live in constant fear that you're gonna find somebody else while I'm gone. You're so beautiful, and smart"—Hans looked down at the knife dangling in my hand—"and strong. Why would you sit around and wait for me?"

"I'm not strong," I admitted with a sniffle. "I'm fucking scared."

I'm scared to be here by myself.

I'm scared of the dark.

I'm scared to lose you.

I'm scared I already have.

Hans took another step toward me and held out his hand in a silent request. I wasn't sure what he wanted, so I gave him my free hand.

The knife, I kept.

Hans lifted my knuckles to his pale, chapped lips and gave them a gentle kiss. "I'm sorry I scared you," he said. "C'mere. I missed you so much."

I closed my eyes and let Hans pull me flush against his chest. His arms circled my body. His chin rested on top of my head. It was the second hug I'd received from a man that night, but it felt nothing like the first.

Ken's embrace had fed me.

Hans's drank me dry.

December 2000

Georgia State University
Department of Educational Psychology and Special Education

Dear Ms. Brooke Bradley,

Congratulations! Our acceptance committee has reviewed your application and is happy to offer you admission into the School Psychology M.Ed./Ed.S. program. Due to the high volume of applications, we were only able to accept ten percent of our applicant pool this year, but your grades, test scores, essay, and accelerated graduation rates appear to be exemplary. Please accept our warmest welcome...

I sat, or rather fell, onto the couch as I read the words a second, third, hundredth time.
I got in.
I fucking got in.

I lifted my head and looked around, hoping beyond hope that someone would magically appear for me to tell my good news to, but, of course, no one was home. It was just me and the sad, short, plastic Christmas tree I'd bought at Walmart a few days before. It had about fourteen branches, each of which bore maybe one plastic silver ornament, also purchased at Walmart. The tree made a mockery of Christmas, and I'd kind of wanted to burn it as soon as I put it up.

Fuck this.

I tucked the letter into the back pocket of my jeans, shoved my textbooks back into my backpack, threw on some makeup, and headed over to Jason's house.

In hindsight, it seems like I should have called my parents first. Or Juliet. Or Hans, not that he would have answered. He was "camping" that weekend with "the guys" and wouldn't have "any cell coverage" for "a few days." Which was obviously bullshit, considering that it was "December," and people could "freeze to death" in the North Georgia mountains without the "right kind of gear," which Hans and his bandmates most definitely did "not" have.

I usually didn't even get the courtesy of an excuse—Hans simply left on Friday night, played a show somewhere at some point during the weekend, and came home on Sunday in a shitty mood and reeking of brown liquor—so the fact that he'd felt the need to come up with an airtight alibi for whatever he was doing made me feel physically ill. I hadn't slept all weekend. All I'd eaten was a box of Velveeta Shells & Cheese. The only liquids I'd ingested were Diet Coke, Jack Daniel's, and tap water. And nicotine had officially edged out fruits and vegetables as a major food group in my life.

Jason welcomed me in with his usual slurry, sleepy-eyed greeting. Allen was on the phone, pacing back and forth next to the pool table. The Alexander brothers were more than happy to get me a beer and try to impress me by telling the most embarrassing stories they could think of about one another. And I laughed politely while scanning the apartment for someone else.

Someone sipping purple Gatorade.

Someone with turquoise eyes.

Someone who refused to let me see *Cast Away* for free because I'd called him an asshole.

When he hadn't arrived by halftime, I threw in the towel and left, giving Jason some lame-ass excuse about how I wasn't feeling well.

It wasn't a lie.

I wasn't feeling well.

In fact, I felt like complete and utter shit.

I stopped at the bottom of the stairs to light a cigarette when I heard somebody say, "Hey, Brooke."

No, not somebody.

Pajama Guy.

I looked up to find Ken standing in front of me on the sidewalk. He had his hands in the pockets of a black wool coat that was definitely too nice to be worn with running pants and Nikes.

"Why do you call me that?" I asked, trying not to act as happy to see him as I was.

"It's your name," Ken replied.

"Well, yeah, but everybody just calls me BB."

"Not everybody." Ken's aqua gaze was direct and challenging.

I'd never met anybody so quietly defiant before. It was like he was calling me Brooke simply because I wanted to go by something else.

Who does that?

I turned my head and exhaled away from him. "How do you even know my name anyway?"

Ken shrugged, dodging the question. "Are you heading out?" He tipped his head toward my apartment building. There was a hint of disappointment in his voice that made me want to smile.

"Yeah. The Falcons were up by twenty-one at halftime, so I figured my good-luck charm duties had been fulfilled."

"They'll probably still find a way to lose," Ken said with a smirk.

"Well, if they start slippin', you know where to find me."

That was my cue to leave. That was Ken's cue to go upstairs, but we both just stood there, looking at each other.

"Hey," I said, breaking the silence, "I wanted to tell you thanks again for helping me study. I just found out today that I got into grad school."

Ken smiled. Not with his pretty teeth, but it was a smile nonetheless. "That's awesome. For psychology, right?"

"Yeah. School psychology actually. I want to help kids." I paused, debating whether or not to divulge the rest of that thought to Ken. "Like Knight. You remember him, right? I think he was in your grade."

Ken's eyes hardened. I could see his exhalations in the cold night air, coming out in quick, steamy bursts as his chest rose and fell.

I was beginning to think he wasn't going to speak to me

again when he finally spat, "Yeah. I remember him choking you in the hallway."

The already-frosty air dropped fifteen degrees in an instant. Or maybe it just felt colder, thanks to the humiliation flooding my cheeks. All I'd wanted was to put that event behind me and bury it down deep with everything else Knight had ever done to me, but Ken had seen it.

And that made it real.

I was transported back to C Hall immediately. Knight's steroid-swollen body loomed over me. I could feel his hand around my throat, the darkness tickling the edges of my vision at first, then opening to swallow me whole. I could feel the cold, gritty institution-grade tile under my cheek when I awoke and the splitting headache that followed. But my injuries were nothing compared to the mortification I'd felt upon seeing how big the crowd was that had gathered to watch me get belittled and assaulted by my ex-boyfriend.

"I chased him. I pushed through the crowd as soon as I realized what was happening, but he ran off. Just left you on the fucking ground and ran off. I chased him all the way to his truck, but I was too late."

Ken's eyes darkened with remorse.

Mine filled with tears.

"I looked you up in the yearbook that night and found out your name. I tried to find you at school the next day to make sure you were all right, but I never saw you again. It fucked with me for a long time." Ken's jaw muscles flexed beneath his smooth, clean-shaven skin. "I don't know what bothered me more—what he did to you or the fact that nobody even tried to help."

Ken's aqua eyes bored into me in a way that made me feel

seen. "I would have helped you. If I had gotten there sooner, if I had known, I would have helped you."

Those five little words wrapped around my heart like a bandage. "I would have liked that." I smiled, my face aflame with shame and the prickly heat of unshed tears.

"Sorry if I was kind of an asshole when we first met. Seeing you just reminded me of that day, and I got pissed off all over again."

"Yeah, you were kind of a dick." I laughed, trying to ease the tension as I wiped my eyes. "I'm just kidding. You got me a drink. Anybody who feeds me alcohol is automatically my friend. Even if they are a Jehovah's Witness."

Ken didn't laugh at my joke.

He didn't even crack a smile.

Instead, he asked, "Do you still talk to him?"

"No," I answered honestly, letting my fake levity fall to the ground, "I don't."

I can't.

I want to.

I won't.

"That's good," Ken replied with a curt nod.

We both just stood there, hands in our coat pockets, needing to put our conversation out of its misery but not knowing how to do it.

"Does seeing me still piss you off?" I wondered out loud.

Ken never really seemed all that happy to see me, but Ken never really seemed all that happy.

"No. Fuck no," he answered automatically, his features turning upward. "The Falcons need all the help they can get."

"Fuck you." I laughed.

I reached out to smack him on the chest, but Ken leaned away from me, easily dodging my swing.

"Ugh!" I stomped my foot and crossed my arms over my chest.

Ken arched a sandy-brown eyebrow at me and smirked. "Are you pouting?"

"No." I glared at him.

"You're pouting because I wouldn't let you hit me."

"So?"

Ken smiled and spread his arms. His wool coat parted, revealing a tight white T-shirt wrapped around a slender V-shaped torso. "Here. If it means that much to you, take a shot."

His gaze was challenging, his features guarded. I studied his face, trying to figure out if he really wanted me to hit him or if he was just waiting to make an ass out of me again. As I held his obstinate stare, something unspoken passed between us.

I think it was consent.

Ken was mirroring his stance from the last time I'd stolen a hug from him.

He wanted me to do it again.

I didn't know why Ken couldn't just give me a hug like a normal person, but as I plunged my hands into his coat and wound them around his warm, dryer-sheet-scented body, as I felt his jacket close around my back and his arms tighten like a vise, holding me inside, I didn't give a single solitary shit.

39

I walked home feeling like I'd been put back together a little bit. Like the pressure from Ken's embrace had kind of shored up the loose parts of me that had been ready to crumble. Like maybe I wasn't as alone as I'd thought.

I also felt the power that Knight held over me beginning to lift. No longer would the story of what had happened on C Hall be about the time I got attacked by my ex while a hundred kids did nothing but watch. Now, it would be the story of the time a stubborn football-team dropout with aqua-blue eyes and sandy-brown hair chased him off.

I smiled to myself as I made the rounds, turning on every light in my apartment and triple-checking all the locks. I called my parents to tell them about my acceptance letter. I called Juliet to tell her, too. I did *not* call Goth Girl. She was still on my shit list for telling Hans that I'd been hanging out at Jason's.

Bitch.

That only left Hans. I knew he'd said he "wouldn't have cell service," but it couldn't hurt to leave him a voicemail, right? And besides, maybe he was already on his way home from "camping" and would have a signal.

And maybe I kind of sort of wanted to check up on him a little bit.

I sat down on the couch we'd "borrowed" from Hans's parents' basement—the same one he used to pull outside whenever he had people over—and dialed his number as a churning cesspool of acid swirled in my stomach.

It's fine, I told myself. *He's either going to answer or you're going to leave a voicemail. It's not like you're deactivating a bomb. Jesus.*

Ring.

Ring.

Doodle-oodle-oo.

I pulled the phone away from my ear and listened.

Doodle-oodle-oo.

It was Hans's ringtone!

I leaped off the sofa and listened again, trying to figure out which direction to go.

Doodle-oodle-oo.

I followed the sound into the bedroom where Hans's four-poster bed stood in a state of disarray in the center of the room. The only other furniture in there was a dresser, also "borrowed" from the Oppenheimers, and two cheap bedside tables that I'd bought at Walmart.

Doodle-oodle-oo.

I rummaged through a pile of dirty clothes on the floor of our walk-in closet until I found it, tucked inside the pocket of his dark gray Dickies.

Hans's cell phone.

I sat on the edge of the bed and stared at the small hunk of plastic. I'd never gone through somebody's phone before. Not because I had morals, but because, with the guys I dated, I was simply too afraid of what I might find.

But I was sick of being afraid. I needed to sleep at night. I needed to eat without wanting to throw up. I needed answers. And that little black Motorola had them.

Having made up my mind, I took a deep breath and illuminated the screen, ready to face whatever I'd find inside, but the word *PASSCODE* in all caps stopped me in my tracks. Four blank spaces glowed beneath it, taunting me.

He has a fucking password?

I tried his birthday. I tried my birthday. I tried 1234. I tried his parents' address. I tried our address. I was about to try a ball-peen hammer when the digital clock in the top-right corner of the screen changed from *11:10* to *11:11*.

Eleven eleven.

I pictured the whites of John the Psychic's eyes as he muttered that number to me the winter before. It had become my lucky number, my favorite time, but maybe it was more than that. Maybe that number had the power to deliver me to the truth.

I crossed my fingers, held my breath, and typed in 1111.

It worked.

"Thank you, John," I whispered out loud, hoping that, wherever he was, he could hear me.

First, I scrolled through his list of Contacts. Half of them were girls' names. And by *girls*, I mean strippers. They all ended in *I*. Kandi, Mandi, Bambi, Tammi, Toni, Baloni.

And there, at the bottom, in the V section, was Victoria motherfucking Beasley.

The traitor.

I checked Hans's call log to see when she'd tattled on me, but I didn't get an exact answer.

Because that bitch had been calling Hans almost every day for the last two months.

Bile climbed its way up my throat, burning my esophagus and choking me with its acrid taste. Fifteen minutes here, thirty minutes there, forty-two minutes while I was at work, fifty-nine minutes while Hans was supposed to be in class.

Wait. What? No. No, no, no...

I hopped off the bed in a panic and raced to the dining room. The only furniture in that small space was my computer desk and a chair. My backpack lay on the desk, full to bursting with textbooks and notebooks and supplies of all kinds. Hans's lay slumped over on the floor in the corner. I grabbed it and dumped it out in the middle of the floor. Books and crumpled papers and prescription pill bottles and ziplock baggies full of weed and tiny glass vials with white powdered residue inside tumbled to the ground in an avalanche of truth.

I sank to the floor and admired the pile with someone else's eyes. Someone removed from the situation. Someone who would give me a full report later, when I was ready to hear it.

She looked at everything, taking mental notes for me. She commented that every paper had a failing grade on it, and none of them had a date later than early October. She deduced that Hans must have dropped out right before midterms, which was probably around the time that he converted his backpack into a drug storage unit. Oxycodone, Percocet, Lortab, OxyContin—eight orange prescription bottles in all.

Then that girl went to work. She didn't want to leave a mess on the floor for me to find later. She was far too considerate for that. Instead, she carried the contents of Hans's backpack to the coffee table and arranged everything as if she were creating a beautiful table display at Macy's. She stacked the pristine, never-opened textbooks in the back, for some height. Fanned the stack of papers out in front so that the failing grades were visible on each one. She created an orange pyramid out of the prescription bottles, off to the side for a mid-height focal point, then laid the clear vials in an asterisk shape on top of the papers, for just a touch of sparkle.

Oh!

Running into the bedroom, she came back with the finishing touch. The cherry that would top off her arrangement of lies.

Hans's cell phone.

Now when BB got back, maybe the truth would be easier for her to look at. Now it was pretty. Organized. Under control.

Unlike that filthy apartment.

Maybe I should vacuum, the girl thought. *Mop the kitchen floor. I can't remember the last time BB dusted. Or made her bed. The tile in the shower is mildewed. I could take care of that real quick. Maybe empty the trash cans while I'm at it.*

I didn't feel. I didn't think. I cleaned. I cleaned and I cleaned and arranged and organized until the sun came up and my arms shook from hunger and my eyes went blurry from lack of sleep. Then, I cleaned some more.

It wasn't until the birds were chirping, the sun was streaming in through the spotless sliding glass door, and I was in the middle of rearranging the candleholders on the mantel for the third time when I finally heard his key in the lock.

40

I spun around and watched from where I stood on the fireplace hearth as Hans dragged himself up the stairs.

He was not wearing camping gear.

He was not carrying camping gear.

He was wearing a T-shirt and baggy jeans. He'd pulled a gray beanie on over his shaggy, unwashed hair. And he reeked of cigarettes and cheap perfume. I could smell it from across the room.

I don't know if it was seeing him like that, the scent of Victoria's Secret body spray instead of campfire smoke on his clothes, or the sheer physical exhaustion of staying up all night, but all of my precious defense mechanisms abandoned me at once.

Poof.

Suddenly, it was just me and Hans.

And the pain I'd been running from.

And the truth he'd been hiding.

And an art installation of evidence on the coffee table between us.

When Hans reached the top of the stairs, I watched his

bloodshot eyes travel across the pristine apartment, take in my tortured, sleepless face, then land on all of his lies, now a neatly arranged centerpiece for the sham that was our home.

Hans stared at the pile the way you would stare at your new puppy—if you came home to find it dead on your living room floor.

Hans didn't look at me. Didn't speak. He simply stumbled over to the couch, sat down, rested his elbows on his knees, and buried his face in his palms.

A million questions pooled in my mouth.

Who are you?

Where is Hans?

What did you do with him?

Will I ever see him again?

Are you an addict?

What do I do now?

Why did you do this to me?

But the one I went with was, "Where the fuck were you?"

Hans sighed, long and heavy, and rubbed his temples with his fingers. I was about to repeat my question when he finally admitted, "The Pink Pony."

"Yeah, you fuckin' smell like it. Is that where you met Kandi, Brandi, Mandi, and Sandi? Looks like you've been chattin' them up a lot."

"Baby..."

"No"—I raised my voice and stepped onto the carpet, shoving a trembling finger in his direction—"do not fucking *baby* me. While you were off getting lap dances and doing blow all weekend, I was here, scrubbing your toilet, folding your laundry, and trying to study on zero hours of sleep because I was up all night wondering when the fuck you were gonna come home."

"I'm sorry." Hans shook his head, still buried in his palms.

"*I'm sorry, I'm sorry, I'm sorry.*" I tilted my head from side to side and sang the words in a taunting, whiny voice. "That's all I ever hear from you anymore. You know what I wanna hear? Just once? How about, *Thanks?* Or, *Hey, let's go out tonight?* Or, *Why don't you let me do those dishes?* Or, *Guess what. I'm gonna pay my half of the rent this month?* Oh! I got one! How about, *Hey, congratulations on getting into grad school?* Oh, wait. You don't know about that because you weren't fucking here when I got the letter!"

I took a giant step over to the coffee table and smacked Hans's cell phone off the top of the prescription bottle pyramid. I'd hoped it would crash into the wall and shatter into a thousand pieces, but it didn't. It landed on the fucking love seat with a cute little bounce.

Which only pissed me off more.

Adrenaline was pouring into my extremities. My fists were balled. My teeth were bared. I wanted to yank Hans's head up by his dirty fucking hair and force him to look me in the eye. I wanted to slap him across the face and scream at him for being no better than every other guy I'd ever known. Then I wanted to crawl into his lap and make him hold me while I cried myself to sleep.

But it was pointless. Hans wouldn't fight back. He couldn't. Not only because there was no excuse for his behavior, but also because he was so drunk or high or both that he was having trouble staying upright.

"Fuck this. You're not even gonna remember this conversation.

I'm going to class." I stomped into the dining room and grabbed my backpack.

"Wait." Hans stood up and blocked my path to the stairs, holding his hands out in front of him. "I'm sorry. I am. I know I say that a lot, but that doesn't make it not true."

"M'kay," I said, looking at him with dead eyes.

"I…fuck…" Hans rubbed the back of his neck. "I love you, BB."

"No," I snapped. "You don't. You love what I do for you. You love how I pay your rent and suck your dick and clean your house and keep my fucking mouth shut while you play rock star on the weekends. You don't even love yourself anymore. Look at you."

As Hans glanced down to take in his disheveled appearance, I tried to scoot between him and the wall.

He blocked my path at the last minute. "Don't go. Please? You don't have to go."

"Yes, I do!"

"Are you coming back?"

That one gave me pause. I honestly hadn't thought about it. I had no plan. No bag packed. But the idea of spending another minute in that apartment with that *fucking smell* made me want to vomit. The only thing that would make me consider inhabiting that space again was standing right in front of me, but he was too far gone to even hope for.

"I'll come back when Hans does," I snapped, trying to push past him again.

"What's that supposed to mean?"

I took a step back and looked him square in the eyes. "That means that *you*"—I gestured to the man before me with the sunken eyes and the hollow cheeks and the pants falling off his narrow hips—"are not my fucking boyfriend. I don't love *you*! I love the boy who held my hand and bought me flowers and took me to concerts. I love the boy who once tried to kiss every single one of my freckles. I love the boy who used to stay up all night, writing lyrics while he watched me sleep."

Frustrated, mournful tears filled my eyes as I remembered how happy we'd once been. The hope that we could re-create that summer of bliss, that we could get back there and stay forever, had become a mirage on the horizon of my life. But I'd finally reached the end of the desert, and there was no oasis in sight. Just a year and a half of footprints behind me—two sets at first, then at the end, only one.

"*That's* who I love. Not *you*. I don't even know who the fuck you are. All *you* do is lie to me and leave me alone, and I . . . I hate you."

Tears spilled from Hans's denim-colored eyes in quiet, remorseful streams. "It's me, baby," he said with a quiet sniffle. "It's still me. I'm so sorr—"

"Stop saying that!" I screamed, pushing past him and grabbing my purse off the end table in the living room.

"I can't live without you!" Hans's voice broke as he rushed to block my way to the stairs. The movement only made the pungent strawberry-kiwi-jasmine-pear-rose-gardenia fragrance coming off of him that much stronger. I suppressed my gag reflex along with my tears. "I'll do anything. Please. Anything. I can't lose you. Just tell me what to do, and I'll do it."

I turned to face him, pulling my shoulders back and holding my head high. But no amount of false confidence could keep my chin from buckling when I said the three saddest words in the English language, "No, you won't."

Hans's chin quivered, too. "Yes, I will," he whispered, his words a token gesture without conviction. "Please, baby. Just give me a chance."

"Fine. I want you to choose. Me...or *the lifestyle.*"

I waited for Hans to do what he did best—tell me what I wanted to hear. Tell me that he needed me. That he'd sober up. That he'd spend every minute of the rest of his life trying to make me happy again. Hell, maybe he'd even turn his empty promises into another song. Record it for his next album so that he could make even more money to blow on even more drugs and even fancier strip clubs.

But, in a rare act of honesty, Hans said nothing. He spared me the lie. He let his tears speak for him.

And he let me walk out the door.

41

I only made it halfway to school before my crying fit got so bad that I had to pull over. I wasn't safe to drive. I hadn't slept in over twenty-four hours. I hadn't eaten in about as long. The adrenaline was wearing off, and all that was left was exhaustion and tears.

So. Many. Tears.

There was no way I could go to school like that, so I turned my car around and headed home.

Or at least, headed to what I thought of as home.

My parents welcomed me with open arms, but it was clear that my status in their household had permanently shifted from *resident* to *visitor* while I was gone.

It had only been four months since I'd moved out, but in that time, my mom had rearranged my bedroom furniture, taken down all four hundred of the photos, magazine clippings, band posters, and drawings that I'd wallpapered the room with, and painted the whole thing pastel blue. Then, as the final touch in the generic guest-room look she'd been going for, my mom had hung a framed print of Van Gogh's *Water Lilies* above the bed.

I was officially homeless.

As much as I wanted to just curl up and die, being in that room only depressed me more, so I sat at the kitchen table instead, sipping the wine my mom had given me to help me "calm down."

She'd tried to give me a Xanax, but I'd told her, "No, thanks."

If I saw one more orange prescription bottle that day, I was going to lose my shit.

Again.

"Honey, are you sure you don't want to come into the living room and watch TV? You look so bored in here."

I glanced down the hallway into the living room where my dad was quietly strumming a red Fender Stratocaster while he watched the daily doom and gloom on CNN.

"Nah, I'm fine. Just need to think."

My mom smiled and sat across from me, her own wine in hand. "Pretty sure I've never said those words." She chuckled. "Most of the time, I'm trying not to think."

"Maybe that's my problem." I smiled back weakly.

"Yeah, I'm pretty sure you do enough thinking for the both of us." Her long red hair was loose, and she'd changed out of her teacher clothes into a T-shirt with the Hindu goddess Ganesh on the front and a pair of yoga pants. "So, what are you thinking about right now?"

I sighed and felt my eyes begin to sting before the words even came out. "I'm just wondering... if I should have tried harder. You know?" I glanced down the hallway at my dad playing that red guitar, so kind, so sensitive, so lost to his passion. "I should have gotten him some help. Or gone with him on the road more. Or... I don't know... supported him more. But I just gave up."

My chin—my stupid, traitorous chin—wobbled uncontrollably as fresh, hot tears began to flow. "I love him so much, and I just walked away."

My mom reached across the table and squeezed my hand. She bore witness to my pain, sat in it with me, and stayed strong so that I could safely break.

Once my cries dissolved into whimpers, my mom refilled our glasses from the bottle of merlot on the table, stroked the back of my knuckles with her thumb, and said, "Honey, I know you love him, but you did the right thing."

I looked up into eyes just like mine. Earthy green. Tired. Sad. A little drunk. Haggard from the agony of loving a musician.

"I love your father. I do. He's a good man, he loves me very much, and he gave me you." She smiled with glistening eyes and squeezed my hand again. "But if I had it to do over, I'd marry a fucking accountant." She laughed, wiping an errant tear from the corner of her eye.

"You're so much like me. I was always attracted to the cool guys with the cool hair and the cool clothes—the bad boys, the musicians—but this is what they turn into." My mom rolled her eyes in the direction of the living room. "Your father hasn't worked in almost three years."

I blinked at her. "Really?" I hadn't realized it had been that long.

"Mmhmm. And before that, he hardly kept a job longer than a year. I didn't want to be an art teacher. I wanted to sell my paintings in galleries, but somebody had to pay the bills. Damn sure wasn't gonna be him."

"If it makes you feel any better, you're a really good art teacher."

My mom smiled. "Thanks, baby. It's fine. It's a good life. I can't complain. But I want so much more for you. Do you know why we named you Brooke?"

"Why?"

"Because Brooke Bradley sounds like a movie star's name. When your dad suggested it, my exact words were, 'It's perfect. If she becomes a movie star, she won't even have to change her name.' Then you came out, singing and dancing and being outrageous and making people laugh, just like we knew you would."

My mom squeezed my hand again, the warmth in her heart making up for her ice-cold fingers. "You have always been the brightest thing in the room, honey, but you dim your light so that your man can shine instead. Don't do that, okay? You deserve someone who is going to support you, not the other way around. You're so focused on helping Hans achieve his dreams, but does he even know what yours are? Does he help you achieve them? Does he help you around the house? Does he help you study?"

She kept talking, but I tuned her out for a minute while I thought about what she'd said. *Help. Achieve. Study.* The only person I could think of who actually knew what my goals were and had offered to help me achieve them was that cold, joyless, defiant, Gatorade-drinking, workout-clothes-wearing smart-ass whose hugs I had to steal.

Ken.

I didn't even know his last name, yet he'd been more supportive and helpful than my boyfriend of a year and a half.

How depressing.

"I know he's sweet," she continued, "and I know he's exciting. But sweet and exciting don't pay the mortgage. They don't sweep the floor. And they damn sure don't change the diapers. If you're doing all the giving and he's doing all the taking, I've got news for you, honey." My mom cast one last knowing look at my father then met my gaze with one of sad acceptance. "You're not his girlfriend. You're his mother."

42

I'd lost count of how many hours it had been since I'd slept. Thirty-something? Forty? I was physically depleted. Even my tears had run dry. Yet there I was, wide awake, staring at the glow-in-the-dark star stickers on the ceiling of my former bedroom. They bothered me. I'd been gazing up at those greenish plastic constellations since middle school, but with my bed moved to a different wall, their familiar pattern looked as random as gravity-defying confetti.

Fitting, considering that my whole fucking life had been turned upside down.

I didn't know which way was up anymore. My head told me that my mom was right. That if I went back to Hans I'd be responsible for everything, my dreams would be put on hold, and my role would shift from muse to maid.

But my heart begged me to do something, anything, to take away the pain. I longed to go back to the days when I'd merely been lonely and worried and jealous. Lonely, worried, and jealous felt like an adorable little wading pool compared to the typhoon of grief I was struggling to stay afloat in.

My heart whispered, *Go back. Apologize. End this misery. Please.*

So, they negotiated—my head and my heart.

My head said, *Okay, but only if he calls and really grovels. He's got to work for it. If we go back now, he'll never change. He'll come around. Just be patient.*

My heart sniffled and nodded.

That was it. I'd made up my mind. If Hans called and begged me to come home, if he promised to change, I'd do it. I'd give him another chance. The resolution gave me the peace I needed to finally doze off.

I awoke with a start sometime around midnight to the sound of my phone ringing. A burst of hope flooded my bloodstream. I threw my right arm out to grab the device off my nightstand, but the back of my hand slammed into an unexpected wall instead.

Motherfucker!

Rolling over, I grabbed my whining cell phone off the table that was now on the left side of the bed and answered it on the final ring.

"Hello?"

Anxiety ate away at my anticipation with every millisecond that I spent waiting for a response.

"Hello?" I asked again.

"You picked up."

The voice was not soft and apologetic. It was not groveling or choked up. It was harsh and deep and clear and sliced my hope to shreds with only three little syllables.

"Knight."

"Punk."

I froze, irrationally praying that, if I didn't move, he wouldn't know I was there.

"I didn't think you'd answer."

I swallowed. "And yet you keep calling."

Knight exhaled a drag from a cigarette. I'd know that sound anywhere. "Guess I'm just an optimistic drunk."

I laughed. I hadn't meant to—I'd wanted to be bitter and bitchy and blunt—but it was the first funny thing I'd heard all day.

"How've you been?" Knight asked, his voice severe again.

"Shitty," I answered honestly. "What about you?"

"Shitty."

Something in his tone sent shivers down my spine. I'd become hyperaware of Knight's moods over the years, as a means of self-preservation. They were basically all just shades of anger ranging from everyday irritability to blind, blackout, homicidal rage. And I'd seen them all. Repeatedly.

"Shitty, like *the last time you came back from Iraq* shitty?"

"Yeah. I guess."

Fuck us all.

The last time Knight had come back from Iraq, he'd attacked a complete stranger with a broken beer bottle, destroyed his own tattoo station at Terminus City, and run my ex-boyfriend's car off the road and into the path of an oncoming dump truck while I was inside of it.

All in the span of a weekend.

I tried to force my exhausted brain to tap into the section that housed all of my psychology coursework, but all that came out of my mouth was, "Shit, Knight. That's bad."

"Yeah." He exhaled another stream of smoke.

"Are you seeing anybody for your PTSD?"

"Nope."

"Are you on meds?"

"Fuck that shit."

"Do you at least have somebody you can talk to, when it gets bad?"

Knight didn't answer, and that was when I realized exactly why he'd kept calling me even though I never picked up.

I was the person he wanted to talk to when it got bad.

"Hey, it's okay. You can call me. Okay? I'll answer next time, I promise."

Knight didn't respond.

"Is it bad right now?"

"Not anymore."

I smiled, happy that I'd been able to help somebody, even if it was the same abusive, murderous psychopath who'd given me my own case of PTSD.

"Good. That's good. Do you wanna tell me what happened?"

Knight groaned. "Fuck."

I waited. Whatever he was about to say was going to have to claw its way out of him.

"I...I don't even fuckin' remember."

"Was it a bar fight? Were you hanging out at Spirit of Sixty-Nine again?"

"No, it was a biker bar. I've been ridin' with a guy from my platoon and his MC."

"You got some new friends. That's good."

"I don't know for how long though. I think I fucked one of 'em up tonight. I can't even *fucking* remember, but my knuckles are busted, and I know it was bad."

"I'm sure those guys are used to the occasional bar fight. Maybe you can talk to your Marine buddy about it. He'll understand what you're going through."

"Your boyfriend gonna be okay with me callin' you?" Knight asked, shutting down my line of questioning.

I sighed. "We just broke up. Today actually."

I could almost hear Knight's smirk. "Well, aren't we just a couple of sad sacks of shit?"

I laughed at the truthfulness of that statement. "Yeah, we are."

"Come by the shop tomorrow night."

"Knight...I don't—"

"You're eighteen now. I'll give you some free ink."

"I don't know."

"I'll draw something for you."

"Maybe."

"Or I could come see you at work. Where do you work now?"

I fucking knew it. He'd gone by Pier 1, looking for me.

"I don't know if I'm gonna go in tomorrow. I haven't slept in a few days," I deflected. "Maybe I'll come by the shop if I get some rest."

"Cool."

Neither of us said anything, not knowing how to end the conversation or if we even wanted to.

"Hey, Punk?"

"Yeah?"

"I'm sorry. About last time. About everything."

"I know you are, Knight. I know."

43

The good news was that I did finally get some sleep.

The bad news was that all that sleep had completely replenished my tear supply.

Thankfully, no one ever shopped in the Urban Streetwear section of Macy's on Tuesday mornings because, if they did, they would have left with black mascara smeared all over their new Sean Jean jeans, receipt, and shopping bag. With the entire department to myself and nothing to take my mind off my shit-tastic situation, except for the ten Christmas pop songs that had been playing on a loop since fucking October, all I could do was think and fold. And cry.

When my manager came over to check the supplies at the cash stand, she took one look at my face and sent me home.

Home.

Like I even had one.

I'd been wearing the same clothes for going on three days, so I decided to go by the apartment to pack up my stuff. I grabbed some empty boxes from the Macy's loading dock on my way out the door and prayed that Hans wouldn't be home. I figured the odds were in my favor. He was never around when I lived there, so why should he suddenly turn into a homebody now?

As I drove toward the Midtown Village apartment complex, I cranked up the heat in my car and tugged on the zipper of my flight jacket, even though I knew it was all the way up. I was trembling, and it had nothing to do with the weather. I tried to calm myself down by chain-smoking and visualizing Hans being gone, but when I pulled up to the building and saw his black BMW parked in front, half-lurched up onto the sidewalk with the front windows wide open, I knew all of my positive affirmations had been for naught.

On the verge of a full-blown panic attack, I considered just leaving and trying again later. I wasn't strong enough to handle another fight. I wasn't strong enough to handle the one we'd just had. But when I went to shift my car into reverse, the clock on my car stereo told me to stay. It told me that the universe had delivered me to that exact spot at that exact time for a reason, and all I had to do was take the final steps. It told me that it was 11:11 a.m.

Showtime.

I parked and walked over to my door in eerie silence. The birds had all flown south. The crickets and cicadas had hunkered down for the winter. The kids were at school, and their parents were at work, and the autumn leaves that used to crunch underfoot had all been turned to ash. It felt like the entire world was holding its breath as I fumbled with my key and opened the door.

And once the door was open, once the secret was finally out, the earth let out a collective sigh behind me. Car alarms and barking dogs and highway traffic roared to life as I stared at a pair of black patent-leather high-heel boots lying in a heap at the bottom of my stairs.

I'd never truly lost control before. No matter how drunk or high or upset I got, there was always some small part of my brain that stayed awake to babysit the rest of me. To take my makeup off before I passed out. To bite my tongue before I said anything too hurtful. To tell me to pull the car over before I killed somebody.

Evidently, that bitch was off duty.

I raced up the stairs and stopped at the top, swinging my head from left to right. The place was quiet. There was no one in the kitchen or living room. And my art installation of lies had been pushed to one side of the coffee table to make room for an overflowing ashtray, a dozen empty beer cans, and my now-empty bottle of Jack.

That only left the bedroom.

I turned left and darted into the open door a few feet away, then stopped dead in my tracks when I saw my worst fear, played out in black and white. Black hair—his shaggy, hers long and straight, fanned out over her creamy white skin. My black comforter draped haphazardly over their sleeping bodies. Our generic white apartment walls glowing in the mid-morning sun. And his ripped black jeans in a pile by the door.

The sight of Goth Girl in bed with my boyfriend hit me so hard and so fast that I felt as if I'd been physically assaulted. Everything hurt. Everywhere. Shock socked me right in the gut. Rejection delivered a roundhouse kick straight to my head. Betrayal stabbed me in the back, as it does. But it wasn't until I saw Hans, surreptitiously peeking at me from under his long black lashes as he pretended to be asleep, that outrage cut open my chest and surgically removed his very presence from my heart.

Rushing over to the bed, I yanked the comforter and sheets off in one motion and slapped Victoria as hard as I could on her bare thigh. "Get the fuck out of my bed!" I screamed.

Her dark brown eyes popped open just as I hit her again. *Smack!* My hand left a satisfying red welt on her ivory skin.

She sat up in a panic, flailing as she tried to scoot backward, clearly not problem-solving well in her hungover, half-awake state.

"I said, get the fuck out of my bed!" I reared back and got one last good hit in, turning her milky thigh into ground beef, before Hans's strong arms clamped down around mine.

He dragged me, literally kicking and screaming, out of the bedroom, then turned the lock on the doorknob and shut it behind us. I was locked out of my own bedroom. And Goth Girl was locked in.

I don't know if he even spoke to me. If he did, I was too far gone to hear a word of it. All I remember is screaming obscenities and chucking everything I could get my hands on directly at his head. The heavy crystal ashtray. The remote control. A candleholder. A bigger candleholder. A framed picture of us standing in front of Bigfoot's tire. Hans's textbooks. My empty Jack Daniel's bottle. My ring. I completely destroyed the apartment I'd spent so long cleaning, and Hans just stood guard in front of the bedroom door, deflecting the flying objects with his hands.

Once everything had been thrown and every glass had been smashed and every insult had finally been flung, I collapsed in a heap on the couch, clutched a pillow to my chest, and cried.

Slowly, the rush of blood in my ears subsided and words began to filter in again. The same words, over and over.

"Nothing happened. Nothing happened. I swear, BB. Nothing happened."

He didn't call me baby. I wonder if he calls her baby now.

"Hey, will you look at me? Please?"

I peeked over the top of the throw pillow I was hugging. Hans was sitting on the couch next to me and looked me straight in the eye. He hadn't shaved in days. His eyes were sunken and bloodshot. And he smelled like the bottom of a whiskey barrel. But the emotion pouring off of him was pure and sad and sincere.

"Nothing. Happened."

"You expect me to fucking believe that?" I pointed in the direction of the bedroom door. "Y'all talk on the phone all the time while I'm gone. Why not fuck while I'm gone, too?"

Hans kept his voice calm and steady, as if he were negotiating a hostage situation with an escaped mental patient. "Victoria and I have been friends since middle school. She and Steven broke up a few weeks ago, and she needed somebody to talk to."

"I'm sure she did," I huffed, turning my head away from him.

He was so fucking naive. Goth Girl wanted somebody to talk to, so she called Hans almost every day for two months instead of me or Juliet? Yeah, okay. She clearly wanted his cock, but Hans only ever saw the good in people.

Especially attractive female people in distress.

"BB, look at me."

"Stop calling me that!"

"You told me to stop calling you baby. Now I can't even call you BB? What the fuck do you want me to call you?"

"You can call a cab *for the fucking whore locked in my bedroom*!" I cupped my hand around my mouth and shouted that last part at the locked door behind him.

"BB..."

I glared at him for using my name, and he put his hands up in surrender.

"Nothing happened. I swear. I went to a bar where my buddy works and got hammered. I called Victoria for a shoulder to cry on since she'd just gone through a breakup, and she came up there. We both drank way too fucking much, so I told her to crash here and I'd take her to get her car in the morning."

"You expect me to believe that a girl who's been secretly calling you for months got drunk with you, came home with you, and didn't try to fuck you *in my bed*?" I yelled that last part in the direction of the bedroom too.

"Look at me. I still have my clothes on."

It was true. He was wearing boxer shorts, a T-shirt, and even socks. Everything but the jeans that I saw on the floor. Hans never slept with clothes on.

"I gave Victoria a T-shirt and a pair of shorts to sleep in and we passed out."

Just then, my bedroom door opened a tiny crack, and a pair of raccoon eyes peeked out. "It's true," Goth Girl rasped, her voice sounding like glass over sandpaper.

She opened the door a little more, and I saw that she was, in fact, wearing one of Hans's old T-shirts and a pair of his boxer shorts. Her eye makeup was woefully smeared, she appeared to be even paler than usual, and her thigh had a raised purplish-red patch emblazoned across the front and side of it.

She looked like she'd had an even worse morning than me.

Good.

Goth Girl took a hesitant step out of her prison, then another, then another, until she was standing right in front of me. Kneeling down so that we were eye-to-eye, Victoria took my hands in hers, kissed my knuckles, and began to cry. I didn't know if it was out of remorse for trying to steal my boyfriend, sympathy for the excruciating pain I was in, or mourning for the friendship she'd just fucked beyond all recognition, but I was in desperate need of comfort, so I took it.

Slipping off the couch, I sat on the floor next to Victoria and let her hold me, and together, we wept.

Once we were all cried out, I lit a cigarette and noticed Hans pacing back and forth behind the couch with his thumbnail in his mouth. He looked miserable and confused and utterly fucking useless.

"Why don't you take her home now? I'm gonna pack up," I said to him.

Hans looked up with his eyebrows pulled together. "What do you mean, pack up? What are you taking?"

"Um, my shit. I'm moving out. I'm taking my name off the lease too, so you can do whatever the fuck you want with the place. I don't care."

"You sure you don't want some help?" I could tell by his tone that when he said *help*, he really meant *supervision*. Hans's eyes darted all around the room, taking a mental inventory of what was *his*.

"I'm sure I want you to get the fuck out," I snapped.

As soon as Hans and Victoria were gone, I picked up my phone, dialed Jason's number, and told him I needed to borrow his truck.

My only regret is that I wasn't there to see the look on Hans's face when he came home to discover that he no longer owned sheets, pillows, lamps, lightbulbs, a shower curtain, shampoo, toothpaste, toilet paper, pots, pans, plates, silverware, food, or remote controls.

Fucker.

44

I pulled into the parking lot behind Terminus City Tattoo with my pulverized heart lodged in my throat. Knight's monster truck was nowhere to be seen, but there was a chromed-out chopper parked in its place. It was so weird to think of Knight going from driving something so big to something so small. I wondered what else had changed since I saw him last.

It had been over a year since that horrible night on Mable Drive. Over a year that I'd kept myself safe. I'd avoided his calls, changed jobs, and even changed residences. I'd managed to shake my abuser, yet after one bad breakup, there I was, serving myself up to him on a silver platter.

Maybe he's different now, I thought as I walked around to the front of the building.

Please get back in the car, my gut begged.

Maybe he won't hurt me this time.

Leave. Now. Before it's too late.

I wonder what tattoo he drew for me.

I wonder how long until you're crying and bleeding.

What if I don't like it?

It won't fucking matter because you'll be dead.

Oh God. Am I sweating? Why am I sweating? It's fucking December.

Because you're about to get straight murdered, you stupid bitch! Turn the fuck around!

I stopped at the crumbling cement steps that led to the front door. Terminus City Tattoo was in an old brick building in Little Five Points—a funky, artsy neighborhood in East Atlanta, home to all things weird and wonderful. And dirty. And dangerous. It was where the punks and goths and hippies and metalheads and skaters and rockabillies and skinheads hung out. It was where I used to spend my Friday nights, curled up in Knight's arms on the couch in Terminus City's break room. It was where I had feared for my life on more than one occasion. It was where Knight had shown me his demons.

And yet I returned.

The contrast of the darkness outside with the bright shop lights inside made it so that I could see everything going on through the window. And the first thing I saw was Knight.

He was facing the window, sitting on a rolling stool, tattooing the calf of a skater guy who was reclined in his chair. He looked so different. He'd grown his white-blond hair out and slicked it back. I used to love to run my hands over his baby-soft buzz cut. Now it looked so greasy I didn't want to touch it. And he was wearing biker clothes—motorcycle boots, black jeans, a black Harley-Davidson T-shirt, and a red bandana across his forehead—instead of his usual combat boots and camo pants. His skin looked weathered, aged far past his twenty-one years, and both of his arms were now completely full of ink.

It wasn't until he glanced at the window and sneered at me

with those crystalline blue eyes that I believed it was actually him. I almost jumped back in fear until I remembered that he couldn't see me.

Knight was sneering at his own reflection.

I looked past him, to the empty place where his old tattoo chair used to be. The one he'd pierced me on. The one he'd ripped out of the floor and hacked to pieces with his butterfly knife in a fit of psychosis. I looked at the hallway just beyond it that led out to the fire-escape stairs that Knight had shoved me down. Stairs that led to the alley where we'd gotten into too many knockdown, drag-out fights to count.

It had been over a year since I was screamed at, pushed, squeezed, choked, slammed up against a wall, or forced into sex. Over a year of being called *baby* instead of Punk. Of being touched with reverence instead of rage. No one raised their voice to me anymore. No one raised their hand to me in anger.

And nobody ever would again.

Hans hadn't been a mistake; he'd been a magician. He'd done what I'd never been able to do for myself. He'd shown me my worth. And one day, when I was less angry, I'd thank him for it.

I gave Knight one last lingering glance, trying to remember his features. The sharpness of his nose and cheekbones. His almost colorless eyelashes and eyebrows, always scowling. His thick, scarred hands, so full of talent yet so prone to violence. And the spattering of light-brown freckles that reminded me just how fast he'd had to grow up.

The only picture ever taken of us together still sat in a frame on his tool chest.

But the girl in the photo? She was long gone.

EPILOGUE

Spoiler alert: The Falcons did *not* go to the Super Bowl. Not even close.

Jason blamed their shitty season on the fact that I'd missed their last four games. I think he believed it, too. He seemed really pissed that I hadn't been around. I tried to explain that I'd wanted to come, but the thought of driving past my old apartment and possibly seeing Hans's car there made me physically ill, but Jason was too drunk to listen to reason. As usual.

Instead, I'd been spending my weekends hanging out with Juliet and Romeo, whom I had totally neglected, and redecorating my sad excuse for a bedroom. The first order of business had been to move my fucking bed back to the correct wall. I'd also come home with a lot more shit than I'd left with, so finding places for all the lamps and art and candleholders and pots and pans and dishes I'd stolen had been a challenge.

I ended up hanging the pots and pans from hooks over my bed, the way they do in fancy kitchens. My mom said it was "an eyesore," but it made me smile every damn time I looked at it. It reminded me that I'd finally become the badass I'd always wanted to be. I was done being a victim, like I'd been with Knight, or somebody's plaything, like I'd been with Harley. With Hans, I'd been through heaven and hell, and I'd come out the other side dragging a sack full of Satan's housewares to display as my trophies.

Even so, it'd still taken a solid month for me to come out of my funk. My school and work routines were finally back to normal after the holidays. My bedroom was starting to resemble a place I might want to inhabit again. But what cheered me up the most was the late-night phone call I'd gotten from Hans a few days before the Super Bowl.

It was the first attempt he'd made to contact me since I'd moved out, and he sounded absolutely pitiful. He was *soooo* sorry. Letting me go was the biggest mistake of his life. He wanted me back. Ever since I'd left, everything had gone to shit. He'd gotten a DUI and was probably going to lose his driver's license for a year. Phantom Limb's record label dropped them due to low debut album sales. And, to top it all off, Midtown Village evicted his ass for not paying his rent. I asked if he was living in his BMW, hoping he'd say yes, but sadly, he was back in the castle on the lake.

By the end of that phone call, the last shred of bitterness I'd been hanging on to floated away like a feather on the breeze. I called Jason with a smile on my face and told him I was in for the Super Bowl.

There were a lot more people at his apartment than usual, but Jason, even in his inebriated condition, dropped what he was doing when I arrived to make sure that I got a beer and a spot on the couch.

I decided that I needed to disappear for a month at a time more often.

I had just settled in for a long night of staring at the TV and pretending like I knew what the fuck was going on when something by the door caught my eye.

No, not something.

Someone.

Jason's newest arrival was tall and lean and dressed in black from head to toe. He shrugged off his black wool coat and draped it over an armless chair in Jason's entryway. Underneath, he had on a black button-up shirt with the sleeves rolled up high enough to show off his defined forearms and biceps. His shirt was tucked into a pair of black slacks that fit just right. And, as he walked toward the living room, he reached up and loosened the knot on a stylish, skinny black tie. Above the neck, he had a jawline that rivaled Captain America's, cheekbones for days, and sandy-brown hair that had been styled just like Mark McGrath's.

He looked like a bad boy with a good job and a great body, and I was definitely in the market for one of those.

Slurping the drool back into my face, I planned to either fall on the floor at his feet when he passed and fake a seizure or pretend to be choking so that maybe he'd give me the Heimlich maneuver. Either way, it would end with him thinking he'd saved my life and us forming an instant, unbreakable bond.

I was about to make a dive for it when I heard Allen shout, "Ken!" from somewhere near the kitchen.

I wondered why he was looking for Pajama Guy when he wasn't even there yet, but when Allen bounded over with his arms outstretched and tackle-hugged Mark McGrath's look-alike, I realized that I'd been wrong.

Ken *was* there.

And Ken was fucking *hot*.

It was just like how Superman duped everyone into thinking he was just a mild-mannered reporter by putting on a suit and a pair of glasses. I couldn't believe that Ken had tricked me into thinking he wasn't my type by simply throwing on some running pants and a pair of Nikes. Was I really that shallow? He was smart and good-looking and funny—in a dry, mean kind of way—but I'd completely dismissed him as just some goody-two-shoes jock.

I suddenly had no idea how to act, what to do. Ken was my buddy. I should at least be able to say, *What's up?* but I couldn't. I just sat there, hiding in plain sight, waiting for more signs of Ken-ness. I watched him fight his way out of Allen's hug like a ninja. *Yep, very Ken.* I watched him pull a Gatorade out of Jason's fridge. *Super Ken.* And I watched him smile when he finally saw me from across the kitchen counter.

That *GQ*-looking motherfucker with the black shirt and the black tie and the sexpot hair and the turquoise eyes was smiling...at me. I think I leaned forward and sighed with dreamy hearts in my eyes before I remembered that I was supposed to smile back.

There was nowhere on the couch for him to sit, so I got up. I had every intention of walking over to him and saying hello, but I got weirded out and took a right turn at the last minute, heading out to the balcony to smoke. I hadn't even grabbed my coat first. I was such an idiot.

The vibe outside was totally different. In preparation for the party, Jason had put up a few strings of white party lights and installed speakers that were hooked up to his stereo. Inside, it was loud and bright and warm and chaotic, whereas outside, it was dark and cold and still and melodic. A brooding song by Linkin Park was just ending, so I curled up on Jason's cushy outdoor love seat, lit a cigarette, and enjoyed the moment as much as I could while slowly dying of hypothermia.

The moment didn't last long. Within the first three seconds of hearing the next song, I was already considering throwing myself off the balcony. As if it wasn't bad enough that I'd committed to sitting outside in the freezing cold, the universe thought it would be absolutely hilarious to make me listen to "Falling Star" by Phantom Limb while I did it. I'd been able to completely avoid that song since our breakup, but my time had come.

I sighed and surrendered to my fate. As I listened to the lyrics, *really* listened to them, it was as if I were hearing the song for the first time. It didn't make me sad. In fact, it made me giggle. And then laugh. And then cover my own mouth to shut myself up so that I could listen some more.

"Falling Star" wasn't an epic tale of fated destinies and true love, like I'd made it out to be in my mind. It was a fucking breakup song. It was about a girl who was meant for bigger things than her lover. He'd tried to keep her small, but in the end, she exploded into what she had always been meant to be, leaving him in the dust.

I can tell you when they streak the sky,
Where the falling stars go when they leave the night.
I know how they shimmer, infrared.
I know because one fell and landed in my bed.

I know it's wrong to keep her.
She belongs light-years away.
I know it's wrong to keep her,
So every day I pray.
Don't let my falling star fade away.
Please let this falling star…
Fall for me.

I put my falling star on a leash,
And I tied her to a post on the mezzanine.
She could easily burn through the rope,
But I think she likes the way it feels around her throat.

I know it's wrong to keep her.
She belongs light-years away.
I know it's wrong to keep her,
So every day I pray.
Don't let my falling star fade away.
Please let this falling star…
Fall for me.

I was wrong. She cannot be contained.
She tricked me with her laugh and her falling ways.
I didn't know until it was over.
She's not a falling star. She's a supernova.

"You like this song?"

I jumped, my hands still clasped over my mouth, and turned to see Mark McKen closing the door behind him. He was wearing his coat and carrying mine. A smile split my face wide open, and tears pricked my eyes. I didn't know who I was happier to see—Ken or my coat.

Handing me my shiny maroon flight jacket, Ken said, "It's kinda whiny, don't you think?"

I burst out laughing as I pulled my coat on like a blanket. "It's whiny as shit!" I cackled.

I scooted over to make room for Ken on the love seat, but he retreated to the opposite side of the balcony, just like always.

Never too close.

"So, what's your favorite band?" I asked, taking a drag from my cigarette as if I wasn't in danger of losing my fingers to frostbite in the process.

"Sublime," Ken answered without missing a beat.

Snort. "Sublime? Shut the fuck up."

"What's wrong with Sublime?"

Oh shit. He's serious!

"Nothing!" I backpedaled. "They're awesome."

"Then what is it?" Ken arched a brow and leaned against the balcony railing, enjoying watching me squirm.

I enjoyed watching him watching me squirm.

"Um, *literally* all they sing about is drinkin' forties and smokin' weed."

"And child prostitution," Ken deadpanned.

"Oh, right." I giggled. "How could I forget about 'Wrong Way'?"

"I don't know. It's basically the greatest song ever."

"Hey," I said, distracted yet again by his appearance, "I like your outfit. Why're you so dressed up?"

God, I hope that didn't sound as creepy as it felt.

"I had to work. I'm usually off on Sundays, but a buncha

assholes called out because of the Super Bowl, so I had to go in for a while."

"Guess that's the problem with being the boss, huh?"

"Yeah, especially when all your employees are fucking teenagers." Ken smirked. "No offense."

"Hey!" I laughed and threw a pillow at him from Jason's love seat.

I had terrible aim, but Ken reached out and caught it before it flew over the railing. The movement was so effortless; I think he could have done it in his sleep. He smiled and pretended like he was going to bean me with it, then tossed it gently onto my lap as I squealed and covered my face with my forearms.

Lowering my arms in embarrassment, I locked eyes with Ken, who looked all too pleased with himself. We fell into a comfortable silence just as "With Arms Wide Open" by Creed began to play.

"Oh God. Speaking of whiny-ass rock stars." I jumped up and flicked my cigarette butt into the parking lot below. "C'mon," I said, grabbing Ken by the lapel of his coat and dragging him back into the apartment. It was as close to touching him as I thought he'd let me get. "I can't handle this shit."

Ken came willingly, and I made a mental note.

Weird about hugs. Does not mind being dragged around like a dog on a leash. Interesting.

Jason saw us walk in and barreled over like there'd been a goddamn emergency. "Ken! Ken!" He stopped right in front of us, huffing and puffing. "What's your last name, bro?"

It was a strange question to ask out of the blue, but I'd been dying to know the answer myself. It felt like time stood still, the party drifted away, and the background noise had been muted as every cell in my body leaned forward and listened. I listened as if Ken were about to tell us the winning lottery numbers. I listened as if he'd discovered the recipe for calorie-free beer. I listened as if whatever came out of his mouth next, no matter how unfortunate or unpronounceable or lacking in vowels it might be, would one day be my last name, too.

"Easton," he said.

Easton, I thought. *I like that.*

Ken and BB's story continues in *Suit*.
Available now.

PLAYLIST

Before I wrote this book, I assumed that I would fill Hans's playlist with songs that we'd listened to back then. He and his band were very heavily influenced by Nine Inch Nails, Tool, and the Deftones. But, as the story began to flow, I found myself gravitating toward songs that fit the *tone* of the book rather than the content. Songs about big love. Songs about love gone bad. Songs with the word *star* in them. Every piece of music listed here helped fuel my fingers as they typed out this story. I am grateful to each and every one of these brilliant artists. Their blood, sweat, and tears provided my *Star*spiration.

You can stream the playlist for free on Spotify here: https://open.spotify.com/user/bbeaston/playlists

"24/7" by The Neighbourhood
"A Sky Full of Stars" by Coldplay
"Avalanche" by Walk the Moon
"Bad at Love" by Halsey
"Called Out in the Dark" by Snow Patrol
"Centred on You" by Atlas Genius
"Encore" by Red Hot Chili Peppers
"Follow You" by Night Riots
"For Me This Is Heaven" by Jimmy Eat World

"Grand Theft Autumn/Where Is Your Boy" by Fall Out Boy

"Heaven" by The Neighbourhood

"Him & I" by G-Eazy and Halsey

"I Will Always Love You" by Whitney Houston

"I'm Kissing You" by Des'ree

"Jolene" by Ray Lamontagne

"Konstantine" by Something Corporate

"Love Like Winter" by AFI

"Love Will Tear Us Apart" by Fall Out Boy

"Love Ridden" by Fiona Apple

"Million Bucks" by Smallpools

"Nicest Thing" by Kate Nash

"Night Drive" by Jimmy Eat World

"Outright" by Wild Party

"Photobooth" by Death Cab for Cutie

"Punk Rock Princess" by Something Corporate

"Sometime Around Midnight" by The Airborne Toxic Event

"Sparks" by Coldplay

"Stars" by Hum

"Vowels (And the Importance of Being Me)" by HUNNY

ACKNOWLEDGMENTS

Behind every successful artist, you will find a devoted, loving benefactor. Mine is **Kenneth Easton**. He is the reason you get to read these stories. He puts our son on the bus every morning since I'm usually up all night writing. He makes the breakfasts, preps the lunches, pays the bills, folds the laundry, handles my business finances, rubs my aching neck and shoulders—hesitantly and only when I beg—and picks up all the slack that inevitably comes with being married to a creative type. And he doesn't even complain about it. He is the motherfucking wind beneath my wings, and I cannot wait to tell you the story of how we fell in love. All four pages of it.

My mother is my other ride-or-die. She has always been there, whether I needed her to watch my kids or hide me from the cops. I could tell her I'm moving to South America to start a goat farm tomorrow, and she'd have a FOR SALE sign in her front yard by that afternoon, saying, "Well, if you're moving to South America, I guess I gotta go too. What's the weather like there? Should I buy a new raincoat? Are goats mean? They're the ones that spit, right? No, wait. Those are llamas. Oh shit. I guess I have to start saying *yamas* now. That's how they say it down there, right?" I love that damn woman.

I want to thank **Ken's whole entire family** for knowing what

I do, looking the other way while I do it, and selflessly agreeing to babysit so that Ken and I can fly all over the world in support of it. You might not be allowed to read my books or acknowledge that you know anything about them, but you still support me unconditionally, and for that, I am eternally grateful.

To **Larry Robins**, my talent manager—Thank you for championing my work, for taking me to my first Hollywood premiere, and for being a surrogate father to me when I needed one most. I cherish our friendship.

To my team at **Hachette Book Group** and my agents at **Bookcase Literary Agency**—because of you brilliant, driven, visionary women, these unconventional, genre-bending books are now sitting on bookstore shelves all over the world. Thank you for not only embracing my weirdness, but thinking outside the box in order to preserve it. I couldn't ask for a better team. To **Miles Dale, Stacy Rukeyser**, and the **cast and crew of** *Sex/ Life*—I am beyond humbled to be a part of something so big and important and empowering for women. I bow down to your collective talent, genius, and superior bone structure. To my editors, **Traci Finlay, Jovana Shirley**, and **Ellie McLove**—I give you my messy, bloody heart, and you turn it into an actual novel. Magicians, all of you. Thank you.

To my beta readers, **Jamie Shaw, Sammie Lynn, Sara Snow**, and **April C.**—You girls are my bottom bitches. I'd go to jail for any one of you. But, like, overnight jail, not like prison jail. Basically, I'd get arrested for you, and then let you bail me out, and then I'd let you pay for my defense attorney. But I'd totally take the rap for you. All day, erry day. Thank you for helping take this book from good to great. I love you!

To **All My Author Friends**—In a society that teaches us to compete, compete, compete, you ladies choose to share instead. You share with me your time, your advice, your encouragement, your resources, and often, your platforms to help me succeed in an oversaturated market where so very few do. Thank you for letting this pink-haired, foul-mouthed new kid sit with you. I love you!

To **My Reader Group**, **#TeamBB**—You guys have literally brought me to tears more times than I can count with your support and enthusiasm—not only for me, but also for each other. I grovel at your collective feet. You make me laugh. You share my announcements. You make me teasers. SO many teasers. You make me blush with some of the pictures you post, and you keep my ass in gear. Thank you, for *everything*. If any of you ever need a kidney, I'm your girl.

And to **Hans**—Initially, I was going to thank you for changing the course of my life, but you didn't. You changed *me*, and *I* changed the course of my life. Your love transformed me from a victim into a survivor, a girl into a woman, and yes, a falling star into a supernova. But you and your bandmates also introduced me to bukkake porn, and for that I will never forgive you. Take care, LDH.

ABOUT THE AUTHOR

BB Easton lives in the suburbs of Atlanta, Georgia, with her long-suffering husband, Ken, and two adorable children. She recently quit her job as a school psychologist to write books about her punk rock past and deviant sexual history full-time. Ken is suuuper excited about that.

BB's memoir, *Sex/Life: 44 Chapters About 4 Men*, and the spin-off Sex/Life novels are the inspiration for Netflix's steamy, female-centered dramedy series of the same name.

The *Rain Trilogy* is her first work of fiction. Or at least, that's what she thought when she wrote it in 2019. Then 2020 hit and all of her dystopian plot points started coming true. If you need her, she'll be busy writing a feel-good utopian rom-com to see if that fixes everything.

You can find her procrastinating at all of the following places:
Website: www.authorbbeaston.com
Facebook: www.facebook.com/bbeaston
Instagram: www.instagram.com/author.bb.easton
Twitter: www.twitter.com/bb_easton
Pinterest: www.pinterest.com/artbyeaston
Goodreads: https://goo.gl/4hiwiR
BookBub: www.bookbub.com/authors/bb-easton
Spotify: https://open.spotify.com/user/bbeaston

Etsy: www.etsy.com/shop/artbyeaston

#TeamBB Facebook group: www.facebook.com/groups/BB Easton

And giving away a free e-book from one of her author friends each month in her newsletter: www.artbyeaston.com/subscribe.